FAIZAH MUHAMMAD

The Art of Making a Forgotten Cup of Tea

First published by FazBooks 2025

First edition

ISBN (paperback): 978-1-9193398-1-8
ISBN (hardcover): 978-1-9193398-0-1

Cover art by Amira Kalasli
Agent: Anupama Patel
Illustration by Anupama Patel

This book was professionally typeset on Reedsy.
Find out more at reedsy.com

For Timișoara, the city that raised me.
Thank you for choosing me to be yours.

The following story is inspired by real events.

"The greatest sin of man is fear — the fear of looking straight ahead and recognising the truth."

— Mihai Eminescu,
Romanian poet & novelist

Contents

Playlist iv

I Part I — Frăţie, roşul sângelui

1 Nicolae 3
2 Elena 7
3 Elena 12
4 Robert 19
5 Dragoş 24
6 Robert 30
7 Nicolae 35
8 Robert 39
9 Dragoş 49
10 Elena 55
11 Robert 59
12 Dragoş 64

II Part II — Dreptate, galbenul ogoarelor

13 Frankie 75
14 Frankie 84
15 Elizabeth 93
16 Frankie 98
17 Elizabeth 102
18 Elena 106
19 Frankie 109

20 Robert 112
21 Dragoş 116
22 Elena 122
23 Elizabeth 127
24 Frankie 132
25 Robert 138
26 Dragoş 143
27 Beriță 149
28 Robert 155
29 Elena 161
30 Nicolae 166

III Part III — Libertate, albastrul cerului

31 Dragoş 175
32 Elizabeth 181
33 Elena 186
34 Frankie 191
35 Dragoş 196
36 Robert 202
37 Elena 208
38 Elizabeth 213
39 Robert 217

IV PART IV — Deşteaptă—te, Române!

40 Frankie 225
41 Robert 233
42 Elizabeth 239
43 Robert 246
44 Nicolae 251
45 Dragoş 259
46 The Professor 267

47	Robert	289
48	Nicolae	293
	Epilogue	303
	Acknowledgements	310
	About the Author	313
	Also by Faizah Muhammad	315

Playlist

- *The Lonely Shepherd* by Gheorghe Zamfir
- *Little Dark Age* by MGMT
- *The Hanging Tree* by Rachel Zegler (from '*The Hunger Games: The Ballad of Songbirds and Snakes*')
- *Everybody Wants to Rule the World* by Tears for Fears
- *Zombie* by The Cranberries
- *Way Down We Go* by KALEO
- *LABOUR (the cacophony)* by Paris Paloma
- *Happy Nation* by Ace of Base
- *Pumped Up Kicks* by Foster The People
- *Skyfall* by Adele
- *Daylight* by David Kushner
- *brutal* by Olivia Rodrigo
- *Colors* by Halsey
- *Seven Nation Army* by The White Stripes
- *Dog Days Are Over* by Florence + The Machine
- *Fourth of July* by Sufjan Stevens
- *The Water Is Fine (Crimson Edition)* by Chloe Ament
- *Golden Brown* by The Stranglers
- *Acasă* by Smiley

I

Part I — Frăție, roșul sângelui

Crimson blood of brotherhood

One

Nicolae

Bucharest, Romania — August 1989

Even with every shut door and window in the apartment, the roar of the crowd seeped in from outside. The thunderous screams shook the floor like an earthquake. It fuelled the man with great confidence — especially when he would see them turning up in such significant numbers with no compulsion.

As he glanced at himself in the mirror, the pepper-white consistency of his hair revealed itself from the side of his head. It appeared more silver in some areas than its preceding black colour. He tried brushing it out of sight, not for the first time in the last hour, and failed to remove it once more.

You're getting old.

It sounded like a taunt as much as it sounded like a fact. He didn't know which way he was leaning more towards today.

Nicolae Ceaușescu, the great leader of the Socialist Republic of Romania, put down his hairbrush and pins, watching himself in the mirror for what felt like an eternity. He admired the stern expression he'd perfected for moments like this, practising his body language before the great speech that would take place in only a few moments. He pressed his fist against the palm of his other hand, failing to relax his muscles. He always felt the anticipation rising in the air before a vital announcement or speech — but he *never* got nervous.

That is forbidden, he told himself.

He hadn't abandoned and fled the mighty fields and narrow alleys of the Olt county only to become a coward. There was too much at stake, and he didn't have time to stop and be afraid. Such privileges were reserved for the other Romanians.

The knock on the padded door made him jump a little, waking him up from the daydream that he was lost in. It pulled him out of his own reflection in the mirror.

The reality of what was going to happen struck him once again.

The heat stung his nostrils — not just the humid air of the Capital, but the collective warmth of bodies gathered below. He wished that all of it could be done as soon as possible, for everyone's sake. He couldn't imagine having to stand in a large crowd like the one outside, under the August sun.

The Romanian people's devotion had no limits.

"*Intră*. Come in," he insisted in a raised tone.

Perhaps it was wrong of him to have his back turned to the door when it opened, but he felt safe. It was one thing to be in the streets or in a foreign building, with security lurking in every corner. And it was a different matter when he stood in his own home, in the quarters that belonged to the family alone. He trusted that his men wouldn't even let a flea get past the first set of doors that led to his room without his permission and precaution. The thought comforted him a little, and he noticed his finger growing softer. The tense feeling that was bothering his arm earlier disappeared, and he gave it a good squeeze to make sure.

Nicolae turned his head to face the man standing by his door — a tall man, who knew more about his schedule than Nicolae himself did, or anyone else, except maybe his Leana, the woman who orchestrated Nicolae's movements in the privacy of their room.

Before Nicolae could say anything, Leana's blissful face rose from behind the door frame, and he smiled at her. The many years they spent together had not strained the rope that held them close, unlike so many people they had known over the years.

"They're ready for you," Nicolae's wife said to him, before the other man, Florin, could utter a word.

He could tell that the man did not mind, though, as his loyalties aligned with anything that Nicolae and his wife did. Their guards were as loyal as their two dogs, Corbu and Șarona — the black labradors that no one else fed except Nicolae himself. He almost grinned at the image of his own men walking around after him, wagging their tails at his smallest movements.

Elena — or Leana, as he called her — moved a few steps closer to him, analysing his face. She straightened his jacket slightly, brushing her long fingers over the pins that he wore on his chest.

"They're ready," she repeated eagerly.

He nodded, looking away from her, and at the mirror for the last time.

"Comrade Florin. Escort me and my wife to the balcony," he said, the order carrying the tone of a request.

Florin gave him a nod, waiting for Elena to step in front of him. Nicolae wondered if Leana was still mad at Florin for what had happened a few days ago. He could still hear her screams, loud even in his memory.

All because of a pair of damned shoes.

Nicolae knew that Elena was never graceful in heels. Most people were aware of this, except his Leana, who insisted on wearing a long pair of heels with a thin support on so many occasions.

Only that last week, she had not been so lucky to hold onto the bannister in time, which led to an uncomfortable landing down the stairs. Later, she would blame Florin for trying to kill her, as if the mistake was not her own. Her screams had echoed through the apartment quarters, and Nicolae had insisted that she calm down.

"He tried to kill me, I'm telling you, you cannot trust a man like this to be among your closest protectors," Leana had said, embarrassment painting her cheeks scarlet.

She had pointed hysterically at the wooden door that was designed to keep sound inside, as Nicolae begged her to stop.

Finally, when she wouldn't, he left to see the dogs, leaving her with the solitude of her own embarrassment. He had also reassured a very frightened Florin that he was not in trouble for this, since an act of treason could very well be considered suicide.

"You know how she can get," Nicolae had nodded sadly, handing Corbu a piece of raw meat.

Florin had only nodded, standing a safe distance away from his leader and his hounds.

The balcony was the best place for a public speech, as the square in front of the building could fit a few thousand people without issue — one of Europe's best facilities. Nicolae stepped in first, but he was still out of the public's sight. A few people had perhaps felt his presence, which is why the murmurs had grown louder. He ignored them, glancing at Leana (and her brand new pair of heels), stepping carefully onto the balcony. Although it hurt her pride, Nicolae knew — she accepted a helping hand from Florin. The Ceaușescu couple stood in the sight of the public now, their faces visible to all those below them.

It is a beautiful day, Nicolae thought to himself, the bright Summer sun glowing on the entire building.

As he had practised earlier, he raised a hand to wave at the people, much like a king or an Emperor. His attire and home were fit for the part, as was his nation. His wife, his army, and his hounds. Not just the ones in his backyard, but the ones scattered across Romania, howling whispers of every house from door to door. He was loved by many and feared by most.

So why *shouldn't* he have felt like a powerful man when he *was* one?

The crowd roared in agreement.

Two

Elena

Timişoara, Romania – November 1989

The woman watched the street drown away with the sounds of the November rain, a calm, steady breeze dominating the place.

I ought to have seen it coming, she told herself, cursing at the laundry that she had forgotten on the hanging rope in the back garden.

The garden, if she could even call it more than a patch of grass, was shared with the other neighbours on the ground floor, which is how Elena retrieved what was left of her wet clothes. It was enough of a struggle washing them once; she couldn't bear the agony of doing it all over again.

In times like this, she reminded herself of the many ironies of life. She shared a name with the wife of their leader, 'the face' of Romanian women, an idol to look up to. And with Saint Elena, respectively, the woman who had spread faith among the Romans, yet she found nothing of herself in either of these women. It was almost amusing.

For starters, she did not doubt that Elena Ceauşescu never troubled herself with doing laundry. The same way that she didn't need to worry about the food rations, the electricity rations, and the fear of starvation, as most of the country did. And the Empress Saint Elena, after whom she was named, had it better than them both; she didn't lose faith as often as Elena did, although hardships had knocked on her door often in life. This made her feel a deep sense of shame about her complaints, twisting her stomach into tiny knots.

On one hand, there was her *leader* Elena, whom she would've traded places with anytime. And on the other hand, the Empress who felt gratitude even for the mere breath that she took. Which one of these women did she resemble more, she wondered?

But they had not sinned the way that you did. Your punishment is yet due.

She watched the street in front of her get soaked with rainwater, like a great flood that spread across the paved roads, the small yards in front of the cement buildings, and the holes in the ground that collected all the accompanying junk. If she had the time to exist in solitude for a few moments, distinct from the people around her, she would want it to be in the thunderous weather that cast people away. It seemed to be her nature anyway — as suggested by the empty seat at the table where her husband once sat.

The thought of Darius pulled her body away from the windowsill, and she reached to shut it entirely. The calming sound seemed like a distraction now, and she turned her back to it, now facing the stove. She stirred the big round pot with leisurely motion, calculating whether it would be enough for the entire family.

Dracu' să vă ia. To Hell with all of them, she cursed.

The state, the people, even the rain. The challenges ahead made her wonder whether someone had placed a bet on her — to see how long she would last if everything went wrong. Elena shook her head, moving back from the pot.

The *ciorbă*, a Romanian soup dish that smelt of herbs and garlic, boiled in silence. Usually, when Elena's mother made it, its colour would be blood orange, and the odour coming from the herbs and vegetables alone could fill one's stomach. Now, the dish staring back at Elena was almost transparent in consistency, and apart from a rotting potato that she had cut into cubes and a small pepper, there were no other vegetables in the pot. She found it to be an insult to her dearly departed mother, who would've made something much better with even fewer ingredients. The culinary arts were not for everyone — Elena dwelled on that idea, as she did whenever things went sideways.

She reached for the tap and filled a smaller pot with a generous amount of water, then poured it into the larger soup pot afterwards. What was left of the water, she heated up, putting it into a cup. She put a couple of *tei* flowers in it, letting the tea rest on the kitchen counter.

Although its colour had paled, the water made it seem like there was a lot more soup than there actually was; in all honesty, Elena considered it boiled water with a few vegetables teasing the eater, reminding them of what they could be having. She added some salt to the mixture and let it simmer for a few more minutes.

Sometimes, Elena wondered if Darius had enough to eat where he was. She had heard that the workers in factories had decent salaries, as well as meals, but that living in the factory meant being away from their families. She couldn't bear to tell her eldest, Ioana, a girl of nine, that her father had not sent a letter again. It had been three months since the last one, when Darius admitted to something that she couldn't quite forgive in an instant. It was that stone that she carried on her heart that made her glad that another letter had not arrived. Maybe it would fill her with more agony instead of revelation.

Forgive me, Elena. I am only a man, a human, with the exact needs as before. I wouldn't blame you if this were the other way around. I want you to know that.

The words from his last letter, which she had memorised by now, hung in the air even after all these weeks. He had said that he wouldn't blame Elena if she had broken the sacred vows of their marriage out of the pure boredom of a life away from family, and the animalistic lust that lurked inside every man.

But she knew that this wasn't the case.

The same forgiveness would never be granted to a woman, especially not a married one with children. Elena knew that even girls were not given such blessings, not when words were invented for women like that.

Curvă. A whore, a slut. Perhaps even a bitch.

It never made sense to her why such words were only ever used for women, and why the variety had spread out so vastly. All she knew was that if she had been the one to sleep with another man during her husband's absence, death would have come to her before the shadow of forgiveness.

It was like a curse, though — ever since her husband had confessed to his treachery, Elena couldn't help but imagine this other woman who had replaced her in these last couple of years. While she struggled with the bills because of Darius's delayed letters, containing fewer notes and pennies each time, he had his arms around this woman's waist, imprinting her with a part of him forever.

This haunted her.

Soon, this other woman had grown a face, and a body — she was everything that Elena would've admired in the physicality of a woman. She was voluptuous, with a heavy chest and tender hands, and she would never say no. After all, pleasing was her job, as Darius had admitted, and even after he insisted that it didn't mean a thing, Elena continued imagining this lady.

At last, she christened the woman with a name. Something which was both generic and unique. Perhaps Anastasia, or Parascheva. This woman had *definitely* been struggling as well, just like the rest of the country, which made Elena feel for her. Who knew what the child was going through, and it led her to sell her own body for a meal or the warmth of a coat? Everyone had mouths to feed, bills to pay, and queues to stand in for the division of rations.

But Darius was the one that she could picture clearly in her visions and thoughts.

Because he is real.

Her memories with him, the places where his mouth had once touched and his hands had caressed, were not a figment of her imagination. And those were the parts that hurt her.

Elena wiped away the tear that rolled down from the crystal grey of her eyes, lifting her head upwards, overwhelmed. She had to stop this brisk shift in moods that occurred whenever the memory of her husband came upon her. It wasn't healthy. Now that the money from him had not come for three months, she worried that she might have to start formulating a reply to his letter. Every time she tried doing it, it left her with nothing but blank paper and one of the pens that she used to mark her students' tests.

At least the primary school provided her with some financial stability for the kids, even if their own father wouldn't.

Three

Elena

Timişoara, Romania — November 1989

Once again, she let her worries swim in her mind until the door behind her opened. It led into the small living room where the children, Ioana and her brother Beriţă[1], sat with their homework books in their laps. She turned to see Ioana standing in front of her, holding her book in her palms.

"How much longer till dinner, *Mama*?" she asked, rubbing her left eye with thoroughness.

Elena was in awe of how often she saw her own younger self in Ioana, an uncorrupted child, naive to the world's hardships. She worried about her daughter's skinny arms and thinning form, which could've led to a disordered growth. Elena's uncle Bernard had died of something similar, an illness that her father would often alarm them about. He had told them tales of what used to happen to the kids in villages, the younger ones especially — parents would send them away to other cities, to live with relatives. Or to secure better jobs, like the Professor and his wife dreamed of, they would move to one of the larger cities. Timişoara, Cluj, Bucharest — sometimes the smaller ones like Oradea or Sibiu as well.

[1] Beriţă – pronounced *"Bay-ree-tzuh"*

Elena wiped her face with the back of her palm.

"It's almost done, come. Set up the table," she asked Ioana, forcing a smile.

She watched her daughter reach for the plates and bowls, setting them around the wooden kitchen table. Four sets of knives, forks, and spoons were laid out neatly, and she congratulated the young girl when she was finished.

"Call Berița," Elena said, moving the pot on the table.

Before putting some bread too, she took a peek at the fridge, searching for butter. What was left of the last ration of butter was no bigger than Elena's little finger, and she felt nearly insulted by it. She remembered that her brother had stood in line for dairy products for almost five hours that day, holding the hand of his six-year-old nephew, Berița.

"All for *this*?" he had asked Elena, pointing at the palm of butter that wasn't even enough for a week, and the two litres of milk that they had to use in the next three weeks.

The milk was long gone, but what was left of the butter, Elena kept like a hidden jewel, using very little when needed. The thought of her brother widened her eyes — *where* was Robi?

"Unde e Unchiul Robi, Berița? Where is your uncle?" she asked her son, who had just climbed up his wooden stool to take a peek at the soup.

His blond hair leaned over the pot as he inhaled the scent of it.

"I don't know," he answered plainly, watching the pot with a glow in his eyes.

Ever since their mother had died, Robi had spent more and more time in Elena's company, and with her children, avoiding the cold approach of Elena and Robert's father.

The old man had been known as *"Profesorul"*, the Professor — a respected person in the entire neighbourhood. People still whispered about his linguistic and pedagogical abilities, but they were careful about what they said. The Romanian Security Service, the *Securitate,* was never more than a whisper away from overhearing the wrong thing from the wrong person (or, in their opinion, the *right* thing from the *right* person), which only ever led to chaos.

The only two people who knew about the Professor's secrets were his children; they were also the only two people who avoided talking to him, the scars from their younger years still fresh.

Robert was tall and lean, like their mother, a twenty-year-old boy with a dark bush of hair and green, frozen eyes. Elena had felt bad for the boy — he had been living with their father in the apartment, which was just a five-minute walk from their own building. Who wanted to spend time with that old, grumpy man?

So when Darius had left to work in a factory two hundred miles east of their city, Timișoara, Elena welcomed her younger brother into the home, as if he were her own child. Their father's shadow dwelled between them still — he had, after all, bestowed valuable knowledge upon his children. Elena had concluded though — knowledge was a curse more than it was a blessing. It's why the stupidest people, or the ignorant people, were always the happiest in the world.

It's our secret, Elena. Everything I teach you and your brother. You must never pass it on, unless it is to your own blood.

Her father had uttered these vows to her and Robert when they were young children; of course, the uncommon part about their discussions was that he had uttered things to them in English, after months of teaching them how to speak it. He then repeated the vows, among other promises, in Italian, French, Serbian, Russian, and German. Elena could still understand most of these languages pretty well, having a sharp ear for the different tongues and dialects.

She and Robi would have become valuable assets to the *Securitate,* the dogs that were running the country in the dictator's name. Such talent needed to stay hidden, perhaps only between people who shared the same blood. Elena had forbidden her father and brother from telling Ioana and Beriță about any of it until they were old enough to understand.

After all, such individuals had an unbreakable bond with one another. Blood ran thicker than water.

The Professor's collection of banned books and texts in other languages had to remain that — *his* own collection.

The front door of the apartment burst open, making Elena jump. The first room that the door led into was the kitchen, so their newly arrived was visible to everyone.

"*Unchiul Robi*!" Beriță yelped, bouncing off his stool and into the man's arms.

Robi held him tightly, putting him back down on the floor after a few moments. He tossed his college bag to one corner and talked to the children.

Though Beriță had only seen him earlier that morning, he had already grown fond of Robi, who seemed like a second father to him. Elena recognised the behaviour too, sadly reminiscing on the time that Darius had lost with his kids.

"You're getting heavier," Robi chuckled, taking off his coat.

The hole on the side of his coat's right elbow seemed to grow more visible, and Elena made a mental note to sew it back up.

"Come, eat," she muttered, filling the fourth bowl with soup.

Robi glanced at the pot, in which little was left, so he took the bowl from her hands.

"*Doamne*, Elena. My God, how much will you feed me?" he asked, pouring a little back in the pot.

She knew his act all too well, and the way that he behaved around the table. He already believed that he was making the daily struggle more burdensome by his presence there, to which Elena ordered him never to repeat that. It broke her heart that he pretended not to be hungry, or that he was too full, only for the children and her to have some more left.

"Please, Robi," she pleaded between furrowed eyebrows.

He gave her a nod, but insisted that he was alright.

"I'm going to go see George; he always has his meals at the workshop," Robi said, waving her away.

A dark curl fell over his forehead.

"Cut your hair. You look like a vagabond," Elena said, pushing his hair back.

Robi gave her an amused smirk. When the soup was finished, Elena began laying out the main course. It was nothing fancy — not in the slightest. Salted cow's cheese, tomatoes, some leftover polenta, and a few thin slices of cured meat. To her surprise, her brother got up from the table and reached for his coat again.

"I must get going. George is expecting me," he said, rushing.

George was one of their neighbours from the second floor of the building, who owned a little wood workshop. He let Robi do the occasional assistance and taught him a few things, but more importantly, he paid him for his efforts. The little money that he made, he contributed to the family.

"He'll understand that you were having dinner, Robi. Please, sit down," she insisted again.

But he didn't listen. He walked over to Elena and planted a kiss on her cheek, just as the children did every time that they left the house.

"Stop worrying, Elena," he urged. "And you…" he said, pointing at Beriță. "You'd better leave some for me."

This trick always seemed to work on the boy; whenever his uncle asked him not to do something, he would do it out of pure amusement. Robert used this talent well.

"One day, I worry that the boy will follow you all the way to the doors of Heaven, Robi. He doesn't seem to let you out of his sight for a moment," she told her brother.

Elena stood by the half-open window and watched the boy walk away from the building. Their street, Theatre's Street, ended at the corner where the tram tracks began, where Robi turned right to head to the workshop. Long after Robi's shadow abandoned the street's corner, Elena turned back from the window. The cool breeze felt pleasant.

She noticed that her cup of *tei* tea stood forgotten on the kitchen counter, lost with the conversations and the hustle. She picked up its cold edges and brought the lukewarm liquid to her lips.

When the kids had left for the living room to do their homework, Elena gathered the dishes and pots from the table and drowned them in soapy water in the sink. She let them rest there for a while before rinsing them well, a habit that helped her conserve soap and hot water in case the rations were late or cut off.

She bent down under the sink and took out a small box that was overflowing with bottles of soap and washing powders.

Underneath the hill of products that she had collected over the months, she could feel the wooden cover of her radio, the only item that she had kept hidden away from her entire family—everyone except Robi, who, after all, had been responsible for the purchase.

Her brother had brought home the radio from a merchant at the *Piața*, who claimed that his product was worn out and old, not worth more than a few spare pennies. Robi, however, had other plans for the old radio. He had lied to the man, Elena remembered him telling her, and then took it to George's atelier for repair. In a couple of days, the radio was perfect once again. It even caught waves from neighbouring countries, a situation that Elena wished she hadn't been put in.

She took out the radio that could've been the reason she would be taken to prison one day, or worse, disappear without a trace. Elena placed it on the kitchen counter and looked around for the children. When she was sure that no one could hear her, she turned the first button towards the right and pressed a smaller one on the left.

The familiar sound of static echoed first, and then the radio came alive.

"*Az 1989. október 23-i forradalom lezárásának hatásai...*" Elena heard, and turned it down.

A horrified sound escaped her; she hadn't touched the radio since the beginning of October. All she knew about their Hungarian neighbours was that 'issues' were unfolding there — unrest spreading from west to east. Hungary had escaped their captors. Could her own people do the same?

She listened for a couple of minutes before hiding the radio away again, tucking it behind all the soaps. Then, Elena walked over to the window that she had left half-open upwards, and pushed it into its frame. She twisted the knob, promising to be more careful next time with her surroundings.

What if someone heard me?

She couldn't afford all that trouble, so she decided not to entertain the worry.

Four

Robert

Timişoara, Romania – November 1989

Robert's face lit up at the sight of the old Gothic establishments. Built in defiance of their western sisters, they looked like miracles next to the newly constructed cement buildings. They looked like a miracle in front of the freshly built cement buildings. These new homes stood tall in the city, but took away all the colour that had once been a part of it — they looked like the images of the Soviet Union that Robert had seen in one of his father's old books.

As he walked down the street where his father's apartment was, he couldn't help but look up at the building, a weird feeling that he was being watched dawning over him.

He waved it away with the shake of his head and carried on walking down the cobblestone road, his hands standing firmly in his pockets. The sound of a tram shaking on its tracks in the distance made him look up, and he admired the contents of the city as if he were a traveller here.

George had been kind to him that day, offering him a loaf of bread and some cured meat in addition to the money that he paid him. It made life much easier, not having to live on Elena's leftover food and the little scraps that were swimming in the pots for the kids. The image of children starving made him sick, only because he had witnessed it so often.

At only twenty, he had seen more than most twice his age; the weight of two decades pressed on him like an axe chained to his back. The queue of desperation and how the faces of people would switch every time a newcomer would show up behind them.

Would there ever be enough?

Electricity fading back into its source after the evening lights would come on, just so the saving of it would pay for the country's outstanding debts. Nowadays, Robi thought amusingly, even one's hope was given in rations, no more than a little at a time.

His friends from the University sensed it as well as he did, that the wave of rebellion flying from the east would soon take rest in their country as well, like a dark bird carrying sorrows. Something huge was coming their way, ready to demolish the foundations that the government was standing on.

Perhaps it would come from within.

Robi fastened his pace at the sight of a few known neighbours passing him by, eager not to have to stop and pretend that their chatter brought him some pleasure. It seemed quite beneath him, too, all things considered. To his luck, the two elderly women were too busy whispering among themselves to notice his turned head, and he swept away smoothly. It brought the ghost of a smile to his face, and he carried on walking as if the world was his oyster.

University usually bored Robi. The limitations imposed on learning angered him; sometimes it was simpler to endure boredom than to feel constant frustration. His father had raised both him and his sister to become individuals with intellect, who valued his teachings above all else — unluckily for them, they were born on the wrong side of the world to put their knowledge into practice.

"What's the point of this burden if I'll never use it?" a fifteen-year-old Robi had asked his father in anger.

His father had usually been gentle to them, even when they grew displeased with his teachings.

"*Never* label knowledge as a burden, Robert. I have never struck you, nor will I — unless you ever grow ignorant, boy. No son of mine shall be an ignorant sheep in this unholy land of wolves," his father had replied, a firm hand holding the back of Robi's head.

He had shaken him gently before letting go, and it was a memory that Robi had never forgotten. That was the last time he had complained about it.

Save for the propagandist philosophies that were chiefly pushed down one's throat, there was little that entertained Robi anymore. Even his father's old, worn-out books had been touched a dozen times by him as a kid, and posed as something uninteresting, no matter how forbidden their contents were.

Most of the Professor's books were gifted to him over the years, from a time when he worked with ambassadors and politicians instead of schoolteachers — but Robi never dared to ask questions about that time. And neither did Elena. What was left from their younger years was a wormhole of knowledge that they were forced to live with, the ability to speak languages that would never escape their lips in public, and a mind designed to detect errors in their own everyday lives.

As Robi carried on walking, he couldn't help but notice the tall figure of a man that seemed to be approaching him directly from the shadows. The sun had started going down long before he had left George's place, and now, a dusky hue had overlaid the late afternoon sky. It was hard making out the faces of people unless he was close to them, and he struggled to recognise the man who now rushed even more than before. Robi stepped to one side, and the man mirrored his movements, leaning in close all of a sudden.

The man grabbed Robi's shirt from the chest, pushing him against the brick wall behind him. The boy turned his head around to see if someone could see him, and it was no surprise that he had been deserted; how could he have been so stupid? Robi cursed under his breath and tried pushing back.

Under the streetlight, Robert could see his features clearly.

The silver-grey eyes and dark hair were undeniably his.

Yes, it must be, Robi found himself thinking.

"Dragoș Stănescu?" Robi's tongue escaped, and he regretted being so vocal.

The man, who was certainly no one other than the Dragoș that Robi knew from the building opposite their father's home, grabbed his jacket's collar and pulled him up.

"If you're clever, you'll follow me without doing anything rash," Dragoș spoke. Then, with a heartfelt smirk, he added, "*Tovarășe.* Comrade."

Robi wanted to spit on his face. So what they said about him was true. His father had warned him about the neighbours who might be spying on others and selling information in exchange for a loaf of bread — soldiers of the *Securitate,* traitors. Cheap tricks continuously fed desperation quite suitably, Robi had found. But he couldn't help but feel hatred towards the man whom he once considered a friend. Despite the Professor's warnings, Robi refused to believe every person that his father suspected of being a spy.

And Dragoș was one of those people whom he would've sworn for.

Aș fi băgat mâna în foc. He would've put his hand in fire, as the saying went.

Dragoș was closer in age to Elena than he was to Robi, but when the young men and boys of the neighbourhood would hang out to play games in the Summer or go carolling in the Winter, Dragoș had always been around. Robi had exchanged jokes with him, just as he had with the other boys; they had been responsible for finishing *Doamna* Grădinariu's famous Christmas *cozonac* the previous holiday season. The bread-cake slices were full of walnuts and poppy seeds, treats that the boys hadn't had for an entire year. And yet, he was one of the slaves of the *Securitate.*

Robi wanted to scream.

He remembered what Dragoș had done for Elena when she was expecting Berița, and a faded frown printed itself on his face.

"Of course, Comrade," Robi responded. He was going to be clever about this, he told himself, as he felt Dragoș's grip loosen up, and walked down the street by his side.

When they reached Dragoş's building, the man's grip tightened around Robi's collar once again, and he grabbed his hood violently.

"No need for that," Robi responded, trying to make him let go. Dragoş was at least half a foot taller than him, which made his struggle all the more difficult.

"*Amice*," Robi added. Friend.

Had he not been in the position that made him vulnerable in front of Dragoş, he would've found the irony almost amusing.

Dragoş pushed him up the stairs, turning his head around and peeking at the street. When they entered the building, Dragoş didn't need to guide him to his apartment. Robi knew where he lived, although he couldn't remember ever coming inside.

It's probably full of dead puppies and happiness confiscated in jars.

Robi could find something to laugh about, even in a condition like this; he was truly a Romanian, having been taught from a young age not to make his complaints evident.

The man twisted a metal key in the hole when they reached the second floor, in front of the apartment, to the right. He shoved Robi inside and twisted the key in the lock, sealing the door behind them with a definitive click.

Five

Dragoș

Timișoara, Romania — November 1989

Dragoș Stănescu hated the stench of dampness in his home. It reeked of sickness and death, and with the probability being on the door, it always put him in a bad mood. The sour smell seemed to affect the newcomer, Robert, as well — the boy scrunched his nose, waving a hand through the air.

He was so much smaller than him, Dragoș thought. He was a mere boy in comparison, although he was in fact a man of twenty. Opposed to Dragoș at nearly twenty-nine, the young boy was less stern-looking, with locks of dark hair and a look that told Dragoș that the boy was afraid. He was good at hiding it, but not good enough.

The first room you encountered upon entering was a hallway that led into the living room, and as much as Dragoș hated the place, he was glad it was warm there. He had tried so hard to install a better heating system in the rooms, but even for someone deeply involved with the *Securitate*, the situation was complicated. Contrary to the illusion that spying got you countless favours, even the people who were responsible for pulling triggers were struggling.

His friend looked surprised at the pile of things sitting in his living room — from glasses, cups, and silverware, to old books, and game cards. Properties for other people before they came into Dragoș's possession, most of which he knew nothing about before.

"Take a seat, Comrade," Dragoș teased. This was far too amusing for him. "Or would you rather stand while we talk about your traitorous sister's radio?" he asked.

The boy's eyes widened in front of him, only slightly. It was enough to confirm Dragoș's suspicions. Elena had always been so careless; it was no surprise that she hadn't checked the window before turning on her little device. Ever since being a Securitate agent, he had peeked underneath hundreds of windows, mostly harmless. Now and then, he would discover smuggled items, but that was all. A radio was truly a precious item, and its possession could be held like a lever over someone, which is why he made sure to get to the source first.

When Robi sat down amidst the pile of magazines and books, Dragoș mirrored his movements. He leaned forward, his legs spread apart on the stool.

"Now, tell me, what shall I do with a traitorous whore like your sister?" Dragoș asked.

He hated using such vulgarity, primarily when referring to Elena — but the performance demanded it.

And he was always convincing when he needed to be.

"Punish her, of course. Besides, I don't know what radio you're talking about. I doubt that a woman like her is clever enough to operate such a thing, wouldn't you agree?" Robert responded.

The boy was far too intelligent for his own good.

"Careful now, *băiete*," Dragoș laughed, leaning forward. "Are you afraid, Comrade? Hm?" he asked, teasingly.

"A loyal serviceman of the country has nothing to fear, right? I perform my duties well, even if it means that my sister has to pay for what you accuse her of doing," the younger boy replied, putting on a taunting smirk on his lips.

"So you're calling me a liar? You think I am accusing her of something she did not do?" Dragoș said, adding some ferocity to his voice.

The younger boy's face grew visibly paler as he straightened his posture.

"Comrade…" he began, mockingly.

He did not have time to finish his sentence, as Dragoş interrupted him with a slap behind his head; quick, but not as hard as he would've hit someone that he intended to hurt.

"A boy like you is in no position to mock," Dragoş spat.

"I would never do such a thing, Comrade," Robi said boldly. "I do think people should be punished, as our Comrade Ceauşescu says. Any enemy of the leader is the enemy of our state. And we all admire the great leader, don't we?" he added, with a hand on his chest.

Dragoş watched him quietly for a moment, unmoved by the boy's performance. He had to admit that for any other person, the boy's acting was phenomenal.

But he felt a hole in his heart, in the space where his dignity had once been. He ached at the sight of youth being drugged into the agendas of propagandist ideologies, fearing what would happen if they ever uttered their own truth.

"Coward," he said, mocking Robi back. "And here I was thinking you were one of the good kids… you're at the University, right? I thought so. But you're still a coward,"

Robi watched him, confused.

"Oh, don't look at me like that, you heard me. You are a coward," and without letting the younger boy speak, he added, "You and I both know that we feel the same way about 'our great leader'… you're a fucking liar, and an even bigger coward on top of that," Dragoş finished.

"Well, you just committed an act of disloyalty towards our leader…" Robi said calmly, pointing at Dragoş's chest.

This 'act', perhaps the younger boy suspected, was all that; an act to lure him into saying the wrong things, get him into trouble. Whoever had taught him how to behave in this situation had taught him well, as if they could read the mind of an agent that needed information. Dragoş cursed everything and everyone that he could think of in that moment, and leaned forward, close enough to feel the younger boy's breath on his face.

"*Dumnezeule*, they really fucked up your mind, didn't they? You're in that deep with these pigs?" Dragoş asked. "A young man like you cannot express disagreement because of how much you're in fear of what might happen?"

The younger boy's eyes burned with the same desire for freedom that Dragoş's words were evoking. He could feel it, despite the boy's silence. The older man decided to break it — days later, he would ask himself if this was the moment that had altered everything between them.

"You know what the *Securitate* asked me to do this time? Oh, don't look so shocked! They asked me to spy on all the young kids of the *cartier*, mere adolescents like you, who go to the University... they're afraid that a wave strong enough to take down everything is coming..." Dragoş admitted in a whisper.

"W-what are you saying?" Robi asked him, realisation pulling him back with a jolt.

"I'm saying..." Dragoş whispered unmoved. "I'm saying, I am sick of it. I could tell them about your sister's radio, just as I've told them many things before. But what is the use, boy? I am still stuck in this miserable pile of junk and shit that I never dared to ask about."

Robi looked at him with a straight face, not even risking the blink of his eyes. His gaze pierced through Dragoş, whose flushed cheeks were now covered with the bare palms of his hands.

"Why would you tell me this?" Robi asked. "Even if it was true, why would you risk telling me, of all people, such a revelation? It doesn't make sense, dear Comrade," the boy added, still half-mocking.

"Because, *tovarășe*... I have had enough of this life for a long time. But no one would've listened to me if I told them about this... until now," Dragoş said, rising to his feet.

He picked up a collection of papers that had been sitting lifelessly on the table behind his chair and tossed them in Robi's lap. The boy tried dodging them as if they were loaded grenades, ready to avoid their sight at all costs. But the papers found the touch of his curiosity in the next moment, as Robi looked at them.

"Maps?" he asked, a swallow stuck in his throat. "What does this mean?"

he asked, looking at the little Xs and dots that Dragoş had marked the papers with.

"X marks the spot where our agents suspect that a rebellion will break out. It could be any of those places, or perhaps even multiple locations. The dots represent all the people I know who are definitely involved. So far. I am meant to give this map back to that bitch who plays me like a fool; she has been for years. But instead, this is what I'll be giving her," Dragoş added, giving the young boy the paper underneath the one on top.

"This one has not even half of that…" Robert said, his fingers shaking on top of the paper.

"Precisely. I can mislead them for long enough until I find out every boy and girl's name who wants in on the protests. The real deal, what the students at the University whisper about," Dragoş said, amused at the look on the young boy's face. "What? You think I didn't know what you and your friends talk about behind closed doors? Why else would I be seeking you out like this, *prostule?*"

Robi's face soured at the taunt of being stupid, and Dragoş made a mental note of giving him a new *poreclă*, a slightly unkind nickname given out of familiarity or even humour.

"I am telling you this because if a *răscoală* will start, I don't want it to stop. I am sick of this shit. Everything rationed, my elderly parents not knowing anything their entire lives other than the one TV channel we have and the endless queues for food. I couldn't care less about who is betraying the dictator. You're scared that I could kill you, aren't you? You have a nice radio with many channels, huh, boy? And you're still leaving here in one piece. I don't know what else to tell you; if killing you is what I wanted, you'd be taken in for treachery right now," he said, and patted his shoulder.

Robert's face gave away the chill that he felt down his spine at the mention of the radio, knowing what the *Securitate* agent had on him and Elena now.

"Are you in, boy?" he asked Robi, waving his arm at the door.

The boy was free to leave.

"*Bine*," said Robert, and rushed for the door, picking up his things from the entrance.

"*Țin**em legătura,*" said Dragoș. We'll keep in touch. Whether he wanted to or not.

Six

Robert

Timișoara, Romania — November 1989

"You really need to be more careful with that," Robi patted his forehead with a handkerchief, tucking it away in his coat's pocket.

He hadn't slept all night; thoughts of the revolutionary protests he had considered secret until yesterday churned in his mind with every passing second. And then there was the matter of Elena's radio, which she was planning on taking out once more, kneeling near the kitchen sink to reach for it.

"Why? Has something happened?" she asked, her face looking pale.

"N-no… well, I don't know, something *could* happen, you know? We need to be careful, Elena. People at the university are being more and more paranoid," he said.

"Speaking of which, you haven't gone in what… three days? You really need to get yourself together, Robi. I don't ask much of you around here, but I need you to study. I can't see you wasting away, not when I know what you're worth," Elena added.

Little does she know, Robi thought.

He had been avoiding the chance of seeing Dragoș since the last time they met; Saturdays were always his favourites before that damned agent found him. Now, even the privilege of a nice, quiet walk by the Bega River in the town's centre was an impossible task.

"Why don't you take the kids out? To see *Tata*? Dad hasn't seen them in two weeks; I am sure he could use the company. And you could use a change in scenery," she said, banging a cup of tea in front of him.

"Jesus, Elena…" Robi muttered under his breath, wishing for a slow, quiet nap.

Then he entertained a new thought. Going in public may have tempted Dragoş to see Robi. But the presence of children wouldn't. The agent was bold, but not enough to make himself seen to Ioana and Beriță.

Ioana grabbed her copy of *Moromeții* in one hand and the Collected Poems of Mihai Eminescu in the other, then put on her coat. Robert tied up Beriță's shoes and handed him his coat, as he couldn't quite reach the hanger without stepping on the little wooden stool they kept in the kitchen. He picked up his own coat and bag from the hallway and turned around to find his sister. His half-finished cup of tea stood on the table, and he reached his hand out quickly to finish it in one go.

"Eleno!" he yelled. "*Plecăm!* We're going now!" he added, rubbing his eyes thoroughly.

Elena walked out in the hallway with the thick woollen blanket wrapped around her and kissed the children goodbye.

On Saturdays, his sister would finally have some time just to herself, while the kids and Robert went out around the city, or to see their grandfather. Sometimes, she would spend these days grading her students' work or reading her favourite novels. Small habits that reminded her of what living felt like, before all the worries had taken over, perhaps.

Robert had promised to take the kids out to *Parcul Rozelor* in the city, also known as the Garden of Roses. Despite not being in full bloom as it would have been in the Summer, the park had the Bega flowing through it, the sight of the Cathedral and was close to the town centre. After that, they could see their *Bunicu'* and spend some time at his place. During which Robert would see George.

At least that was what he usually did.

He left the apartment in a hurry, rushing the kids outside — Elena's hoarse voice told them to be good. The cold did not agree with her throat, no matter how much she insisted on drinking tea and wearing warm clothes — a home needed to be safe, which Robert doubted it was anymore. For Elena and for the kids. It ached his heart that there were people out there, just like them, who perhaps had even less than they did; after all, it could *always* get worse.

They left the building and stepped into the street, which, as always, looked the same. Cement block buildings, dark windows, the sound of people walking and talking in hushed voices; all as eternal as the wind calling Robi's name.

To their right, there was a tram station, which connected the entire city through its polished tracks and rattling noises. They would have reached the park in about ten minutes by tram, if they were lucky. The 'Number Two', as they called it, may have already left.

"*Hai să mergem*," said Robert, pushing the kids gently in the station's direction.

He reached out his hand for Beriță to hold, and Ioana, out of instinct, reached out her hand to hold his, too.

They walked with a fastened pace around the corner, crossing the main road. The streets were full of *Dacias* with even-numbered plates, as the laws forbade all cars from travelling on weekends.

One of the days was for odd—numbered cars, the other for even-numbered ones. Robi remembered that when Beriță was born on a Saturday, the man that he was now avoiding had to drive Elena to the hospital because Darius couldn't. The car number plate would not allow it. His sister had sat in the backseat of Dragoș's car, wailing and crying from the ache. Little Ioana was left at home that day, while Robi and Darius tried to comfort Elena.

Now, Robi thought, amused, he would've given a limb not to see Dragoș at all. The man was still not trustworthy, and he was going to stray as far away from him as possible.

Suddenly, Robert's steps were stopped by the firm grip on the back of his neck, hanging on tightly to his coat. The kids stopped and looked at him. Without even turning around, he could tell who the hand belonged to; the other man's voice only confirmed his fear.

"Unde mergeți, copii? Where are you going, kids?" said Dragoș, his icy smile watching the children.

A shiver ran down Robert's spine. All in all, if Dragoș was lying, he couldn't put his niece and nephew in danger. How could he have been so foolhardy? He should have known that even with the kids around, a *Securitate* dog would make himself noticed.

The kids knew Dragoș — of course they did.

In a neighbourhood like theirs, everyone knew everyone, especially when the man had aided them in a time of need. However, people preferred to keep to themselves, avoiding entanglement with individuals like Dragoș. Years of deceit and lies had instilled those habits in them.

His gut feeling told him not to worry, but he knew better than to trust his instincts in a world where they meant nothing. A world that relied on his instincts being wrong.

"*Parcul Rozelor*!" yelled out Beriță enthusiastically, and for once, Robert wished he could have been as quiet as his sister was.

Ioana gave Dragoș a stare, without uttering a single word.

"Oh, *la plimbare*, eh? You kids are taking a nice walk on a day like this?" teased Dragoș.

If Robert didn't know any better, he would have told him to fuck off. No matter how unusual such language was for him, he would've sworn and cursed till the sun went down.

"I am only taking the kids out to get some fresh air and see their grandad, I never realised they passed that as illegal too?" said Robert, leaning in closer.

The kids looked amused, even Ioana, smirking under her breath.

"No, of course not, Robi. You wouldn't mind if I joined you, no? And on our way back, I think we can all treat ourselves to some *Scufița Roșie*!" Dragoș chirped.

Scufița Roșie was the only sweet brand available for kids to buy; a bar of waffle and milk coated in a thin layer of chocolate. It was shaped like Little

Red Riding Hood, the fairytale character. Robert did not plan on standing in any queues for two pea-sized pieces of chocolate, even if Dragoş made him do it.

The cold brown eyes, the dark chestnut hair, and the intimidatingly athletic figure all melted away in the face of the children. Dragoş seemed to have won over both children with that bold promise, which, in a world where your next meal was not assured, felt glorious.

Chocolate was only available near holiday seasons, and sometimes, if Elena made bargains with colleagues or neighbours near the kids' birthdays. People always helped if they could; it was one quality that they had naturally developed.

Who would help the helpless, if they weren't going to help each other?

"Of course you can," said Robert, trying not to hesitate.

Causing a scene on the street would only draw more attention to him, and worse, the children. So, he went along with whatever twisted game Dragoş had in mind.

He scowled at Dragoş's face once the kids turned around and headed to the station that they knew like the back of their hand, while he was left behind with someone he could only describe as a sadist.

"Lighten up. No serious talk in front of the kids," said Dragoş, leaning into Robert's left ear.

Great. More talk later.

And somewhere behind that calm façade, he knew trouble was waiting.

Seven

Nicolae

Bucharest, Romania — November 1989

The fly kept landing on his skin — like it knew something he didn't. Its wings buzzed louder than the voices around the table, louder even than the accusations he tried to forget. The damned creatures were just like 'the Six' that had been causing havoc all around the country for the last few months, enough even to dominate his restless sleeps at night.

Nicolae Ceaușescu palmed his forehead subtly while the politicians spoke in hushed voices, waiting for him to command something. Usually, a leader's posture alone was enough to convey silence and fear across a room — his body language had to speak louder than his words ever could.

However, the headache had worsened since morning. His age played a factor, too, he thought.

The end was so near he could almost touch it; like a mystery hidden behind a veil, which he was stretching his small arms towards, trying not to fall over the edge in the process.

His people, the ones he had done all this for... they were turning against him.

In the privacy of their homes, they cursed him. They said he was a maniac, a *dictator*! He, who had paved roads, given the people free homes when they needed them, made the country stable and independent? The people's ungratefulness had no boundaries — he was generous to them, like a father. He had given everyone of them a job and taught them how to do it. They called him "*Ceașcă*" in mockery, like the Romanian word for cup. He only wished that they could all forget what they claimed he had done — leave him behind on the kitchen counter so that he could cool down during all this heat.

And now *his own* greatest six members from the Communist Party had made up all these lies about how he had committed crimes that were unheard of! The whole world had heard the broadcast and made their loyalties evident.

"Six men who had dined at the same table as I, and had broken the bread that I had brought from my home. Do you understand what is happening here?" he had asked Leana when she was complaining about some nonsensical thing.

"That happened because you have too much trust in people," Leana had said, holding his chin in her hands. "Tell me, Nicu. Are you afraid now, knowing that you have to present yourself in front of a nation that hates you?", she had smirked.

His anger often came accompanied by sadness.

"We said we would make history together. And that's what this is. With the good and the bad," he had tossed her hand out of the way.

Elena Ceaușescu had seemed unbothered by the gesture.

"I know you're frightened of what follows. That's why I insist, Nicu. You need people that you can trust even in the dark," she had lowered her head. "You must punish them, my love."

Then, reaching into the pockets of her coat, she had handed him a little locket hanging on a thick, black string.

"I got this from *Baba* Dafina for you," she had uttered, lowering the totem into his palm.

Nicolae was aware of Elena's adventures around the Roma neighbourhoods, as she went there at least once a month — disguised and with her head lowered, in the absence of her husband. The women forbade a male presence in many homes, but even so, their voodoo and tricks never immensely impressed him.

He clutched it between his fingers.

"I don't believe in all this pagan nonsense," Nicolae had replied, handing it back to her.

"Dafina says she sees ten swords in our future. Her mother says it means that our armies will grow, but she says it could symbolise d—"

"No more," Nicolae had put his hand up in protest. "I don't need this right now."

From the corner of his eye, Nicolae could have sworn that he had seen Leana murmur something into the locket before tossing it into her purse.

That had been the end of it.

The meeting hall was still thundering upon the fly's buzz, until Nicolae had already had enough of it. Without intending to, he slammed his fist into the wooden table, sniffing loudly.

The room went silent.

"Do all of you think that I haven't read the contents of the terrible 'Letter of the Six' yet? We didn't come here to discuss what has already happened. My interest is in what we will do next. What do you, my advisors, consider that I should do now?"

The politicians, advisors, and, last but not least, Leana, watched as his mouth twitched at the mention of the letter. His vision felt like a lens of spiderweb covering his eyelids, and he shut them tightly to clear his head.

You must punish them, my love.

Leana's eyes met his, piercing through the sizzling heat inside of him.

"Despite what you have advised, Comrade," a younger member let out a cough, "Punishing these people won't do us any good. Not when the entire world is watching us."

Nicolae wanted to laugh — only that they would start calling him a madman too then, if they hadn't already.

"This is our country. We don't owe them anything— absolutely nothing.

We don't have any debts to anyone, nor do we have any poor relations. Only a fool would start a conflict that doesn't have anything to do with them," Nicolae's crystal clear voice echoed in the hall.

He could hear his wife's voice in the back of his head, guiding each word that came out of his mouth, as if it were her own. As he glanced over at her, she looked pleased.

"And the leaders from the rest of the world won't put themselves at such a risk. Historically, we never started any wars — we only defended ourselves. In a month, no one will even remember what happened in a country like ours, insignificant to the West," he raised his hand, so no one would dare interrupt.

No matter how well-intended their advice would have been.

"We won't let anyone beat us," he added, nodding at Leana.

The words had sounded much more believable when she had uttered them to him, in front of their son, Nicu, and their daughter Zoia. Their oldest son, Valentin, had been away again — doing whatever he pleased, as was his way. The memory only assured Nicolae that he had done a good job in picking his youngest son as his successor; at least he could deliver such speeches as well.

The meeting hall was soon crowded with people exchanging glances around the room, all of them avoiding Nicolae Ceaușescu's gaze. Except for that little fly.

It seemed to hang on to Nicolae's flesh, as if he were a corpse.

Eight

Robert

Timişoara, Romania — November 1989

Timişoara had been blessed with numerous architectural wonders, thanks to the Austro-Hungarian influences it faced in the 19th century. The sights around him were vastly different from the village he grew up in, which, to Robert, felt like a completely separate world. The buildings in Timişoara were grander, their shapes mirroring the Austrian buildings he had seen on postcards.

The archway doors sometimes had buds of ivy and little leaflets growing around them, the statuettes of Gothic creatures hanging from the edges of the windows, in front of their caramelised frames. The buzzing of trams rattled through every street, connecting the townspeople from every corner in a matter of seconds. Preserved on the side of the town centre's roads were street lamps from the time of the Austro-Hungarian Empire.

After all, Timişoara was the first city in Europe with permanent electrical facilities, starting with the lamps on the paved streets. It felt like a shame to Robi that such a gift was now being rationed, as if the wonder of it being available all around the city seemed like a foggy memory. His favourite part about the city was where he was taking the kids now (and Dragoş, against his will).

The river Bega.

From a distance, it resembled a thin azure layer flowing through the rock-hard, cemented city — like the drying drops of hope and liberty draining through the hardened hearts of people, despite the cold wind around them. People sometimes sat by the river on benches or picnic blankets, admiring the sights of the gardens around them, close to the Viennese and Parisian-style buildings.

The ride on the tram was pretty quiet, especially for someone like Dragoş, who seemed to have a lot to say; he engaged with the kids more than he did with Robert, asking them about their favourite games and stories.

"*Mama mi-a citit Capra cu Trei Iezi*," said Beriță, referring to the book Elena read him the other night.

It was by one of the most popular Romanian authors, Ion Creangă, a story about a mother goat and her three kids. The three goat-children invited a wolf inside their house, without realising that he wasn't their mother. It was a tale of deception and a lack of trust, urging children not to let anyone in until they were certain.

The kids didn't need to be told again.

"My mother used to read that to me too," said Dragoş.

Robert found the comparison almost poetic.

"And you, Ioana? *Tu ce citești?*" the man asked.

Ioana handed him her two books, and he let out a surprised chuckle.

"You actually understand what he says?" he said, pointing at the Collected Poems.

Ioana responded with a smile.

"*Cobori în jos, Luceafăr blând, alunecând pe-o rază. Pătrunde-n codru și în gând, și norocu-mi luminează*," she recited.

Dragoş put on an impressed grin.

"Hey, Robi, you didn't tell me your niece could recite Eminescu so well?" Dragoş demanded, impressed.

"Blaga, Alecsandri, even prose… Ioana's the prodigy," said Robi, sitting opposite them on the tram chair.

He hated sitting in the opposite direction of the way they were heading;

it made him dizzy. But he would rather have kept Dragoş under his sight.

He was glad to see Ioana talking to someone about her interest and finally coming out of her shell a bit; he just wished it wasn't someone blacklisted by the *Securitate*.

They got off at the corner station right in front of the Orthodox Cathedral, which was the tallest one in the country. Despite not being built more than forty years ago, it kept the grandeur of the city alive through its brick walls, sharp towers, and earthy tones.

The walk from behind the Cathedral and into the park was a short one, with the sound of the river flowing nearby in a melodious manner. Dragoş insisted that while he and Robi sat down and enjoyed the sights, the kids would walk around the park and do their own thing.

"Nu mergeți departe. Stay close by, and don't go too close to the river," said Dragoş.

Robert felt his face grow hot at the sound of this man showing care for his niece and nephew. Winning trust in their world made winning the lottery without a ticket look like a simple task. What kind of monster did that to children?

When the kids got far away from their earshot, Dragoş spoke, as if reading Robi's thoughts.

"I know you don't trust me. I don't expect you to. I need you to do what you're told and when you're told it."

Robi let out a sigh.

"And does that not make me a coward? That's what you called me, right?" Robi replied.

Fricosule.

"Lying makes you a coward, Robi. I want you to be honest if you want a good future for yourself. And for them, more than that," Dragoş said, pointing at the kids.

Speaking this way in public was risky, but their benches were far away from any other person's earshot, and the low tone of their voices kept them discreet. Robert gave him a nod. It was more than enough for Dragoş to understand that, perhaps for the first time in a long while, he had found the possibility of making a friend.

Or an acquaintance, if he was being realistic.

Sure, it started with threats and deceit, but someone was going to help him put an end to what was happening in their country. Double-crossing the intelligence was going to come with a price; if, of course, he was going to be caught, Robi told himself.

"How long have you been doing this?" asked Robert, without saying the 'S' word.

After a moment of silence, Dragoş got up from the bench. Before he went by the riverside where Ioana and Beriță were splashing cold water on each other, he turned his face away from Robi's.

"Far too long."

The way to the kids' grandfather's house was relatively easy, as they had taken the same tram to get there and now took it back home. They stopped at the same station in front of a row of cemented block buildings that shadowed several small entrances, some with queues of people standing outside, waiting for rations. The tram rattled away loudly, as Dragoş knelt in front of the kids.

He pushed a hand into his coat pocket and pulled out two pieces of round solids, wrapped in a drawing of the character Little Red Riding Hood. Beriță exclaimed loudly at the sight of the chocolates, almost wanting to snatch them from Dragoş's hand. Still, he patiently waited, just as Ioana did.

"Because both of you have been such good kids today, here's a little *gustare*," he said, handing them the treats.

He smiled at them through his chilly, grey eyes, which masked his proper form, and shook hands with both kids.

Robert patiently stood by them, waiting for Dragoş to give the kids a gentle reminder of how to serve the great leader with proper respect so that they could live happily.

When he didn't say it, though, Robert thanked Dragoş briefly and walked to the building to their left, which looked identical to all the other ones apart from the large oak that was planted outside. They went inside, while Dragoş stood and watched them.

"Ioana?" muttered Dragoş, watching her enter the building while Robert held the door for her.

She turned her head, chewing the solid waffle.

"Next time I see you, recite me some *Scrisoarea a III-a*," he said.

Ioana gave him a short nod and went inside. Robert followed, ignoring Dragoş.

His father lived on the second floor, in the apartment to the right. Before the kids even reached there, the door had been opened, with *Bunicu*'s wrinkled face watching them as they climbed the stairs. He resembled Elena, with the same dark brown hair that almost all of them had, except Beriță, who bore a resemblance to Darius, with gold strands of hair and a button nose. Robert climbed the stairs at a slower pace than the children, trying to look out for unwanted surprises.

Ever since Robert had recently tried to make his father warmer towards Elena, he seemed to have started growing colder towards both of them. Robert had no clue why Elena and his father were the way that they were. Nor did he ever ask.

"I saw you little *șoricei* from the window!" said their grandfather, hugging the kids.

That is how he always was around Elena's children: warm, kind and welcoming. Then, his face shifted into a calm look.

"*Săru-mâna tata*," said Robert.

His father nodded at him and gave a low grunt, which sounded, if Robert really tried lying to himself, like a 'Hello' and a cough.

"Kids, why don't you go inside the *sufragerie* and see what I have for you two!" said the kids' grandfather, and let them go into the living room.

Robi smiled at the thought of them enjoying the warm *tei* tea after walking around on a chilly day like that, which he could already smell from the kitchen. The kids' hurried footsteps rushed into the living room, and Robi's father leaned back to shut the door behind them.

"Robert, was that Dragoș Stănescu I saw with you?" he asked, once the children were gone.

"Yes," said Robert, while helping himself to some water.

His father, for as long as he could remember, never asked him or Elena if they would like anything, unlike what he did with the kids. It was a small gesture that would have meant the world to him if he had ever been able to do it.

But his father, the famous Professor, remained a mystery.

"Be careful of what company you are keeping, Robert, especially around Elena's children. They shouldn't be around a man like that," he warned him, in English.

It was his way of reminding Robi of the people around them and what they knew about their family. Sometimes, Robert wondered if their father regretted teaching them so many different linguistic and philosophical concepts, letting them read books from far and wide. Sometimes, knowing less was actually a blessing.

And yet, Robert hated that for once, he agreed with his father. Dragoș should have been away from him and his family.

Damn that fucking radio.

"I know, but it was nothing. I promise you," said Robert, as he placed the glass in the sink. "I need to get going, but I'll be back for the kids in a bit. Elena needs me to pick up some *unt.*"

His father nodded knowingly.

"I hope you understood me, son. Stay away from Dragoș. He only means trouble."

Robert nodded. He left the apartment with a short goodbye and headed downstairs. He jumped off the stairs, almost flying above each step, in a hurry. What he was hurrying to, he did not know. He felt a desire to escape the reality his father had presented to him. He flung the door open and made his way to the street.

He didn't find it even slightly surprising when Dragoș walked out from behind the giant oak tree and walked alongside him, as if it was the most natural thing in the world for them to be in each other's company. He had been waiting for him.

"How's your father's English?" said Dragoş, keeping up with Robert's hurried footsteps.

"What?" asked Robert, stopping instantly.

"His English. Your father was once 'the professor' in this neighbourhood, you know? Everyone knows he had a good ear for English, French and Russian back in the day," he said casually.

"I don't know, nor do I give a fuck," said Robert, walking away.

If someone was going to put his father's life in danger because of that, he didn't want to have a hand in it.

"Jesus, you have a temper in you, kid. That's for sure," said Dragoş. "*Calmează-te.*"

"You have been following me around for two days, trying to win my niece and nephew's sympathy by manipulating them with the few things that still make them happy, and now you are threatening my father. In what world do you think that will keep me calm?" said Robert, almost as a whisper.

Dragoş almost laughed.

"I have been watching your back for two days because otherwise some other *Securitate* asshole who probably knows about your indiscreet sister and her radio will report you, if they haven't already. Your niece and nephew should be even more protected because they are not of age yet, and I know for a fact that no one will spare them if they come after you," he spat back. "And enquiring about your father's English isn't a threat. It's a precaution, *prostul naibii ce ești,*" swore Dragoş.

The breeze whistled between the buildings around them, and although they were far enough from the direct window sights, Robert couldn't help but feel like he was being watched. Dragoş, despite being a trained agent, didn't have the power to hear through walls and windows from the streets.

His enquiry about his father's English felt rational to Robert, who tried letting out a breath.

"Why the chocolate? And this sudden care for us?" he asked. "I don't understand what you want me to do, without being a little sceptical."

Dragoş widened his eyes in disbelief, muttering a swear under his breath.

"Come with me," he insisted.

For the first time since they had started talking, Robert felt like he was not being ordered to do something.

Dragoş was begging.

Dragoş's apartment was the same as the other day, when Robert was certain that the damp, mouldy walls were going to be his last sights before dying. Despite being smaller than his own home, Robert thought it was colder there than anywhere else he had ever been.

While Robert stood in the hallway and watched the place more carefully now that he felt safer, he heard an older woman's hoarse voice coming from the back of the place.

"Dragoş, *mamă*, is that you?" she coughed.

Immediately, Dragoş made his way to the back rooms, where Robert assumed that his parents were resting. He heard the low tones of the old couple talking to their son, and then a phrase that surprised him.

"I brought my friend, the Robert kid from Number Three. You remember the old Professor's son, don't you?" said Dragoş.

Robert dared to peek behind the ajar door into the back rooms. The sight left him speechless for a moment, which felt like eternity.

The wrinkled face of the old woman looked cold and pale, as if she had been awakened from a deep, death-like sleep. The freezing temperature in the apartment made her look almost ghostly, frail, and small in front of her son, who was helping her into bed by holding her arms.

"Of course, I do…he looked just like Elena, the girl…" said Mari, her legs bent to one side, as she tried heating her core with the blanket that Dragoş put on her.

As if she had passed out, her eyes closed dully, while her son watched. Robert thought how, despite resembling death so uncannily, Mari looked peaceful, like a ray of warm light in the middle of the cold, shallow apartment.

Dragoş walked towards the door behind him, where it used to be his own bedroom once. Now, he had told Robi, he found that keeping his parents in separate rooms when one or the other got ill was a better idea, protecting the other from being sick too. His father slept on his childhood bed, resting his head on a pillow diagonally placed.

Dragoș lifted it and straightened his father's neck to avoid a cramp, letting him sleep.

"No fever. Thank God," Dragoș whispered lightly.

Robert stood as still as a statue when Dragoș walked back into the hallway.

"What, you thought I was a cold-hearted bastard?" said Dragoș amusingly.

"I still think that you're a cold-hearted bastard," said Robert. "Perhaps just one with a family to look after," he added next.

Dragoș glanced into the back rooms.

"They've been like that for so long, it feels difficult to remember what they were like before this," he replied.

Despite the tension between them, the hate Robi felt for a traitor like Dragoș, and his annoying presence that he couldn't rid himself of, the younger boy felt a slight ache for him.

For the man who was trapped in his childhood home, the boy who had to become his parents' guardian because of their illness and was reporting on people around him to secure a decent meal. It had come to this for how many people, he wondered. How many people were making difficult decisions to protect their loved ones, the vulnerable ones?

"I'm sorry for doubting your intentions," said Robert.

He didn't even know if he believed it. But it felt like a consoling statement, which was all he could give Dragoș. And of course, the truth about what was happening at the University.

Dragoș nodded and walked to the kitchen, instructing the other boy to follow him. Then, he pointed at some of the things in the kitchen.

"I probably have too much of this anyway. Ever since I started this job, I have been getting way too many 'presents' from them. God knows who they really should go to or who owned them once, but now I want you and Elena's kids to have them," he handed him a box with silverware. "Be quiet about this. If anyone asks, say you got it from an older couple who wanted to get rid of it," Dragoș warned him, letting the silverware jingle at the bottom of the box.

Robert did as he was told and picked up the silverware. After receiving boots, a clock, and a worn-out set of paints for the kids, he headed home.

He hid everything in a box and bags that Dragoș had given him, without stopping to talk to anyone.

Nine

Dragoș

Timișoara, Romania — November 1989

Of course, Dragoș knew that his new friend was being watched by others as well.

When Mari and Vasile Stănescu's son was born on December 1, 1956, the entire building welcomed their newborn with gifts and wishes for health and a long, prosperous life. It was more than unusual for a woman in her mid-40s to be able to conceive, let alone give birth to a fully healthy baby boy. Which is why, for all the love he had suddenly brought into their grey lives, all the *dragoste*, his parents named him Dragoș.

Naturally, the boy seemed to be loved everywhere he went, with the weight that his name carried. All the elderly women would spit little drops on his forehead with a light '*Ptiu!*', praying not to bewitch the little boy whom they adored so much.

"*Să nu te deochi!*" they would shower their blessings, which was followed by a recitation of prayers and forehead kisses.

This gift from God meant even more to them when Mari was told that she couldn't have more children, in a world where such a regular occurrence was labelled a curse or a punishment. Now, the people around her murmured tales of '*Poor Mari*', '*Only one child*' and '*How unfortunate for the little boy to grow up alone*' right in front of her, while she pretended as if she couldn't hear them. It did not matter.

Her little boy was more than enough for her.

When his elderly parents started going out less and less because of their worsening conditions, it was only natural for Dragoş to pay them the respect that they deserved. One thing after another led to him never moving out, never starting his own family, bearing only the guilt of his parents needing him now that they were growing old.

The gossip of his mother and father's misfortunes in life slowly turned into praise for him, admiring the couple who raised such a boy, who sacrificed everything for his parents' lives. Naturally, rumours spread quickly in an intimate setting. One thing that Dragoş was certain about in his life was that, whether you went through good times or bad, the people around you would always find a way of labelling your situation to match their gossip. Something that would sell, no matter how unbelievable. And, from the time his parents could barely leave the house on their own, he stopped listening to what was being said about Mr and Mrs Stănescu.

So, when the *Securitate* targeted him as a safe ally for themselves, he couldn't refuse them. It was ridiculous how it had all started.

It was a sunny afternoon in either 1981 or 1982; Dragoş hadn't written it down. The little shop that his parents were running, selling bread and pastries, had been in the family for almost three generations, with Dragoş being the fourth. Although on most days the shelves were empty and filled with dust, the family's pride were the days when the bread was in full stock on the rows of wood aligned on the walls, with queues of people gathering up behind the door.

It was on one of those days, in the height of summer, that Dragoş was running the shop on his own, as it usually was now, since neither of his parents went out much. *Mama* with the aching knees and sore throat from the slightest cold, and *Tata* with diabetes and a bad back. Now, it had become a routine.

A woman who was about his own age, who had been standing in the queue for about twenty-five minutes, finally got her turn to buy bread. Dragoș rapidly handed her one of the many loaves from the display behind him — the aroma of freshly baked bread filled the air, enchanting people who stood behind the glass frame.

"Luați, doamnă," Dragoș hurried, handing her the bread.

But she stared at him through her blonde hair and blue-grey eyes with a blank expression, and said, "Are you Stănescu Dragoș?"

"Yes, *doamnă,*" he had said, trying not to sound impatient.

The queue on days like this was long enough, so he didn't need interruptions.

"I think we need to talk, Mr Stănescu," she said, pulling out a little yellow card and placing it on the counter in front of him.

'Departamentul Securității Statului' it read, in thick bold words, under which her name was written calligraphically.

'Florica R Lupu.'

His first instinct was to run as far away from the shop as he could.

After all, she couldn't outrun him, *Securitate* or not. He wanted to run away from this life that he was leading, looking after the shop, his parents, the wretched place he was sick of. Perhaps the countryside would be kinder to him; he could grasp it, even as he stood there in the cold, trembling from anticipation— the familiar smell of the fields of Banat, once golden in their colour. Miles away from the web of the city lies.

But something had told him that sometimes, running away from something was the same as running towards it. He only needed to be clever about it — and now, he was cornered.

So, he had closed off the shop at the woman's demands and hurried the people out of there, despite the loud curses and complaints that some of them were shouting at him. The bread was going to grow cold, but the desperate people would return as soon as he opened the door, even if he sold them bread as hard as rocks, with mould on every corner.

Florica looked pleased.

"What can I do for you, *doamnă* Lupu?" he had asked, maintaining his calm and cool state.

He tried studying her with his sky-grey eyes, realising that there was no escape from becoming utterly inhumane anymore. Things that were once just rumours to him seemed to gain shape quickly. The illicit voices that people had warned him about; *he* was one of those voices. He was the shadow that would replace the light in other people's lives.

After all these years, he couldn't even remember what Lupu had asked him on the first day they met. So much had changed since then; for a start, his family was looked after and fed, while the others were left to starve and die out. It was an uneasy reality that he faced once he realised how many people were being brainwashed and manipulated by the Intelligence. The old man who sold flowers, the woman who had twin girls, the couple that rarely saw their kids, whom he recognised from their appearances… all of them were leading separate lives, reporting on the people around them. The commonness of it scared him the most; where had the loyalty gone? Where had *his* own morals gone?

He was never asked to report anything on children or even face the possibility that they would harm them until now; with or without that occurrence, he wanted to get out. Deep down, he had always known that his actions had consequences that others would face.

Like *that* woman — he had never seen her again after he had reported her.

She had claimed, as he struggled to remember the exact phrase, that she would have killed Ceaușescu and fed him to her dogs if she ever got near him. What upset him then was that despite sharing the sentiment, he had been cowardly about it, like a submissive bitch on the leash of a tyrant, a dictator. Instead of accepting his own feelings, he was butchering the people who dared to say what they really thought. Florica had laughed about the woman's claims, but Dragoș had never seen her outside or at work afterwards. God knew where they had taken her and what they had done to her, all thanks to his sharp ears.

After deciding to mend things, he tried to forget all the harm he had caused to people. The evil that he had been a part of. Sometimes, the nights grew lonely and the thoughts loud — he had considered doing a lot more than running away.

More than once.

But he had a family to feed, a life to lead… and besides, he was taught that it was a major sin. There was no peace, even in death.

He knew for sure that the people he had betrayed to the *Securitate* would have done the same to him in a heartbeat, without ever thinking about anyone else but their own families. It was the monsters that the society was reaping in the blissful land of the Communists.

Divide and conquer.

The doorbell rang at precisely three o'clock, nearly awakening Mari from her deep sleep. Her husband was out cold in the room next to her, and her son, who was watching over them both, sat at the kitchen table with a Kent cigarette stuck between his lips.

Kents were as valuable as gold in their country, and in exchange for a couple of boxes, you could get anything from an extra loaf of bread to a few minutes of lust and ecstasy in a deserted alleyway. Mari would have scolded Dragoş for wasting the Kents like that; little did she know, he could obtain ten boxes within the next hour, and no one would bat an eyelid.

Dragoş let Florica in before she could continue ringing the bell like a maniac; he always considered the possibility of his apartment being bugged, but thought how deep in he was with the fuckers. He was basically one of their 'buddies', if such a rank existed.

Indeed, in the first few months, he would have been closely watched. But just like any institution or organisation, even a jungle like the *Securitate had its* official and unofficial ranks, with secrets being sold to some people. In contrast, others were left in the dark. Dragoş believed he was one of the luckier ones; telling himself such a thing made it easier sometimes.

Florica's inquiries only confirmed it.

"Well? What did the boy say?" she asked agitatedly without greeting him, picking out her own Kent.

Dragoş picked up the lighter and bent closer to her.

"He agreed to report everything to me. Any news about any goddamn traitors," said Dragoş, trying to emphasise the last bit.

Florica looked pleased.

"Well, then. I look forward to hearing your developments," she said.

She turned around and walked towards the door; their usual meetings never lasted much longer than this anyway. Everything was brief and quiet, as if it were their own existence. Dragoş let out a cough.

"He is my contact, *doamnă* Lupu. I advise against intimidation or violence in this case. The boy has agreed to cooperate," he added.

Florica straightened her blonde-dyed hair with a quick hand, puffing out some smoke. She turned around on her heels as she leaned on the door and smiled at Dragoş. She licked her horrible lips as she got lipstick smudged over her teeth. Florica considered her last words.

"Greet your mother from my side. *Să ai o zi bună,*" she said, with a twisted gleam in her eyes.

He didn't let his face give away the gulp that sat in his throat, stuck and tight. It suffocated him to smile and wave at her, but putting on a show was what he *had* to be good at. Dragoş had been in the job long enough to read her like a book.

Especially when she threatened him.

Ten

Elena

Timişoara, Romania — November 1989

Elena, surprisingly, had not inquired about the silverware anymore. She had picked them up gently and placed them on the top shelf above the kitchen counter, out of sight. She was growing frailer and thinner day by day, with most of her own rations going to Ioana or Beriță, and sometimes to Robert. And with her husband gone for so long, the hopes of having all of her family in one place left her even more heartbroken.

Elena's thin fingers were now covered in oil from cleaning old pans. After all, she couldn't use the same oil for so long, no matter how little was left in the short bottle. She washed her hands thoroughly and decided to prepare something for the next day, as it was Sunday. For Christian Orthodox people like herself, it was the holiest day of the week, when everyone would rest and enjoy a family meal, after visiting the church in the morning.

Ceauşescu and his wife had been against the practice of religion for as long as Elena could remember; it was discouraged in every form. From demolishing religious institutions to banning traditions on religious holidays, the dictator left no room for people's free will to be expressed, even in such an intimate matter, between oneself and a higher power. He had even taken out the icons of religious figures from the walls and replaced them with a portrait of himself. Going to church, no matter how widely ridiculed, became more than just an act of Christian duty; it was a form of rebellion against the leader who would have frowned upon their actions.

It became a little voice among the rest of the oppression, where people could gather in front of a symbol that gave them hope, despite everything. So, Elena, although never being overly religious herself, preserved the tradition of going to church to feel the rays of liberty now and then. And perhaps one day, her children could have succumbed to the temptation of freedom and made all of the country feel as open as the halls of prayer made her feel.

She called for Ioana to help her prepare the *mămăligă* for that evening. It was thick, cooked cornmeal, a necessary replacement for bread. On the table was a piece of chicken, which was to be divided among all of them. It couldn't have been more than a handful, so Elena boiled it and shredded it into a large bowl before adding it to hot water for soup. There was a cube-shaped piece of salted *brânză*, a traditional Romanian cheese, that would pair well with the cornmeal. On a good day, baked fish would be accompanying this combination, but that was an impossibility right now.

This was all they were going to eat.

"*Vii la biserică cu mine mâine*. Come to church with me tomorrow," Elena asked her daughter.

Ioana shook her head.

"We have another workshop tomorrow morning; lessons about sewing," she responded with genuine pity in her voice.

Some people believed that compulsory Sunday workshops were deliberate — Ceaușescu's way of highlighting his disgust towards the 'ancient' ways of religion. If he thought it was not right, the children of his country should have been kept far away from it; and so, Elena's burning desire to take her children with her melted away like dewdrops on a sunny morning.

She hid her displeasure, cursing the entire system for the first time that day. There was a tension growing inside of her, a sense of hysteria, that made her think she would go mad any day now. Everything in her life was being disrupted by someone who seemed not to give a damn about her, her family, or anyone around them.

When she lived in the village, it was the farm animals that mattered; anyone who had more than a certain number of chickens, cows, and even crops was legally obligated to give a portion of them to the government. People didn't own anything, not even things they invested time and resources into. Their own homes were in danger of being snatched away at any moment. And while the regime assured that everyone would have a job, no matter how big or small, people had no reason to go to work and enjoy what they had.

Their lives were a monotone routine, a dreamless sleep of grey and white.

"We saw Robi's new friend today," Ioana told her.

"What?" Elena responded, her head clouded with the memories of another lifetime.

"Dragoș, his name is, I think. He is Robi's new friend."

"Not Stănescu, is it?" Elena asked, remembering the tall figure of a man she once knew.

"I don't remember his surname. He gave us chocolate," Ioana smiled to herself, letting her cheeks grow redder.

Elena watched her daughter's face glow at the thought of the present from the mystery man who was undoubtedly Dragoș Stănescu, the man who had driven her to the hospital when Beriță was going to be born. Since then, though, Elena had seen him creeping underneath windows as a means of walking around to his building, probably peaking into people's homes and gathering information. She could never be too sure, and most people that she saw made her think that they were connected with the *Securitate* or the government in some way.

Why would Robi hide this?

"Listen to me, Ioana," she knelt close to her daughter's face. "I don't want you to tell this man anything if you ever see him again. Did he ask you anything today?" she asked eagerly.

"No, he was very nice, *Mama*! He listened to me reciting poetry, and told me that—" Ioana continued, but her mother, shaking her shoulders, interrupted her.

"You have to be more careful, silly girl! You never know who is listening to other things about us. What if he is a bad man?" Elena murmured in her ear. "Not a word about this man anymore, Ioana," she told her, patting her lightly.

Elena was sure about two things, from the evident disappointment on her daughter's face; Ioana had grown fond of this newcomer instantly.

She was also sure that her brother was hiding a terrible secret from her.

Eleven

Robert

Timişoara, Romania — November 1989

A few hours had passed since Robert had brought the kids back home from his father's house. They were happy as always to see their grandfather, Ioana, even returning with another book under her arm. He sat behind his thick Economics book, sketching something on a piece of paper. The shape finally seemed to resemble what he had intended.

A map.

Dinner had gone smoothly. As smoothly as it could have gone, ignoring the elephant in the room. The fact that their food was growing shorter by the day, and that it wasn't going to be long before everything they had in front of them right now was going to fade away. Robert, despite the apparent tension in the home, smiled and thanked Elena for the food.

"Săru-mâna pentru masă," he said. Kiss your hand, an expression for gratitude and respect.

He got up from the table while the children were still eating the rest of the cornmeal. With a steady hand, he put the plate on the counter, with his sister's agile eyes watching him.

"Where are you going?" she asked.

He was already reaching out for his things from the table.

"Oh, it's nothing…just seeing George again…" he stammered.

Elena's right eyebrow arched. In an instant, he knew that she was aware of the lie he had told. Of course, he was going to see Dragoș, but how could he tell her this without making her weak frame panic beyond measure?

Her pale eyes watched him now, steady and ready to ask him where he was really going. It seemed that more and more clandestine conversations were taking place between him and Elena, with the children lost in their own little matters. Ioana, however, shifted in her chair slightly, her eyes watching Robert and her mother slipping away from the room.

Elena stood in their living room now, where the chilly air made her hands tremble; she seemed to ignore the aching movements of her arms, which were straining in their joints.

"I know you're going to see that *vagabond* from across the street. You think the kids don't tell me who they see when I'm not around, Robert?" she said, a cold note in her voice.

Robi felt its iciness more than the plain freezing air around them.

"I didn't mean to hide it from you, Elena, but he and I are…" he said, but her fury interrupted.

"Are what?" Elena raised her voice, watching the kitchen door, "Friends? You want to befriend, what? An obvious danger to this family?" she asked.

Robert felt bizarrely defensive about Dragoș. He had misunderstood him entirely, as Elena was now. He couldn't be mad at his own sister, not for something he too had done.

"You know what I mean, Robert. If Stănescu finds out about the abilities we can offer, he won't hesitate to put this entire family at great risk. You can't go around trusting anyone," she insisted.

He knew what she meant — Dragoș obviously knew about their father's language skills.

But if anyone suspects more than that...

Elena and Robert possessed the same abilities, but they were a secret. No one knew about it, not even the children. In their younger years, it was another way of expressing their distaste for the regime's strict ideas on foreign languages and books. Twisting this could make it seem like they were traitors, engaging with the enemy of their country, sympathising with someone other than the great leader.

"He doesn't know anything about that, Elena," Robert promised.

Elena straightened her back and pulled her cardigan closer.

"My dear *frățior* has forgotten what our father always told us about dogs like your new friend?" said Elena.

He hadn't, in fact. Their father had a proverb of sorts about the *Securitate,* a humorous way of warning his children.

"Sometimes, you see a person coming from a distance and think that it is just another human being. Then, they get closer, enough for you to see their badges and uniform, and you realise it's a bitch from *Securitate,*" he had said.

It wasn't a lie — Dragoș could have known about all their endeavours and previous experiences without uttering a word about it to Robert. The people from the *Securitate* were better actors than those Americans that he had seen in forged tapes that his friends at the University owned.

"And yours doesn't even wear a badge. He pretends to be a wolf in sheep's skin," she said, glaring at her fragile, bony hands.

"Something *huge* is about to happen, Elena. There is a minuscule chance of it, but I am willing to take it. You have to trust me, please..." he reached out his hands to hold her arm.

"You do what you want, Robi," said Elena, with the same chillness in her voice, pacing back. "But keep this family out of such affairs," and she walked out, followed by one of the children calling her.

Robert stood there for only a moment, thinking of how wrong he could be about Dragoș and this entire matter with the students.

He picked up his keys and headed for the door anyway.

Dragoș's list of names was neatly written and laid out in alphabetical order — all Robert had to do was tick the boxes next to the names if the said person was involved with the hushed movements of the students. It wasn't a secret between them; something was going to happen, even the *Securitate* knew that by now. Dragoș knew that his employers would have hired hundreds of other people to do things within the students' divisions, but if even one of them turned to the right side...

There were whispers of revolutions and a change in their leadership at Robert's University. The students desperately wanted to be given the opportunities that their parents had been robbed of.

The youth always saw things differently. The generation before them had been submissive, but they wouldn't be.

Which is why Robert brought the map, which he had drawn, alongside a few notes on the students he knew. Teaming up with the 'rats' of the *Securitate*, who wanted to leave the regime's clutches, and the students who were already planning a movement, was the only chance they had.

The youth had been hiding these desires from their families, ignoring the unfairness around them until it was indeed unbearable. Robert thought about what his father would have thought of him at that moment.

The names of all the students were laid out beautifully, with photos and ages next to them. In Robert's mind, he felt a little uneasy about how much Dragoş and his people seemed to know about the students; some of these young people were his friends, people he had grown fond of. If he were selling them to the wrong people, he would come to regret it for the rest of his life.

The silence between them grew uncomfortable as Dragoş shuffled from one corner of the room to the other, stepping beside the endless rows of paper.

"So what now?" Robert asked, aligning the last photo.

The photo of a young boy stared back at him with bright eyes and a pair of thinly outlined lips. He felt his stomach turning at the sight of his face, and the thought of what horrors awaited the young boy in the next few days if he was wrong. He shook his head, trying to get rid of it, whispering a grunt under his breath.

Then, suddenly, the image turned into a much different one, within the four walls of his own mind. If he were right about helping out Dragoş, the boy would grow up into a young man with freedom; he could see a family around him, who were passionate travellers and learners. People who weren't bound to the strictness of a dictatorship. For his own sake, that was the image he held onto, more than the first one.

"Now, I need you to make it as vague as possible that you're interested in such a movement. If I am correct, which I usually am (at this, Robert rolled his eyes), those bastards will send someone else to talk to you as well. You say exactly what you tried feeding me; most of the rest are just as gullible as Ceaușescu himself," laughed Dragoș.

"It's funny, isn't it?" Robert said after a short pause. "The most loved people often feel like the loneliest, and the most hated ones delude themselves into thinking that the world accepts them as they are. "Truly evil people never seem to think that they are hurting others, do they?" he said.

Twelve

Dragoș

Timișoara, Romania — November 1989

Dragoş fell silent for a short moment before laughing it all off as a joke. The chillness of what Robert had just said ran down his spine, like a shiver loaded with fear. Because he, too, had hurt countless people, never counting himself as one of the 'evil' ones.

Maybe it was his turn to.

"Look at you, *domnul profesor*!" said Dragoș. "Like father, like son. Both damned fools are too clever for their own good," he shook his head.

Robert smiled and got up from the pile on the floor.

"Unfortunately, it is Elena that you have to watch out for. She's probably smarter than both me and my father. Too bad she has to hide it away most of the time."

Dragoş got up with him.

"Don't think that I forgot about her. I know that all three of you share a great deal of pride amongst yourselves. You're a real pain for intelligence services when you're more intelligent than they are," he said.

But, despite what the circumstances were, Robert didn't look threatened.

"Yes, you are right about that, I am afraid. The three of us are *egoiști* when it comes to our knowledge. I sometimes wonder if that's the reason my sister and father cannot stand each other. I wonder why it is, though."

"Oh?" Dragoș raised an eyebrow.

"I have never known Elena to place a toe out of line, just like her own oldest child. Both are perfectionists to the bone. That's what my mother was like," he said, with a sad smile. "She was so much like Elena and Ioana, and they're just like her… but not *her*. You know what I mean?"

Dragoș lowered his gaze. He could never understand what such a sentiment of loss felt like when his own parents seemed to have never been out of his own sight for as long as he had been alive.

Sometimes, he imagined what his own separate life would have looked like. A life where he wasn't a spy, where he could have his own family, perhaps. He had once heard that Ancient civilisations believed in the next life; if such a thing existed, he wished that in the next life he would have entirely different circumstances altogether.

"Well, we can't all have what we want. Sometimes, *putem doar să sperăm,*" he said. "You know what we say. *Speranța moare ultima.* Hope is the last thing to die."

"*Dar tot moare.* And yet it still dies," Robert continued the proverb.

Dragoș laughed at its irony and how it mirrored their position so well. Every Romanian person had felt hope at some point in their lives — until it died out, like a mirage on sand. Robi gave him a short nod and headed for the door — everything about the boy seemed blue. His work there was done. Outside, Dragoș could hear the sound of cars passing on the street, despite the late hour.

"I'll see you tomorrow, *puștiule,*" Dragoș said almost kindly.

He turned to the photos and placed them in folders.

Robert walked out the door unaccompanied. He didn't even turn his head back at Dragoș when the man watched him from the golden gleam of the kitchen light, anticipating.

The sound of the telephone ringing loudly awoke him suddenly from a dreamless sleep. Dragoș ran to the kitchen, nearly tripping on the mess on the floor. Someone had put a blanket on him while he was asleep.

He picked up the telephone, holding it tightly in his arms. His hand had gone numb while he was asleep, and he tightened his palm again and again, until he could get rid of the feeling of pins and needles in his skin.

The phone rarely ever rang, mostly when the neighbours' relatives from other cities called to check in on them, or to tell them about someone's death or birth. Their home was one of the few in the neighbourhood that had a telephone, a gift given to him a week after he met Florica.

"*Alo, da?*" Dragoș enquired, his voice hoarse.

He let out a light cough.

A voice he recognised instantly spoke from the other end.

"*Ora trei. Cod roșu,*" said Florica.

Code red — he had to see her at three o'clock today. He glanced at the clock quickly as he put the phone down. 2.05 AM. The short notice only meant that the situation would have been a code black if it had been reported a little later. An orange or a yellow he had dealt with before, but red was new territory for him.

He tucked a few papers into the pocket of his jacket, a pen, and put it on. Then, with fastened steps, he went into his parents' room. He had nearly forgotten about them and their prescribed medications waiting on the living room table.

His mother and father were both awake in their own bedroom, wrapped in warm clothes. This usually happened when the night chill awoke them from deep slumber, placing them into a new kind of nightmare while their eyes were wide awake. Their pale faces turned to him and smiled.

They look exhausted.

"Oh, you're awake," his mother said, her voice weak. "Already?"

"I'll be back around the morning. I need to meet a friend first. They're in trouble," he said, then placed their medicines on their nightstands.

He kissed his mother on the cheek and ran out the door, as fast as he could.

"You should sleep," Dragoș added.

"It seems like that's all we've been doing… for so long. Perhaps it's time to wake up, son… *să ne deșteptăm…*" his mother held his arms.

Her son watched her with might — maybe she could feel the wave that was knocking on every door, right around the corner. The sentiment of change was too strong to ignore, regardless of age. He squeezed her arm back in response.

"Protect that boy, Dragoş," she whispered, referring to Robi, and tucking herself back into the bed.

Dragoş dimmed the light in the room, promising his mother that he would.

His mind raced to Robi, to what may have happened to him. If the boy had slipped something to his employers by mistake, he was running towards his own death. Or worse — something about stopping the students' movement was going to be put into motion. He lit a cigarette to calm down and made his way to the spot where Florica and the others usually met.

From the outside, it looked like a broken-down warehouse at the edge of town. Inside, though, it was much more solid than it looked, and acted as the meeting spot for Florica, him, and a few other people he had only met a few times.

He didn't know their names, as they didn't know his. Once, he had seen one of the men, a tall guy with a bald head, in a shop in town. Although he had recognised Dragoş too, they both pretended like they had never seen each other in their life. It was an uncomfortable meeting, but pretending was what they excelled at.

It's what their lives *depended* on.

He stepped inside the warehouse and put his arms to his side, waiting to be approached by someone who would check him for weapons and wires. Two men with fat faces came to the door where he stood and emptied his pockets. They looked at the papers and pen that he had tucked in, which were harmless in their eyes. One of the men handed him back the papers, and the other pushed him into the room in front.

He let out a sigh. All of this toughness was unnecessary. He had been there plenty of times for them to remember him. He walked into the room, ignoring the men behind him.

Inside, Florica sat at a desk and looked through a few papers, one of which was a newspaper.

"Hello," she said without looking up.

Dragoş hesitated.

"What are you doing?" he asked, in a casual tone.

"*Îmi văd de treabă.* As you should mind your own business as well," she said.

Her tone was always cold towards him. Harsh and hard to decipher, especially in a moment like that. Florica could very well be watching him get eaten by sharks while smoking her cigarette with a neutral expression, probably wondering what to have for dinner later.

Despite everything, the picture amused him.

"Why did you call?" he said, trying to act normal.

Nothing about any of this, his life, Florica, his work, none of it had been a regular sentiment.

Florica stopped looking at the papers and got up.

"Because, *dragă*, we have a code red," she said condescendingly.

She always did when she called him *'dragă'* — dear.

"I know that! But what is it that couldn't wait?" Dragoş said agitatedly.

He felt uneasy at how Florica smiled at him through the slightly overlined lipstick, watching his anger getting fuelled by how she kept him on his toes. She was enjoying this more than she should have. In another life, maybe she would have been his friend. Perhaps they would've teased each other on matters that didn't determine someone's life or death, like ice cream flavours and movie nights.

She pointed at two pictures that stood on her desk, of a man and a woman.

The woman had dark chestnut hair and green eyes, with full lips and wore makeup on her eyelids. He had never seen a woman wear such a thing on her eyes; Romania had a limited supply of cosmetics, as it had with most things. Most people could barely afford the bare minimum, so the luxuries of extravagance were reserved for special occasions. Her features were also easily distinguishable from those of others. Ceauşescu's regime favoured the traditional woman: modest and hard-working, far from being in touch with her femininity, unlike the 'Western' fashionistas, who were 'consumed' by vulgarity and colour. Dragoş wondered whether Florica's limited views had called a code red for the woman's attire alone — such an exaggeration wouldn't have been entirely out of the question...

The man had blue eyes and a long Northern nose, like an emperor from one of his novels. He too had the same chestnut hair as the girl, only a little lighter, nearly auburn in colour. From the background of the mugshots, he could tell that they were foreigners. If they were code red, they were either from the far west or rebels from neighbouring countries.

"These are two writers from England. They say that they come in peace, but we aren't so certain after we found this in the man's bag," she handed him the newspaper she had been studying.

It was written in Hungarian, which he knew Florica could speak. Never did he question her on it; Romanians had a good ear for Slavic, Uralic, Germanic and Romance languages, as many of them had family members in the bordering countries. It was the Western countries that people frowned upon, with their ideologies and libertarian views that put the great dictator in danger.

"It speaks of the rebel movement happening there. Led by students," she said with disgust.

"So what? The two seem like Western hippies who are looking for something exotic to fuel their spirits... The man picked up a newspaper on his way here on the train. Are you going to condemn someone for that?" he said.

A small part of him wished that Florica would be right — that they were involved with the Hungarian revolution rumours. Or at least, they were interested in it.

"I am telling you, Dragoş, we didn't call code red for nothing. Foreigners and their ideas will eventually bring down this country, I'm telling you," she said.

Dragoş couldn't help but laugh. She looked at him, surprised.

"I am sorry, but anyone could swear you're the same age as my mother," he tried being subtle.

The truth was that he found her ideas about foreigners amusing. One way or another, it was the people of Romania who would bring their own independence to the world.

No one else.

Giving so much credit to people who had not even done something like that only showed how much faith these traitors had in their own people.

"Well, your mother is right then. These outsiders should be exactly that. On the outside," she said.

Dragoș studied the photos.

"I see why you would find this threatening, but why call me?" he said.

"Well, the foreigners stupidly asked one of our guys if he knew anyone who spoke English. Of course, they talked more in signs than actual words. What a small world!" she let out a laugh. "And can you guess where I suggested they should go?"

"I-I... I don't know..." Dragoș said, feeling his heartbeat stop.

"Oh, come on, dragă! The Professor, of course..." she chuckled. "This is going to be so much fun. I have placed everyone exactly where they need to be to gather all the information. The foreigners, the Professor, your boy..."

It took every ounce of his strength to hide his reaction. His mind rushed to Robert, Elena, the kids... everyone who was in danger. If Robi's father was going to be involved with outsiders, the entire family could have been hurt. The *Securitate* didn't care whether you were a child or an adult; if you posed a threat to them, you were going to be eliminated. So far, the Professor had given them no reason for them to arrest him or even question him; they had set up a trap just for him, and he was going to fall right in it...

"Oh?" was all he could say. "Robert's dad?" he asked, as if his heart wasn't sinking at the thought of what might happen.

Everything was growing hot all of a sudden, with his temple drowning in cold sweat. His mouth was dry, and his throat felt heavy. This felt like a cruel joke from the Universe. So much for the hope that died last. It only took a couple of hours for his hope to perish beyond reach.

"Yes, the very same one. I believe the foreigners will be looking for someone to get on their side if I am right, so I will need you to keep an eye on them as well as our student boy," and she walked towards the door, lighting another cigarette.

She said all of that with the casualness of talking about the weather.

He thought about the sharks again, but this time it did not amuse him in the slightest.

Dragoș rushed outside, the adrenaline flowing through his veins. Everything seemed heavy around him, the trees floating in the dusk light. He could feel a heavy scent on the street, something metallic and cold that smelled like dried blood. He tried to take his mind off the games his own fear was playing, and rushed back to the neighbourhood.

For as long as he could remember, Theatre's Street was a peaceful place, with the occasional drama that every neighbourhood had. Old women poking their heads out of windows, watching people's movements, the sound of women screaming at children when they got into nonsensical fights, and so on. For the first time, he feared that rumours of a disappearance in their own neighbourhood were going to come true.

If, of course, the Professor was foolish enough to tell the foreigners that he would help them with whatever bucket list box they were here to tick. How did one escape the danger of death and disappearance, when it was all that the enemies were relying on? Surely, he needed a miracle for things to work out. He hadn't prayed in a long time, but he hoped that Heaven's door wasn't entirely sealed for even someone like him.

He made his way back into the neighbourhood, glancing over his shoulder occasionally. He always wondered if Florica had people watching him as well, counting his steps and tracking his movements. It wouldn't have surprised him, which is why, whenever he went out doing something that could've been seen as suspicious, he made up a story worth believing in his mind beforehand.

If someone caught him creeping around the Professor's apartment, he would tell them he was spying on the old man, trying to decipher what plans he was making with the foreigners, if any. With light steps, he made his way into one of the buildings. As much as he wanted to feel like he was doing the right thing, he knew what all of this looked like…

He felt like a rat doing this, a man so little that he didn't deserve the label of human — he curled his fingers in the pocket of his jacket, and waited for daylight.

II

Part II — Dreptate, galbenul ogoarelor

The golden land

Thirteen

Frankie

London, United Kingdom — November 1989

The silence had become deafening. Deafening enough to, bizarrely, become louder than any sound the man had ever heard before. Two hours after midnight had already passed, but his azure-grey eyes teared with nothing but awakening.

The sweet anticipation of the sleepless.

The rest of the world was fast asleep and quiet. And yet, there was restlessness inside him, between the peace around him. Like a dying star, ready to erupt at any moment. Very little felt mundane at work for the man, who was now rubbing his forehead thoroughly, with his gaze fixated on the floor. He widened his eyelids after rubbing his eyes as well, protesting against the voice in his head that insisted that he go home.

Almost there, he told himself, as he straightened his back against the chair and leaned forward, in front of the screen that he had been staring at for nearly fifteen minutes. It was finished. The words on the screen were as still as ever, ready to be printed on paper in a few hours.

The man's face felt numb and heavy, but he knew that no matter how bad it got, he could never sleep. It was like a disease of some sort that aided him in staying awake for long hours, despite his body slowly begging him to rest.

It had worked out in his favour so far, pushing him to be present for longer hours than any other journalist at his station.

Sometimes, even beyond his physical presence — sometimes, even momentarily, Frankie Hannigan would find himself picturing the lines that his next article would feature, even when he did not have a story to chase. The thirst for one never stopped him from writing down the words and phrases he had printed in his mind, devouring each sentence with delight. He chased stories like children chased after lost balls in long, deserted playgrounds.

Only in his journalism world, the playground was real life, and the ball was made of fire. He felt the desire to be burnt, left in flames with every touch; the adrenaline of getting into a territory that people rarely had access to. In his mind, Frankie saw the world unlike anyone else, unfiltered and raw, as if everything happened to him, not to the people he wrote about.

As it was only natural, the office around him had been empty for a long time; everyone had gone home to their families and friends.

But who does a foreign correspondent go home to, he would joke.

For Frankie, the office was almost his entire life. There wasn't much else to go home to, or even a 'home', for the matter. Of course, he had his cosy apartment on Camden Road, which was his house, theoretically, and had been for the last two years.

But it wasn't a home, and a deep feeling told him that it would never be. How could it, when the rest of his adult life was spent in New York City? But in times when he missed home, he remembered why he wanted to leave so desperately, why the job of foreign correspondent was his escape ticket from the hellhole that had become New York. Returning there would bring him nothing but sorrow and a profound longing for the way things used to be.

A loud ringing sound made him jump, waking up every little part of him that longed for the sight of a warm bed, as his body ached and dazed. He picked up the telephone that sat on his desk, its echo leaving a mark on the silent room. He felt startled and guessed who it could be.

"Go for Hannigan," he said, his words carrying a rasp.

Frankie ran his right hand through his fair auburn-brown hair, with the telephone leaning in his left hand. A man's voice spoke in a fading tone on the other end, with a cheerful note in his voice.

"Frankie, m'boy! How are ya tonight?" said the man.

Frankie sighed silently and closed his eyes. Despite being friends, it seemed like a bad time for John Brown to call. He leaned back against his chair and put his feet up on the desk in front of him. After all, there was no one around to tell him off for it.

It had been a little over two years since Frankie had been offered the foreign correspondent job at his station back home in New York. It was already 1989. At the time, Frankie was going through what he would later describe as the hardest time of his life. So when they offered him the job, it felt like the answer to all his prayers.

It seemed to him at the time that running away from home was the only way things would get solved, the only way he could forget about everything. Little did Frankie know, some demons never stop chasing you, no matter how far away you run — especially *your own* demons.

"John...hey..." he said finally, the words coming out quieter than he intended. He palmed his forehead, tired. "How are you?"

The man on the other end did not seem to notice Frankie's disinterest.

"I am doing excellent, Frank! Same old, same old 'round here, you know what that's like... but what's new with you? I haven't heard from you in a while, mister foreign correspondent!" said John with glee.

Frankie moved around in his chair and stared at his worn-out Converse All-Stars, the feeling of night catching up with him. John had always been a little overwhelming to be around, mainly because he could never tell when someone *really* didn't want to continue the conversation. But Frankie owed a lot to him, which is why he tried making an effort every time.

"I'm well, thanks. I got back from Paris last night. And I finished writing all the reports for the entire trip just now, they'll be neat for the archive when I send them over," he said.

That should be enough of an update for the guy, Frankie thought.

"No, no Frankie, I don't mean your work!" replied Brown, audibly smiling,

"How are things with *you*? Are ya doing alright over there?"

He found it amusing sometimes how the people he had once known better than he knew himself were now replaced by figments of what their past selves resembled, and only their appearances had remained unchanged. He knew all too well that appearances were often deceiving, which is why he was so good at doing it himself.

"Yeah, I've been good. Paris was nice," was all he said. He liked being a mystery to those around him, who seemed to understand very little of how his life was going.

Frankie took out his box of cigarettes from his back pocket, which now gave him a little ache since he had been leaning on them for so long. Trying to pay attention to John, he lit a cigarette, his eyes still on his All-Stars.

"Good, Frankie, that is good. I wanted to talk to you about something, thought now would be a good time to call ya," John insisted in a low tone.

His voice faded away even more. Frankie pushed the telephone closer into his ear to hear him better, only to meet the low static of the phone.

He drew in some smoke, and with a deep breath, he replied.

"What is it, John?" the silence in the room dawning on him once more.

His friend stood silent for a moment, almost as if he was collecting his thoughts and preparing to display them to Frankie, in an attempt to sell him a proposition.

A little over two A.M in London means nine P.M. in New York, Frankie realised. Frankie could imagine John, with his prominent jaw and perfectly trimmed hair, in his apartment in the Upper West of New York. This was past Brown's curfew, as well as his own. A call at a time like that felt ominous, although John knew how late Frankie usually worked.

"*The Daily Sun* has been ahead of *The Evening Star* and *Walter's* for over a month now, thanks to every growing story ya gave us back here! Their foreign correspondents must have no clue about how the heck ya do the job y'er doing...or the poor bastards don't even have people abroad reporting things back to them," he said.

Frankie was aware of the competition between these companies even before he started working for *The Daily Sun*. Their rivalry was unmatched in the world of journalism. The fast-paced workplace had not suited many, but people like Frankie and John were dedicated to staying on top. It was one of those things that started as minuscule and amusing, but it escalated to something that made people forget how they even arrived there in the first place. Frankie was thrilled when he discovered the little tricks *The Daily Sun* would use to attract a larger audience. It felt like being part of something, a secret inside joke or a club. And ever since, he had remained vigilant to keep being a part of it.

"Well, I am glad to hear that, John," Frankie responded.

"I need you to keep an eye on things over there in Europe a little longer," John said in a low tone.

And there it was, the news that Frankie was awaiting. He would have bet anything on it. They wanted him abroad for good, for all he knew. His contract specified a certain number of months, but given the progress he showed as an investigative journalist overseas, he knew they would have wanted to keep him there longer. Still, he made an effort to appear flattered.

"Wow, I don't know what to say. Are you sure?" Frankie smiled to himself.

He didn't feel upset by it, nor was he too glad. In fact, he felt *nothing* towards it.

"Of course I am, Frank. There aren't even a quarter of journalists out there with your dedication. Actually, your *stubbornness*!" Brown laughed.

"Well, the stubbornness is the Irish in me!" and he blew in some smoke, gently coughing.

John sighed, chuckling softly.

"Well, I am glad you're happy about it, Frankie. I wasn't sure how you'd take it," he said. "Either way, you're doing a great job there, and you were great here, so I have no complaints."

Frankie smiled again.

"Thanks, John," and they exchanged a few farewells and parted their own ways, leaving Frankie's office buzzing with silence once again.

The walk home was straightforward even on the worst of days, when darkness and fog covered the London streets like the smoke of a burning flame, deadly and immortal. Initially, the English capital sometimes appeared to Hannigan like a maze. The concept of blocks was completely lost there, every alleyway leading into a new neighbourhood entirely, and the sight of stone buildings centuries old.

Growing up in New York came with few benefits in this case; a big city didn't frighten him in the slightest. In fact, it felt familiar and good, like a New York away from New York.

His apartment was a ten-minute walk from the office, and at that time of the night, the cold breeze was his only companion. The low whistle of every passing motion awoke him even more, a deep, shallow feeling inside him surfacing. Differing dreams from reality had become strenuous at that time of the night (morning, in fact). Frankie wrapped his coat more tightly around his torso and continued walking down the street. The passing people paid little attention to him; they were all travellers in their own little worlds, living while the day was at its prime.

He passed by a few places that he recognised and knew, but they seemed ordinary to him now. Sometimes it scared him. How quickly the new had shifted into the ordinary. How distant were the memories of these places that once excited him. When he first moved there, everything felt like a shiny new toy that he could show off, but despite getting used to this life, he had something at the age of thirty that most people didn't get to experience even in an entire lifetime. The privilege of not knowing what tomorrow might bring.

The wind's cries were still following his footsteps until he reached the street that he had grown so familiar with. There were trees planted every few feet, shading the apartment buildings. The cold had rid them of their dark green garments, but the ancient branches still watched over residents. The street had several newly-built houses and apartments that were painted in bright pastel colours, lively even in the coldest of Winters. Like most nights, it was quiet after midnight. And Number 248 was the place he called home.

Frankie made his way to the door with silent movements, exhaling a cloud of cold breath into the air. He fished out the bundle of keys from his coat pocket and let himself in after jiggling them to find the right one; the sound of them travelled across the neighbourhood. Paying little attention, he stepped into the dim corridor.

The apartment building consisted of three apartments, with his room located on the first floor. On the ground floor lived an elderly couple who slept as early as eight in the evening on weekdays. He was careful not to wake them up every night. The occasional snoring suggested that they weren't the lightest of sleepers. Above the first floor, there was a room identical to his, home to some teenager who, in an attempt at rebellion, moved in with a couple of friends in the capital. Frankie had only spoken to him a couple of times when they bumped into each other in the corridor or on the stairs.

The way three people were living in an apartment designed for no more than two people amused him slightly — the way the young made the most of something like that.

The setting of the apartment reminded him of the old Sherlock Holmes films he had on VHS a few years ago, but in this film, Sherlock lived without Dr Watson and had few mysteries to uncover, apart from the news articles. The typical London-style buildings were cosy and felt almost homely, especially when he spent more time there than at the office. Jokingly, he once wondered how unusual his colleagues would find him if he moved into the office rooms with a tent and just never left. Had anyone been insane enough to do that? It would have saved him a lot of money, which he was sure about.

Frankie left his coat on a hanger in the corridor that most people in the building used (apart from the teenagers, who rarely wore coats, he noticed), and walked up the stairs on the left. The second step creaked lightly under his boot as he quickly stepped on the third one; then he reached out his hand for the wooden railing, the surrounding area becoming darker. The way to his room smelled damp and cold, and with the constant darkness, he was sure that a colony of mushrooms would rise from his floorboards one day. When he reached his floor, he unlocked the door and walked into his apartment, thinking not for the first time that night that he was glad to be here.

The apartment had a gentler smell of sourness, with the only mouldy smell coming from the toilet window, where rainwater would collect if Frankie were not careful. The rest of his place smelled of smoke and cinnamon, the fireplace's ashes hinting at the warmth he desperately needed after coming home. He put some firewood in the small chamber by the armchairs, which loosely resembled a living room.

Except, of course, it was not a room, but an extension of the hallway where he was standing earlier. The kitchen was separate, standing behind a wooden door. Through the kitchen, a corridor led to his bedroom, which had a toilet in it. Other than acting as a way between his living room and bedroom, the kitchen was unused and empty, except for the cupboards and drawers that had bags of crisps (as the English called them, opposed to the American 'chips'), sweets and unused cups and bowls. Many of the items in the apartment were already there when he moved in, and most of his personal belongings still rested on shelves in New York. If no one had stolen them, that would have been the case.

Matching colours and decor seemed like alien concepts in Frankie's apartment. There were many different colours and patterns spread through the place, suggesting a certain indifference to such things. The walls in the main entrance and living room area were a pale, blue-green colour, while the bedroom walls were covered in a red-leaf pattern wallpaper. Taken out of context, the two rooms could have belonged to two entirely different places.

But it did the job.

There were no flowers or frames in sight, the only thing remotely close to decoration being an old clock that watched over him from above the fireplace. Frankie did not remember where the clock had come from, or even if it was there when he moved in. Like so many things in life, it somehow just was there, as if it always had been, from the beginning of time. And its presence made sense, although it was not something that could be recalled.

Frankie lit another cigarette and let himself fall back on the armchair in front of the fireplace. Soon, dawn would gently knock on his window, awakening the busy city. Or in his case, simply greeting him once again. He had not slept in two days, which was not atypical; he watched the calm flames of the fire tremble in front of him.

He melted away in the hot breeze, not remembering why he woke up on the still armchair in a couple of hours.

Fourteen

Frankie

London, United Kingdom — November 1989

The next morning, he found himself guiltily waking up at the sound of the TV noises playing loudly in the background. He glanced at the ceiling, the realisation coming to him in an instant. With fastened movements, he checked the large clock, which read '07:03'. Then, with a sigh of relief, Frankie walked to the bathroom to freshen up.

Lately, his own memories had become increasingly hazy. He couldn't tell night from day when he thought of the office, and falling asleep usually meant passing out from exhaustion. No matter how much he neglected the heavy feeling on his chest, the sharp pains and the tiredness, it had become the bane of his mortal existence. He had trouble sleeping since college, where late nights and the desire to stay ahead of the curve sometimes left him awake for a few days at a time. But this was different — he was not only suffering physically, but there was a profound feeling inside of him which, he thought, would make him slip off life one day.

He shook his head as he saw his reflection mimicking him in the mirror; then, palming his face, he got into the shower.

At 8:00 A.M, he was already off the tube at Oxford Street, heading into work, like he usually did. Office hours didn't officially start until nine, but old habits die hard. He made his way to the door until a sight, or rather, a person, caught his eye. She was as vicious-looking as ever, underneath the dark hair, dark lips, and hazel-green eyes. Even that morning, as peaceful as it had been until that moment, seemed spoiled now that she was there.

"Miss Sturridge," said Frankie, watching her approach him.

"Hannigan," she said, with a sharp touch in her tone.

Elizabeth Sturridge seemed to be the only person who had not warmed up to him, despite how long he had been in London. But, if he thought about it better, it could've been his fault as well. After all, they had an equal say in insulting each other's personalities.

It had been his first week in London, and in his defence, everyone did it. Everyone got drunk and occasionally got a little silly. Perhaps silly enough to go back home with Lizzie Sturridge under their arm, without being able to keep away from her dancing eyes, their gleam inviting him into a trap that neither one wanted to escape.

Frankie hadn't realised where the problem would be rooted until the next day, when he woke up tangled up in his bedsheets, his face nuzzling her soft hair. It had been unbelievable.

Frankie had actually *slept* that night.

But for reasons he couldn't explain, he had watched her walking away from his living room window, not uttering a single word about what had happened.

Lizzie Sturridge had despised him since.

Their one night together in London, on the first week of Frankie's arrival, was the first and last time that they had ever been kind to each other. Perhaps more than kind at times, he could recall. And thus, a chain of petty arguments had started, which had caused enough havoc in the months to come; everything from missing files to a small fire that had started in front of Lizzie's office.

Of course, typically, they would both have been fired, and Frankie would have been on the next flight to New York, spending less than a month in London.

But their bosses had agreed; losing a good journalist was bad enough. Losing two could be their doom. They were never assigned the same project, and, as a precaution, both of them were aware of the other's timetable. They avoided each other at all costs, hence avoiding any unprofessional occurrences from happening again. The second time, they were *definitely* going to get fired.

Now, Lizzie watched him, her dark eyelids demanding more.

"What are you doing here, Miss?" said Frankie, trying to seem casual.

The last time he had spoken more words than that to her, they were at each other's throats.

"Funnily enough, Hannigan, I happen to work here," she said sarcastically.

Frankie waved his arms.

"Look, I am just tryin' to be nice," said Frankie.

"Well, that's a first!" she laughed, even more sarcastically.

Frankie had never thought that what started as a petty fight between coworkers could have had such a profound impact, especially on him and another person. As far as he was concerned, Lizzie could have been anyone in the world. What made her different from the rest of the people he knew was the annoyance she knew how to cause in every room that she walked into. He wondered why she couldn't just move on from the silly thing as if nothing had happened.

"Miss Sturridge, this question has been dwelling on my mind for quite some time now, and I have been meaning to ask…" and he paused to turn his head closer to her. "Why on Earth are we still hung up on what happened such a long time ago? I know they say that first impressions are last impressions and all that crap, but I was never one to believe in that. I don't think you ever truly know someone until you take the time to know them, and every argument, every fight, everything uncomfortable…I think it takes you a step closer to knowing this person. And I think that for both of us, we gotta try harder to stop being so…difficult," he said.

She paused to light her cigarette.

"You think that because you're this New Yorker with a shitty background, who made it in a place like London, you somehow get to be right about everyone around you. You judged me long ago, Hannigan, but so did I."

Lizzie took a deep breath, studying Frankie's puzzled look.

"So forgive me, Francis Hannigan, for holding a grudge with someone who doesn't feel remotely sorry for how they are, and want to make their sad, miserable consequences disappear simply because they wished them away," she said, walking towards the building door.

Frankie couldn't believe it.

The sinking feeling in his chest began to feel deeper, as if it was being challenged. He felt caught out, seeking defence from Lizzie, who figured him out so well. Perhaps she was right; maybe he had been pushing himself to do so much lately so he could feel power over his life, and even the people around him.

He just wished no one else would have said it out loud to make it accurate.

The day went by as usual, as Frankie stood at his tiny desk and took notes about a case he had been looking forward to. A safe distance away from him, out of his sight and earshot, Lizzie Sturridge was probably doing a similar thing.

It almost made his heart jump when one of his boss's assistants, Sam, walked up to his desk and patted him gently on the shoulder.

"Jesus Christ, Sam," he said, shaking off the feeling.

"Mr Berkshire would like to see you after lunch," she said, ignoring Frankie's reaction.

He gave her a nod and watched her leave the room.

Ross Berkshire was the leading businessman with journalistic skills sharp enough to make anyone applaud him; he never made an error in his judgments, a streak that he proudly mentioned to everyone, which is why working for him was the opportunity of a lifetime for young journalists.

Berkshire was shorter than the average guy, a little over five feet. His head was naked on top, but he grew generous sideburns and hair above his ears, along with a moustache that brushed over his thin lip when it was overgrown, hiding it away. He wore oversized shirts that highlighted his robust torso, and tight leather belts around his khaki trousers. His office was always choking with the smell of strong, pungent cologne.

Berkshire's office was the most spacious one in the building, much bigger than the little desk cubicles that the rest of the journalists were given. The way to the office was through a long corridor passage, with light mustard walls and framed certificates and newspaper cutouts staring back at you from every spot. As expected, most of them featured Berkshire's name, or a photo of him smiling mindlessly while shaking the hand of some guy whose name he couldn't remember. The black and white contrast gave the corridor an aspect of mystery — if it wasn't for the thunderous sound of the radio, echoing from Berkshire's office.

The man's eardrums can't possibly be working right, Frankie would think every time he walked down that arcade.

Berkshire had a reputation for his niche traits, which made him seem almost comical, in a cartoon-like way. But amongst all of them, Frankie despised the music more than anything.

That afternoon, the words Frankie could hear even before stepping into the mustard corridor were amusing (*'You were handsome, You were pretty, Queen of New York City'*), a popular Christmas song that year. Despite the volume, he could have sworn that he heard Berkshire humming and singing along to the jolly tune. Frankie sauntered towards the office, hands in his combat trousers and his head lowered. He could feel the urge to drink a cup of coffee, although he had promised himself to cut off caffeine. Perhaps one cup couldn't hurt?

He reached the door on the right, where the music was as loud as it would be in a club at night, the sound of walking and tapping coming from inside; the smell of Berkshire's cologne drowned him even at the doorstep. Frankie knocked (punched, actually) the door in front of him, the sound of the frame shaking under his fist.

"Come in!" yelled a loud voice from inside, proceeding to turn down the radio music.

Frankie opened the door, the smell of cologne getting stronger. He coughed lightly before greeting Berkshire, who stood behind the desk.

"Afternoon, Sir. You wanted to...uh, see me?" said Frankie, running a hand through his hair.

He flinched his eyes at the sight of the bright, cold Winter light devouring the room, letting itself in through the three windows in front of him. Berkshire's office was warmer than the rest of the building, as the heat of the room rose to Frankie's forehead. And although he hated the smell, the loud sounds and the brightness in the room, he wouldn't have entirely hated having an office like that to himself.

"Yes, Mr Hannigan. Please, take a seat!" replied Berkshire loudly, as if the music from his radio was still playing, while pointing at a chair in front of his desk.

Opposite the desk and chairs on the right, a set of cupboards and drawers was filled with files and papers. Some were so full that they wouldn't close properly, with sticky notes marking each set.

The walls had shelves with tokens, trophies and artificial plants, giving the office a more human touch. But like everything with Ross Berkshire, it was the aspect that counted more than the real thing.

Frankie pulled the chair in front of the desk and sat down, relaxed, the stench of cologne still tickling his nose; Berkshire walked behind him to the file drawers, hunting for something.

"A cup of tea, Mr Hannigan?" said Berkshire, accentuating vowels the way Northerners did in their speech.

"No, thank you, Mr Berkshire," hesitated Frankie, hands on his knees.

Then a silence fell in the room, the only sound being the low hum and buzz of the radio, playing something popular and catchy again. Berkshire was occasionally flicking through the files behind Frankie, muttering something under his breath. Then, the older man poured himself some tea, leaving it to brew on the desk.

The young journalist started bouncing his left leg, hitting the carpeted floor with the bottom of his All-Stars. It was an old habit that he had never outgrown, ever since he was a schoolboy. The nerves just seemed to grow more and more.

Outside, a car's horn screeched loudly.

"Seems like those new meds are working fine, Francis," Berkshire said.

"Yes, thank you. Can you tell me what all this is, Mr Ross?" Frankie asked.

Ross Berkshire took a sip of his tea.

"I can never quite figure you out. A man like you — always so good at his tasks and missions, yet with enough issues to make some shrink out there very, very wealthy."

Frankie frowned in annoyance, and rightfully so.

"Did you call me here to taunt me about things that I disclosed to you in private?" he asked.

Berkshire laughed.

"Quite on the contrary, Mr Hannigan. I admire your courage, I really do," he said. "You can barely sleep, and when you do, it's because you pass out from the tiredness. The white light, loud noises… even if a bloody pen is clicked too loudly…It's enough to push you over the edge with your stress levels. And yet you manage just fine, even on potentially life-threatening missions."

Frankie straightened his back, as if preparing to defend himself.

"I picked this job for a reason, Sir. I wouldn't have done it if I thought that I couldn't cope with the race in here," he told Berkshire firmly.

"I am sending you abroad again, Francis. And I need to know if you can do this — that's why I wanted to see you right now, before assigning anything to you officially," Berkshire said, brushing a finger on the edge of his teacup.

Frankie looked at him pale — the offence was too great for him to bear.

"When have I ever demonstrated that I am not able to do my job correctly? This is such bullshit… what, one time? *One* time, I had an incident on the job, and you want to sit there and insult me!" he lost his temper.

Although Frankie was awaiting the worst, his boss did not look angry at him.

"Your work is always good, even when *you're* not doing so well. This time, I want to ensure that what happened last time never happens again. You had a panic attack, Francis. That's not uncommon — but it's a risk that I cannot afford on this next mission," Berkshire took another sip. "You'll be travelling into dangerous territory, and there are very few journalists reporting from this place. I can't tell you too much, in case you want to decline. But I want you to know that no one will blame you if you do."

"Call it what you want, Mr Ross. I'd like to know what I'm investigating," Frankie added with confidence, although his palpitating heart said otherwise.

Then, after a moment which felt like an eternity, someone else knocked on the door.

"Ah, yes! Come in," said Berkshire, laughing out loud.

To Frankie's surprise, the person who walked into the office was no one other than Lizzie Sturridge. The look of shock reflected on her face as well as his own, and before either one of them could say a word, Ross Berkshire jumped in.

"Now, before either one of you can say anything..." he began, but jumped back when Frankie stood up.

Lizzie let out a tired sigh.

"You?" asked Frankie, not knowing *what* exactly he was referring to. "You must be out of your mind, Mr Berkshire."

"People in glass houses and all that," mumbled Lizzie.

She palmed her face at her own remark, staying silent afterwards. Ross Berkshire stepped back into the spot between Frankie and Lizzie.

"Mr Hannigan, as I was saying before..." and he pointed at Lizzie to take a seat next to Frankie, "I have called both of you here today to discuss your next assignment, since you're both going to be on this project."

Despite her best efforts, Lizzie looked at Ross with confusion, while Frankie lowered his head, anticipating the worst.

"I thought we weren't being assigned the same projects to avoid conflict," said Frankie in a low voice.

For once, Lizzie seemed to agree with him — she nodded silently.

Ross Berkshire placed a couple of files in front of them and sat down in the chair behind his desk.

"Mr Hannigan and Elizabeth," he said, addressing Lizzie by her first name as he usually did. "You lot really need to figure this bickering out quickly. Neither one of you is a child, may I remind you!"

Frankie had quickly learned that Berkshire seemed quite fond of Lizzie from the beginning, for reasons he could not fathom. Right now, though, this was the least of his worries.

Berkshire watched them both, from left to right, then right to left — hands on his hips, as if he were a mother scolding her kids.

"I needed *both* of my best journalists here today for this project. You're investigative journalists, for goodness' sake — quit acting like high school girls out to pick a fight," he told them.

Frankie got up.

"Not to be a complete dick, Mr Ross, but I will not be taking this project after all," he said.

Lizzie looked at him with a mock-surprise expression.

"Frankie letting someone down? Shocker!" Lizzie scoffed.

"I don't want any part of this," Frankie protested, looking back at Berkshire.

This time, though, his boss *was* angry — the man's cheeks had reddened, his breath growing into a pant. Berkshire put both of his hands on his hips.

"Sit. Down," Berkshire thundered as Frankie was headed for the door.

Frankie turned around, but didn't sit; he crossed his arms.

"You are one stubborn man…" Berkshire added, to which Frankie sat down, looking obviously displeased.

Ross Berkshire gulped his final sips of tea and tossed a file labelled '*CONFIDENTIAL*' between Lizzie and Frankie. Lizzie was the first to pick it up.

"Oh my God," an exclamation escaped her.

Instantly, Frankie knew that London was soon going to become a distant memory.

Fifteen

Elizabeth

London, United Kingdom — November 1989

"Abso-fucking-lutely not," Lizzie responded sharply, standing up, the file falling on the desk. "I am no longer a foreign correspondent; I have no business going to the other side of the continent."

"Yes, but you were before. New York, Paris, Melbourne…you were our girl for many years before you came back, Elizabeth. And you were good at what you did, no matter what you think of it," said Berkshire.

Hannigan's eyes sparked the same confusion as everyone else who had come across Lizzie; they all wondered why she *wouldn't* have been proud of such a record. Over a decade of experience, ever since she was fresh out of school. And to think that London was Hannigan's first city as a permanent foreign correspondent.

By the looks of the papers lying still in front of them, the next place for both of them was Bucharest.

"Why this place?" asked Frankie, pointing at the paper.

Lizzie scoffed.

"Because the place has low media coverage, despite being a crucial place for the development in the fall of the Communist bloc. The few predictions out there claim that Romania will most likely be next in the list of Eastern countries to fight against the communists," said Lizzie, pushing her chair in. "I need time to think this over before I agree to anything, Ross," and she made her way to the door.

"Of course, Elizabeth," was all that Berkshire could say, while Frankie's agitated leg bounce absorbed every little detail of their next adventure.

"Both of you remember 'The Letter of the Six', I'm sure... well, now we need to know how a few people disappeared without any trace in just a few weeks?" Berkshire asked.

Lizzie placed a couple of papers on the side of her coffee table, where her hot cup of tea almost spilt. She leaned down, marking the papers with a neat 'X'. Naturally, the young woman had read them, and the marking helped avoid confusion.

And she knew how much she needed to avoid confusion — of any sort.

Naturally, she was working out in her mind *how much* confusion she would have to deal with if she took the assignment from Ross Berkshire. In that moment, the fact that the American was assigned to her was the least of her worries.

Lizzie had lived in London her entire childhood — first with her mum in Covent Garden, near the West End, then near King's College after she graduated. She liked that part of London, no matter how much she would curse the big city atmosphere sometimes. But this was before she took the job at *The Daily Sun*.

There had always been one thing dwelling on her mind, though, like a parasite that couldn't let her go. She always wondered if growing up in the West End was to blame for it, as did her mother, because, no matter how hard Lizzie tried, she couldn't put her heart into anything other than the art of theatre and dramatics.

It was carved on her soul, a feeling that she couldn't shake at all, and what broke her heart the most was that, despite not enjoying her career in journalism, she was good at it. One of the best, if she took her boss's word for it.

How much better could she have been if she had done what her *heart* desired?

She had always wondered if that was the reason she worked as a foreign correspondent for so long. While she never stopped to dwell on the past, she did wonder from time to time why she had never really tried settling down, moving from city to city, as if she were immortal. As if her own life wasn't going to end one day, without the happy endings from the plays that she was so fond of.

Of course, Berkshire had a hand in her life decision, too, perhaps more than anyone she had ever known. But she liked forgetting that fact even more than her own meaningless existence, with a job that she hated and dreams that she could only touch in her sleep.

Lizzie picked up the telephone cord and cradled the telephone in her hand as she stepped closer to the sofa in her living room. The flower print on her sofa matched the baby pink curtains, and the carpet's light tones highlighted the colour of the furniture. She hated the decor that had been trending in that decade; all bright neon colours that hurt your eyes, and things that stood out only because of how bad they were. At least the tens of medals, trophies, and certificates that she had accumulated over the years smiled back at her right now from every corner of the room. She rang the number that she knew by heart ever since she was a little kid, and put her bare legs up on the coffee table.

"Hello?" said a voice on the other end, almost like a song.

"Hey, mum," said Lizzie, smiling to herself.

Her mother was so much like her — the same pale skin and dark hair, and the air of someone who belonged anywhere else except the life that they were leading. Lizzie always believed that her mum would have made a lovely TV star, someone who was always in the limelight, constantly surrounded by others. Or was this just her own wish, to be the person that everyone watched — even if it was just for a little moment?

"Dearest! How are you, Elizabeth?" she asked.

In the background, Lizzie could hear a bell ringing, her mother calling for tea.

"I am doing well, mother, I just…I needed to talk to you," said Lizzie.

She shifted her position on the sofa, putting her legs to the side and leaning her head on the sofa's armrest. On a really tiring day, she would have fallen asleep right there and then.

"What is it, dearest?" her mother asked.

So Lizzie did something that brought her comfort, something that most people her age had stopped doing long ago. She told her mother everything that had been on her mind from that morning.

"And what does Berkshire think you should be doing?" her mother asked calmly.

Sometimes, Lizzie forgot that Berkshire and her mother shared so much history — the product of it all being *her*.

"He thinks I should do it; he didn't even bat an eyelid when they asked him to assign me on this," Lizzie said. "I think he forgets that I am not just his employee," she said bitterly.

"Ah, that is what's bothering you…I see," her mother sighed in understanding.

"Perhaps. I just thought that I could finally let go of all of this," she confessed. "Maybe even start over, without moving away somewhere far away all the time. I have the money, you know."

Lizzie could hear her mother pouring tea on the other side of the line.

"Well, we both know you were never one to care for money, Elizabeth. Or for settling down, marrying a stable man. These things were never going to be yours," her mother said.

There wasn't any anger in her voice, or even the hint of a condescending tone.

"You're a free spirit, dearest. You wanted to go to many cities and see the world and then become an artist who could rely on the past at least, if the days got heavy."

"You're right. But will that day ever come?" Lizzie asked.

"Only *you* can decide that. I cannot make these decisions on your behalf, Elizabeth. I am only telling you to do what makes you happy," her mother replied calmly.

Lizzie thought about it for just a moment. Then, considering her options, she sat back up.

"Okay. This is the last time I'll go away, Mum. After I am back, I'll tell him that I am done with working for him, and find something else to do," her voice sounded decisive.

Deep down, she didn't know if this was really what she wanted — how could she? The truth, as Lizzie believed it, was that no one ever really knew what they wanted. Not until they made a choice, then realised that it was the wrong one, or the right one.

Surprisingly, her mother seemed to disapprove of it.

"Don't do anything rash until you get back from this trip of yours. See how you feel afterwards," she told Lizzie.

It seemed wise, Lizzie thought.

"How's that neighbour of yours, Diana Wilson?" Lizzie asked.

She vaguely remembered a woman with flashy attire who had offered Lizzie a job when she was still at King's — Diana, the lady who lived on the floor above Lizzie's mother. She ran a cultural magazine.

"Oh, she's fine," her mother said. "She is in Oregon, helping family. I think she mentioned something about a distant relative being in rehab over there."

"Jesus," Lizzie replied, picking up her cup of tea.

"Yeah, you never know with that one..." her mother agreed. "She's always out somewhere."

"It's better than not doing anything at all," Lizzie suggested.

"True — but remember, Liz, you still have plenty of time. Please give it to yourself, don't take it away. We don't need to think of Diana Wilson or a new job right now. Enjoy the moment before it dissolves away," the older woman said.

Lizzie needed the reassurance; it was never too late to start over. She had enough time to think about what she wanted to do.

After promising her mother that she would visit her before leaving for the Eastern bloc, Lizzie put the phone back in its place. She picked up the papers from the coffee table and put them in her bag. Then, with careful steps, she made her way out of the apartment, heading back to the office.

Sixteen

Frankie

London, United Kingdom — December 1989

Berkshire always stayed at the office after hours, a fact that made Frankie feel uncomfortable. He did not dislike Berkshire necessarily. However, he found some of his habits quite irritating, almost as if it were a challenge to see how long people would last on the job.

As he sat at his usual desk that evening, writing down everything he could find about the place where he was headed, Berkshire's usual movement could be heard from the opposite corridor. He was surprised that the usual loud music was not playing, and the sudden silence made him shuffle. Frankie could never quite put his finger on it, but he found the quiet very bizarre. Even at home, he needed to leave the TV on whilst having dinner, or the radio when he was showering. He wondered if this had always been his habit, or if he had only recently noticed it.

And despite his feelings towards Berkshire's attitude, he wondered if the man constantly had loud music playing in his office for the same reason.

Did he, too, find the voiceless to have a louder voice than the living?

He got up from his desk and decided to go outside to smoke. A well-deserved break seemed necessary — and his back pain only confirmed it.

As he approached the back door, he heard a familiar voice.

"Mr Hannigan, wait a moment," said Ross, standing still.

Frankie turned to face him.

"I just spoke with Elizabeth. She has agreed to go on this little journey with you."

Frankie was surprised. He tried to hide his genuine feelings, but Berkshire seemed to share the sentiment.

"I know, I wasn't expecting it either. Elizabeth is a difficult person, trust me on that," Ross said.

"What changed her mind?" said Frankie, remembering Lizzie's strong reaction.

He could only assume that she hated her time travelling around the globe back when she was doing it as a foreign correspondent. Something had to motivate her this time.

"Oh, I wish I could tell, Mr Hannigan. I am glad she did, though, because both of you will be able to bring back something incredible to this station," he said.

Frankie nodded, feeling the cold breeze on his face from the ajar door.

The man found himself on the platform twenty minutes before their plane was scheduled to depart, taking them to Berlin first, from where they would be entirely on their own. Next came the train ride through Austrian fields, followed by the Hungarian territory that had recently declared its freedom from communism.

He watched Lizzie carrying her books in her hand, with a light rucksack hanging off her broad shoulders. He had even offered to give her a hand, which she had declined with a polite nod. Once the airport checks were through and Ross had left them to their demise, Frankie put his head back on a chair in front of a local coffee chain, letting the white light in the distance pinch his eyes.

"Wake up," Elizabeth's calm voice had insisted, giving him a flashback of something that he didn't want to remember right now.

"I *am* up. What are you talking about?" Frankie insisted, staring into the ceiling again.

"You blacked out again," she whispered knowingly.

He sometimes wished that he hadn't become so open about everything when he got drunk. And besides, how on Earth did she still remember everything that he had confessed?

"Why do you still know about that?" he groaned, hoarse.

"I like to think that you black out like that every time that you're being a real asshole," she pushed a smile. "Makes me bear you a little more."

"Ah, yes, that's what we all want to hear. *You become bearable when I have something to pity you for*," he rubbed his eyes hard.

Lizzie stood up from her chair, picking up her bags.

"Come on, I don't think Ross will allow another one of our messes to get in the way of his plans," she smiled, and Frankie was relieved that it was going as smoothly as he could have hoped.

Not too much later, he sat in his seat and read the pamphlets brought by Lizzie on Romania and the communist countries neighbouring it. She had been more than prepared for this, he had admitted to her, and in return, had received an eye roll for an answer.

"We need to dispose of this shit in Berlin before we get on the train. Can't be seen lurking with things against their *beloved* ruler," Frankie told her.

"Yes, most of it is junk anyway," she said. "I suppose you knew nothing about Romania until Ross told you about the mission?"

"Ross? What is up with you calling your boss by his first name? What are you, his prize student?" Frankie demanded.

Lizzie tossed it as a joke.

"I don't blame you for not knowing, it's the American flaw…" she chuckled.

"And yet I didn't have to shag anyone to get this job," Frankie's words escaped.

Instantly, he regretted his ability to vomit out all his thoughts at once. He laughed it off, pretending it was a cruel joke — which, to a certain extent, was true. The woman looked at him with disgust, perhaps even a mixture of shock and anger.

"Ross Berkshire is my father," she said plainly.

"I'm sorry, I didn't know," he admitted, not certain of what else he could have said to mend the situation.

"Doesn't that excuse take the crown? 'I didn't know'... but still, you dared to presume despite that ignorance that you are so full of. Anyways, I do not wish to speak of it," she raised her hand in defence.

"I won't bring any of it up," Frankie promised.

The sound of the plane's engine revving up agreed.

Elizabeth had been asleep for most of the time that they were flying, while he had been writing down every small notion from the material in front of him before he would bin it. He knew little about the eastern part of the continent, save for the history between his own country and Russia. There wasn't much else that he could have helped with on this investigative project, where the two had to uncover the inner breaches of intelligence.

Sometimes, he feared for his life — especially in times when he was going undercover like this, as they were at that time. Lizzie and Frankie were going to pose as writers from England, both of whom were passionate about poetry and writing, and as their cover required, they had to appear as a couple.

Berkshire had insisted that this was going to make their cover much more believable, but Frankie doubted that it was necessary. The communists were brutal, not unintelligent; in a situation like this, Lizzie and he weren't allowed to keep anything that could link them to their real lives, to avoid the possibility of getting into trouble.

In less than a few weeks, he would be back home, he told himself, where the comforts of his own space were made available at all times. He hoped that the tales about the east were simply that: *tales* of how everything was bad. He wished that they were all exaggerated, as he flicked through the experiences of others who had travelled to these places.

Soon enough, the bump of the plane's landing shook him in his seat, as he tucked away the materials.

Seventeen

Elizabeth

Europe — December 1989

Then came the train ride.

Lizzie had travelled by train before — all around Europe, in fact. But to the American, the sight of trains and people, merging with the fields and buildings, seemed like an endless dream. She liked the feeling of not having to explain herself to strangers in distant lands and foreign countries; they would never know what she was truly like. Perhaps this was the only part of her job that she would truly miss.

"I never thought it would be so lovely," Frankie admitted, squatting down on the train platform as if he was about to collapse.

"The German countryside… they say it is one of the most stunning in the world," Lizzie said, dropping her cigarette on the platform, then crushing it with her heel.

Frankie stood up, shaking his legs.

"Look, I'm sorry about what I said before. I was way outta line…" he said, putting on an apologetic look.

"I told you, I do not wish to speak of it," Lizzie said. "Berkshire may be my father, but that is *not* why I got into journalism. Regardless of what you think," she added.

"I know, I know..." Frankie said. "I shouldn't have assumed."

"But that is what people have always done, Francis... they see a successful woman in a man-dominated field, and they assume it is because of a man," Lizzie said in frustration. "And I am sick of proving them otherwise."

It was true — she didn't want to tell anyone about Berkshire being her father for that exact reason. They would have assumed that she got the job because of him, and not because she was truly good at what she did. And no matter how many good articles she would have written, or topics she would have investigated, people would have still been hell-bent on believing what they wanted to.

"Anyway, I am leaving after this trip. For good," Lizzie sighed. "You'll get rid of the competition once and for all," she smiled.

"Why?" Frankie demanded.

"I can't keep working here — my heart just isn't in it the same way anymore," she confessed. "I am not one to do things unless they are done out of pure pleasure."

"A hedonist? Never would've put you down as one," Frankie laughed, his hands on his hips. "Well, good luck, Miss."

"You know, you can call me Liz," Elizabeth smiled, and the sirens announced the arrival of an incoming train.

By the time their papers were in order and they were ready to leave, both Frankie and Lizzie were exhausted. The journey had proven to be tedious — the long and winding road ahead of them had become one with the sky, and they were not sure of how far their final destination was.

Now, the woman in front of them looked at them with widened eyes and overlined lips — her appearance resembling that of a madman. In fact, there was an alligator-like resemblance to her as she held a cigarette between two fingers. She didn't give them her name, and as far as Lizzie was concerned, the lady could have been the Queen; she had been holding them up for long enough.

"Miss, we really need to go; we have to catch the next train to Bucharest," Frankie protested, not for the first time.

The woman spoke no English — but seemed to understand a great deal. She mumbled something to a man next to her, who pointed towards the direction of the ticket office.

"For fuck's sake…" Lizzie swore, wanting to punch the woman in the face.

Instead, she gave her a sweet smile, as if it was in gratitude.

"Where do you think they're taking us?" Lizzie asked, feeling foolish about her question.

"No clue," Frankie responded honestly, "But I reckon we won't make the train to Bucharest unless they let us go in exactly three minutes and twenty-two seconds," he eyed his wristwatch, shaking it a little.

The mission had been a disaster from the start, and they hadn't even arrived at their destination yet. As they walked into the ticket office, Lizzie could smell the blue of the walls, touching her nostrils like a punch. She wanted to cover her nose, but it would've been too evident, she presumed.

"Sit," a man with a large moustache told them, the new office being the size of a small cubicle.

They did as they were told, holding on to the dream of leaving — maybe never to return here again. Behind them, the office door creaked loudly; the woman shut it and sat down behind them like a guard dog.

"You come to Romania for?" the man asked, his accent thick and a little rough.

"We write," Frankie imitated with his finger and palm, as if they were playing a game of charade.

The man nodded knowingly.

"You go *București?*" he asked.

"Y-yes," Lizzie coughed.

The other woman murmured something in Romanian to the man, and he gave her an approving hum.

"You no go *București,*" he said finally, then pointed at the ground. "This… *Timișoara*. You…" and he continued pointing, trying to tell them they had to stay.

"Why?" Frankie asked.

The man shook his head.

"No," was all he said, and he stood up. "Go," he pointed at the woman who was now smirking like a snake, her vision widened once more.

She led them outside the office and to the exit. The entire station was about the size of six platforms back at their train station at home, but the intimacy of a few small offices showered an eerie aspect over the place.

Outside, a red car was parked next to a bridge — a model that Lizzie did not recognise. The other woman twisted her keys in the door and indicated for them to get in.

"This doesn't make any sense," Lizzie whispered, as they lifted their bags in their hands, to put in the boot of the car — at least it would buy them some time to think, she thought.

"I know, but what can we do? Maybe they found out we're… You know," Frankie said.

It was impossible — and where was this police officer lady taking them now? A prison cell? A dungeon? Or to the side of a deserted road, like in the mafia films, to shoot them in the head and push them into the river?

Elizabeth Sturridge did not want to die; so she did the only thing she could do, and stepped into the car, giving the officer a beaming smile.

If only they gave out Academy Awards for these performances.

Eighteen

Elena

Timișoara, Romania — December 1989

"Oh dear…" Elena muttered, thoroughly rubbing Berițā's fingers with spirit alcohol.

The boy's inked hands looked as guilty as his lowered gaze implied, which made Elena pity her son. His other hand was bruised violet, from the cracks of his teacher's wooden ruler against his tiny, round knuckles.

"All this because the boy cannot write with his right hand!" Elena added, frustrated, as she looked at her younger brother.

Robi had an amused smirk on his lips.

"*Lasă, învață și el.* He will learn how to write with the right hand; this is the least of his worries," he smiled.

"How absurd is it, though? Everyone has to be the same, identical… we're *not* the same, what difference does it make if the boy writes with his left hand? Doesn't this make Berițā who he is?" she said, pointing at the sink so that the boy would wash his hands.

In the attempt to write with the hand that physically ached, the boy had made a right mess on his hands, clothes, and his poor mother's kitchen tablecloth.

"This is all ridiculous, Robi. I can't even take Ioana to church with me, my son can't write with his left hand... we can't go out and buy ourselves what we like!" she demanded.

"Of course, Elena. But all this will change soon. You know it, but we must be patient," Robi said, looking back at his own papers and pens.

"Ah, because that vagabond of a friend of yours promises so? We have more chances of getting Beriță to write with his toes by then," she whispered.

Her brother rolled his eyes.

"You need to stop detesting him so much," Robi snapped. "He is not all that bad."

"And how do you know that someone like that is trustworthy?" she asked.

"I feel it, Elena," was all he could say before someone's keen knocking interrupted them, followed by the doorbell ringing.

"I will get it," Elena got up from her seat, scolding Beriță to stop splashing water on the floor.

She jolted the door open, which was opulent in its appearance but weak in its structure.

Dragoș wanted to burst in — in fact, he was ready to. But he stopped suddenly, taking a step back.

"Unde e Robi?" he asked, looking pale and sickly.

Elena wanted to shut the door and pace away from it, but Robi's shadow appeared by her side, as if summoned by the man who had uttered his name.

"What's wrong?" her brother asked.

Dragoș looked around, his eyes pleading; this wasn't the kind of conversation that he wanted to have outside. Elena stepped aside, alert, letting him into her house.

"Beriță, du-te fă-ți temele. Vin și eu imediat. Go, your homework won't be done by itself," Elena said, looking at her son.

He left without hesitation after greeting the newcomer. Elena looked at Dragoș — the dark circles under his eyes seemed wide and deep. Had the man slept the night before?

"Who do you think you are?" Elena asked, repulsed by his presence. "You come into *my* home, pretending like everything is fine, and that you're welcome here?"

"Elena..." Robi wanted to stop her.

But she had too much to say.

"*Nu ți-e rușine*? You come into a family like ours, that barely has enough to make ends meet, and use it to your advantage! I don't care what you want from us; we will not give it to you," she said, feeling a rock fall off her chest full of burdens.

Dragoș looked at her with sadness, his furrowed eyebrows waiting to plead. Once he knew that she was done talking, he leaned closer.

"*Tatăl vostru este în pericol*. Your father is in great danger," was all he could utter before the doorbell rang again.

Nineteen

Frankie

Timişoara, Romania – December 1989

"No, thank you, I don't want tea," Frankie said – not for the first time.

The Professor insisted that they had something, considering that it was their first time visiting his home. *'Planted'* was a word that Frankie would have instead used. Visiting and being deliberately put in places of inconvenience were two entirely different things.

Lizzie, on the other hand, seemed fine. He watched her reach for the plate with hardened biscuits, putting down her cup. If this was all part of a greater act, he had to applaud her for it.

"Please," the Professor insisted, and Frankie picked up the jug full of water, just to rid himself of the old man.

The Professor sat down on his armchair, which cornered the coffee table on two sides. The decor in his living room was cosy and rustic, with numerous porcelain trinkets scattered throughout the space.

"The Romanian police... they like to know what people are doing, you know? I owe them a debt from a long time ago... they still ask me to help with translations and whatnots," the man explained, not mentioning anything about the Intelligence in those parts.

"I see," Lizzie said, coughing. "Well, we've told you already. We write. We want to go to Bucharest," she added.

"Yes, I know," the Professor raised his right hand. "But I cannot let you roam around wherever you like until they are certain that you are safe. For Romania," he told them.

"How come you are mixed up in all this?" Frankie asked, not certain *what* exactly he was referring to. "A man of your education doesn't have a place among the officers and the military, I wouldn't have thought."

The old man raised an eyebrow in suspicion.

"They know I can help linguistically. That's all. I give them the translations, and occasionally, I read a paper or two that they can't decipher — they keep my son and daughter out of trouble when needed. I am sure that a man of *your* education understands these situations quite well," the Professor said sourly.

Frankie nodded, then stood up.

"Hm. Well, unless you can tell your friends that we want nothing more than to get to Bucharest, we'll need a place to crash. Know any good hotels?" he asked, not sure about how serious he was.

"I am not the same man I used to be, sir," the Professor admitted, "I cannot simply give the police orders. Especially not if they suspect you. But I can help you with a place to stay. I will be leaving town tonight for a few days. You can stay here until then. My daughter lives across the street, and she can help you until I return. How does that sound?"

Frankie and Lizzie exchanged a look that conveyed the same message — they were not going to leave this place anytime soon. For all they knew, the old man was a psycho.

"Sounds perfect," Lizzie smiled.

Frankie wanted to applaud her once more.

The new building was spacious and cold, with hollow spaces that felt like a void between the concrete. The Professor led them to his daughter's home, a woman of about thirty, named Elena. Whether she spoke any English or not, they didn't dare ask.

"Elena!" the old man shouted.

A stranger on the other end opened the door and stared back at them with curiosity. The Professor exchanged a few words with the young man, then turned to Frankie, nudging him to go in — and despite the shuffling, he had noticed the Professor staring back and forth around the dim hallway, perhaps scanning the space for nosy neighbours. Frankie kept his hands in his coat pockets — not for the cold, but to stop them shaking. Every Romanian voice felt like a gun clocking in the dark.

The first room they entered was a modest kitchen, where a woman (who was presumably Elena) stood by the table, accompanied by another man. This was her husband, perhaps?

The Professor looked at the other man with an intense glare, as if his presence surprised him. And although neither Frankie nor Lizzie could understand the language that the others spoke, their tone of voice was evident.

The old man was the first to speak, pointing at the other man, as if inquiring about his arrival. The woman then said something, but the Professor gave her a cold look, followed by a sharply delivered insult, Frankie thought. The other man, who was much taller than everyone else in the room, remained silent.

The man who had opened the door for them interjected then, trying to calm down the situation between them. When the room seemed calm again, he turned to the newcomers.

"I'm Robi," he said, shaking Lizzie and Frankie's hands respectively.

They didn't need to be told that he was the Professor's son — close up, his eyes looked exactly like his father's.

Twenty

Robert

Timișoara, Romania – December 1989

Yes — of course, he trusted Dragoș with their secret.

Although his father's face looked paler than before and evidently cross, Robi ignored him. If this was the danger that Dragoș had come to warn them about, he had already proved his loyalty to their family. Now, it was time to be clever and play the game that had been laid out for them by the *Securitate.*

His father scolded him; he should have been wary in front of Dragoș, a stranger. Who could have possibly asked him to spy on others if needed? But those days were behind Dragoș now, Robi knew. A lot of things were behind all of them, and the only way was ahead.

"*Dumnezeule.* My God, Robi. Have you learned nothing?" his father demanded, looking hurt.

"*Domnule profesor,*" Dragoș began, but Robi's father raised a hand — curt and final.

"I do not speak to people like you, Dragoș. Don't be fooled, I know a great deal about your *aventuri*. The adventures that you tell no one about… You think you're so clever, son. But be aware. We all know what you are," Dragoș said.

All this tension made Robi's stomach twist in hunger — he pulled out a couple of chairs in distraction, waving his hands so the new guests would sit down. They didn't need to be told twice; there was a particular curiosity about their faces, something that seemed out of line. But perhaps Robi was being paranoid. The better question was, why was the infamous Professor hanging out with a couple of tourists?

As if he had read his mind, Dragoș addressed the same question to the old man. His father was growing impatient.

"You're also clever with the ways of questioning a man to make him confess, I see," the old man said to Dragoș, with a hidden smirk. "You reek of them, boy. I won't be answering anything to you."

The words hung in the room like smoke. No one breathed. Even Dragoș, with all his masks, flinched.

"*Tata...*" Robi begged, his face flushed.

The Professor sighed, pulling out a stool from under the table to sit down. Elena, who had been watching all the exchanges quietly, walked up to the stove and put some water on it to boil, perhaps for tea.

"*Poliția...* they asked me to 'befriend' the strangers for a while, until they can clear up their papers. Something in the system flagged them... I don't know anything else. I have helped the police before, Robi. It was only to protect you guys, you know how these things can get. Some more than others," he shot a despising look at Dragoș.

"*Trebuie să plecați.* You have to leave town as soon as possible... I think they want to frame you," Dragoș whispered, his eyes widening.

The look of fear on his face was a new shade for Robi, who had only ever seen the man as a strong, courageous figure. Now, in the face of regret and potential war, he seemed like nothing more than a frightened child who wanted to run away into the distance and hide away from all the monsters. Everything about Dragoș was growing grey, from his face and hair to the smoke that he filled every room's air with when he walked into it.

"I have to leave anyway," the Professor said, not looking at Dragoș's face. "I am going back to our village for a few days, to see my nieces and nephews," he added.

"Good," Dragoş nodded. "Ask the foreigners to get on the next train back home if they want to live," he said to Robi.

"*Nu*," Elena coughed, making everyone turn their heads towards her. "No one will let them go until their papers come clean. Let's be realistic now."

She poured some *măceșe* tea into small cups, taking out the saucers that were only ever seen when guests were around.

"Elena is right," his father said, surprisingly. "They can stay at my place for as long as I am away, until things get clear."

Elena turned to the foreigners and handed them the drinks.

"Seems like all you people do around here is eat and drink," the man said, who sounded American.

Robi recalled the film he had watched with his friends, hidden in the basement of their college, passing forged tapes from one room to another. It was something about the air force, if he remembered correctly — this new man who stood in their kitchen sounded like Tom Cruel, or Cruise, whatever the actor's name was. The intrigue of this somehow piqued his interest.

"Make yourself at home," Elena told them in English, then introduced herself.

"I'm Liz," the woman said. "This is Francis."

"You can stay at my father's apartment until he comes back," Robi nodded at them.

They both thanked them in unison.

"*Fii cu ochii pe ei*. Watch them closely," Robi told Dragoş, smiling as if they were exchanging regular remarks.

"I don't have a choice," Dragoş told them in their language.

"I want to know everything," Robi whispered in the man's ear.

Robi's father leaned forward on his stool behind them, then stood up.

"Right, I am going to go. *Am multe de împachetat*. I have a lot of luggage to pack," the Professor said.

Elena nodded at her father.

"*Ai grijă, tata*. Be careful," she said, then smiled at the foreigners.

They stood up from their chairs, but Robi put his hands up.

"My friend can take you home, please. Stay a little longer," he insisted.

The Professor gave him a puzzled look.

"Are you certain, Robi?" the Professor asked in Romanian.

"*Ai încredere.* You have to trust me," Robi nodded.

The Professor gave him a low hum, then said his farewells. After hearing the thud of the door shutting behind his father, Robi pulled the stool and sat on it.

"Tell me," he looked at the American, "What kind of things do you write about?"

Francis gulped his tea and put his cup down.

"All sorts, really. Art, literature, culture…" he said too quickly, shying away from looking directly at Robi's eyes.

Robi recognised the body language of a nervous person all too well — he had done these very same things when Dragoș had put the fear of God inside him.

"What about politics?" Robi asked, leaning closer.

The man furrowed his eyebrows. The sound of the woman's cup chiming against its saucer sliced the tension in the air.

"We're artists. We don't get involved in… other things. Look, you can tell your father that we will be on our way home as soon as the papers get cleared. Okay? We don't want any trouble," Francis insisted.

"N-no… our father won't know about it. We were just curious, that is all," Robi gave him a wink and patted his shoulder.

The man sneered at him between grinding teeth.

"*Dragoș, du-i acasă, te rog,*" Robi told his friend, feeling a rush of adrenaline inside him.

Dragoș would take the newcomers home, and no more secrets would be kept from them. They could be one step ahead of the *Securitate* at all times — and their work, the students, the protests… it would all carry on.

The only mystery left was why the American was so determined to lie to him.

Twenty-One

Dragoş

Timişoara, Romania — December 1989

For a five-minute walk, Dragoş had surely dragged the way out, leading them towards a few side alleys that no one ever took. For starters, no agents or curious observers would follow them through these deserted ways without giving themselves away. And it also gave Dragoş time to watch the two writers closely.

Of course, he couldn't exchange a single word with them — but this was part of the experience. His sole focus would be their behaviour, without being influenced by the twist of a clever tongue.

Their steps were slow and confused, lacking any calculation. To some extent, they had no choice but to trust Dragoş, even if they wanted to run away. Who knew what else the 'police' had told them when they arrived? It wasn't uncommon for people in Romania to be blackmailed, especially when informing on someone else was involved. Perhaps the so-called clever agent that Florica had mentioned in their last meeting had asked them to do much more than wait for the next train to Bucharest.

Dragoş wasn't taking any chances — he fastened his footsteps.

Around the corner, a yellowed tram passed by. The foreigners stared at it with admiration, as if the rust on it was in fact gold. It made Dragoş scoff;

the strangers were such a funny bunch of people. What seemed to him like a small, minuscule detail about his city appeared to them like something fantastic.

He led them to the Professor's apartment building, then took them inside. The humid air was pleasant in some way — different from the stillness that was trapping them outside.

He nodded at them as he walked back downstairs, uncertain of how he would say 'goodbye' in their language.

Florica Lupu stood by the corner shop with a file dangling under her arm, while she stared at the building in front of them. Dragoș tried to hide behind the pole that illuminated the street, but it was no use. People passing by were too frightened to glare at him anyway.

"What did you find?" she asked, pretending to continue flicking through her file.

"They're staying at the Professor's," Dragoș answered truthfully, knowing that this kind of information would get passed around to Florica through other sources too.

"Hm," she said, showing no interest.

"Can I go now?" he asked her, feeling a surge of boldness.

"Just a moment," she said, dramatically slapping her file shut. "Do you know anything about the boy's colleagues yet? Any information on their so-called movement. Anything?" she said, veiling her desperation with attitude.

Was Florica begging?

"Nothing yet," Dragoș shrugged. "As far as I know, the boy is all bark no bite."

"Something is going on, I know the students are planning something... but I can't put my finger on it until one of them slips," Florica rubbed her hand against his. "And besides, I think those two at the Professor's place are journalists... why do you think we're keeping them under close watch? Just one wrong confession and I can have the Professor and his entire family arrested for treason."

What?

With a steady hand, she gave Dragoș a paper bag. He didn't protest; he held it open. She suddenly pulled the collar of his shirt in the alleyway behind them, their back against two thick walls that belonged to someone's apartment.

"A bag with medicine for Mrs Stănescu, more than last time. A few boxes of cigarettes and a... present," she clicked her tongue.

Dragoș inserted his hand in the bag and felt the paper-like texture of money massaging his fingertips. He watched Florica lean in.

"*Pentru toată munca ta grea, frumosule,*" she bit her lower lip. "For all your hard work."

She drew herself close enough for him to feel her cold, minty breath on his cheek. Then, she planted a small kiss on it — a chill travelled across Dragoș's body.

Then came the unexpected.

His mouth found hers in between shaky, tense movements. He kissed her like he hadn't kissed anyone before, his lips and tongue possessing a will of their own. Dragoș exhaled sharply into her mouth, trying to catch his breath — this couldn't be. He paused for a moment, searching for an explanation on her face. He had dropped the paper bag somewhere behind them, letting the wind whistle against its contents.

"Is this real?" he asked, as if from behind the bars of a prison, trying to hang on to the last thread of affection that was being paraded in front of him like a toy.

She smiled — and not in a wicked manner either. It was the kind of smile he had never seen on her face, one that radiated something other than hatred. Before he could say anything, she pulled the collar of his shirt closer, as he palmed the wall behind her with his entire force. He remained unmoved in the position, dancing around with her tongue — at one point, he could have sworn that he heard her laughing under her breath, running her thin fingers through his hair. Dragoș pushed a hand down her back, then brought it up to her chest.

He felt a gulp escaping his throat, and he sighed into the cold air. Then, as if he were in a daydream, he kissed her again.

Dragoș had never been so miserable.

With the opportunity to walk out of all this business hanging so closely, he didn't want to risk anything that he and Robi had planned and put together. And yet, he hadn't hesitated in front of Florica's demands. He had never been *so* deeply entangled with the intelligence community or the police.

And she paid you, as if you were her whore. As if she knew I wouldn't decline the opportunity.

As he paced back to the Professor's apartment with a brand new idea in the back of his mind, all thanks to Florica's lovely demands, he pictured what he would do after all this was over. When Florica and everyone else finally stopped terrorising the people of the city, and the students' protests began a domino effect, leading to the country's change.

When Ceaușescu would finally be imprisoned or replaced, *what* was left for Dragoș?

He couldn't leave his parents alone at home; this much he had decided long ago. But at least he would have time for more people in his life; would he even need the bakery? He could get a new job… maybe even something that he actually enjoyed. People had always told him he had a talent for the culinary arts — being a chef somewhere in town was a good backup plan.

At least he had lots of time until he had to make such decisions.

When he arrived at the Professor's apartment, he instinctively looked around the street to make sure that no one had been following him there. Then, he shut the main door of the building and rushed up the stairs.

Lately, all of his days had been moulded into one feeling — he kept getting senses of déjà vu and other similar recollections, but couldn't remember much about his days. He was too caught up with the work that he had set out for himself.

Dragoș panted heavily in front of the Professor's door, waiting for the man to let him in.

"Ce dorești, Dragoș? What do you want?" the Professor asked, squeezing the door handle tightly.

Dragoş wanted to chuckle at the sight of his white, bloodless fingers that were clutching the door — as if Dragoş was the wolf from Ioana's storybook, and the Professor and foreigners were the goat children that had been hiding away.

"I have to tell you something important," Dragoş leaned closer. "*Vă rog,*" he begged.

The Professor hesitated — but when Dragoş was ready to turn on his heels and go back downstairs, he stepped away from in front of the door.

"*Hai,*" the man told him, holding the door tighter than before.

Dragoş looked pleased and anticipatory as he marched forward. He found the foreigners sitting down in the living room, their notes and papers spread out on the coffee table in front of them.

"*Bună,*" he mouthed, feeling slightly stupid.

Languages had never been his strong point; when all of this was over, he wanted to be able to change that. He had often found English to be a sweet-sounding language. The man, Frankie, looked at him and nodded. A mixture of fear and confusion reigned on the people's pale faces. Dragoş sat down in front of them, trying not to seem like a threat.

"*Zi, Dragoş,*" the Professor followed in. "What do you want to tell them?" he asked, then explained something in English.

Dragoş let out a cough, rubbing his hands thoroughly; Christ, was he *nervous*? This was a dangerous shot, but he was willing to take it.

"Tell them that I do not care what kind of writing they are experienced in… or what they are here for… I need them to write about all of *this,*" he waved his hands around.

The Professor raised one of his eyebrows.

"I'm not quite sure I follow, Dragoş. What do you want from them?" he inquired.

"Oh, stop pretending to be so naive. You know exactly what I mean," Dragoş stood up. "Don't think I don't know about all your 'banned' books and stupid endeavours, old man. You're in on the 'Revolution' talks and protests as much as any of those students out there that everyone knows about, but no one wants to mention."

The Professor sighed.

"*Stai jos*. Please, sit," he insisted. "You know what doing this means. Are you ready to have that kind of risk on your head, boy? I have lived my life… I don't care about my books or what they want to take me in for. But you? You're a young man," the man added with pity.

"All my life, I have only ever done wrong things, Professor," Dragoș said. "Please. I need them to want to stick around at least another day or two and write about this place. Even if three people hear about it, it is something. You know that the lives we are leading here are full of injustice," he elaborated.

"You have a bright future ahead of you," the Professor said, giving him a sad smile. "I see it."

Then, to Dragoș's surprise, the old man began elaborating in English to the strangers.

Twenty-Two

Elena

Timişoara, Romania — December 1989

"You did *what?*" Elena demanded again, bewildered by the man's presence in her home.

She had never seen and heard of him as often as she had in the last week, and something told her it wasn't going to stop anytime soon.

"I know, I know," Dragoş interrupted. "But I think this is our shot," he said.

Robi stood in the corner, palming his face.

"I thought you were the clever one," he said. "I don't want to die this way, Dragoş..." he added, half-jokingly.

"Stop exaggerating. None of us is dying like this. This is the best idea I have had in months," Dragoş said, sipping his tea.

Elena scoffed.

"You're lucky it was our father that you asked this... if it were anyone else, I would have been ready for the *Securitate* to waltz in here any second now," Elena told him.

"They agreed to help, okay? Come on, Elena, don't be so rude. Let them in here. They don't know what we're saying anyway," Dragoş asked.

She remembered the man and woman who were sitting in her living room right now, beyond the closed door that separated it from the kitchen. They were not Romanian — not even Hungarian or Serbian, if that mattered. They had come from the West.

And the West only meant trouble.

She walked over to the next room and nodded at the two to come in — not without noticing how her youngest, Beriță, had been sitting on the carpet with the woman. The other woman let go of the toy train that she was holding in her hand at the sight of the boy's mother, perhaps anxious enough as it was. Elena found the woman's lacy attire odd. The man's printed clothing wasn't any better. At least, if they didn't want to be noticed, they could have made an effort to blend in, like with less colour and flair.

The last thing Elena wanted was for them to feel like hostages, so she smiled encouragingly.

"Bye," Lizzie winked at the boy before leaving, who carried on playing as before.

"Come on," Elena said, letting them in.

When everyone settled down into their chairs, she looked at the two strangers with courage. After all, if it wasn't this, something else was bound to have killed them. They were playing with fire. But Elena wasn't frightened of getting burned.

Eventually, all scars healed.

"We need your help," she said confidently.

The man nodded at her.

"That much is certain. Your father already told us. But with what, Miss?" he asked. "We write about the finer things in life."

"Liar," Robi smirked.

"I beg your pardon?" the man asked, his cheeks reddening.

Robi picked up a notebook from the table — it had beautiful, leather covers, and it looked almost new.

"I know this is bad, but I looked through your things. You think an officer who knows a little bit of English wouldn't understand what you're saying here?" Robi said, pointing at the papers full of neat, black ink.

"You're writing about 'The Letter of the Six'," Elena murmured, her eyes widening.

Her brother turned to Dragoș and told him — *Scrisoarea celor Șase*. The letter that had made Romania get global coverage for the first time in years.

"Why?" she asked.

Frankie remained silent. He rubbed his forehead thoroughly, looking frustrated.

"We're journalists," Lizzie said, surprisingly, making Elena shift her gaze towards her. "Look, we want to leave. Please. Don't tell your police friends about us... Many people are waiting for us to get back with a good story, but I am not sure if we can even get back at this point."

Elena put a shivering hand over her mouth.

"Can you write for the newspapers? Tell them what is going on in Romania?" she asked, with the thought of it being too good to be true.

And when something was too good to be true, it usually wasn't true at all.

"Ye—yes..." the woman said. "We have to document our time here. Everything that can help write a strong political article," Lizzie added.

"Can you write about us?" Robi asked.

Frankie laughed.

"Look, kid, we can't write about every Tom, Dick, or Harry that wants to be on the news. We have a task to complete," he said.

"What, Mr Francis, is more important than writing about the suffering of a nation? Or more noble?" Elena asked.

Francis looked at her with a considering glare; the unexpected wave of realisation over his face unveiled his fears. He did not know what to answer either.

"I suppose I can't say anything except the fact I know for sure. Journalism isn't noble. If anything, it is the least noble thing in the world. I tell you, every story I have ever written about — I don't even remember those people's names. They're just another number on my record," the American said, listening to his own words as if they were alien.

Elena lowered her gaze to her lap, where her hands shuffled, as if she were one of her students. The chilly air around her suddenly made every inch of hair on her arm rise.

"What would you know about nobleness, then?" she muttered, moving away from the man.

How foolish she had been, thinking that this foreigner was actually ready to extend an olive branch. For all the years that the rest of the world had left Romania forgotten and cold, like Elena's cup of tea that she had left to brew on the other side of the table.

"Wait," the other woman said, looking at Elena.

Elena faced her — Lizzie's piercing blue eyes turned to glass.

"I'd like to write about you," she admitted.

Francis turned to look at Lizzie, and Elena could sense the tension rising to her cheeks. The Englishwoman looked as though she was about to cry.

"I want to write about this city, Frank," she said, trying to reach for his hand. "This is my last job."

Francis nodded knowingly.

"You're jeopardising everything. You know that, right?" he asked.

Elena wanted to interrupt — did the man really think that they were dangerous? She could vouch for almost everyone in the room, save for Dragoș, that they were not going to spill about this to anyone.

"Stop it, Frankie," Lizzie said. "I'm tired of pretending like I want to write about what Berkshire tells me to write about. I didn't even want to come here. At least if this is my last time, I want to do it my way."

Francis — or Frankie, as Lizzie called him — palmed his forehead. Then, he let out a forced laugh, as if all of this was utterly ridiculous. Elena wanted to punch him in the throat. How could a man be this difficult?

"Jesus," he laughed again. "You know, he asked me to protect you? And then you are trying to pull some shit with these people… f-for what, huh? To be all high and might? High and mighty Lizzie Sturridge, everyone," the man started clapping.

Robi looked at him, amused.

"I wouldn't be cheering if I were you," he smirked. "You're relying on us to keep you safe, remember?" Elena's brother smiled widely.

But Frankie ignored him.

"What's the matter with you?" he asked Lizzie. "We have a task here."

"Oh, stop it, Frankie. You and I both know that no one will give a *shit* about another story involving faceless politicians that they have never heard of. 'The Letter of the Six' was Berkshire's way of sending us here — I'm telling you, he wants us for his *best* project yet. A simple piece about what everyone is already talking about isn't new or original," Lizzie said mockingly.

"Yes!" Robi jumped, making Elena's heart pound. "The girl gets it. The real story is here. In this city."

Frankie looked at the boy with disinterest.

"Well, what have you got? Give me your best headline for a story that will get us out of here?"

Elena raised her palm before Robi could speak.

"How about 'Europe's Last Dictatorship'?" she asked. "Anything along the lines of making this final."

The next sound was the click of Frankie's pen jotting down her suggestion, his eager eyes waiting for more.

Twenty-Three

Elizabeth

Timişoara, Romania — December 1989

"Wow, you really enjoy this, don't you?" the younger boy asked sadistically, as she wrote down a little bit more of what he had told her.

A lot of it had made her sick — the thought of children starving, people living in fear of the intelligence lurking by, and the unforeseeable future of the people of that country. She had written down details from people's daily lives, trying to make it seem like stories.

Some of it was described like someone's daily routine — written with enough charm to convince anyone that she was rooting for the 'bad guys'. Then, a better idea came to her mind; she started jotting down quotes next to each sentence, famous words from prose, theatre or literature that would remind her of what she was trying to express.

"I don't enjoy any aspect of this job," Lizzie responded truthfully.

"Oh?" Robi asked, looking down.

"Not anymore. I want this to be my last job," she explained. "Then I am done. So let's make it worth it."

"At least you're able to make these choices for yourself," the boy told her. "Most people here just get sent off to factories or the army."

"Not you, though," she raised an eyebrow in suspicion.

"Our family was full of nerds, like you call them… I couldn't be any less than them, could I?" he asked, chuckling.

"So if you could do whatever you wanted, what would it be?"

The boy considered.

"I would be on TV. And not on the kind of shows they play here on our channel… Do you know that Romania only has one channel? It's ridiculous. I would be on a talking show of some sort, or a film…" he smiled.

"That's a nice dream to have," Lizzie said. "I myself want to be in the performing arts. Theatre and all that."

"Well, Miss Liz… if nothing works out for both of us, we could always start our own circus. Perform there," Robi said, amused.

Lizzie laughed.

"I think this place can teach you a thing or two about performing in a circus," Lizzie scoffed, writing down another sentence.

"You have no idea," Robi agreed. "One time, my sister and I had to pretend that we were our neighbours when we went to buy some food around Christmastime. You see, they were out of town… gone to their family in Maramureș, which is very far away from here. So their rations would have gone to waste, or someone delivering them would have taken the rest home. So we took our chances, put on a slight disguise. It worked pretty well… for three days afterwards, though, we didn't even leave the house. We were too scared that someone would find us out and call us thieves."

Lizzie shook her head.

"Technically, that does make you thieves. But not in the typical sense," she said.

"This is one of the biggest problems we are facing in the world today… We like blaming the lower class and working class people, or in Romania's case, a *large* part of the population, for 'stealing', or 'spying', or whatever other sin we have committed. But you see, Miss Sturridge, no one is looking into *why* these people do these things. We are being forced into doing bad things just so we can survive, a game of hunger and poverty. Instead of punishing the poor or the weak, why does no one stand up to the people who oppress the rest of us?" Robi asked.

"You're not wrong, Robert. But it isn't enough to stand up to the system if it is corrupt from within. I bet you there are people here that won't let things change so soon, with or without Ceaușescu," she nodded.

"Easy with the names now," Robi looked around the kitchen cautiously, although it was just him and Lizzie there.

"I apologise," Lizzie said. "I don't think I say his name right anyway."

She had noticed some of the pronunciation differences that she would have ignored before; the people here spoke her language fluently despite never learning it within the comforts of formal education, and yet she couldn't help but butcher every attempt that she had made.

"Don't worry. Romanian is a difficult language. You know, we were taught that our language is derived from Latin, just like all the other Romance languages. However, one of my father's books claims something else; some people have researched the origins of Romanian and believe that it is even older than Latin. Or at least it existed around the same time, and somehow managed to survive all these years," Robi told her.

"Fascinating," she said, writing that on her paper.

Robi gave her an approving nod.

"Tell me about this 'revolution', or 'protests', and all this buzz around it. I know your sister and Dragoș are trying to have a conversation about it in the room next to Frankie right now, but I want to hear it from you. You're a different age from them, too," Lizzie explained.

"Well, if the Revolution is your thing, Dragoș is your man. Shame he only speaks a few words of Russian, and nothing else. I'm sure Frank over there is getting some of it right now," Robi shuffled in his chair. "What's the thing between you two anyway?"

"What do you mean?" Lizzie asked.

"Oh, please. Come on, you know." Robi arched his eyebrows.

Lizzie coughed.

"Well... we sort of had a thing, a long time ago. Not that it is any of your business," she smiled. "But we also work together. And for most of the part, we can't stand being in the same room... he's too different," she said.

"Hm," Robi hummed. "Not if you ask me. You two are alike."

Lizzie didn't want to know what he meant by that. But the boy proceeded anyway.

"You're both passionate. *Very* passionate. It's just not about the same things, I think. You think you have to prove something, you know?" Robi said.

Lizzie looked at him, surprised.

"And here I thought you wanted to talk about your home and life," she laughed.

"I do. What else do you want to know?" he asked, smiling coyly.

"Tell me about the kids. What is life like for them?"

Robi considered for a moment. He got up from his chair, moved over to the kitchen counter, and hopped on top of it.

"They go to school. It's rigorous over there... even what they learn has been filtered a million times to make the leader look like a saint. You know, I shouldn't tell you this, but they suspect that the leader's wife isn't even a real chemist. That he bought her a degree as a present. In one of her interviews on TV, she called carbon dioxide 'ko-two', or *'co-doi'* in Romanian," Robi laughed.

Lizzie did too — the possibility that politicians might purchase qualifications instead of earning them would have explained *many* historical occurrences.

"The kids are good, I don't think they understand a lot of what is happening. Ioana, the older one, has started asking questions about some of the things happening around here. Like she asked her mother the other day, why do we have to stand in queues for so long, instead of just walking into shops and buying them like we should? And Beriță is still adjusting to all this," he admitted.

"How old is Bay-ree-tzuh?" Lizzie asked, wondering whether she had said it right. "What does his name come from, even?" she asked.

"He's six, and oh... his birth name is Bernard. His great-grandfather on his father's side was Austrian, so they named him after him. And also my uncle, who died a long time ago," Robi said.

"I see. Bernard," Lizzie smiled. "When he was playing with me, excuse me for noticing, but… he had some bruises on his hand."

Robi put his hands up.

"That would be his teacher from school. He is left-handed, and that is not allowed," Robi said.

"What?"

"We're all the same, remember? 'Equal', if you like," he mocked. "So writing with the left hand, instead of the right, doesn't make Beriță equal to the rest anymore. It doesn't make him superior or inferior either — just different. And that is dangerous."

Lizzie nodded silently, remembering the perfect quote to add to this collection of stories. Her words flowed neatly on the paper, writing a single sentence that she could recall from her years studying English Literature.

"ALL ANIMALS ARE EQUAL, BUT SOME ARE MORE EQUAL THAN OTHERS."

Twenty-Four

Frankie

Timișoara, Romania — December 1989

The suffocating air made him take his coat off, nearly tripping on the children's toys on his way to the hanger.

"I'm sorry about that. We don't get heating all the time. It's being rationed like everything else, so we're making the most of it," Elena justified.

"It's okay," Frankie said.

He hated knowing that everyone in that apartment saw him as a big asshole and nothing more — even Lizzie.

Actually, *especially* Lizzie.

What did the rest know about not being able to sleep at night, or even drift off for a while, having to rely on his emptying bottle of pills? The Professor's apartment had been more than comfortable, and the sofa where he had crashed was old, but still usable. All of it was much better than what he had back in New York, too.

He wished he could word what he was feeling better — the fear of failing at this job, which was all he had in the entire world. Could he ever give up on this, the way Lizzie was going to?

"Now, where were we?" Frankie looked at his notes, his palms growing sweaty.

Most of the revelations there were enough to shock any normal person; he couldn't imagine the process of rationing everything from food to electricity back in London, or anywhere else he had been. The woman had told him the amount of food they received monthly for a family of four. Frankie wanted to say to her that he had spent that much in a few weeks by himself, and he was just one person. Instead, he continued writing the rest, thinking of how he would tie this in with the story about 'The Letter of the Six'.

"Dragoş says that the Revolution will start once there is a good enough reason for people to march in the streets," Elena told him. "It's worth it... If you decided to stick around for a little while longer. Can you?" the woman asked him hopefully.

"I don't know," he answered truthfully. "I would love to get this story out to the world, Elena. I really would. But I don't know..."

"I understand," Elena nodded. "Well, Dragoş also says that this story will be bigger than everything else you have ever done. And that you will see."

Frankie nodded and wrote his final bullet point.

"I'm sorry, I need something desperately. For... for my s-sleep," Frankie interrupted, shutting his notebook.

"You cannot sleep?" the woman asked him, her voice soft.

"No," he shook his head. "I have had this problem for ages, not just now," he added.

Elena jumped from her chair.

"Come to the kitchen, I will make you some tea. It's perfect for insomnia. It's made out of *mușețel*, I don't know how you say it in English. I hope you join us for dinner," Elena smiled, walking into the kitchen.

Frankie followed, with Dragoş lurking not far behind.

"Get off," Frankie heard Elena telling her brother, who was sitting on the kitchen counter.

The young boy, whom Frankie tried to read like he did most people, got up from the counter and raised his hands.

Dragoş laughed, saying something in Romanian.

"You really don't have to make us dinner," Frankie said, remembering Elena's offer.

"Oh, yes… You really don't have to. We have some stuff at the Professor's apartment, he told us we could have it," Lizzie added.

"Nonsense," Elena said. "You are at my house as a guest for the first time… well, properly, anyway. I can't just let you go away empty-handed. That is never our way. You have come to Banat."

"That is very kind," Frankie pushed a smile, accepting the cup of tea that Elena had made him as a remedy for all the sleepless nights. "Thank you."

Elena shook her head.

"Just say *sănătate*. You never thank someone for medicine here," she laughed. "I would have to tell you that it was my pleasure in return, which is wrong…"

Frankie nodded.

"Good to know," he smiled back.

He gave it a good sniff — it was chamomile tea.

If it didn't make him sleep, at least he could relax for a while.

The dinner laid out on the table consisted of everything from cured meat and a few slices of cheese to a thin liquid that tasted like soup. It didn't have any meat or vegetables in it, acting more like a broth than a regular soup. Still, it tasted like a dish made out of love and at home — and both were things that Frankie longed for.

He couldn't help but notice that despite how little food there was on the table, everyone had somehow managed to get their hands on enough not to feel hungry. The two young children were fed first, upon the insistent nudges of Dragoș, the man who joined them for dinner.

Frankie had some suspicions about him — perhaps he was military, or undercover police? The man kept looking over his shoulder, even when he had taken him and Lizzie home. There was something he was afraid of, but they would not be told about it anytime soon.

"Thank you for this, Elena," Lizzie said.

"It is our pleasure," Elena nodded. "I think you guys should get back home soon. Geta is coming over soon. I don't want her asking questions."

That made Elena's brother exchange a few words in Romanian with

Dragoș — it was difficult for Frankie to understand, especially when the language always sounded very loud and expressive. Even with the tone of voice, he couldn't decipher what they were all talking about most of the time. But not speaking gave Frankie time to do something much more difficult.

It gave him time to think.

How were they ever going to escape this place?

Even if Frankie and Lizzie had been cleared to leave for Bucharest or out of the country, the matter of *this* story was still there. Whatever had possessed Lizzie to take it on needed to be stopped — but what could he do? He had promised Berkshire that he would take care of his daughter, but also not mess up the whole thing. Lizzie was going to leave anyway, but he couldn't let her sabotage his job just before she left the place entirely.

Frankie walked over to the sink and put his plate in, letting it clink against the other dishes in there. He gave it a good rinse before turning towards the door, where Lizzie waited for him with her coat on.

Dragoș lurked nearby, waiting to leave with them, as if he were their escort or bodyguard — Frankie didn't like the feeling at all. In that moment, the best thing for him was that the chamomile tea was finally kicking in, it seemed. His muscles were more relaxed, and the headache was almost gone.

The Professor's apartment was clean, although a weird smell hung in the air outside the apartment door. The hallway and elevator were full of dust and were poorly lit, which made the rest of the block-filled neighbourhood look dingy. Frankie couldn't imagine living there for the rest of his life; it would have been too much.

"You don't even have Coke here? Can you believe that?" Frankie asked Lizzie to peek through the Professor's fridge.

He took out a plastic bottle with no label on it and put it on the table in front of them.

"People here don't even have what to eat, Frankie. I think that fizzy drinks are the least of their worries," Lizzie replied, not taking her eyes off the notes in front of her.

"What is *up* with you? Giving up what we came here for in the first place just for a sob story?" Frankie demanded, putting both of his hands on the table.

Lizzie looked at him — not furious, but with a pale shade of remorse on her face.

"My father sent us here to get a good story. It doesn't *matter* if we can't write about the Six," she said. "Come on, can you really not see the bigger picture here? Berkshire told us about the revolutions happening in the neighbouring countries. We know, even better than they do, that a revolution will take place in this country, too. It's an inevitable domino effect."

Frankie shook his head.

"Whatever. When we get home, you can get brownie points from your father despite fucking this whole thing up, and I'll go back to writing some good articles," Frankie said, his eyelids feeling heavy. "Now, what is this drink?" he said out loud, undoing the lid of the plastic bottle.

"You're unbelievable, Frankie... your *arrogance* is the first thing that will get us killed, if we're ever in that position," Lizzie said in annoyance, watching Frankie pour a clear liquid that looked like water into his glass.

He gulped the drink down his throat, then smacked the glass on the table with a bang. Had it been any louder, Frankie would have broken the glass — the drink was *strong*.

"*This* has alcohol!" he shouted, looking at Lizzie's amused face. "Oh God, that burns... and it tasted like shit..."

"Karma..." Lizzie smiled, tiptoeing into the bedroom next door to sleep.

"What kind of people put alcohol in plastic bottles?" he asked, throwing away the rest of the drink down the drain.

He paced over to Lizzie's bedroom and knocked on the door — he felt like a fool.

"I'm sorry for bringing up your dad in everything," he admitted, looking at her from the ajar door. "I get frustrated when he does pretty much anything... I have been in this job for so long, and I have nothing else to do.

I don't know what to do if my work goes sideways. I have all my faith in one thing, and that is journalism," he added.

Lizzie looked at him from the edge of the bed; it reminded her of the morning when they had—

No. He couldn't sit here and recall the past.

"It's alright, I'm used to you being a dick by now," she smiled. "You put too much pressure on yourself, Frankie."

"Maybe I do. But I have never known any other way."

"Well, then, consider this journey a changing experience for both of us," Lizzie said.

He considered, then nodded.

"Goodnight, Elizabeth."

"Goodnight, Frankie," he heard, before he shut the door again.

Twenty-Five

Robert

Timișoara, Romania — December 1989

Robi read over both Frankie and Lizzie's notes once again, trying to decipher some of the 'code' words that they had used to make it all confidential. He liked their writing style, even if it was a little unconventional. This was the 80s after all, and things were changing for everyone, everywhere. Even people's tongues had changed, like his father liked reminding him so often.

The articles were going to be good, this much he could guarantee. The man and woman were sharp and knew how to twist words to make them sound like something else, and also the same, both co-existing chaotically. These notes had only been written in the last week, until the foreigners finally received their clearance for leaving the country or going to Bucharest if necessary. Robi handed them over to Elena, who was translating each paragraph for Dragoș.

Seeing his sister grow closer to the man who had not long ago been nothing more than a simple stranger made him feel safer; if Elena had it in her to forgive a man like Dragoș, then everyone could. His friend had dodged any unwanted meeting with the police, intelligence, or other associates of the regime that could have posed as a potential threat to the family.

"Here," Elena handed the last bunch of notes to Lizzie, who folded them back into her bag.

"Thank you for writing about us, truly," Robi said, putting his right hand over his chest.

"Let's hope that we can find the right home for this," Lizzie told him, pointing at her bag.

Underneath the kitchen table, Beriță pulled the woman's sleeves, trying to get her attention.

"*Hai să ne jucăm*," he said, revealing his blond head from under the table, and hopping into Robi's lap.

"He wants to play with you," Robi explained.

"Aw, of course," Lizzie said, reaching for Beriță's hand.

The boy had grown fond of this woman, and why wouldn't he, Robi asked himself. Lizzie was from a different world, the kind of woman that wouldn't have hit Beriță for not writing with his right hand — the young boy, just like his sister, didn't have the best of luck at building friendships. What kind of fate did his nephew and niece have! Beriță was playing with his toy trains alongside a woman who was leaving by tomorrow evening, while Ioana adored Dragoș, a double agent of the *Securitate*.

Lizzie hugged the boy and took him to the living room, where it was warmer than the kitchen anyway. Ioana left with them, holding on to her new book — "*Dumbrava minunată*" by Mihail Sadoveanu, a gift from Dragoș. She gave him a smile and a wave, which was more of an interaction than anything she said to the kids at school.

"I have to go now," Robi got up from his chair. "I am meeting with a few others from the University to see what else we can do until we can strike."

"Robi has a date…" Elena chuckled, making Frankie palm his mouth.

Despite the hostility that the man had displayed a few days ago, they had quickly gotten over Frankie's bizarre obsession with his assignment. He was a good man, perhaps — somewhere underneath all the boundaries.

Way, *way* underneath.

"Yeah, yeah," Robi waved his hands, blushing slightly.

Ana was only his *prietenă* — they were friends, nothing more. On his way out, Robi could still hear his family and friends laughing out loud, and Dragoș imitating the sound of kisses to mock and annoy him.

The young people of Timișoara were talented and creative; their own peers had demonstrated this much. He enjoyed it when they roamed the streets in groups of four or five, like they were now, walking through *Piața Unirii* — every single alleyway had its secrets and beauty. The square consisted of many churches, historical sites, and architecture that the Austro-Hungarians had built. He pictured what the future would look like when Robi and his friends would be the ones to run the place. Maybe all these buildings would be renovated in different colours, and more people would visit their country.

They walked through the centre, all the way to the nearest tram station. A few trams were stopped in front of them, waiting for passengers to hop on. They all rushed across the street to jump in, nearly tripping on the way there. When they were finally seated, Robi and his friends couldn't help but laugh — they were puffing loudly, as if they had just run a marathon. Sitting down on the tram seat, Robi couldn't help but think of how much he would miss this moment when it would be gone, as he often felt.

"*Unde cobori?* Where do you get off?" Robi asked Ana, leaning in to whisper it in her ear.

She smelt of peaches and summer, and Robi could drown in it forever.

"*Piața Maria*," she smiled, shying away from looking into his eyes.

"I'll come with you," he said, coughing out the hoarseness in his voice.

A couple of minutes later, the tram stopped at the station, and Robi and Ana got off; they waved at their friends, who were still sitting in the yellow carriage. He extended a hand to hold hers, and she accepted. It didn't take long for them to cross the street and walk over to the other side, where Ana's eyes couldn't get off the crowd in front of them.

Robi shifted his focus — *what was happening?*

A large crowd of people were gathered under a balcony, right across the tram station of Mary's Square, all looking up to the sky for answers.

"Come on, let's see what that's about," Robi told Ana, tightening his grip around her fingers.

When they gained a clearer view of the balcony, they could see a pastor standing at its edge, his hands placed firmly on the railing. He wasn't dressed like an Orthodox priest, but his attire was still religious.

"That's László Tőkés," Ana whispered. "I know of him. We go to the church where he works."

Robi had almost forgotten that Ana's mother was ethnically Hungarian, as was the man who was standing above them. László Tőkés was surrounded by people on all sides of his balcony and behind him. When Robi gazed down, he saw men in uniform standing outside the building's door as well.

Securitate.

"What's happening?" Ana asked a woman who was standing next to them.

"They're taking pastor Tőkés away, they're forcing him to leave the city entirely," the woman said with fear, holding back tears that she was ready to spill at any moment.

"But that's not-" Robi wanted to say, but was interrupted by László Tőkés's crystal clear voice ringing around the square.

"I stand here, before you, dear citizens — not as a politician, but as a servant of God..." László began, and everyone else stopped talking. "God's home is, and will always be, a place of truth. Of sincerity. And the truth, no matter how much some people want to reduce it to silence, they won't succeed. The authorities want to remove me from this place, from this church, not because I broke any of the laws. Not because I am some criminal. No... only because I spoke up against injustice. Because I said that *we*, the people of this country, have to be free, live, bow down to God, and talk without any fear," the pastor continued.

The crowd began murmuring loudly. Robi watched with widened eyes.

Was this heading in the direction that he was hoping for?

"*Nu vă cer violență*. I am not asking you for violence. Or war. What I ask is much more challenging to offer. Courage. Stay in peace, in faith. Stay, not just for me, but also for yourselves, and for our children, for the future of this nation. I can distance myself from here, but I cannot erase the truth. And I cannot erase God. Stay strong, and do not be afraid," Tőkés spoke before being dragged away from the balcony.

"Robi?" Ana's voice brought him back, as Robi had blocked out the inaudible chanting.

She squeezed his arm, and he looked at her, feeling something profound in his bones. Was this excitement, or anxiety? He didn't have time to debate because the man in front of them had already decided it for him.

"*Jos, Ceaușescu*! Down with Ceaușescu!" the man shouted with all his might, trembling from fear.

"*Vrem alegeri libere*! We want free elections!" A faceless voice shouted from the other side of the square.

He didn't have to say it out loud because the tears in Ana's eyes were proof enough to back up his hope and suspicion.

The Revolution had begun.

Twenty-Six

Dragoș

Timișoara, Romania — December 1989

A riot because of the pastor — who would have thought?

Dragoș stood with his hands on his hips, wondering what was next. The British woman, Elizabeth, had already asked about whether he had known anything about the pastor's eviction.

"Nu," he had responded honestly. "But I know someone who does."

Where was Florica?

And why had she ghosted him for these last few weeks, despite the growing tension around them? He kept wondering. He wanted to ask her what she knew, but perhaps staying away from the other intelligence agents was the safer option right now. He was ready to be seen — and declare his loyalty to the people who truly mattered: the people of Romania.

Elena's home was not large enough to contain all of them in the kitchen, but they had tried to make space between the corridor as well, sending the children to their rooms. Dragoș rested on a stool by the door, leaving the kitchen seats for Lizzie and Elena to sit on, while Robi and Frankie occupied a chair and a stool, respectively. Outside, the occasional sound of something crashing in the distance made them all exchange looks from time to time, although they weren't too sure about which one of the sounds they should have been cheering for.

Dragoş watched Elena's pale, confused expression as she leaned on the table to speak.

"We're not going to win this by staying here," she said in Romanian, then repeated it in English, her voice trembling.

Dragoş wished that he knew how to speak the language that would've helped him understand Frankie much better. Talking to him and Lizzie through hand gestures and drawings had been exhausting. Perhaps, when all this was over, they could keep in touch, and Dragoş would learn English; they could exchange correspondence from time to time, and maybe one day they would even visit their home in England. Elena would teach him English by then, he imagined.

"You're right," Elena's brother approved, explaining to the foreigners. "But you cannot come, Elena."

This time, he only spoke in Romanian.

"De ce? Crezi că nu pot sa ajut? You think I am incapable of helping this cause?" she demanded, looking hurt.

"No, no... Elena, you have two little children who still need you, and they will need you long after the revolution is over. What would happen to them, think! Please, Elena, stay here," Robi said, standing up. "We'll go join the revolution with the other students, okay? When we're back, Elena, we can see if it's safe for you to come too."

Then, Robi turned to Lizzie, and although Dragoş understood little of what he was uttering, he could read Lizzie's response quite well. She, too, wanted to go with them, but Robi was right about this. It wasn't safe for anyone out there, let alone Lizzie and Elena — women that the *Securitate* would take advantage of if they could. He didn't even want to picture the atrocities that they would do to the women.

His mind raced once more to the thoughts of what Florica was doing at that time, knowing that havoc had started. Knowing that many of her own people were going to turn on her within hours.

He shook his head.

"Look, Robi, we need to get going," he said to the boy standing. "Come on," he said, standing up.

"How will I know that you're alright?" Elena asked them, looking from Robi to Dragoș with a hint of eeriness.

"You will know if we're *not* alright for certain. Until then, assume that we are alive and well," Dragoș told her, putting on his best humorous tone.

But she watched him with the same eagerness as before — perhaps there was something *more* here for Dragoș — a way for him to be a part of the family truly. There was a mixture of dread in her face as she looked at him pleadingly, begging him without words.

She begged him to come back alive, willing to risk it all herself.

"Take care of my brother, please, Dragoș," she asked, hiding away a shiny pearl rolling down her cheeks.

"Stop worrying, we'll be fine," Robi insisted, and then proceeded to pat Frankie on the back.

The two exchanged some words with each other, while Lizzie watched their faces with a sad smile.

"*Unde pleci, Unchiul Robi?* Where are you going?" Berița asked from the kitchen corridor.

"I thought you were in bed!" Elena yelped at him, sounding almost playful.

She picked up her son, letting him say his farewells to the men.

"I am going out, but you have to stay here until I get back," he insisted. "Stay with *Mama* and Lizzie, show Lizzie the rest of your cars, okay? I'll be back before you know it."

"But you said it's dangerous out there! Why are you all leaving?" Berița asked, looking like he was about to start crying.

Dragoș paced forward then, holding his arms out at the boy.

"We are going to make sure that danger stays out there, Berița. But we'll need a big, strong boy like you to look after *Mama* when we're out. So promise me, you won't leave, yes?" he asked him, facing the boy who leaned against his mother's arms.

"Okay," Berița agreed, as the trick worked perfectly on him.

The young boy spread his arms towards Dragoș's neck and gave him a tight hug.

"I promise," the boy whispered in Dragoş's ears, holding on to him.

Dragoş felt the space inside him that had been filled with doubt for so many years, emptying itself, as the blood rushed to his cheeks. He furrowed his brows, making his cold fingers tremble.

How many young boys like that were going to be the new face of their country one day, he asked himself.

He was making all of them promise that they would look after what he was leaving behind, like a treasure left for the youth. In his own heart, he felt like making amends was plausible.

Next came the hug from Elena and Lizzie, who were trying to hold back tears. No one said that this was possibly the last time they would see each other, for what could be forever, but they were all aware of the circumstances. Dragoş couldn't help but laugh at the irony of it; when the foreigners could finally leave, or go to the Capital, all hell broke loose to keep them in Timişoara.

Even Elena's six-year-old was clever enough to deduce that something was going to be terribly wrong out there, no matter how hard he tried to keep his childish wonder from ruining it.

Dragoş was the first one to leave the front door, looking around for any attackers on the street who were likely to grow violent towards anyone; there were always those who didn't give a shit about the cause that people were fighting for, but were the first to flood the streets with terror. Some people enjoyed the sound of chaos reigning from east to west and used the shield of the revolution as an excuse for their actions.

Behind him, Frankie followed closely, clutching his bag tightly. In it, there were still records of what had been happening in Romania during the days when Lizzie and Frankie had arrived a few weeks ago. Now, there would also be records of the revolution.

Robi was the last to follow them outside, his fast footsteps carrying the most noise. Dragoş gave him a warning stare, urging him to be quieter as he left the apartment. The last thing they needed was a nosy passerby watching them leave and head to the apartment to find the girls and the kids.

The boys began walking, since they couldn't be too sure about the deserted trams. There was a slow, comfortable silence between them, with the winds of Winter howling through the buildings and streets.

The streets of the centre were full of people chanting the banned anthem of Romania, *'Deșteaptă—te, Române!'* on the top of their lungs, marching down the small cobbled alleyways with their flag in their arms, while the military seemed to be out of sight. Dragoş had tried to stay out of sight, avoiding the large crowd, which gave him a nervous feeling in his stomach.

There were too many gathered in front of the Cathedral, en route to the apartment where Elena, Lizzie, and the kids were hiding out. Dragoş wondered how many people in the crowd had left families back home, just like he had. His mind had also dwelled on his parents' condition, who were staying with his cousin Geta until the streets were safe again. The road from the Cathedral to the opera house, which was at least a mile away, was full of people — all gathered by the hundreds. Anger was drowning the city, as the people paced with the eagerness of their freedom.

The bridge where the revolution had started near *Piața Maria,* they had seen, was full of people who had been singing and chanting. Some were even crying and laughing at the prospect of freedom and hope that would come with the conclusion of this revolution. László Tőkés's balcony was like a memorial for the people, as they were looking up to see the place that had sparked it all.

Frankie walked towards Dragoş now, who had paused by the Cathedral, holding an arm to his chest. The banned anthem had become the people's hymn — it echoed in the sky, their words piercing through with an impact more substantial than the Communists' arms.

The foreigner handed him a flag, and although Dragoş knew that this wasn't his fight to win, he admired the young journalist for participating in this way. He was risking his life for people that had no connection to him, in the most noble of ways. He accepted Frankie's token with a smile, raising it to make the hole that had been carved through it evident for everyone else.

As Robi appeared by his side, Dragoş raised his arms to the sky. In the eye of his mind, he pictured Ceaușescu himself looking down at him through the cut flag, hearing his voice over the thousands of people shouting out.

"Deșteaptă-te, Române…" he began singing.

He didn't pause until the sound of bullets flying to his right began.

Twenty-Seven

Berița

Timișoara, Romania — December 1989

Six was an old age to be.

He had realised this when Dragoș had trusted him to look after *Mama* while the other men were away. He would look after Lizzie and *Mama*, as well as Ioana, showing them his collection of cars and books, while the occasional thud from outside would occasionally distract them.

He wanted to do that too, since it meant talking to Lizzie, and Berița liked Lizzie a lot. She was nice and friendly, unlike his sister Ioana, who got annoyed with everything he did. Although she didn't understand everything that he told her, she always had a sweet, red smile on her lips, and she liked his collection of toys very much. Lizzie would watch him write and spell, sometimes draw, and then they would play together. He had friends at school too, naturally — but none of them cared much about playing with him.

Once it was safe outside again, Robi could take them all out with him, and they would invite Lizzie to the town square. Berița would show her Bega, the surrounding buildings, and oh! The Cathedral, which he loved so much. The stairs of the Cathedral had been his companions as a young boy, too, back when Robi had taught him how to walk. Of course, he didn't remember much of that, the same way he didn't remember *Tata*, but *Mama* had told him that this had been the case. He remembered things better now, just as he would remember Lizzie for many months after she went back home.

What he couldn't understand was why everyone wanted him to stay indoors for so long, when he was old enough to take care of *Mama*? Why couldn't he go with his beloved *Unchiul Robi* to the town square to see what the hassle was about? He asked himself a series of heart-wrenching questions that troubled him deeply as he gazed out the living room window, watching Dragoș and Frankie walk around the corner, followed by Robi.

His body shuffled up and down the sofa as he looked at the men walking away; they soon disappeared beyond his eyesight, although he could deduce where they were heading. The trams were not functioning, he knew that much. But the walk to the Cathedral was straightforward, following *Bunicu's* apartment's path to the tram lines, all the way to the bridge where he had heard that the 'revolution' had started.

He didn't know what a revolution meant, but he knew it was serious; people never told Beriță too much, but they said Ioana much more. She was the one to tell him what was going on out there.

"It's crazy what is happening out there, Beriță... they're all fighting Ceaușescu!" Ioana had whispered to him in the living room when the rest of the adults were gathered in the kitchen.

Beriță had heard this name plenty of times — *Ceaușescu*. And sometimes '*ceașcă*', which Beriță knew was referring to the same person. But for the life of him, he couldn't tell what the *fuss* was around this guy.

Everyone said his name day and night, as if they were fearful of him. He didn't fear Ceaușescu, though — if Robi and the others were right, this man was going to be gone very soon.

Mama had forbidden Ioana and him from going to school for the next few days, until it was safe again. She would've never let them miss a day of school unless it was necessary. She was a teacher, like his *doamnă* at school, and she wouldn't have let him miss a day either. Beriță could already write all the letters of the alphabet, with a few minor mistakes in the lowercase ones; the Bs and Ds looked identical to him.

"Hey..." he heard Lizzie calling from the door, as she pointed at him towards the kitchen.

He jumped from the sofa, feeling an adrenaline rush in his veins, and he ran to the kitchen door. Lizzie kept pointing inside toward her, where *Mama* stood by the window. Her eyes were crystal clear, awake and alert.

"Listen, Beriță, I need you to do something for me. It's a quick and small thing, okay?" *Mama* asked, and he watched her with widened eyes. "Dragoș's parents are staying with his cousin Geta, here on the third floor. You know *Tanti* Geta, yes?" she enquired.

"Yeah, of course," Beriță confirmed. "What is it, *Mama*? Is Dragoș okay?" he asked, feeling a little scared.

"Yes, darling, of course they are. But you have to give them this paper from their son; he asked me to pass it on to them when he leaves. Can you do this for *Mama*?" she asked.

"Yes, *Mama*," Beriță responded, taking the note from her hand and squeezing her palm.

"Beriță," *Mama* called out after him.

He turned to face her while Lizzie handed him his coat.

"Come back quickly," she asked him — but the truth, he knew, was that she didn't want him lurking outside the building.

"Yes, *Mama*. Bye, Lizzie," he said, which was one of the first things that he had learned in the last few weeks.

"Bye, B!" Lizzie said, as she had nicknamed him.

He looked at *Mama* and Lizzie, waving eagerly at them. He would come back soon to look after them again, as he had promised Dragoș.

Finding *Tanti* Geta was easy, since he had visited her during Christmastime last year with Ioana, when Robi had taken them carolling. All he had to do was knock on the door and utter his name when it stood ajar, suspended between the metallic chain that held it locked. He could smell something sweet baking in the oven, and for a moment, he forgot about the frightening realities taking place beyond their doorstep.

The woman opened her eyes as soon as she saw the fluff of blonde hair growing on his shoulders; he wanted to let it grow longer until he looked like Robi.

"Please, come, come," the woman insisted.

But Beriță took a step back and handed her the note.

"From Dragoș, for his parents. Mama said I have to go now. I'm sorry," he answered sincerely.

"That's okay, sweetheart. Please tell your mother we thank her," Geta replied, as she locked the door again.

As soon as the woman's frame was gone and the knob was clicked back into its lock, Beriță ran back down the stairs to the ground floor, where his home was. There, in front of the steps, he had a clear view of the front door of the building that invited people in and out of the place. He walked past it and to the home door, which stood shut, and paused. He looked at the view outside, rethinking Dragoș, Robi, and Frankie out there, participating in the 'revolution'. And of Lizzie, Ioana, and *Mama*, who thought that he was at Geta's.

I could miss for a bit until Mama starts growing suspicious, right? Geta could've invited me inside...

He headed to the front door of the building and held its knob tightly. There was nothing wrong with having a little bit of fun if no one could find you out, he realised, and headed for the street.

Beriță was surprised to see that the trams were, in fact, still transporting people from one corner to another, as he hopped onto the 'Two', and stood by a metallic pole with his hands wrapped around it tightly. The surroundings had never looked so empty before, he thought, until he reached the centre of the city and got off.

Here, the station near the bridge overlooking Bega was crowded with more people than Beriță had ever seen. More than at Christmas, or on the national days that were compulsory for them to celebrate. They all shouted the exact words over and over again, a word that seemed new to him.

Liberty. Freedom.

The boy sneaked in through the large group of people, some of whom were singing a song that he did not recognise. He didn't know how time worked exactly, but was fearful that he had been gone long enough for Mama to realise that something was terribly wrong.

He rushed to the Cathedral, the view was clear to him then, and tried running past every large and small person while taking a glance at their faces. One of them had to be Dragoș or Robi. Maybe even Frankie. They had to be there, he could *feel* it.

He reached the Cathedral and looked around, trying to make out a face in the crowd full of flags and shattered glass. And then, for a brief moment, he thought he spotted *Unchiul Robi*'s jacket, standing out to him in the crowd. That became his reference point, as he followed him to the monument standing tall above the burning city.

When he arrived at the door of the Cathedral, after climbing up the steps, he almost couldn't believe his eyes. To his left, Dragoș stood with a lifted flag in his arms, while Robi and Frankie held one each a few steps beyond him. Between them, a few young men and women stood on the steps, repeating the exact phrases and demands over and over again.

He began running towards Dragoș, without taking notice of the man's surprised look. It wasn't aimed at him, after all.

It was aimed at the military tank that had just pulled up in front of the Cathedral building.

Beriță shouted Dragoș's name, worried that the man was going to be angry at him for breaking his promise. But he would explain himself, and everything would be okay again. He saw Dragoș and Frankie both turn their heads towards him, surprised that they could hear him over the noise that had just fired from the military tank. Beriță ran towards them, walking on the very same steps that had meant so much to him and his family.

Then came the bullets.

A sharp jolting pain impacted Beriță on the chest, making him jump back towards the building. The sound of something firing about a dozen times per second, combined with the screams of those around him, made him panic.

What had just pierced through his flesh?

He brought his sleeves to his chest, letting them soak in the fresh, crimson blood that was flooding out of him like an open tap of water. Then he saw Dragoș's face kneeling over him, but he couldn't understand what he was saying; the screaming and shouting were far too loud, and for reasons unknown, Berițâ wanted to shut his eyes.

Then everything went silent for the last time.

Twenty-Eight

Robert

Timişoara, Romania — December 1989

He didn't realise how long he had been sitting still.

Robi lay flat on the Cathedral steps, with Frankie's arm hovering over him with tightness. His own hands held his ears, pressing them to avoid the sound of bullets passing above them like missiles in the sky. He could feel himself trembling under the weight of his friend, fearful of what was going to happen if either one of them raised their necks a little too high.

His first thought was whether Frankie and Dragoş were alright, and the other man's reassuring grip holding his jacket made his heart sink. Robi couldn't see Dragoş over the steps, and as the sound of guns firing from the tank in front of them began to fade out, he dared to look around him, shaking from head to toe. The screams of people around him were lower now — some shouting names, others running far away from the military personnel that had started aiming their guns and weapons at the civilians.

"Are... are you okay?" Frankie shouted in his ear, and it came across as a whisper.

Robi whimpered, pulling back from his grip. An irrational, animalistic thirst to escape overcame him, and he gathered his body up on trembling legs, trying to take a look around. Then he fell back to his knees, ready to crawl on all fours across the Cathedral's floor.

The military had paused their fire, moving their tank north, towards the National Theatre. The pets of the *Securitate* were armed, looking around with grins and pleasure; this wasn't outrageous to them. The people begged for mercy, most kneeling by their injured bodies. He didn't want to think that a lot of them were possibly corpses, as he watched the citizens wailing and screaming while holding dear ones at their chests.

When Robi spotted Dragoş in front of the Cathedral steps, kneeling, he felt quite relieved. The danger hadn't been obliterated yet, but he had to know that his friend was alive and well.

Or if he wasn't.

Robi crawled down the steps with an arm under his stomach, trying not to alert anyone. He ignored the red spillage on the steps that led to the bodies, which were now being embraced by people who had, only moments ago, been standing.

"Dr-Dragoş!" Robi shouted from the steps, letting himself fall on his face.

He landed on the concrete beneath him with a gentle thud, and he could sense Frankie's leather jacket touching his leg behind him. The men approached Dragoş from behind, pulling his sleeves. The man seemed to be bending down over a body beneath him, holding his arms bent up to his knees.

"Dragoş!" Robi called out again, wiping away the tears and sweat that had assembled around his eyes.

He lifted himself from the steps, getting a view of Dragoş's face and body, and for a short moment, the body was buried under Dragoş's. While Frankie tried pushing him down again, peeling to the ground, Robi pushed Dragoş's arm aside, making way for the horrendous sight in front of him.

The shock only lasted a split second before realisation hit him through the chest, just like the bullet that had carved his nephew's heart. Dragoş had been protecting the body of none other than Elena's son, Beriţă; the question of how the boy had reached there and why he didn't even arise at first.

His first concern was whether the boy was still alive and breathing, as he pushed Dragoş aside.

"Beri...Beriță..." he stammered, trying to reach the boy with his cold fingertips.

The boy's golden hair covered his shut eyes, and Dragoş pulled his body up so that Robi could reach him. He wanted to feel his pulse under his ear, but his arms felt frozen at the touch of the boy's skin.

"Hey... hey... shh..." Robi picked the boy up in his arms and started hushing him, as if the screams and cries around them were all the boy's.

Frankie arrived at the boy's side and brought his hands to his mouth, letting out a silent gasp. Dragoş's arm pulled the child back, and Robi pushed through to touch him.

"How? Why?" he asked out loud, trying to grab the boy from Dragoş's arms.

"Let go, Robi... " Dragoş held back his own tears.

"How the fuck did he arrive here?" Robi shouted, holding his face close to Dragoş's.

The concern of those around him was non-existent, as he felt his stiff limbs grow heavy and fall to his sides. He couldn't care less about what he was sounding like in that moment, sitting there on the hard floor with the movement crowding around them.

"How?" he repeated, holding Dragoş by the collar.

"I think he followed us," Frankie whispered from behind, who had been silent until then.

Robi hadn't uttered anything to him, but he had felt the man's genuine passion about their cause reflected through his actions — he had protected Robi from the guns firing around them. How many men, he asked himself, would have drowned themselves for him, catching bullets in the face of the military?

"Fucking damn this..." Robi said to Frankie in English, trying to pick up the corpse.

The lack of circulation in his palms had caused them to harden, as he found it troublesome to pick Beriță up.

"Come on, we have to take him home... Elena, she could, she could solve this, right?" he asked the men, in both languages respectively.

"*Lasă-l*, Robi, *te rog*. Please, let go..." Dragoș begged him, picking up Berița's solid body from the concrete floor. "*Îmi pare foarte rău*," he added.

He was sorry for his loss. *Loss*.

Robi hadn't seen it as that until the first shade of pity and condolence, said by Dragoș, was spoken out loud. He pushed the men back as the tears that he had been holding in started flowing down his reddened cheeks, which burned with heat.

The leader, who was hiding in the capital or somewhere else, miles away from where they were, was probably laughing at this. When he had joined the revolution with the students, he hadn't suspected that it was going to escalate like this and become a vast, massive event within a few hours... large enough for the cowards of the *Securitate* to bring in the military.

To shoot at innocent civilians, even at children.

Berița shouldn't have been outside, wandering the streets during the revolution. However, he shouldn't have been targeted by the military either; they were supposed to be the people who protected the people.

Not the tyrants.

Robi felt like exploding there and then, melt away, and take all the people around him with it all. Was there a point in carrying on with this 'revolution', now that the innocents were being killed around the city? Who knew how many more tanks were settled around the town, willing to take out everyone if they had to...

"Robi, please... *ascultă-mă*. Listen to me, please, Robi," Dragoș said, taking his own ghostly hands and placing them in Robi's.

Words echoed around his ears, although he struggled to fathom them.

"I can't-" Robi started, letting more tears swim around his trembling eyes. "I have to find Elena... she can find a solution, I'm sure she can. He can't be dead, Dragoș. He cannot be..." he shouted, not being able to hold in any of his emotions anymore.

Robi lowered his head into Dragoș's sleeves, screaming into the cloth that touched his face. He rubbed his eyes against him, crying loudly. He couldn't tell after a while which pleadings were his own and which ones belonged to other people; all he felt was Dragoş's strong arms holding him close, letting him drop his sorrows into his shoulders.

He didn't know how long he had stood there, stable and relaxed, leaning on his friend's chest. The next time that he had looked up was when Frankie had given him a gentle thud on the back, as someone else had called out.

"Please, let us help..." a woman's voice said, and Robi glanced up to face him.

The daylight had blinded him so suddenly that he couldn't see the woman's face properly; shutting his eyes and holding them against Dragoş for so long had affected his vision. He rubbed his eyes thoroughly, feeling their dampness on his fingers.

As he got a clearer view of the woman speaking, he noticed her paramedic uniform.

"Please, may I?" the woman approached them, now being the centre of attention.

"Where are you taking him?" Dragoş asked, putting a hand between the concrete and the dead child's body.

"The-the hospital, sir. *Spitalul Județean.* They are offering treatments there to those injured and identifying the dead in the morgue. You can let your boy rest there until the entire family is ready to make arrangements for him..." she murmured, looking anxious at the sight.

Good, Robi told himself.

If *she* felt horrified, could she imagine what the boy's mother had to live through? No one should have witnessed the sight, but this was now their truth.

This is Ceaușescu's legacy.

Robi considered it for a moment, as his arm rested over Beriță's frozen skin. He hadn't noticed that the boy wasn't even wearing a coat until then, which made his imagination escalate. The boy's frigid body was sitting in the morgue, as lifeless as his own leaders had been when they allowed the firing to start.

He didn't — couldn't, let Elena see the boy in that way.

"No, no..." he began to grow angry at the man for even daring to suggest such a thing.

"Robi," Dragoş held him tightly, and he couldn't move forward. "Please, help me lift the boy," he added to the woman, holding Beriță's arms.

The newcomer leaned down and held the boy's legs — he wasn't heavy, but the woman's frail hands would've struggled. Dragoş held the boy until they walked to the small ambulance parked on the corner of the street. Robi looked at the motion happening around him, noticing the people that he had not paid attention to before.

Wailing, crying, the sound of crashing against concrete solids.

They were the city's new anthem.

"Frank?" Robi asked, feeling his throat irritated.

Frankie looked at the boy's face, puzzled, his eyes painted with bloodshot.

"Go home, please. I can't tell Elena, I don't know how…" he said, looking at him with a furrowed expression. "The… the hospital is not too far from here. I can walk there with Dragoş. Bring Elena and the others. Please,"

"Okay, okay… hey? Be careful out there, I don't know how many of them are still marching the streets," he admitted.

"You are the one who should be careful. And maybe don't tell Elena anything just yet…" Robi told him, pushing his shoulders.

He was confident that the American could look after himself, though, without getting lost in the city that was on fire right now. The way had been straightforward enough for the man to remember, too. In a few moments, his sister would find out, which was the reality that he feared the most. He thought of her eyes freezing at the sight of her dead son.

And the world around them still had the nerve to keep spinning on, as if all was well.

Twenty-Nine

Elena

Timişoara, Romania – December 1989

Twenty-two minutes.

It took Elena exactly twenty-two minutes to start suspecting that something had gone terribly wrong at Geta's. The woman rarely invited people inside her home for long, let alone while an entire protest was happening outside. In all possibilities, Geta would've invited little Beriță inside the apartment and then politely nudged him away with a plate of delicacies for the family.

Twenty-two minutes had gone by, which made Elena grow more and more suspicious by the second.

"I am sure he is fine, Elena. The boy hasn't left this building; he's probably still upstairs," Lizzie told her.

The other woman's thick accent was slowly becoming more understandable for Elena, who, until then, had struggled to distinguish the words that the British tongue uttered.

"I don't feel good," Elena said, handing Lizzie a warm cardigan from her own wardrobe.

The woman had brought enough clothes to last her for a few days, but Elena was happy to lend her the wool scarves, cardigans, and mittens knitted by her elderly relative, who worked at a factory. Lizzie accepted with a smile and nod. When the other woman had confided in her that she feared that her monthly cycle was soon to start, Elena had also made her cotton pads to wear and carry.

"Elena, you should rest," Lizzie suggested, pointing at Elena's bedroom.

In the children's bedroom, Ioana was tucked in bed, ready to be called for dinner when the men were going to return. Elena considered joining her daughter, but the uneasiness of where her son was kept her on her toes.

"No. I must go look... where Beriță..." Elena stammered, shutting her wardrobe door.

She rushed to the kitchen, leaving a standing Lizzie in the hallway, who didn't follow her out of the front door. Elena hadn't even taken a coat with her, she realised, as she shut the door behind her and felt the cold breeze through the ground floor of the building.

Her feet rushed up the stairs and on to the third floor, her heart knocking against her chest with great might. The woman's bruised knuckles found Geta's door with more power than intended, as she was ready to call out the other woman's name.

"Coming, coming..." Geta's voice came from behind the wooden door.

Geta opened the door, letting it settle into the half-open position, clasped between its metallic chains.

"Elena, hello! Come, come..." Geta said, trying to break the door out of its locks.

"No, no, I insist, Geta, it's alright. Could you please ask Beriță to come home? Dinner will be ready soon," Elena said, placing her hands awkwardly by her hips.

"Beriță? I'm sorry, Elena, I am not sure I understand. Your boy was here, but he left. About half an hour ago, if not more. He gave me a letter for Dragoș's parents..." she explained.

"W... What... What do you mean? You don't know where Beriță is?" Elena's bewildered eyes demanded.

How could her boy not be in there? He certainly wasn't at home, and she would've seen him in the building if he was wandering around; it wasn't his way to listen, she knew this much.

For her own sake, she prayed that he hadn't gone anywhere else.

"I'm sorry, Elena. I really, truly… I don't know. You can come inside, but I assure you, the boy is not here," the woman added.

Elena wasn't going to insult the woman by going through her home, peeking under the table for Beriță, like a cat chasing a mouse. This wasn't a trick, or the woman would've said so after seeing the mother's worried look.

"I'm sorry, I didn't mean to trouble you…" Elena said, hiding her face away and running back down the stairs.

Her eyes felt stained with tears, but she could not tell for what reason. She only knew the reality of what her feelings were telling her mind in that moment — she wanted to run away, to hide her vulnerability from everyone around her. She had felt something else in Geta's sad eyes in that moment, something that she recognised whenever she would tell her brother that a new letter from her husband had not arrived in months.

It was a form of pity, and she was fearful of the reason behind it.

"Elena! Elena!" Lizzie's voice startled her as Elena walked down the final flight of stairs.

Lizzie was running up towards her, holding her cardigan and loose trousers as if they were a ball gown that was holding her down. As she got closer, Elena could see her flushed cheeks, their rosy consistency causing her a shortness of breath. Lizzie looked as if she had been running, although she had not been out of the apartment for long.

"Elena…" Lizzie paused suddenly, looking at Elena. "It's Beriță, come quickly," the woman said agitatedly.

"What happened?" Elena asked, rushing downstairs.

"It's Frankie… he'll tell you," was all Lizzie could say.

Again, she saw the same look in the other woman's eyes, who looked carefully around Elena's movements as if she were a piece of glass, ready to shatter. She wanted to shake away that feeling, but all she could think of was Beriță, which caused her stomach to twist. She reached the apartment and found the door wide open, while Frankie visibly shook around the coat pockets and gathered dimes from them.

"What do you think you're doing?" she asked, holding his arm with all her might.

"Elena, it's Beriță... he's at the hospital," Frankie said.

She held a hand to her mouth to hide away her gasp, while the man proceeded to tell her what had happened.

"I can't tell you whether he is still... the way I had seen him," Frankie said, referring to Beriță's state. "I think he was alive. When they took him, I mean. We have to get to that hospital, though, to see him..." he said, while Elena was gathering her things from the kitchen, looking for dimes herself.

The woman had felt goosebumps on every inch of her body while Frankie recalled the events of what had happened. Her boy must have slipped outside to follow the men, especially her brother. He idolised Robi; what could she do — but there was hope that the boy would be treated well, as they spoke, which was what she wanted to hold on to.

I have to be strong for my son now.

She needed as much change as possible to give to anyone willing to do her a favour, which is what Frankie had done too. They placed the money in one purse, while Lizzie watched them.

"I have to tell Ioana I am going to go see her brother... I can't take her with me," Elena said, thinking of Beriță in every moment.

"I will bring her, Elena..." Lizzie said. "You should go," she added, looking at Frankie with a stare.

"Thank you, Lizzie, thank you!" Elena said, holding her arm tightly.

Then she proceeded to write down the address of the hospital on a piece of paper for her and planted it in her palm.

Elena hated the smell of hospitals. It reminded her too much of her late mother's final days, which had been as uneventful as any other days in her life, only full of pain that no one should ever have to bear. She remembered her sickly, thinned face, still managing to slip curses at Elena through the small lips.

Now, the place was crowded with family members of victims who had been shot, some dead, some alive; she walked around, wondering what the sights had looked like for these people. The leaders had lowered themselves beneath the earth that they stood on, shooting at civilians marching on the streets. Even her own boy had to be in one of these rooms, she told herself, marching down the hospital corridor.

She spotted Robi and Dragoş standing by the exit of the last door, both looking as ghostly as the dead.

"Where is he?" she asked, and was met with their tearful eyes.

Seeing the men upset only made her own heart sink beneath the freezing floorboards; were the sick really being kept in these conditions?

"They're not letting anyone enter the morgue, Elena. Official command of some sort," Dragoş told her.

The morgue.

"Why the morgue? Where is my son, Dragoş? Frankie said he is here, he is fine, where is he? *Unde este*?" she asked, her pitch hysterical.

"You didn't tell her," Robi said in a thankful tone, standing up in front of Frankie.

"Tell me what?" Elena asked her brother. "Dragoș..." she stepped away from between Robi and Frankie, who were talking in murmured voices. "Dragoş, tell me where my son is. Please. Tell me he's fine."

She looked into his eyes, while he looked away from hers in the split second.

"Beriță is dead," Dragoş said in a calm voice. "He was shot through the chest and killed instantly. Frankie... *nu ți-a zis ca să nu intri în panică. A murit, Elena*. He didn't tell you so that you wouldn't panic. He died, Elena," he said, his face growing wet.

Elena found herself kneeling on the hospital floor, unconscious, with her chest aching.

Thirty

Nicolae

Bucharest, Romania; Tehran, Iran — December 1989

"You have to start being more careful. We cannot keep doing this, you know? Your men are outside protecting you for a reason," Elena Ceaușescu whispered in his ears, close enough for him to feel her warm breath. "We have to leave this place. For a while."

The people were *obviously* angry at him.

Nicolae lowered his head, remembering the screams and shouts that had accompanied his public appearance. Most of them were going to spend the night in prison, tortured beyond any hospital's abilities to mend them. And here he stood, debating whether running away like a coward was on the table.

He could remember his August speech now, where the world felt like his own playground — the people below stashed on top of one another like ants, holding up the Romanian flag.

Now, the same people were marching below him, parading with false gratitude. Now and then, one of them would burst towards him, expressing their hatred louder than the rest.

Had he been oblivious this entire time?

Leana tapped his forehead gently with a cloth.

"No one cares about anything more than they care about you, my love. You are their hero, you have given them everything," she lied, rubbing his cheeks with her knuckles.

He tossed his head back, moving away from her touch.

"You know you don't believe that, Leana. They hate us for what we did. For what we're doing," he said, trying to calm down. "There is a fucking revolution happening on the other side of *my* country!"

His breath grew heavier, the blood rushing to his cheeks. He had never spoken to her this way before.

"You know it, my dear. We have been doing this for far too long," he admitted, feeling his skin lose colour.

His wife stepped back from his armchair, his words making her flinch.

"You are an idiot if you truly believe that. Look at what we've built. An empire, a kingdom... they will remember you for centuries after you're gone. Your legacy will be unmatched," she said, her eyes widening.

In the corner, Florin gave them a low grunt. He had seen the people's anger, too, Nicolae knew. The way his bodyguard's arm had protectively rested over his shoulders at the sight of the sea of people in front of their home, the reassurance was enough for him to trust Florin with his life.

"What do you think?" Nicolae found himself asking Florin, who was watching the turmoil from his window seat.

"For once, I think I agree with her," he pointed at Leana, who looked puzzled.

Nicolae heard Elena's sigh escaping her, as she smirked under her breath. She turned to face the painting behind her, standing above their fireplace; she had won the argument.

"Absolutely not," Nicolae insisted.

"For your safety. Who's going to rule these people if there isn't a person like you to do it?" Florin demanded.

"I am not a coward," Nicolae found himself shouting. "*Nu plec cu coada între picioare.*"

He had never raised his voice in front of Florin before, but Leana had flinched, as it was her way.

"No one said that you are. You're not running away. You are protecting yourself," Elena suggested, kneeling by his armchair.

Sometimes, he forgot how much ambition the woman in front of him had. Perhaps even more than he did as leader of the state. She knew how to orchestrate their moves like a silent mastermind who would've made a better leader than himself. He often found himself doubting his own potential like this in front of hers.

"Comrade Nicolae, if I may..." Florin began, standing up.

Nicolae wanted to let out an amused laugh. One change in tone made the man's entire attitude shift in an instant. And the people said that fear wasn't the best governor.

"Elena suggested Iran... that might not be entirely bad for you, you know? Tehran is a safe place to travel to, considering our relations with the Arabs. They will keep us under their protection," Florin spoke, as his leader nodded.

Nicolae considered — Timişoara was drowning away in spilt blood, the blood of his own people. Unless he wanted to join those poor, unfortunate numbers, he had to think fast.

"Get the helicopter ready," he ordered. "This is strictly a diplomatic meeting, tell them," Nicolae barked, feeling a new surge of emotions in his veins.

He hadn't felt this in a long while, not since the countryside sights in Oltenia were his only familiar terrains. But he recognised this new need very well; after all, we all hungered for it.

It was a need for survival.

Nicolae sat in front of his bed, arm resting against the desk to his side, as the view of Tehran looked almost like a film from where he stood. The sound of a city, loud and buzzing, was precisely what he loved about leading; knowing that all of those voices, noises, and buzzing whispers could not have been so peaceful if it had not been for someone like him on top of it all, leading the people to their glory.

The few hours in Iran had done him well, with the warm December sun shining on his face like a new ray of hope, the people around him unaware of what was going on back home. He felt more certain now than ever before that the phase that was taking place in Timişoara was simply a bump in the road. Every great leader experienced great loss, greater wars, and the greatest challenges. It was these things that built them into the men that they were remembered for, he told himself.

Timişoara needed military involvement, which was the latest update he had received from his friends back in Bucharest — the men he had left in charge during his absence. He hadn't denied them anything, except an unambiguous instruction to avoid shooting at anyone who was on their leader's side, anyone who was chanting his name while the rest opposed him. As for the rest, he had not clarified anything, which now worried him, picturing the city drowning in the overlapping sounds of bullets, disrupting the beautiful melody of a living city.

Elena's hurried footsteps caught his attention as she entered the en suite with rushed movements, almost as if she was ready to jog across the room. She paused by the telephone on their nightstand, and without uttering a single word, she began dialling a number on it. The click of her fingertips echoed in the near-empty room, where a bed stood between her and her husband, who waited to guess what she was doing.

"Leana?" he demanded, as she was shaking while the phone tried reaching the Romanian line.

"Oh, my!" she shouted, as if she hadn't noticed him sitting there until now.

She turned her startled face to him, and dangling the phone on her shoulder, she twisted her lips into a smirk.

"Your military people have really outdone themselves this time," she said, praising him.

She let the phone hang close to her ear, as she looked straight at him, ready to talk.

"More than forty civilians dead in Timişoara, Nicu. Shot by your men. I must say, I am rather proud of their efficiency. But still, we got our hands *really* dirty this time. Kids and civilians, you see," she muttered, looking at him with slight disgust.

Suddenly, the phone was answered by someone on the other end, presumably Leana's assistant.

"W-what are you talking about?" Nicolae asked, getting up from his chair.

It shouldn't have shocked him. It was a perfectly expected turn of events, and even *he* had predicted some civilian casualties would come from this riot. Still, more than forty people were dead? His skin crawled at the image of such brutal bloodshed, all done in his name. His Leana, trying to make things right.

In his name.

"Yes, this is me," Elena confirmed to the male voice on the other end, reading out her security number to assure that it was her. "I want you to listen very carefully to what I have to say about your brutal attack on the people," she said, putting on her best raised tone.

She looked Nicolae in the eyes, knowingly.

"You're going to gather all of those dead fuckers, take them to *Spitalul Județean*. If I remember well, it is the closest hospital, and also the biggest one, correct?" she asked, catching her breath.

He suddenly remembered their property in Timişoara, on *Bulevardul 'C.D. Loga'*, in front of the school of the same name. Not far from the hospital. When the person on the other end gave her an agreeing hum, she continued.

"You will take them there, and keep them there. Keep them until nightfall, without a single person going in or out of the goddamn hospital. Our men will come at night, and they will handle it from there. They will take all the corpses to Bucharest, lay them in a pile, ready to be cremated at *Cenușa*. No one will know about this... situation,"

Massacre, Nicolae thought.

That's what it was, in fact. And now, there would be no evidence that it had ever happened. A bizarre, unorthodox sense of pride overcame him, as his eyes gleamed with his wife's every word.

"They will handle the corpses, identified or not. Make sure no one comes looking for the dead. We have to make up some believable stories about them... some fled the country during the revolution, others moved abroad, things like that, okay? Do your best."

"Do we have your permission to proceed?" the man enquired politely, his voice flat.

"Yes, for God's sake, yes!" Leana yelled. "You have my approval for every stage of this operation. Now get the hell on with it, yeah?" she said, hanging up the phone.

Once again, she had proved to be a better leader than he. While he had stood here, looking at Tehran from the small window in front of him, Elena had been controlling the significant affairs. She had tried mending everything — things that he should have been doing.

"What is that?" he repeated, trying to put some confidence into his tone.

Leana walked closer to him then, stopping by the nightstand on the other side of the bed. Nicolae hadn't noticed the vase of freshly cut roses resting there — perhaps left by a servant, in the early hours of the morning. They were thirteen in number; odd and lucky, just like they were, he thought.

Leana plucked a white rose from the vase and pushed it closer for him to smell.

"Oh, darling..." she smiled. "That's *Operațiunea Trandafirul*."

Operation Rose.

"Operation?" he demanded further.

Leana placed the rose in his open palms.

"We can't leave evidence, so I took the necessary decisions," she said, twisting her wrist as if she were in pain.

Nicolae was bewildered.

"At *Cenușa*? You think the people will forget their dead so soon? All because of László?" he asked.

Leane picked up her overnight bag from across the room and pulled out a small box of powder. She opened it, then started tapping her nose thoroughly.

"They won't know that they're dead. Already, General Milea has started to make their documents, papers which show that they have actually fled the country," she said casually. "Do you think my nose looks too powdered?" she asked.

Nicolae palmed his forehead — he felt ill.

"Leana, Leana... you spoke to the General before coming to me?" he asked, feeling nauseous. "*Kids*, Leana? Kids have died, too?" he asked, recalling what she had told him.

Elena Ceaușescu looked annoyed, as if his reaction had come as a burden.

"The sacrifice offered by them will build a country for others, tens of thousands of children. Come on, Nicu, don't be like this. It's only a small thing, in the grand scheme of things," Leana said, trying to console him.

A whimper escaped Nicolae — that's when he realised that he was crying.

"Call our children, I h-have to tell them..." he said, trying to gather himself a bit.

"Nicu and Zoia? They already know. And Vali... no sign of him, as usual," she said, hunting for her lipstick at the bottom of her bag.

Nicolae Ceaușescu watched his wife, letting the contemplation settle in.

Was this how his legacy would be remembered?

III

Part III — Libertate, albastrul cerului

The clear skies of freedom

Thirty-One

Dragoș

Timișoara, Romania – December 1989

Dragoș had held Elena in his arms long enough for her to regain consciousness. Her damp face had been caked on his shoulders, the exact spot where her brother had mourned the loss of his nephew earlier. It seemed that Dragoș's place had been fitted perfectly among the mourners, as he didn't dare utter a single word of remorse about the boy's passing.

What good would have come from it?

Someone needed to be here to hold the hand of the people who had lost something irreplaceable. Something that Dragoș, or anyone else, couldn't ever make up for.

"Elena..." Dragoș whispered in her ear, leaning down.

He could feel her breathing on his neck as she remained still and quiet.

Robi saw his sister's motion from the far end of the hallway and marched down between the other people to see her.

"How is she?" he asked, probably wondering where Frankie was.

Both Robi and Frankie had gone to separate wings of the hospital to find the morgue, or perhaps a nurse who could help Elena's weakness. The women and men of the hospital had their hands full with the injured, as many more came in through the front door like a flood.

"*Slabă*. She is weak, and her condition is worsening. See if you can bring her something," Dragoș said, placing a warm hand over Elena's.

"Look around you. There isn't enough for the people here," Robi waved around, pointing at the people waiting in long queues.

Frankie's sweat-filled face revealed a sad look from the exit door near the hospital's entrance, where a half-broken sign coloured in neon green lit itself above his head. He ignored its blinking as he sat down next to Dragoș.

"No…" was all Frankie could say to Dragoș, which let him know that he had no luck finding any sign of where they were actually keeping the dead here.

The hospital's real morgue was underground, but the doors that led there had all been locked, with no exit on any side. Some of the people whispered about how the bodies were hidden in one of the hospital's wings, some between the living that were being treated. The *Securitate* wanted to stop the identification process of the people, which radiated an air of fright in the cold, humid corridors; how many people were already dead, and no one knew about them?

"I'm…I'm okay…" Elena's weak voice spoke back to Dragoș, sending a shiver down his spine.

He moved aside to give the woman some space while she tried to rise to her feet. Her eyes looked like they had been swollen from being rubbed and pressed down for too long, while her fragile form seemed to shake ever so slightly against Dragoș's jacket.

"Robi, *ajută—mă*. Help me up, please," Elena extended her arm towards her brother.

He picked her up gently, and Dragoș and Frankie mimicked her movements.

"Where are you going?" Dragoș asked, as did Frankie; he couldn't know for sure what the other man had asked, but it was a safe assumption.

"I have to find my son," Elena replied, and turned to speak something to Frankie, too.

There wasn't an inch of the hospital that hadn't met the sound of Elena's soles, and with them, the men's. Dragoș's ankles ached from all the motion.

As he passed an elderly man who was holding a cup in his hand, he realised that neither of them had found the luxury of a drop of water since the morning. The hospital was short on supplies, which were already reserved for the ill. Dragoș wasn't going to be the one to steal from their mouths.

"Where is my son? Where is he?" Elena's voice echoed in the new, dimly lit corridor, the only space that Dragoș couldn't remember from all their rounds around the place.

He must have zoned out long ago, thinking of the streets where he should have been parading, or the bullet that he should have swallowed instead of Elena's young boy, who was dead somewhere in these walls. When he glanced at Elena, he realised that she had been grabbing on to the collar of the nurse whom she had yelled her demands at, addressing her with as much anger as a grieving mother could carry in her voice.

"I'm… I'm…" the nurse stuttered, as Frankie tried to unclasp Elena's tight fingers from around the nurse's collar.

"Elena, let her go," Dragoș said softly, placing a firm hand on Frankie's. "Where is the boy?" he asked, stepping in front.

The nurse's face looked familiar as Dragoș leaned closer to look at her face.

"She took him," Robi said, rushing past Dragoș. "She's the one who took him! Dragoș, it's her…" which confirmed Dragoș's suspicions.

Dragoș had helped her put Beriță's body in the ambulance, which had later brought him here. During a time of revolution and civil conflict, even nurses were taking on the role of paramedics. If leaders and protectors could do the job of mercenaries, perhaps even the people could lift a finger to help each other out.

Dragoș looked at her eagerly.

"I'm sorry. The boy is in the morgue under the hospital," she said with honesty.

Dragoș leaned closer.

"How do I get there?" he asked, pleading.

"I don't know what to tell you… We're not meant to. I haven't gone down there, and as far as I know, no one else has. We can't let anyone in there, I'm sorry," the nurse answered, turning her back on them.

The woman's white uniform paled away behind the corner, as Dragoș remained motionless. He jerked his arm into the wall nearest to him, trying to push it forward. There was nothing left here for the grievers, he knew, but couldn't bring his lips to speaking the words out loud.

"We can't just stay here," Robi said to him, patting him on the shoulder. "The people are crowding up even more than before, and it's not safe for so many of us to be in one place."

As if the boy had read his thoughts. Dragoș nodded, and walked back to Elena, who was resting on a chair.

"Elena, *trebuie să plecăm*," he insisted. "We have to leave, it's not safe here anymore. Please…" he begged.

"No… no…" she shook her head, saying each refusal louder than the last. "I am not leaving my boy here with them, Dragoș. I can't. He has no one here…" she said, referring to her son as if he were still alive.

The thought made Dragoș's chest ache. Elena's denial was only normal for the shock that had just shaken her entire body to its core.

"I am not leaving him, you understand? He has no one here, and oh… his father… what will his father say?" she asked Dragoș in a praying tone, as if he held the keys to all the world's greatest mysteries.

"Elena, people around you are looking, please…" Dragoș whispered, instantly regretting it; it wasn't his place to tell a mother how to grieve her lost child. "We'll stay, alright?"

It seemed to soothe her a little, as she stopped holding him with force. He had a bitter feeling on his numb face, as his dry mouth swallowed in emptiness.

"We have to wait for them to let us in… but when will that be?" Robi asked no one in particular.

"It doesn't matter. *Tu poți să pleci*. You can leave, go home. See Lizzie and Ioana…" Elena murmured, as if she was remembering them for the first time.

"No, Elena. I am not going to leave you," Her brother urged, holding her arms and hands with his own cold ones.

Dragoș looked at the two siblings, the young man and woman who still found some shade of unity in this palette of dark words. The man took a step back, looking at them from the outside of this bubble that he too felt like a part of — perhaps it was his newfound fondness for Elena that made him feel like he was part of the family to the two. Or maybe it was the loss of the boy, who Dragoș had seen running towards him before the bullet had cracked his chest like a wooden doll.

"Go, Robi… I'll stay with her. Take Frank, too. I'll stay," he said, not believing the words himself at first.

Dragoș had been undercover for the *Securitate* for so long that he had forgotten what doing anything else out of his own wish was like; he couldn't care about being seen out here with Elena, the known '*traitor*'. Even if someone from the cowards' department had seen him now, he was sure that they had bigger problems on their hands. He had to find Beriță, no matter what was going to happen to him. No matter what Florica could do to him if she found out that he had turned on her long ago.

"Go," he insisted, and when Elena did not protest, Robi put his left arm around Frankie, whispered something in his ear, and the men headed out the hospital exit.

The green light in the hospital maintained the same hue at all times of the day, whether it was evening or morning. Dragoș's divided mind couldn't tell the time, but the hunger inside his body could. There wasn't anything to eat around, although more patients had spun in and out of the halls around them.

Elena had remained unmoved since her brother's departure; apart from sitting down on the empty seat by the exit, where a young boy and his brother slept on the three chairs opposite them. The older one kept the younger one's head in his lap, tightly holding the boy so that he wouldn't fall.

Dragoș was puzzled by the people around him. The chaos had not been contained in the slightest; the television people had walked in and out of halls, places where injured victims were willing to speak openly about the attack that had scarred their bodies. Some claimed it was better than the mountain of scars that the government had been printing on their minds. And yet, their hope had not yet died.

Occasionally, Elena would find pleasure in holding the sleeves of a nurse or member of staff, pleading that they would let her into the morgue. They would all repeat the same thing that they had heard a hundred times before, ringing through their eardrums like a stolen poem.

Finally, Elena and Dragoș remained unmoved in their seats, while the motion around them carried on escalating.

Thirty-Two

Elizabeth

Timişoara, Romania — December 1989

Once Elena and Frankie had left, Lizzie had sat down at the kitchen table with her palms holding her head, as her face grew damper with each sigh. Frankie had lied to the mother of the dead boy — and for good reason. If Lizzie's heart was sinking now, at the thought of Beriță's cold body hitting the ground after the bullet wound, his mother's pain was unimaginable. Her chest ached for Elena, for Ioana — even for the boy's father, although Lizzie wasn't too fond of the stranger.

"Liz?" Ioana's voice made Lizzie get up from the chair instantly, wiping away the rows of tears that had marked her cheeks with the back of her sleeves.

She couldn't let the girl see her this way; for once, even Lizzie seemed to be at a loss for words. But the girl was clever; she knew this well enough. She would know that something terrible had happened, and Lizzie didn't want to make the poor girl suffer more than she had to. Perhaps for a bit of while, Lizzie could keep the girl sheltered from the trouble of what was coming. She could let the girl live in this illusion, even if it was going to cost her a lot afterwards.

"Yes, yes, I am here," Lizzie said, smiling and turning to the door, where

Ioana stood by the door frame.

"Mama?" she asked, and Lizzie understood.

"No, Mama... Mama go..." Lizzie tried to express with her hands, pointing at the window. "With Frankie," she added a nod, to seem convincing.

All the years of acting couldn't have stopped Lizzie from letting out a suppressed cry then, and she held it in by hiding it with a cough. The girl watched her knowingly.

She was a clever one, *far* too clever even.

Lizzie forced a grin as she turned to the stove.

"How about some *supa?*" she asked, pointing at the soup that Elena had left on the low fire, recalling the word in Romanian for it.

Ioana gave her a nod and took a seat at the table.

"Liz... Beriță?" she asked next, remembering that her brother was missing from the kitchen table.

She jerked up from her chair, ready to find her brother.

"No, no..." Lizzie tried stopping her until the girl finally paused. "Beriță is with Mama. Mama..." she pointed eagerly at the door.

The thought soothed Ioana, it seemed, as she remained unmoved for the rest of their time together. Lizzie had poured herself some hot water in a cup, instead of the potato soup, and she let it brew on the counter after dropping chamomile petals in it.

When the girl was finished, she reached her arms out to hug Lizzie, a gesture that surprised her. She had kept the woman at arm's length until now, as she did with most people — except the other man, Dragoș, who could bring a smile to the young girl's lips in an instant.

"Aw, you sweet girl," Lizzie whispered when the girl let go.

She wished then, with her entire might, that she could keep Ioana protected from the bad news that was going to shock her to the bone, even if it meant staying in the wretched apartment forever. She could let it be just the two of them like this forever, allowing the girl to wonder where her family went and keeping promises of their return, to hide away the dreadful reality that waited outside the doorstep.

But the wicked occurrences of the world always seemed to happen to the most innocent. Lizzie's last trip as a foreign correspondent, this eventful stay in Romania, had been her most significant witness to support that.

Frankie returned at some point in the evening, accompanied by the young man Robi, who followed him with dragging footsteps. Lizzie had heard the doorbell chime from the kids' bedroom, where she and Ioana were sitting under the warm blanket on the sofa bed. Ioana had a book tucked under her elbows, while Lizzie sipped the tea that had grown cold on the counter.

"Where have you been? How is everything?" Lizzie rambled on with more nonsensical questions, wondering whether this had all just been a terrible nightmare.

Sleep came way too easily in the chilly apartment where the heating had refused to aid them on these cold December days, and so Lizzie was eager to hope. She had tasted it, here between the Romanians. Hope was on their tongues and lips, and their hands and feet, somewhere so deep in the texture of their skin that even the great dictators of this place couldn't strip it away from them. Lizzie had grown addicted to this hope, looking out for the brightest star in this night's sky.

"Elena is with Dragoș now… they won't let us enter the morgue," Frankie said.

Morgue.

The word cut her like a knife. The little boy, whom she felt like she had known for a lifetime, was now piled up in some frozen room, among the other dead? The image made her stomach twist and roll, and she felt sick. There was nothing inside her stomach to let out, though, and she forced down the warm bile that had risen to her throat. Lizzie's cold fingertips shivered.

"Why are you two here? We should be doing something; we can't let the boy rot away in some dingy hall! He was a child… just a young boy…" Lizzie tried to hush her cries again.

Frankie reached out a warm hand as he grabbed her shoulder.

"You have to go, Lizzie," he demanded in a low voice. "I can't keep asking you to hide away in this apartment when I know how much good you can do out there... we both can. Or at least we can try," he added, holding her chin between his knuckle and his thumb.

"I will stay with Ioana, now... and I think it's time. I need to tell her," Robi added.

Lizzie wanted to plead, with him begging him not to tell the little girl about the monstrosity of the world. She was far too young to lose her faith in people already, the same people who had let her brother die like cattle. At least cattle served a purpose in their death — what sin had the boy committed, that his right to serve a purpose in this world had been stolen away so soon? The boy had barely lived, Ioana had barely lived, a voice cried out in Lizzie's mind...

Robi sniffed forcefully and exited the kitchen, leaving Lizzie alone with Frankie.

"Are you ready?" Frankie said, holding both of her shoulders now. "Liz, this is unlike anything we have ever seen or will ever see... we can follow Beriță's family in this situation outside now. Write about it," he insisted.

Lizzie's nauseous feeling returned to her chest.

"This isn't just another story for me to chase, Frankie. They're grieving people... how can I follow them around, knowing damn well we're going to use their stories as a means of making ourselves successful?" Lizzie shook out of Frankie's grip. "Beriță was just a *child*."

She could feel her vision growing blurry in the pale light. Frankie reached for her palms again, holding them tightly.

"Elizabeth Sturridge, you are one of the greatest, if not the greatest, journalists I have ever met. I know you are going to do something out of this story, to help this grieving family if you can. If this case means as much to you as I think that it does, you know that we can do more good from out there than from in here, or from back home. We can actually raise some awareness, Lizzie..." Frankie said, his eyes gleaming under the kitchen light bulb.

"I don't want to profit from this, Frank. You can tell Berkshire this was all your thing, I barely did anything," Lizzie said, the words sounding like a different language to her.

Her competitiveness had always gotten the better of her, long before she had become a journalist. Now, Frankie, her so-called nemesis from work, a man that was like a mirror being held up to her own face, watched her with the same disbelief that she could feel then.

"I don't want the money either, Liz. It's not about any of that anymore. This is the biggest injustice I have ever come across in this life, and I pray that we can at least make amends for it by providing Elena and her family with some comfort," Frankie uttered.

From the other side of the apartment, the loud bang of a door echoed, followed by Ioana's unfamiliar wails. The quiet child's voice shrieked from the far end of the place, and Lizzie accepted it as a command to step to the side.

She shut the door behind her with ease and faced Frankie. Lizzie had vowed never to do such a trip again, no matter how much money they were going to offer her for it. If this was to be her last one, she could make it worth the effort and time, like she had wished to in the first place.

Who cared about the story that Berkshire wanted, which revolved around the political situation? Lizzie had learned, she told herself, that the real challenges are never a country's politicians or leaders.

It's the people who made the place; their leader was simply a reflection of themselves. The Romanian people were liberty seekers, free-spirited, and kind-hearted. There was no way that their leader could get away with the murder of innocent children without facing the consequences that he should've faced long ago.

"I will come with you. But we're changing the story, Frankie," Lizzie said, reaching for her notepad from her bag.

Thirty-Three

Elena

Timişoara, Romania — December 1989

"Eat this, here," Dragoş insisted again, when Elena didn't offer him a reply.

The look of the stale *covrig* made her realise how hungry she had actually been, and as much as she wished that she could refuse them, she accepted Dragoş's friendly hand. He had been there next to her for more than a couple of hours now, letting Elena rest her head on his shoulder when needed, and following her around each time she needed to call out to another doctor or nurse.

Finally, when the clock had struck eleven o'clock in the evening, Dragoş had asked her to follow him to a nearby corner shop that was selling old bread, rock-solid pastries, and moulded pretzels. He had overheard a young nurse telling her friend about it right next to them, seconds before Elena had asked this woman how to get into the morgue as well. The cries and mourns of the people made the hospital a dreadful sight, and escaping into the street even for a moment came like a slight relief to Elena.

"Thank you," she said to Dragoş apologetically, as she bit through the concrete *covrig*.

"You're welcome," he replied, keeping the change from the shop in his pockets.

"You should go home soon," Elena told him, as they began approaching a bench in front of the hospital.

"Madness! I won't do that just yet, Elena. You can't be here on your own," he told her. "If I leave, you're coming with me," he said, eating the pretzel in his hand with such hunger as if it were some rare delicacy.

"Dragoş… you've been more help to my family than I could ever be able to pay back. When this is all over, and I find my son, I promise you… I will make it up to you," Elena told him.

She still felt as if she could find Beriţă; she would be able to mend his torn body like a needle going through a ripped-up cloth. Mothers had inexplicable power, gifted to them by nature; could it defy death, she asked herself? The acceptance of what everyone around her already knew came to Elena with considerable difficulty. She wasn't going to let her son stay dead, not when her mind had her convinced that he was alive in her head.

"Nonsense, Elena. You're like my family, too, now. You and Robi, the kids… maybe even those foolhardy foreigners who don't seem to know when to stop. In the family, we don't have to pay each other back for anything, there's no *rânduri*," Dragoş said, pulling himself closer to Elena.

The temperature had dropped more than before, with the dusky sky above them threatening a storm.

"When Beriţă was born, you remember I couldn't go to the hospital on that day? Our car, well, Darius's… it didn't allow it with the number plate," Elena began, not knowing why she brought that up herself. "And you had so much urgency to reach the hospital on time, perhaps more than anyone else other than me… the pain of giving birth to that boy came so many hours before I got to hold him."

And the pain of losing him will remain even years after I get to hold him for the last time.

"You were so worried that the boy would come before his time was due, I remember that much. And my mother, she remembers you better than even I…" he said. "You were always a good mother to them, Elena,"

Had she wanted to hear this? Elena had never heard her own husband tell her that she was a good mother to the kids — let alone *her* father, who constantly reminded her of the past. Of course, Dragoș was unaware of this past. Maybe for a bit longer, she could keep it this way, she convinced herself of this much. She took another bite from the solid, stale bread.

"I hate all this... waiting and nonsensical procedures. I want to hold my boy again, Dragoș, and I don't care how many people try to stop me," Elena said after a while, as she could feel a slow rush of energy pumping through her veins.

"We could return tomorrow," he mumbled his suggestion, as if he wasn't convinced of it himself. "Perhaps it is worth staying here for a little while longer, though... if you want, of course."

Elena felt a surge of pain, aching her deeply, in her left arm and hand, and back at the centre of her chest. It was as if someone had poked her heart, digging sharp fingernails into her core. Her boy was here, at this wretched place, and as people told her, he wasn't alive anymore. Perhaps the shock hadn't settled in just yet, as her constant fidgeting and demanding had kept her on her toes.

She couldn't leave Beriță here, on unknown territory and between enemies. Her little boy had been killed, murdered; what she should have been doing was going to the authorities, begging them to release the boy's body and every other deceased person's — but here she was, sitting on a bench in front of the hospital. The irony of it all was that the authorities were probably going to have her arrested, instead of helping her get her boy back. And here, a traitor of the law like Dragoș was next to Elena, ready to mend her wounds.

Even those that no one could see.

A welcoming sight caught Elena's eye then, who had been listening to the whispers of the night, carried away by all her thoughts. Dragoș made the reigning silence feel comfortable between them, without insisting too much effort on her behalf. The newcomers spotted Elena first, as she did them, and she rushed towards them before Dragoș could even see them.

Elena embraced the other woman with a new form of relief, and Lizzie did the same, whispering words of apology, her face soaking Elena's shoulder with tears.

"I am so sorry," Lizzie repeated, as if she couldn't convince Elena of it.

The woman held Elena's face in her hands, covering her ears as if she was protecting her from the damn noises. Frankie, on the other hand, patted Elena's shoulder — the man hadn't spoken much since he had come for her at the apartment. When the woman let go of Elena, revealing a tear-stained face, Dragoş was the first one to break the silence.

"Ce fac ei aici, Elena? Ask them, what are they doing here?" he asked, shaking Frankie's hand.

Elena could sense the worry on Dragoş's face, even in the darkness surrounding them. Elena asked them, a little confused herself. The writers, she knew, were looking for a story to tell when they went back home. But was now really the time for them to start working?

"I want to help you," Lizzie said with a genuine expression. "Please, don't think that this is for a story that we will sell when we go home... I want to help you and Beriță. People should be aware of what happened here. If you think I should go home, I will walk away right now and leave. Whatever you say. It's your word," the woman insisted.

"Stay," Elena said finally, putting her frozen hands in her pockets. "We can use your help," she admitted.

She didn't want to exploit the events that were going to scar her forever, not when she hadn't held her son yet. If Lizzie and Frankie could help her even slightly, she would gladly accept their assistance. They may have been foreigners, placed here out of a simple task or job, but their hearts were in the right places, and Lizzie had loved her boy. In the short time that Elena had known her, the other woman had proven to be not so different from herself.

They were both fighting to thrive in this world of illicitness, where men held up guns to the heads of children and women with the promise of protection. Lizzie was perhaps the closest thing Elena had to a sister, a companion of the same shut well where the sunlight crept in seldom, but its prisoners had each other, despite it all.

"I think we should try to go inside once again. Directly to the morgue if we can find the entrance," Frankie suggested, pointing towards the hospital.

Dragoş gave an agreeing hum, although he couldn't respond to the other man.

"*Spune-i să vină cu mine. Mergem împreună.* Tell him, we'll go together," he nodded at Elena.

"Go with him," Elena instructed Frankie, holding Lizzie's arm tightly.

"Okay," Frankie nodded, turning to look at Lizzie for a little longer than he usually did.

It was a subtle nod in her direction, but not nuanced enough for Elena not to notice; the two had inevitably become inseparable. Elena couldn't help but turn to look at Dragoş then, who, her eye caught, had already been looking at her this entire time.

Thirty-Four

Frankie

Timișoara, Romania — December 1989

He hadn't blacked out even once in this entire journey, which was more than he had wished for. In his awakening, though, he could only think of the white, thinned faces of the people near the Cathedral, all of them queuing up in front of the missiles and tanks.

When had it turned to this?

Frankie fastened his pace to keep up with Dragoș, as they rushed back into the hospital to get answers out of someone. Elena's son was dead, and the sight of his lifeless body resting on the stairs of the building, over a pool of his own blood, would haunt him for many days to come.

He felt an intense coiling in his stomach, making his head rush each time — he didn't want to see Beriță's body again. He wished that he hadn't come to this place, that everything here would have been just like any other regular assignment that he had done in the past — all of this had been too much. If he could have gone back in time, he would have told Lizzie's father that he wasn't fit for the job after all.

But this was not about him.

If he had come this far, he was going to write about these people; he owed it to them. He had been with the other revolutionaries, like soldiers down in the trenches together, brothers in arms. He wouldn't forget the sentiment now, just because the adrenaline rush was gone.

"Where to?" he asked Elena, who was looking as determined as ever.

"I'm not quite sure," she said, squeezing her hands into tiny fists. "The morgue again?"

She asked Dragoş something in Romanian — the same thing, Frankie assumed. The Romanian man replied with something brief, causing Elena to stop abruptly.

Frankie eyed the clock on the wall to the side; it read '03:22' in the morning. The time had flown by too quickly — more than twelve hours had passed since Beriţă had been taken away.

"He thinks we should split up," Elena said. "You and he go to the morgue below, where they're probably hiding away the dead, for God knows what reason. And Liz and I will find people. Witnesses, the injured, anyone at all…"

She swallowed dryly, looking like she was choking. Frankie placed a firm hand on her shoulder.

"Whatever you say," he nodded. "Be careful," he added, feeling slightly stupid.

Of course, they were going to be careful — but knowing that he had told them to made him feel better. Unity was their only strength in that moment, alongside her sister's empathy, and they couldn't get enough of both.

It wasn't convenient that Dragoş spoke a total of three words in English, which was more than what Frankie knew in Romanian. Still, they talked through hand gestures well enough — actions had always spoken louder anyway. Frankie followed Dragoş down a row of outdoor stairs that led to the exit, only for the other man to abruptly stop upon reaching the end of the third floor. There were still two floors below them, but Frankie didn't dare look down — he hated heights. Instead, he focused on Dragoş, who leaned over the barrier, reaching for a forgotten window.

Dragoş had longer arms, but Frankie was more skilled with things that required discretion. He tapped the man's shoulder, wanting to give it a go

— he understood what Dragoş was trying to do.

The window was opened enough for them to reach their arm on the other side and twist the handle to open entirely — Dragoş made way for Frankie to stand in front of him and lean forward. This window definitely led to a different wing of the hospital, an area that had been sealed off from every other side.

Frankie leaned forward, trying to reach for the handle, stretching out with every ounce of power that he had left inside of him. He leaned over the edge, feeling his body bend a little too far. Then, a hand grabbed his jacket with confidence, holding him tight enough not to fall.

Dragoş kept holding on to him until Frankie could lean over with more trust, trying not to look down during the entire process. He could feel the handle in his hand in the next few seconds, and he twisted it as quickly as he could.

"Yes, I got it!" he chanted, knowing that Dragoş understood his tone of voice.

Dragoş pulled him back then and stepped in front to push the window open for them.

Then came the more challenging part.

The gap between the stairs and the window had gone unnoticed when Dragoş was holding Frankie, but now he had to *actually* jump over the space to get into the building again. He could have asked the man to go on and unlock the door, which could have acted as a safe passage for Frankie from inside the hospital, but how? There was nothing that he could do, not even tell him about the pit in his stomach that had deepened at the sight of the ground underneath.

Dragoş looked at him and murmured something. He pointed at the window with intensity — there wasn't much time before they could be discovered. People were patrolling around the building all day long, and although this exit had been left unmonitored for a while, someone was bound to stumble upon them if they hadn't rushed.

Frankie leaned over again and put his arms over the barrier and on the hospital wall. There was no grip on the thing — the paint had left a dry, crusty texture, which was painful to touch. The journalist bent his body again and put one foot forward, hoping to reach the windowsill that was visible to him, about three feet away.

Oh God, did he have to jump?

He could have thrown up then, the image caressing his brain like a curse. A fall from that height could have been fatal, depending on how he would land, and what on…

There was no going back now — the only way was forward. Frankie tightened his muscles into a running position, keeping his balance as steady as possible. Then, with a silent prayer in the back of his mind, he leapt onto the platform. He would've nearly lost his balance, but his shorter stature allowed him to be quicker — he leaned forward as quickly as he could, landing in the room that Dragoş had just helped him unlock.

Then came Dragoş's turn. The other man hadn't hesitated as much as Frankie did, despite having no one to hold on to him from behind. He placed one firm arm on the wall, just as Frankie had, then jumped. But Frankie could feel it even before Dragoş had decided to leap — there wasn't enough power in his jump.

The other man's physique was much fitter and stronger, but he was too big to lean forward so quickly. He would have hit his head on a wall instead, with his legs dangling over the edge.

The American's move was done swiftly — just as the other man had acted when Frankie had nearly gone over the boundary of the exit stairs. He grabbed Dragoş's arms, reaching to tighten his grip around his torso and pull him in. Dragoş held him back, and with one push, he fell on the floor beside Frankie.

"What the fuck," Frankie grunted, his head resting on the floor.

He could feel his heartbeat racing — his ears ringing loudly. He sighed, feeling the cold breeze from the window touch his face.

They were not going to perish today.

Dragoş's arm found him in the next moment, pulling him up from the floor.

"*Mulțumesc*," Dragoş told him, his eyes gleaming in the pale moonlight.

Frankie didn't need to use a dictionary to understand this one — the sentiment was mutual.

"Thank you, too," he told Dragoş, then raced to the door of the room.

Thirty-Five

Dragoș

Timișoara, Romania — December 1989

The way down the new set of stairs had proven to be much simpler, as Dragoș and Frankie galloped down as quickly as they could. There wasn't a sign of life in this area of the hospital, which led directly to the underground area as a safe passage into the morgue — and as Dragoș had realised, it had been left unguarded, too.

The hallways were dark and dusty, and although the electricity should have been back and functioning there at that time of the morning, the entire place was pitch black. He hoped that a *strigoi* wasn't going to sneak up on him from behind in such a morbid place, and he made a cross for the first time in years. Then, as if by luck, he spotted a bright light at the end of the staircase, all the way down at the bottom.

He dared to look around the open rooms, just as Frankie was — but in the green hue that came from a streetlight outside, everything just looked abandoned. Dragoș didn't want the last sight of his life to be a dark, dingy hospital. Instead, especially in a time when he could see the uncovered mattresses, the uncleared spillages, and all the accumulation of dirt, he prayed that he would go away anywhere else except that place.

When the men reached the small tunnel leading to the underground area, they had to duck to fit — this section had probably been sealed off long before it was used as a morgue. The plastering stunk of fresh paint, and as the two knelt to walk, Dragoş could feel the wall's wetness on his icy tips.

They weren't the only ones taking this route.

Frankie turned to him and mumbled a curse word out loud, showing him his wet hands. No — all of this had been arranged for someone else to come through, and very recently as well. The only fear that Dragoş had was that he would stumble upon the people on their way back up this way. Then what would they do?

As they approached the underground section, the gap above them grew enough for both of them to stand straight. Dragoş had to tilt his neck to see what was happening below, while the passage curled up like a ball in front of them. He stuck his ears to the thin walls, curious about what awaited them on the other side.

Could it be?

The chatter sounded muffled, but it was undoubtedly human chatter. Someone on the other side of that wall was talking. Dragoş could sense his brain growing increasingly alert by the second. He gently tapped the wall for Frankie to listen to it too.

The American's eyes were widened.

Dragoş tip-toed slightly forward, standing on the edge of the new wall and the rest of the corridor that led to the opposite side of the morgue. From there, the open space allowed the sound to travel a little more clearly.

"*Du-i pe toți la mașină, am spus.* Take them all to the car like I told you to," a man's voice echoed insistently.

Dragoş felt his heart racing faster, each second weighing on his shoulders like a burden. But he had to know what was going on. He leaned in closer to the wall, stepping in front and around the corner. In that darkness, he wouldn't have been visible to some sleepy passerby — it was the only chance he could take in that moment.

"*Hai,* quicker with that one. Careful, you don't want to drop him again, do you?" the man's voice added. "What are you looking at, Doctor?"

Dragoş could see the shadow of the man from the crack in the door, his own hand firmly placed over the wet wall. Frankie squatted down and watched their back, as well as the opposite side of the corridor, for other people.

"N-nothing, *nimic*... I was treating this man not too long ago, and he has a pulse. He isn't dead," the Doctor's voice was much younger and distinguishable when he spoke.

Dragoş heard the echoes of the other man's footsteps approaching the Doctor. Something clinked and fell on the floor, making both Frankie and Dragoş jump.

"*Ascultă-mă*... we were given orders to get rid of the evidence. I won't risk a national uprising because of some *tâmpit* in a white coat that can't differentiate between the dead and the alive. Are you fucking stupid? Hey, *Radule*, come here and check this one's pulse. Show our lovely 'Doctor' here what it means to be deceased," the man said.

A different set of footsteps then proceeded, which gave Dragoş more new information about the space they were trapped in — there were more than two people in this corridor. In the matter of a physical fight, Frankie and Dragoş were goners.

Am belit-o.

And two, he knew that the dead were being trapped here alongside some potentially injured people. They were being relocated, though, so that the 'evidence' could be destroyed. As he dwelt on the possibilities, a third man's voice interrupted.

"*Dumnezeule. Este viu*. This one is alive, he is twitching, look..." the third man said.

The shadows of the three figures danced around the room, all approaching a faraway point where the injured person was laid to rest. Dragoş wanted to move farther down, but feared that his own shadow would pop up in front of the other people.

Gunshot.

The sound of it was loud enough to make him and Frankie kneel and cover their ears. The sound seemed to keep on ringing for a few moments after it had passed, as Dragoş trembled over the weight of the journalist. The screams of the people inside the morgue gave him an approximate number of people in there — six or maybe five, including two or three women.

"*Gata. Acuma e mort. Puneți-l cu ceilalți.* It's over, he is dead. Put him in the back with the rest," the first man said, pacing towards the exit.

Dragoş stuck his back to the wall and held Frankie's arm for balance. The officer, as Dragoş could see, was heading in the opposite direction, where a white plastic door led to the exit a couple of steps above them. He sighed in relief, then straightened his back.

"*Vă rog, domnule.* Please, we want to check the pulse of the rest of the injured. Some of them are alive, sir... You cannot take them like this. God will punish you for this," a familiar woman's voice cried out.

There was silence for a moment, then the sound of a simple click, followed by the woman's wails.

Had someone loaded their gun?

"Oh, look, she has pissed all over the floor. I am not going to kill you, you dumb *curvă*. The gun is a gift. A token, if you may. It's what you can do with the rest of the injured in here," the man called Radu replied.

Dragoş heard the gun land on the table, making the woman's wails louder.

"Let's go," an older man said, causing an entire group of military personnel to exit the morgue.

In the dark, it looked like seven or eight at least, making Dragoş swear at his lack of judgment. The last twenty minutes had made him feel sicker than he had in years — never in his life could he have taken somebody else's life with such ease. The rest of the people in the morgue were quite probably doctors or medical personnel. How many of them were siding with the enemy, though?

He slid forward in the dark, crawling out of the passageway. Frankie held on to Dragoş's jacket in the dusky surroundings, trying to find his way around. Dragoş was on all fours, creeping away like a burglar or a thief. He hated it.

"*Doamne,* oh my God..." the crying woman's voice came out weak.

It made Dragoş stop. They had to get out there without being seen. He rubbed his palms against the floor beneath him, trying not to make noise. Frankie did the same, Dragoş could feel. They reached the crack of the morgue door, their only source of light; it was dim and lifeless, and something about it reminded Dragoş of his parents. Were they well, he wondered? His stomach twisted in response, his body not coping with the weight of the anxiety — there was something else at bay here, he could smell it.

He extended his neck towards the door, trying to see a sign of the women left inside. From this new angle, he spotted one, and — no, it couldn't be.

The paramedic.

No wonder he had felt that her voice was both familiar and unappealing. He had spoken to her on multiple occasions, ever since she had carried Beriţă's body into the ambulance. Now, she was right there in the morgue, aiding the mercenaries in hiding away their crimes, like dust swept under the carpet.

Dragoş arched his back and tried melting away into the concrete behind him, but it was useless. And then—

Her eyes were teary and grey, her face swollen from all the crying. She recognised Dragoş, too, he knew — but she didn't show any sign of shock. She masked it with more tears, turning to face her friend, the woman whom Dragoş couldn't see. She even held on to the other woman's elbow tightly, guiding her view away from the door.

She was doing it for him.

Dragoş crawled as quickly as he could, all the way past the open gap of the door; Frankie did too, and they stuck their backs to the wall on the other end of the space. It was almost over.

"*Hai să vedem ce putem face…* let's see what we can do," the paramedic's friend insisted. "Please don't cry."

Dragoş put a finger over his mouth, advising Frankie to keep quiet. If someone had walked in on them, they would have been cornered by military and hospital staff on either side. He couldn't sabotage anything, not when they already knew more than anyone else in the country.

Frankie was ahead of Dragoş this time, sliding away at the edge of the wall. They approached the next quicker than they had before, the urgency tingling every bone in Dragoş's body. He seemed to have grown numb around the wrists and palms, their colour turning blue. The new staircase led up, where the people from the military groups had gone — they couldn't go up there, but going back wasn't an option either. That's when Frankie's insistent hand became evident.

To the left, Dragoş noticed, there was a path leading to the other wing of the hospital — in the same direction from where Dragoş and Frankie had initially walked down. Surely, a different exit was waiting for them on the other side. These old hospital buildings usually had multiple entrances, and under the exit staircase that they had broken into, there must have been a door.

Dragoş stood up, his back stiff from being on the ground for so long. He held Frankie up, the other man's hands shivering — whether it was from fear or the cold, Dragoş didn't know how to ask. They had to make a run for it now — the most crucial part of their endeavour had proven to be the conclusion, where both of them were inevitably hoping not to get caught.

The men raced down the cobbled floor, the windows above them being their only source of light. The underground had already suffocated their lungs enough — the mixture of scents was sickening — chalk and blood, ashes with dirt.

Seeing a different exit on the opposite end was a relief. Dragoş pounded on the door, expecting it to be locked. But it opened with ease, letting in the fresh December air — while Dragoş and the journalist landed on the concrete floor.

Dragoş lifted himself from off the ground and headed for the grass patch in front of him — without having time to catch his breath, he stained it with vomit and bile until his stomach had twisted inside out.

Thirty-Six

Robert

Timișoara, Romania — December 1989

The cold water was, for once, refreshing against his skin. After all the sticky tears and sweat stains, he needed something to keep him awake for the next few hours. It was almost four in the morning, and there was no sign of his sister or the others — he had to know what was happening.

Ioana had fallen asleep with ease, although he hadn't thought it would be possible for her to get rest in such a troubling time. It had broken his heart to watch her cradle herself into her brother's side of the bed, holding on to his old toys as if they were made out of gold. Perhaps she could still sense his presence from afar, although he had been very clear about what had happened to Berița.

It wasn't the whole truth, though.

Sure, he had told her that he had died in front of the Cathedral, and that he had been a victim of attacks. But he hadn't told her that it was the country's own protectors that had killed Berița in the name of the law — and now, his frail body was rotting away in a dingy hospital corner.

No.

He had told her that her *Mama* was with Berița now, making all the arrangements to lay him to rest. It was enough of a pain that the young girl had to adjust to living without her baby brother, the one that she had known better than anyone. Robi's chest ached at the anxiety of not knowing where Elena and Dragoş were — but thinking of losing them forever? He didn't even want to imagine that life — it would have been lacking everything that had been good about his current day-to-day moments.

There was nothing else for him to do at home; he had to go out and be of use somehow. If the others were in trouble, they would have needed a hand like his to rely on, someone to pull them out from whatever pit they had been thrown into.

With the flick of a switch, Robi turned on the bedside lamp next to him and pulled out a notepad from his drawer. He picked up Ioana's *stilou* from the table and struggled to get a grip around it, as he hadn't used one since he was a kid — then, with as steady a hand as he could keep, he wrote down a little note for his niece:

Plec. Trebuie să o ajut pe Elena. O trimit pe Geta să vină până după—masa la tine.

It ached him to tell her that he was leaving to help Elena, but at least the girl could rely on her neighbours to come and take care of her. Even the Professor had still not heard of Beriță's death, not from a member of the family at least. He felt that writing a note to let the Professor know about their whereabouts was appropriate enough, so he took out another piece of paper.

Tată,

Ioana are nevoie de tine. Cu toții suntem la spital cu Beriță — mama sa îl caută în morgă. Sunt sigur că știi deja ce se întâmplă.

R.

He folded it and tucked it in his jacket's pocket, wondering whether he could have made the note longer. Ioana was going to tell the Professor everything anyway, and Robi had no time to waste — he had already hung around long enough.

As he got up from the bed, he clicked the lamp switch to turn it off again and placed the note for Ioana on the fridge, clasping it with a thick magnet. He walked out of the apartment for the first time since he had lost a family member in the great war that had unfolded outside.

The street was quiet and empty, except for the bum on the corner of the street who was sitting with a bag under his head and a carved blanket over his legs. He hadn't been there before — Robi felt an urge to ask him who he was, why he was on the streets… but he had learnt his lesson. Instead, the boy crossed the street over to the other side, where the road with the trams became visible.

Theatre's Street had never known such turmoil.

On the main roads, some cars were still circulating, and even a couple of people were heading for the centre. He did not doubt that new protests would soon emerge.

The Professor's building seemed closed off from the rest of the occurrences happening outside, and for a split second, even Robi got lost in the feeling of living the same as before. He wanted to pretend like this visit to his father's home was regular, and Ioana and Beriță had already run up the stairs to get there ahead of him. In the back of his mind, Beriță's laugh could still be heard, his shut eyes holding the vision in them for as long as he could hold it there. In his head, he was just as alive as ever.

He gathered the strength to walk up those stairs just as he would have every time, his head lowered. The ache in his left hand had made it grow numb, as he clenched it in frustration. The surroundings were freezing — he could only wonder what the people out on the streets were feeling.

His heart nearly jumped out of its cavity when the Professor's demanding expression caught his eye from behind the wooden door of his home.

"Oh-" Robi exclaimed, putting up his fist in defence.

"Come in. *Te-am văzut.* I saw you when you were coming up," the Professor said.

Robi's shortness of breath made him exhale out of his mouth — the panic was about to settle in his mind anytime now.

"Why are you awake?" Robi asked his father as he walked into the corridor.

"I could ask you the same question, young man. I think your mind has gotten to your head, boy," his father exclaimed, lowering himself down on a stool.

"What was I going to do? Start the revolution from my bed?" Robi asked, frustrated.

His father shook his head.

"You're ready to throw it all away just like that, Robi? You know I can't protect you or anyone else. If you go back out that door and to the protests, only God can save you," the Professor said. "Think of the child—"

"Beriță died," Robi spat.

He could feel the little soul he had left inside of him slide away once again, as if his life was the one that had been taken. The Professor looked at him in shock.

"-Beriță..." the Professor whispered, as if remembering the boy for the first time in years.

"He died because of those fucking maniacs who are shooting civilians. You understand that, father? *Children* are being killed... did you not tell me you didn't want your son to be a 'cowardly sheep in this land of wolves'? Now's the time to bring them down... for what they have done to Beriță, and to every other innocent," Robi shouted.

The Professor looked hazy.

"My grandson died?" he asked, a shiny tear rolling down his cheek.

Robi could feel his face losing its colour — he placed a firm hand on his father's shoulder.

"Yes," he said, wiping away a layer of water that led to his own eyes. "I am sorry, father... but his death can't be in vain. Elena is at the hospital right now, she is looking for h-his body. Dragoș is there too, and the foreigners..." he added.

The Professor sniffed loudly, trying to get his form back together.

"y-yes, I returned this evening and didn't find anyone here. I was worried, too... I don't know what to say anymore. Your friend, Dragoș — it's impressive that he is helping you with whatever the heck is going on out there. I never thought that his and your plan would be this effective. Luring the students into fighting back. It was a clever strategy," the man mumbled.

Robi's body grew cold, as if all his blood had just been drained out of him. Amidst all the chaos, he had forgotten the most crucial part: the revolution had begun.

"How do you know about the plans?" Robi asked, turning on his heels.

The Professor looked down at his shoes.

"W-well, even a blind man could tell that you were planning something. Why else would you be hanging around Dragoș? I always suspected that there was something off about him... "

"He helped us get Beriță to the hospital," Robi said, waving away all the thoughts of the revolution and their plans. "That is what I know him as. A man of honour."

"Christ, Robi..." the Professor said, grabbing his handkerchief from his left pocket. "He turned against his own now, at a time of distress? What kind of a person does that?"

Robi shook his head.

"The kind of person that wants a change," Robi answered. "The Intelligence has tortured him enough... You should know what the system is like, *Tată*... what are you even talking about? It's like I don't recognise you anymore."

The Professor tutted.

"Your friend is a liability. He has already cost us Beriță... had I known that you were stupid enough to leave in front of a six-year-old boy. And that you told him where you were heading..." The Professor's eyes grew teary again.

Robi had had enough of this — whatever his father was going through, it had to wait once everything had calmed down.

"Dragoș didn't cost us Beriță! The army did... how can you even blame him for that?" he asked.

He headed for the door with courage.

"Be careful," the Professor warned his son.

Robi didn't need to be told twice. His father shouted over the sound of the keys clinking in the knob.

"Not everything is what it seems, Robi."

Thirty-Seven

Elena

Timişoara, Romania — December 1989

Dragoş and Frankie walked up towards her and Lizzie on the eastern side of the hospital, where a few patients were being treated for heart illnesses — Elena drew a sharp breath in, wondering what had taken the men so long. When they approached them, she could see Dragoş's expression looking ghastly; the morning hours were still dark, and his words would soon be darker.

"We have to get out of here. Now," Frankie said, holding both of their arms.

What had they done?

She searched through Dragoş's face for an answer, but watched as his lips quivered.

"Tell me, Dragoş. *Spune-mi, unde e copilul meu?*" she asked, shaking his shoulders.

Dragoş leaned closer, as if he was about to embrace Elena.

"*L-au luat.* They've taken everyone away, Elena," he whispered.

She put a hand over her mouth. If they were being taken to a new morgue or worse, she had to find him. An address, something... she was sure that the men must have returned with something.

Her last hope couldn't have just ended like that.

Just as Elena wanted to ask them another question, she felt a tap on her shoulder.

"Excuse me..." the woman in the nurse's uniform said. "T-this is for you."

The same woman that Dragoş and Robi had recognised as the paramedic who had taken Beriţă to the hospital — she handed Elena a folded paper.

"*Hei*! *Stai*... wait..." Dragoş said, his voice sounding rough and drained.

The nurse looked at him.

"I won't tell..." she whispered. "*Îmi pare atât de rău*. I am so, so sorry."

"I know," Dragoş said. "I just wanted to say thank you. *Pentru tot*," he said, leaving Elena even more confused than before.

The woman walked away, leaving Elena with a piece of paper to read when she could escape the suffocating building. Perhaps it disclosed a location or information about where the cadavers were being taken.

Her hope was still not lost.

Elena wiped away the residue of tears in her eyes as she sat at their family's kitchen table. Her father had been there earlier, too, listening to everything that Frankie and Dragoş had witnessed. It was enough to shake Elena's world entirely, and oh! Poor Ioana — the young girl hadn't seen her mother like this before. Elena had to be strong for her girl in this moment, but she didn't know where to summon the strength from. The only thing left now was the letter, which she had anticipated from the moment it had found itself in her pockets.

She hadn't dared to open the letter when she was still outside — not after all the sights of people burning down cars, breaking into shops to steal, and attacking anyone who got in their way. She had even avoided the gaze of the man who was stealing cigarettes from beyond a broken glass window, and carried on walking with the rest as if all was normal.

She unfolded the letter, feeling everyone's warm gaze focused on her. With a cough, she began reading the things witnessed by the nurse, and didn't stop until she needed to catch her breath again.

Dear doamnă,

I am sorry for calling you that. I suppose I never asked for your name, and now I probably never will get to hear it either. This is the last piece of evidence tying me to this place, because I am leaving first thing tomorrow morning — a group of us is fleeing to Vienna for the remainder of this chaos, and we'll see what happens next. In all honesty, I'm not sure if I will ever return. I trust you to do with this letter what you know is right.

I wanted to tell you, from one mother to another — I know what happened to your son. And I know that your husband and his friend (the men that had come down to the morgue earlier this morning) also know parts of this Operation. I am sure that some of it you have already heard... but I cannot leave knowing that I never tried to help a fellow human being in a time like this.

Yesterday, the military began shooting people on the streets... we were all told to go out and help, as most of our oaths and morals guided us to do in life. I am a simple nurse, but something possessed me when I heard what was going on in every part of town, so I left with the rest. Your boy's body was one of the first that we took to the hospital.

This much you know for sure, as do I.

What came next was gruesome and vile to admit to, but I can't go to a confession booth and tell a priest any of this. This kind of sin... You don't confess to it so that you earn forgiveness. There is no forgiveness for it.

They asked me to take the bodies of the dead down at the morgue, and the injured in the hospital wing that is being renovated right now. It's not finished, and there is limited access from that side — but judging by where your two friends were waiting, I think they broke into that part of the building. They arrived a little late, though — a lot of the injured were there. The ones that didn't seem to have a real chance at surviving; they were waiting for the kindness of death to take their misery away, finally.

I should have questioned it. I should have known that the fraieri *were up to no good. We were being told what to do by superior members of staff, who were getting their own orders from others. Men I had never seen before were waltzing in and out of the room as if they owned the place, and told us not to let anyone in. So I did what I was taught to do. I obeyed what I was being asked to do, as someone who had no absolute authority in the place.*

Around three o'clock, the head nurse in our wing told us to head down to the morgue because the police was there. I asked myself then — why would the police come? Why so late? Where had they been all day long, when we were all trying to get the dead and injured some identity confirmation? I carried on without saying anything...

When I went down to the morgue, the miliția *was the one calling all the shots. That's when I understood what was going on — we were helping them get rid of the evidence of what their people had done. Don't believe what anyone tells you. It was always the military that attacked the people during this riot, and no one else.*

Your boy, I am sad to say, did not live — but he did deserve a proper burial. I found out yesterday that they are taking the dead to a crematorium in Bucharest, where they're going to get rid of everyone. I have a friend in Bucharest who will receive a letter about this and might be able to visit the crematorium to ask around for witnesses who have seen them. I swear to God... there were some living people there too. Depending on how long your two friends were there, they would have heard all the commotion. Perhaps there are records of them, including pictures, documents, and even testimonies.

They asked us to shoot the injured. They made us put them in their cars at gunpoint, despite knowing better. And perhaps there is no forgiveness for this. Such a nation is doomed to suffer — I don't know how these people will be able to live with themselves. I know we will be haunted by it for as long as we're alive. I am trying not to make it sound as bad as it is because I know you are a mother. You won't see your boy again, because they turned him to ash and dust. I hope you can find it in your heart to forgive what I did.

I am a coward who is running away. Maybe this chance was worth a shot. I could sleep better at night if I lied to myself that you were better off with my confession.

Thank you for understanding.

Elena folded the letter and turned around, twisting the stove to turn it on.

She grabbed a matchstick and lit up the fire in the biggest circle, then put the letter in it.

As she watched the paper turn to ash in front of her eyes, she prayed that a hellfire as hot as this one would reach all the people that had brought this upon her — the doctors, the army, the police, Nicolae and his wife.

And that fucking nurse.

Thirty-Eight

Elizabeth

Timişoara, Romania – December 1989

The events of the last week made Lizzie sick – and not just in a way that made her throw up every piece of food that she tried keeping down. She couldn't breathe without feeling a sharp ache in her throat and chest, or the tingling in her fingers, making her palms go numb whenever she tried moving. In her sleep, she only saw pale, white faces with no names calling her name – she didn't know what it could mean.

The skin on her hands was cracking, and their lack of composure was alarming; the cold had been harsher than anything she had ever fathomed. And for the first time in her life, she had bled without having access to any sanitary products – she had been lucky that Elena had taught her how to use cotton as a replacement for tampons. Even Lizzie's eyes, down to every capillary, had sensed the weight of the world around her, which was making her labour for more.

She had seen conflict and problems, but nothing this close. She was affiliated with the revolution and its heroes in a way that very few journalists had ever managed to… some would have called her brave for it.

But she wasn't, in fact, courageous.

She was ready to flee this place and never return.

Elena's letter burned away in front of her, and Lizzie stood closer to make sure the woman wouldn't burn her hands. She was too close to the fire — but to Lizzie's surprise, the other woman drew out a thin stick from her pocket, and leaned closer to the stove with it between her fingers. Elena brought the cigarette to her thin, trembling lips and inhaled the air with a cough.

"What?" Elena asked, catching Lizzie staring at her.

"N-nothing… can I have one?" Lizzie swallowed dryly, not sure of why she was nicking a fag right now.

The heavy smell of smoke was almost distracting — Elena handed her one, and Lizzie placed it between her lips before leaning in front of the stove to light it up.

"Thank you," Lizzie muttered, sitting back down. "Frankie and I should get going… back to the Professor's."

"No," Robi spoke from behind the kitchen table, cradling an asleep Ioana in his arms. "Dragoș and I will sleep at my father's apartment tonight. He is leaving again… and I don't really want to be here for a while. Dragoș needs a safe layer where no one will find him," he added.

"That's fine," Frankie said, surprising Lizzie. "We could crash in the living room."

Elena nodded, exhaling thick smoke.

"Go," she said to her brother. "What else can I tell you to do? You've already made up your mind anyway… I know you'll go to more riots, Robi," she said, her words incoherent.

"I have to go…" Robi began, but Elena put her hand up to stop him.

"Grieve in your own way. Go."

Robi put Ioana's head on the support behind them and reached under the table to get out. His hair had grown down to his shoulders, and his grey eyes looked cold and lifeless. Lizzie knew then that the young boy was ready to leave the front door on his own — he had changed, just like everyone else in that room. He looked like a different person altogether from the boy who had sat on the kitchen counter and laughed with Lizzie about the regime's policies.

As she watched Robi and Dragoș leave the apartment, she wondered when she would see them again. But of course — she hadn't even told Elena yet.

"Listen… Elena?" Lizzie asked, looking at Ioana, rubbing her eyes in her sleep.

"Hm?" Elena answered, smoking by the window.

"Frankie and I are leaving for Bucharest," she told her. "We have decided that it is the best way to find the conclusion to our story about the crematorium. And the revolution overall, Elena."

Elena didn't say anything — she stared out of the window as mindlessly as ever. But she *had* heard her. Lizzie couldn't pretend that this entire game of guilt and pity wasn't draining her. Of course, she felt for Elena — but how long could she have stayed in Timișoara?

"You too?" Elena asked, and Lizzie could hear her grinning.

"I told you… We're doing this for the people. So that their stories get told. What do you want me to write about from here, Elena? I have nothing to do… It's driving me crazy. All I think about is those people that were murdered and then taken from their families, and here I am with a weapon mightier than any sword the world has ever seen," Lizzie clicked her pen repeatedly, and got up from her seat. "I can find out what happened to Beriță. Where he was taken."

She touched Elena's elbow, making the woman flinch — too much had bruised the woman. She couldn't tell the distinction between what would leave more scars and what wouldn't. She turned to look at Lizzie and tapped her cigarette on the edge of the windowsill.

"Will you write about me? And about my boy?" Elena asked, and Lizzie nodded.

"I promise. Everyone will know what happened to the victims of this military operation," she added. "But I need to know the ending of it. How it all happened after they were taken away to Bucharest."

To Lizzie's surprise, Elena's arms extended to embrace her.

"Thank you, Elizabeth," Elena said, her head nestling on Lizzie's shoulder. "You cannot go alone, though. I will not allow it."

"Elena, you have done enough… really," Lizzie said, breaking the hug to look at Elena.

"Take Robi with you. Please," Elena insisted. "How else would you go around Bucharest on your own? It is far too dangerous..."

"I will ask Frankie. I think he wants us to go to the Embassy there," Lizzie admitted. "Then home."

Elena nodded.

"I'm glad there is still an escape for you, Liz. You won't remain frozen in time like me..." Elena masked her sobs with another cigarette.

"You're not frozen, Elena. You will come out stronger on the other end of this, I promise you," Lizzie whispered sweetly. "You know it."

Elena nodded, lowering her head — Lizzie gave her a moment to herself, leaving her in the same kitchen where they had spent so many of their days together.

Thirty-Nine

Robert

Timișoara, Romania — December 1989

"Are you certain this is what you want?" Frankie asked for the fourth time, to which Robi rolled his eyes in annoyance.

"Please, Frank. I can at least try to bring back my nephew's ashes for Elena to bury him. Give him an Orthodox burial… God knows how that would work, though. I don't even want to think of it right now," he said, tossing a pack of dry crackers across the table.

"These are stale," Lizzie told him — not a complaint, a mere observation. She dipped them in her cold cup of tea, trying not to look too displeased.

"Blame Dragoș," Robi said, lying flat on the Professor's sofa. "He has been eating all the leftovers."

Dragoș mumbled from the kitchen at the mention of his name.

"*Taci*… just stop making excuses. We all know you love eating all the sweets," Robi smiled, allowing the grief to melt away like a candle at someone's *înmormântare*.

"Will he be alright without you?" Lizzie asked, eyes dancing over to Dragoș's direction in the kitchen.

Robi shot a glance at Dragoș, who sat all alone at the kitchen table, under a dim light. He wore one of the Professor's old bathrobes and ate out of an old bucket of cream cheese, since 'it was going to waste anyway'. Next to him, he held a glass full of *pălincă* tightly — his fourth or fifth from that morning, Robi guessed.

"He should be. I didn't know he ate when he was upset," Robi raised an eyebrow.

"Or stressed out, anxious…" Frankie said.

"You seem to be better, though," Robi told Frankie.

The American breathed in deeply — he shuffled his hands in his lap.

"Y-yes, I must say that is true… I have been able to sleep better at night."

"I know," Robi smiled. "I heard you snoring this morning. Since when did you realise this?" he asked curiously.

Frankie paused, gathering the words in his mouth carefully.

"I… I think it was ever since the night at the morgue. It's very strange. I don't know what it was about that night that made me relax down to my last bone," Frankie said, sitting up straight.

Robi nodded knowingly — he had noticed it too.

"Your brain… it needed to rest after that. Perhaps the shock never settled in," Lizzie guessed, dipping another cracker in her cup.

"The last time this happened, I had been at a funeral. Someone close to me," Frankie explained. "It didn't last long, though… and I never shed a single tear."

A second later, Robi heard Lizzie's cracker split and splash into the drink, leaving the young woman with frustration painted across her face.

"Is it bad that I never cried again either?" Robi asked bluntly. "After all of it, I never broke down again in the last few days… not even when I saw his toys or his old clothes. The things that carried his scent. I didn't feel the same sadness… I feel something else. A sort of hole…" he pointed at his chest.

"Emptiness," Frankie sighed.

"Yes. Like there is nothing there anymore," Robi explained. "Dragoș seems to try to fill it with food. I don't know what to do."

"Everyone grieves in different ways, Robi. You mustn't feel bad for not doing what you thought you would in a situation like this, or what is normal to do by most standards… unless you're in the same situation, you can never tell," Lizzie said, fishing her moistened cracker from the bottom of the cup.

Robi nodded. Of course, he loved his nephew. *Of course,* he wanted to honour his memory and those who had died alongside him. But not weeping did not change the guilt that he had buried deep within himself, all the way down to his heart. It ached in moments when he last expected to be struck by the hurt of loss — when he walked up the stairs to go home, or even allowed himself a short moment of joy in the middle of Hell.

Robi jumped from the sofa.

"I'll pack the rest of my things. We have to be quick today," he said, shuffling over to the kitchen.

Now, he saw the kitchen table layout clearer — there was a jar of pickles, an old piece of bread, and a slice of something that looked like it was picked up from behind the furniture after six months of rotting away in silence.

"*Dumnezeule…*" Robi said. "Do you want to be able to move from here without needing a crane? You just gave '*îngrașă porcul în Ajunul Crăciunului*' a whole new meaning."

Dragoş gulped down some *pălincă*.

"Christmas is still a week away. God knows if you'll even be here for it," Dragoş said bitterly.

"I told you… You can come with me. In fact, I insist. But it's dangerous, especially if your friends find us," Robi admitted.

He wanted his friend to accompany him. But Dragoş would wait for him here — where Elena and Ioana needed him, and where the danger was containable. They would see each other in the next couple of days — Robi repeated it out loud for Dragoş.

"Yeah, yeah…" he said. "I don't know what I'll do on my own," Dragoş added.

"You'll stay here, where it's safe. No one knows about this place… your parents are safe. Elena and Ioana can rely on you for help. Isn't that true?" Robi asked, trying to make Dragoş lighten up.

He wondered how much of this was actually getting through his fogged mind, clouded by the glasses of liquor that he kept devouring.

"I need something to do… something I can rely on while you're away. It's like…now that the riots have expanded everywhere, I don't have anything else to look forward to," Dragoş explained, coughing down more from his glass.

Robi and Dragoş had been together when the radio announcements were being made in Elena's kitchen — the radio that had sparked the beginning of an unusual, yet beautiful alliance. There were protests, riots, and fragments of the Revolution scattered all over the country — București, Cluj, Iași… all the significant cities stood united against a common enemy, ready to demolish the years of injustice that had broken their bones and scarred their skin.

"They'll put the dictator on trial soon enough, you'll see. It's bound to happen. Then, we're free!" Robi turned his elbows outwards, as if he were performing a trick. "We can do everything we want."

They would have all the time in the world after this — and although it was juvenile of him to feel like this, he vowed to become immortal. Metaphorically — of course. He'd live for the martyrs in more ways than one. So would Dragoş. And what happened to Beriță — this trip to București would account for that as well.

The crematorium on the other end was waiting for them. Then Lizzie and Frankie would write about everything and send it over to their correspondent in England — for this, Robi would lead them to the British Embassy in Bucharest.

He laid the plan out to Dragoş, who nodded drunkenly.

"When are you back, though?" he asked.

Robi palmed his face at the stupidity of his friend's question.

Why did I let him open more bottles of alcohol? And is that the plum rum we got from the village last year?

"Dragoş, Dragoş…" Robi said. "I will return. Please, will you stop making me feel bad for going? I have to help them get this story out there, beyond the Romanian border," he pleaded. "I will feel better if you give me your 'blessing' for this instead of being so difficult… and stop drinking away your sorrows. There isn't enough alcohol in all of Romania to drown away those."

Dragoş gave a low chuckle.

"Go," he said. "I can't stop you even if I wanted to. You'll be closer to him, though. *Ceaşcă*," Dragoş laughed, referring to Ceauşescu by his satirical nickname.

A cup of tea.

"So? It's not like he'll personally lean down to kick me in the balls, Dragoş. Your paranoia is getting out of hand, God…" Robi wanted to laugh.

"I'm just saying," Dragoş raised his spoon, waving it around like a madman.

Robi sighed. This was too complicated — when it didn't have to be in the slightest.

"I'm coming back in less than a week. We'll spend Christmas together, how about that? Give you something to look forward to. *Un eveniment*," Robi said, trying not to mock.

He patted Dragoş's shoulder.

"Thank you. For everything," Robi said.

"Oh, no, no… you're making it sound like farewell. That's what I don't want," Dragoş punched the table, making the spoon and glass on it ricochet.

"It's a 'see you soon', Dragoş… not a goodbye," Robi said. "Okay?"

"Fine. But you'd better call when you can," Dragoş said. "Or else I'll assume you *fraier* got your ass killed somewhere in the Capital," he laughed.

"God, always so dramatic," Robi scoffed, embracing Dragoş.

When he finally let go, he smiled at him and plucked a kiss on his friend's forehead — his fellow soldier, returning home from the Great War.

And they would never go back to the bloodshed of the Cathedral's steps, Robi promised himself silently, like a whisper beating through his chest.

IV

PART IV — Deșteaptă—te, Române!

Wake up, oh Romanian!

Forty

Frankie

Bucharest, Romania – December 1989

Frankie hated the smell of trains. The vigorous, metallic rasp in the air made his stomach twist; the emptiness inside thudded continuously.

He hadn't eaten for almost fourteen hours – when they had left Timişoara, Robi had packed some stale leftovers for them. Food that would have otherwise been consumed by Dragoş, the tall, grey man, fuelled by his own grief and anger. The food had run out pretty quickly among the three of them, especially after Robi had offered some bread-cake, or *cozonac*, as Robi called it, to the passenger sitting next to them. The man hadn't declined it, not even out of politeness, which made Frankie pity him more later on.

Despite how slow they were going, the journey hadn't tired him in the slightest. He managed to sleep through the slopy track roads, the winding turns on the way, and the cold air that had filled the compartment at night, through the cracked window. Now, Lizzie's head rested on his shoulder, and Robi's leg touched the edge of his seat, extended all the way to the top. Frankie had wanted to move, but felt too awkward to – he put his head back on the compartment's wall, and tried drifting back to sleep.

I haven't slept this well in years.

Was it the fresh air? The tiredness? The shock and exhaustion? Whatever it was, he was thankful for it, and was certainly not looking forward to returning home, where he had known nothing but the lonely sleepless nights in the heart of London.

The train's sound was comforting, although it was old and carried way too many people on board. Apart from the hunger that he couldn't wait to satisfy, Frankie Hannigan was actually *enjoying* the mission that he had set out for himself. He hadn't felt this excited since his college days, when he had quit being the paper boy in his old town, and had moved to the Big Apple for a new life.

He would work from morning till evening on a new story, researching old ones, and coming back on top with something even better — before he started chasing the desire and ambition that had driven him to London. Young Francis wrote about all the things that were missing from the world: love, compassion, empathy. Feeling them all so deeply again reminded him of the boy he once gazed back at in front of the mirror, a kid no older than twelve, who wrote about the local drug store's missing cough syrup mystery as if it were the most remarkable story ever told.

He had overheard the cashier talking about it, then rephrased everything to fit his first-ever little article. Perhaps he ought to frame that, he told himself now, not feeling like sleeping at all.

"Hey," Robi whispered in front of him, his voice sounding pleasant.

Frankie had an excuse to shuffle a little, letting his numb legs shake.

"You need to wake her up," Robi said, checking if the man next to him was indeed asleep.

Throughout the trip, they had avoided talking in front of the man in the compartment — who knew what trouble would be waiting for them if someone had suspected them. They were lucky enough to sneak on the train without being noticed by anyone; all the focus was finally on the Revolution and its development. Frankie looked out of the window through furrowed eyebrows, the new sign in front of them speaking clearly.

They were in Bucharest.

If Timişoara had been chaotic, Bucharest was Hell. Frankie covered his face at the sight of smoke and dust settling around the groups of people in the town squares, with Robi making way for him and Lizzie to pass.

The streets were *loud*, louder than any city Frankie had ever witnessed. The people could no longer be silenced, especially not after the events that had unfurled in Timişoara. The rows of newspapers at the stand in front of Frankie only confirmed his suspicions — people were aware of what was happening. He picked up one of them unknowingly, in awe of the graphic detail in which everything was described.

He handed it to Robi, who was nervously clutching a cigarette in his hand, rubbing his hands to warm them up from the cold. Lizzie watched him curiously until he finally offered her one, too. Cigarettes as a luxury; Frankie could almost laugh.

"What does it say?" Frankie asked.

Robi stared at it for a while, as if zoned out.

"Only half the truth," Robi said, rolling the newspaper, then putting it in his back pocket. "The other half is still here, at *Cenuşa*. We have to find it before we're too late, if we aren't already..."

"We need to get to the Embassy first, Robi," Lizzie demanded, smoking anxiously.

She had smudged her mascara over her eyelids to seem a little in touch with the cold — Frankie wanted to help her rest now, keep her away from the harsh weather. They hadn't had a hot meal or a warm bath in more than two days, with the lengthy journey still hovering around them.

"Fine, we will," Robi said. "If my directions are correct, we should be there soon. The British Embassy is meant to be right around the corner."

Frankie nodded and tried to lead the way; the cobbled path made it difficult to walk, as if he were sliding on ice. Suddenly, he found himself covering his ears at the too familiar sound of a gunshot — from the direction of the Embassy's street. Frankie ducked behind a brown *Dacia*, covering Lizzie's shoulders with his left arm, and tightening his grip around Robi's coat with his right. This couldn't happen, not again.

With slow steps, Frankie's body rose above the cars that had been sheltering them, and he turned his head to look around. Suddenly, he missed his friend Dragoș too much, remembering the man who had helped them get through the turmoil back home. Who would hold them now, without the other man's strength there to drag them up?

Lizzie butted her cigarette on the door of the car, letting the cremated ashes slip on the icy floor.

"You okay?" he asked her, letting his hand slip into hers.

She nodded and sniffed, letting out a sigh of relief.

"Are we ever going home?" she asked, rubbing her thumb against his hand.

"I believe this might be our best chance yet, Liz… we just need to stay alive until everything settles."

"You're right. But the memories of here… I cannot forget them, no matter how hard I try to focus on our story and on leaving. I feel like a hypocrite, at the end of the day," Lizzie whispered, following him down the cobbled path.

Robi slid by them, trying to get ahead.

"If we're lucky, you two can go in and stay there until they send you home," he admitted.

Robi pointed at the eggshell white building in front of them — Frankie disapproved of the sight ahead. *Securitate* guards, military personnel, and a few other men in uniform all lurked close by; the high alert on this specific side of the street seemed unnecessary. People were being shot down by these same groups all around the country — were they trying to keep the people in the Embassy as hostages?

Frankie was bewildered; he carried on stomping down the road until he was close enough to the military to see them face-to-face. Behind him, Robi had shouted something inaudible, which he had chosen to dodge. He wouldn't let the fear get to him.

"Hey!" Frankie shouted at the personnel inside the Embassy.

The military tried pushing him back, while he tried reaching for the bars of the wall in front of him. He heard them clicking and panting closer.

Are their guns loaded?

Frankie tried getting the attention of the people inside, beyond the useless rows of men who stood like scarecrows in a cornfield. Someone pushed him back again — harder this time, his ears ringing from anger.

"I am a journalist from England," he put his hands up in protest.

Surely, they wouldn't shoot a foreigner.

Or would they?

"What are you doing? Are you out of your mind?" Lizzie yelled at him, pulling his elbows back.

He was almost crossing the line set out by the people in front of the Embassy, as if breaking in.

He could see a man in a blue suit beyond the tall walls, looking at him with a confused glare — he oversaw Frankie. Then, leaning down to speak to an officer in a black uniform, he addressed the officer. Frankie didn't need to hear him to know that they would be let in. The men in front of him lifted their heads at the shouting of the man in the black uniform.

"You can go," a tall guard spoke in a strange accent, watching Frankie from head to toe.

Lizzie held on to Frankie's arm.

"All of us?" Frankie asked, looking around for Robi.

The guard looked down at him.

"If they're with you, yes," he said.

The gates opened, allowing them all to walk in as if this were their own home — including Robi. He kept quiet, not letting them know that he wasn't in fact a journalist, or from England, like Frankie and Lizzie were.

"Frank. Frankie Hannigan," he shook the man's hand.

"Michael Shortridge," the man nodded.

"Thank you for having us here today," Frankie added quickly, leaning back into one of the uncomfortable plastic chairs they had to pull out for them.

Looking around the relatively new building, it was apparent to Frankie that everyone there had gathered around for the same reason as they had. There were twenty-five, perhaps thirty people sitting in every corner of the open hall — all of them were trying to get the next flight out. Luckily, there weren't many of those around anyway; when he caught a young teenage boy staring at him angrily, Frankie was sure that the boy would fistfight anyone in the room to get to the other side of the continent. As would many of the others, for sure — he had to play his cards right if he wanted to be guaranteed a safe exit out of the country as soon as possible.

"Listen, I'd like to call someone, Michael… can I call you Michael? Look, I want to know a way to get back home as soon as possible, but I also want to hear a story on the other end. I am a journalist, you see—", Frankie blurted.

"That won't get you any brownie points," a voice mocked him from behind.

The teenager stood up and walked a few steps closer to Frankie, extending an arm for a handshake.

"Tim Collins. From *The British*," he shook his hand firmly. "I apologise for staring at you earlier, I recognised your partner out there. Miss Sturridge. You work for Ross Berkshire, don't you?" the boy made himself comfortable on a plastic chair next to Frankie.

Frankie looked around, as if seeking some help from Lizzie — but she was standing in the far left corner of the room, with Robi hanging around her closely. Wing around her closely.

Were they going to lure someone before Michael finally gives me the time of day?

"Y-yes…" Frankie smiled. "I am terribly sorry, lad, but I am trying to get us back home here," he scoffed, pointing back at Michael.

Michael raised his head from a bundle of papers that Frankie hadn't even acknowledged before.

"Mister Hannigan — if you can't already tell, the situation here is filled with tension. Those men are lined up so that they don't let anyone flee the country, so you or your friends won't be getting home anytime soon. I am terribly sorry," Michael dipped his head back between the papers once again.

"You have to be in contact with someone from London, you have to…" Frankie said, giving the newcomer an insistent look.

Tim raised an eyebrow.

"That is what I have been saying…" Tim laughed.

Frankie shot him a glare — the boy needed to be quiet, for his own sake.

"The Foreign Office in London has been in touch, yes, but Mister Hannigan… we have about thirty more people like you in that room over there. All panicking, begging their employers to get them home. Some are trying to reach Her Majesty and get her to send help," Michael laughed. "I am afraid that the best shot we have is to wait until the storm has cleared out."

Tim clicked his tongue.

This fucking kid.

"Look, I need to speak to Berkshire. This boy just told you that he knows us, my partner and I. If there's anyone that I trust for this, it's Berkshire…" Frankie felt like he was begging.

"I am sorry. You are welcome to stay here for as long as you wish, but we aren't allowed to let anyone make calls in this building," Michael looked at him apologetically.

Frankie stood up and thanked him, and to his surprise, Tim imitated his action in unison. He headed towards Lizzie, not paying much attention to Michael or the Collins kid — there was no way they could contact Berkshire without the Embassy's help.

Robi and Lizzie looked at him eagerly, even before he had approached them. He didn't like having so much rely on him alone; there needed to be a way for they to get their problems to Berkshire. A way that preferably didn't include pigeons and handwritten letters.

"Well?" Lizzie asked, watching him walk towards her in sheer disappointment.

"No luck," Frankie shook his head. "The—"

"Jesus! Is that you, Timmy?" Lizzie shrieked suddenly, reaching out to hug Collins.

"Liz!" Tim hugged her back.

Robi and Frankie exchanged a look of confusion. *Trust me, I am thinking the same thing*, Frankie wanted to tell him.

All in all, he found it amusing.

"This is Little Timmy," Lizzie grinned. "He is my mother's only nephew — the spoiled one in our family."

Lizzie embraced him again.

"Look at you all tall and mighty, out here on a mission? Why are you here?" she asked.

"Well," Tim scoffed, "You know that our parents have always taken notes from each other about how things need to be done… mother thought it'd be great for me to come out here and do something different."

"Oh, lovely," Lizzie nodded. "Very good… I see you've been doing some research?" she eyed the notes emerging from his back pocket.

"Yes, yes," Tim nodded, swallowing dryly.

Frankie furrowed an eyebrow.

"Can we see what you've been doing?"

"W-well, yes, sure…" Tim said, looking around the room. "I have been looking at the political activity here in the Capital… as well as a few rumours that I have heard from other people, none of which are confirmed yet, though."

Frankie watched him draw out the papers between bony fingers, handing them to Lizzie.

"Here," he said.

Lizzie glared at them for a moment, then passed them around to Frankie. The only sentence written on the paper on top was in thick marker, dark enough to stain the documents behind it.

"I CAN HELP YOU MAKE THAT PHONE CALL."

Forty-One

Robert

Bucharest, Romania — December, 1989

The streets of Bucharest ricocheted the heavy rain across the alleyways, the pouring water splashing every inch of the pavement. Robi's nostrils flared at the smell of damp, cold air. He flinched when an unfamiliar stench wafted above him in tease, and he leaned closer to Lizzie to get a better view of what was going on across the road.

The umbrella wasn't much help, but at least their hair and tops were dry enough not to stain their skins, as the road grew wider from in front, and all the collected water began flooding the side of the street.

"How much longer till we're there?" Lizzie asked, shouting above the singing of the clouds.

Robi kept searching for any sign labelled *Cenușa* — the Romanian word for ash.

Where there is smoke...

"I don't know," Robi eyed his map again. "I think it is around the corner," he mumbled, tucking in their passes to get back into the Embassy.

He felt the glossy texture of the paper on the tip of his fingers, pushing it further down to the bottom of the pockets of his coat.

"You said that three corners ago," Lizzie shouted again. "Jesus," she cursed under her breath, hiding away her box of cigarettes from the drops spitting from the edge of their umbrella.

"I don't know who to ask," Robi said, stopping abruptly.

He looked around the road, noticing how empty it seemed without all the millions of cars that usually flooded the streets of Bucharest — they carried more might than the flood that threatened to invade every inch of the city soon. That's when the iron gates of *Parcul Tineretului*, The Park of Youth, led him to a clandestine corner that shied away from the main road.

"Come on," Robi led Lizzie to the opposite end of the park's gates, stomping through the muddy, wet puddles.

Lizzie hurried alongside him, tightening a fist around the bottom of the umbrella — Robi lowered his grip from above, close enough to hold her hand between his own fingers. He ran quicker, careful not to trip or lead Lizzie down a path that would end with both of their demise.

Each beat against the rocky pathway yelled out his nephew's name, loud enough to silence the pouring rain that had finally agreed to wash his sins clean. He wanted to cry, to scream — some strange grain of hope had been laid down at the bottom of his pit, a shadow that had only been tormenting him for the last few days. This was the final opportunity God had given him; a last chance to not go back home empty-handed.

As if his prayers had been answered, Robi spotted a tall Gothic-like building sitting alone in the middle of a deserted plot of land — the grass around it had not been cut in months. It looked like a chapel, its round dome weighing down on the rest of the building. It made a horrible sound every time the water dripped down along its edges, as if there was no room for it to leak anywhere other than the mud and grass, which yielded thick ragweed and wildflowers.

Cenușa looked dreadful.

For a passerby, it was nothing more than an old, forgotten building resting at the edge of the park. Perhaps a place for all the drunk punks who consumed the most foul substances to hang around, the place smelling of dirt and mould.

"This is it," Robi promised, feeling his breath grow shorter.

"Are you certain?" Lizzie asked.

"I have never been more sure. You have to trust me," Robi urged.

He raced over to the steps of the crematorium, its structure resembling that of a church in an almost eerie manner. Robi wasn't sure of what he was expecting, but he knocked on the door and waited patiently, feeling his heart pounding in his throat. He was afraid to let a single word slip from his mouth, expecting bile, sweat, and blood to rise all the way to his frontal lobe.

Lizzie placed their umbrella in the shade of the building, placing it upside down — she rubbed her hands thoroughly, sniffing from the chilly air. Her lips had parted, bleeding from within; the Winter knew no friends.

When the unlocking sound from within echoed in the small area, Robi placed both palms on his forehead, as if preparing for the worst. He would have raced to the gates of Heaven if it meant getting Beriță's body back — thankfully, the wrath of the Capital was as far as he had to go this time. The face that emerged behind the door made his stomach twist, and he could have sworn that he was experiencing hot and cold flashes from merely walking in the rain.

"*Da*? Can I help you?" a small, angry-looking man asked, coughing.

"Y-yes..." Robi stammered. "I want to see my nephew. He was taken here a couple of days ago," he added.

"Hmm..." the midget grumbled, unclasping the lock on the door. "I don't think I can help you much, to be honest," he added. "We get too many bodies every day, lots of unnamed *bucureșteni*... especially nowadays."

"My nephew was one of the martyrs in Timişoara," Robi blurted, water dripping down his face from his wet temples and hair.

The short man's eyes widened.

"I am sorry... I don't have any people from Timişoara here... you have the wrong place."

Robi unwrapped the envelope that had been sitting in his back pocket among the thick passes and the map. The paramedic's letter was hanging between his frozen fingers. Then, a new idea came to his mind as he recalled his first encounter with Dragoş, the only person who had ever tried to bully him into getting answers for the fun of it.

"The authorities in Timişoara know differently," Robi bluffed. "I would know, since I was involved in the cover-up, *domnule*."

Robi was surprised at how easily he could lie to someone's face like that; the words were coming out of his mouth like a fountain of water, as if it were the most natural thing in the world. He cursed the illicitness that he had adopted in these last few weeks, like a child under his wing.

Twenty-three million people in Romania, and forty-six million faces.

"But you said you had a nephew here…" The man raised an eyebrow, unlocking the door once again.

"I had to make sure we didn't hire imbeciles for the job," Robi coughed, his mouth going dry. "*Prostul naibii*, you were ready to give us away, weren't you?"

"N-no…" the old man said.

Robi chuckled, as he channelled Dragoş's mannerisms for this conversation. If he had to play a role, he would do it well.

"Well, are you going to keep us out here for the rest of the day?" Robi asked, allowing the man to review the paramedic's letter.

The man clutched it tightly.

"If you already know that the bodies were handled here, why are you still lurking? Wasn't it enough that your friends have been enquiring about this every single day? I wouldn't be surprised if your Elena came here tomorrow to look at the bodies herself," the man scoffed.

"Elena?" Robi asked.

"The Mother of the Nation? Your Elena, the leader's Elena…" the man said, as if explaining it to a schoolchild.

Their fates intertwined — both an Elena, both depending on Cenuşa.

Robi would have laughed if it didn't mean looking like a maniac.

"Are you fucking dumb?" he asked instead. "The person who wrote that letter! How many people do you think they told?! We need to be careful that people like you aren't ruining all the work that we laid out so perfectly!" Robi yelled, grabbing the man by his shirt's collar.

He didn't want to hurt him — God, he would *never*. However, he tried to make a lasting impression.

"F-fine…" the man stammered, as if choking.

Robi let go of the grip he had on the man's collar and snatched the letter from his hands.

"Lead the way," Robi ordered in a shaky tone.

He turned to Lizzie and brought a finger to his lips, telling her to hush. His cover was strong, and the possibility of holding Beriță in his arms was closer than ever.

The still air inside made his face scrunch, as the dust on the windowsills and the cheap washing liquid on the marble floor made him feel nauseated. The place smelt of death and unhappiness, even the midget looking as if his days were full of the sorrows and burdens of the world, leaning on his bald head like a knife.

"You know, I saw it too…" the short man coughed as they approached a tall door labelled *'CREMATORIUM'*.

"Saw what?" Robi covered his face, the heat on the other side feeling unbearable.

The old man shrugged.

"In your letter… the woman said she knew that some of the people were still alive," he swallowed dryly, taking out a handkerchief. "I did too. The people… some were twitching…"

The old man turned behind them and retched on the floor in the corner. He wiped his mouth with the handkerchief, his face covered in sweat.

"I am sorry…" he whimpered, a tear rolling down his face. "Your friends knew my wife, my granddaughter… they knew their names… so I didn't tell anyone, not even my priest! But God knows I needed to let it out, I couldn't bear it…" the man sobbed. "There was one man who I hear screaming… his horrible sound…"

The old man imitated a low cry, as if he were being burned alive. Robi wanted to hold his skinny figure and embrace the pain that they shared — the old man had a few years ahead of him, and they would all be full of guilt and grief.

"At least it's made me see something before it has even happened," the old man sniffed, pulling the door that led to the hot room open again.

"What's that?" Robi asked.

"What my screams will sound like when God makes me walk through the gates of Hell."

The old man turned his head and opened the hot room, letting the flames spit from beyond the crematorium's wall.

Forty-Two

Elizabeth

Bucharest, Romania — December 1989

Her eyes had swollen up from the heat and the dust — or perhaps it was the crying that did it. She had once prayed for opportunities like this to present themselves in the world, where she would document the real torment that most societies were shielded from. Little had she known that the path that led to self-destruction often came with a false, plastic valour; in the face of the great crematorium, her spine had bent itself forward in defeat, as she brought her knees to her face, and hushed away her crying.

Robi had gone in — *of course*, he had.

But it had been up to Lizzie and the old keeper to pull him out of the hot room; otherwise, he would have burnt himself severely. He had wanted to hold on to the rods of the big, metallic door that protected the flames from the rest of the rooms, maddened by the thought that his nephew had been burned away in a big pile of corpses. The image was enough to make Lizzie's stomach twist, as she scolded her urge to puke out her morning coffee, just as the crematorium's keeper had.

She sheltered her face behind the crematorium's stairs and underneath its roof, as if she were hugging her own composure. She had been waiting for Robi for ten — perhaps fifteen minutes. The crematorium keeper had asked her to wait outside by simply gesturing at the door and mumbling something, but she had understood anyway. Now, in the light of the grey sky and its thunderous roars, Lizzie found herself more awake than ever.

Her arms felt like they were being stabbed with needles and pins all over them, while her cold toes had gone entirely numb. And yet, the touch of cloth against her entire body seemed new and foreign, as if this had been a unique experience.

She thought of the young boy whom she had known for a very short time. The six-year-old who, in only a few weeks, had taught Lizzie the joys of writing with your left hand in a world where everyone wanted you to do it with your right. The struggles of playing with your toy train right before supper, making everyone trip on the carpeted floor. Even the small illicitness one could find in following their uncle out on the street, even when told not to.

The innocence of that boy had amounted to ashes that had been mixed in the room of the crematorium, with other people and their lives, all resulting in dust and old memories. Everything had been destroyed — all evidence except the paramedic's letter to Robi and Elena.

Not all.

She raised her eyebrows at the feel of her notepad resting behind her coat's front pockets, nudging her slightly. Then, with the swing of her arm, she rushed back inside to get Robi.

It was time to return to the Embassy.

Lizzie had to speak to her father — she just had to. Whether the Embassy and all the people inside it allowed it was a separate question. But she knew that if there was anyone who could have made this story accessible fast, it was Berkshire.

She showed her pass and Robi's to the tall security man at the entrance, then rushed into the Embassy's building. She nearly tripped on the stairs, which had a dark, black shine from the rainfall, her reflexes making her jump. Robi grabbed her arm, though, and the accident was avoided.

"Thank you," she patted him.

"You're welcome," Robi coughed, his face still stained with crystal-coloured tears.

She squeezed his arm tightly.

"I am sorry about what happened, and having to bring you back here. I know you want no part of it," she whispered, opening the big door in front of them.

Robi held it open for them both, as he tilted his head to one side.

"It's okay," he said, cradling the little jar that he had in his hand, a gift from the crematorium's keeper.

The dark grey ashy colour made Lizzie's stomach twist — but at least there was something for a funeral. It may have been a scoopful of sandy dirt, but Robi held it with the tenderness of rocking a newborn to sleep.

"I have to speak with Frankie, I must," Lizzie sniffed, parading into the Embassy's building.

"I know," Robi admitted. "It's the only way."

He nursed the jar under his elbow and took a step towards Lizzie. She grabbed the metallic rod of the staircase, trying to pull the weight of her body upwards, all the way to the top floor. The slippery soles of her heel did not help either.

"Here," Robi gave her a hand, which she accepted with a polite nod.

"I think Frankie can find a way to reach my father. I will send him all my notes. The things I have been documenting in the last few weeks. And Timmy? He is a gem, you ought to keep that one around, I'll tell you..." she whispered in his ear. "Do not lose hope, Robert. I promise you, this incident will get a lot of coverage."

And Elena, Ioana and Robi would live with more than just a half-full jar of ash.

Tim held out his palm again, as he had been for the last fifteen minutes. He grabbed the hammer from Frankie tightly once more, like a child helping his father out with a house chore. Lizzie wanted to burst out laughing at the sight of her little cousin doing something that required even the slight touch of manual labour, a vision unaccompanied by her close family and relatives.

"How much longer are you going to need me for?" he asked Frankie in a neutral tone.

"Not too long," said Frankie, who was standing on a small ladder, leaning on the Embassy's back door.

Under the roof of the office building, there was a shallow opening between the top of the roof and the brick lining underneath it. On the bottom, a thin layer of mould had started growing. But to hands that had been used to labour, who had even plastered walls, smelt the cough of cement after pouring it from a bag, and knew how to measure with the eye alone, the wall had obviously been put up recently. Whatever they had tried covering up with the old, damp brickwork was not going to fool people for too long. From the buzzing of wires inside the wall and the guards' frequent returns to the other side of the building, Frankie assumed that there must have been a functioning telephone there for unknown reasons.

"How the hell did you even spot that place? Do you walk with your head like this?" said Tim, stretching out his neck upwards mockingly.

"No, Collins — I am simply a more attentive journalist than you are. And I am older", said Frankie, fishing for the hammer.

He had seemed to find a new type of annoyance in 'Timmy' — a sentiment that hadn't poked him since he and Lizzie had left London together. Tim swore under his breath while handing him the hammer again.

"There's so much bird shit up here, Christ!" cried Frankie, laughing.

Tim gazed up at him, bored.

"Frank, we need to go, come on," he urged.

The people inside could have approached this opening any time, Lizzie realised. There was too much at stake — if the Embassy had kicked them out for being nosy in all the wrong places, they were as good as homeless, in a city where havoc ruled.

"Hand me the wooden plate," said Frankie, ignoring his comment entirely.

Tim did as he was told, and Frankie proceeded to unscrew the metal bars above them. The opening, as small as a trap door, was large enough to accommodate a person. The look on Tim's face was priceless as Frankie proceeded to pick at the side of the opening, trying to expand it. The weight of the bars collapsed underneath the bricks, allowing the opening to become wide enough for both Frankie and Tim to jump through. Robi, who had been silent until then, began clapping slowly, one thud at a time.

"Come on," Frankie laughed.

Lizzie looked mesmerised by the old telephone that rested on the desk in front of them, the door locked from the outside. With Robi prying close by, they were sure that there was enough time to reach Berkshire in London. Tim handed Frankie the notes — he gave a low nod. It was time to call her father and tell him everything.

After letting the phone ring for about forty seconds, Frankie was ready to back away. Tim raised a palm, though, urging him not to.

"Hello?" said a familiar voice on the other end. "Go for Ross," he barked.

Lizzie let out a delighted laugh — she palmed her mouth in surprise. For a second, she thought that tears of joy would escape at any moment, but she avoided the relief of contentment.

"It's me," Frankie coughed. "I am calling from the British Embassy in Bucharest."

Then there was a long pause.

Too long.

"You blew it, didn't you? You blew your cover and everything?" Berkshire demanded, sounding upset.

"What?" Frankie raised his voice, outraged. "Trust me, this was the safest thing to do."

"I will trust you when you put Lizzie on the phone," Berkshire said.

Frankie sighed, handing the telephone to Elizabeth.

"B-Berkshire?" she asked, her heartbeat fastening.

"Lizzie? What is going on there?" her father demanded.

The high-pitched tone of his voice sent an alarmed concern through her, masked with the unwillingness to speak further. Lizzie told him then — everything that had happened in the last few weeks. She tried using codes and phrases that would be hard to decipher if someone had bugged the telephone. But ultimately, she had to tell Berkshire about *everything*. She couldn't believe how long she had waited for the phone call — she told him about the Revolution and how the dead had been burnt and forgotten at the crematorium in Bucharest. She saved the details about Dragoș, Robi, and their families for now; those things could have waited.

The danger couldn't.

"Hmm..." tutted Berkshire. "That's all solid, Elizabeth. Just not something I would want to print right *this* second," he said.

Lizzie heard his lighter flick, as she assumed he was smoking now.

"What?" she asked.

"You can write all the tales yourself when you come back, Elizabeth. This whole thing will settle soon, you'll see. Call me when they have imprisoned the king," he coughed, referring to Nicolae Ceaușescu. "Until then, anything you tell me is speculative. Unless, of course, this movement is affecting one of our own."

Is he being serious?

She had known her father and people like her father for the better half of her life — getting into journalism meant that she had always been aware of how the story could be twisted into different versions of the same thing. More often than not, the original tale would be left out entirely from the final product. To most, this was a harmless method of selling something — at the end of the day, journalists, like any businessman or salesperson, were also selling a product. Perhaps the most valuable product of all — *information*.

Raw and unfiltered when exposed to first-hand, but processed by a hundred different lenses when a journalist touched it. What Berkshire was suggesting wasn't unusual at all — it was a fabrication of falsehood, perhaps a pile of misinformation. But not a new technique in the slightest.

"You want us to make shit up? Really? With everything that we already know?" Lizzie could feel her blood boiling.

Berkshire sighed.

"You have to seem more vulnerable. Like you're not calling me from the safety of an Embassy — you don't seem like someone who is in the trenches,

Liz. It would get passed down like ordinary news. Something slightly more exaggerated and… it might just sell," Berkshire said.

"People got cremated," Lizzie replied. "After being brutally murdered. By the army. What can be worse than that?"

"I'm sure you'll think of something," Berkshire said.

Before Lizzie could question him further, the telephone went flat, falling dead in her restless palms.

Forty-Three

Robert

Bucharest, Romania — December 1989

The crowd had gathered under Nicolae Ceaușescu's home, like ants demolishing a great molehill. Although they had been unsuccessful in convincing Ross Berkshire in England about their experiences, something larger was at play here.

He held the ashes in his jar closer to his chest, trying to shield them from more trouble. Of course, it was absurd — but he had to hold on to the one thing in his life that he could take back to his sister, an explanation for the pain that he had caused until then. Beriță was the one thing that they *had* to hold onto, the reason for everything that they were doing here. He had grieved his little nephew in the most uncommon ways — and closure didn't seem anywhere near him yet.

Robi looked up to the sky, waiting for the great dictator to come to the window and make his little speech, like a schoolchild reading a poem off by heart. He had very little faith that the crowd would be impressed by anything that he had to say, especially after what the nation had endured in the last few days.

"What are we going to do?" Frankie leaned in and asked him, looking at him with foolhardy temptation.

Robi eyed his clenched fists and the little bump on his forehead that looked like a lump the longer he stared at it. Frankie placed a firm hand on his shoulder.

"We cannot cause a scene, no matter what Ross wants. This isn't a movie, like one of your American stories… Frankie, we *cannot* be like this," Robi wanted to toss away his hand from his shoulder.

Frankie tutted.

"Geez, you're all the same," he laughed manically. "The real world — the journalism world," Frankie articulated, "That world relies on certain improvements from exterior factors. If one of *us* isn't in the middle of the turmoil, no one will care! *Why* don't you get that?"

Robi wanted to smirk, but his lips betrayed him, curling into a puny frown instead.

"Because there's an '*us*' now, right?" Robi asked. "It was always about that '*us*'? Was it, Francis?" he demanded, hurt.

Frankie's eyes widened, their spectacle dimming away with each passing moment.

"You *know* that's not what I mean… things shouldn't be like this. But you know as well as I do that *this* is how they are. The rest of the world won't give a fuck about a bunch of random people who got injured, killed, or worse in an attack happening miles away from their homes. It isn't relevant to *them*. However, when someone can associate with a parent, a brother, or a son, it is a completely different story. And it shouldn't be like that," Frankie shook Robi's shoulders. "It shouldn't," he paused. "But it is."

Frankie's arm pulled Robi's head forward, sticking the younger boy's forehead to his own.

"It shouldn't," he repeated. "And I wish I could help you otherwise."

"I know," Robi whimpered, trying to shut away the tears. "I don't want to tell lies, I am tired of them — I don't have it in me."

He let the man pat his back, holding his skull between thick, bone-hard fingers.

"You won't have to," Frankie promised, letting go.

The crowd had grown wilder by the minute — Robi could feel the thunder in his bones. The people cheered and shouted, roaring at the sight of their *beloved* leader. He saw Frankie standing close to the camera operators, and Tim holding out the notepads under his elbow, both in position. The idea was to capture a photo of someone vulnerable (to which they had all agreed that Lizzie was an appropriate subject) in a way that made them look like the *real* victims in this whole situation. The attack had to feel personal and up-close, a feeling that a Romanian's image would never satisfy the people in the West.

He had heard of it before — the way history had been manipulated and served on a silver platter for the wealthy to digest, without causing too much discomfort. The journalists weren't there to make people uncomfortable — *no*! Their fundamental role, Robi had concluded, was to show the version of a story that *their* audiences would buy and talk about, tossing their words across the dinner table like the side dressing of a salad. It would become regular gossip, just another 'trendy' thing to worry about. And now, he had the privilege of experiencing the media's exploitation first-hand. Not just the exploitation of himself, but also of his friends — he doubted very much that these journalists were even aware of this manipulative thread that they were sewing the story of their lives with.

Still, he comforted himself. *They will talk of Beriță, of the military operation. Of everything else that has occurred.*

The heaviness on his chest seemed to lift with each passing thought, as he gathered closer to his fellow revolutionaries. All of the facade would be worth it, he agreed. If, and only if, Beriță's story and the tales of the crematorium would be told.

There, in the pit and darkness of the Palace, he waited for Ceaușescu's beak to poke out in cowardly movement. For a split second, he drowned away the sounds around the space, focusing all his willpower on the man that had emerged from behind the maroon curtains — in this light, the dictator looked different.

Ordinary.

The old man was possibly older than Robi's own father, the old Professor who awaited them back home. His frame was frail and pale, the man's gaze focused on a point in the distance that Robi could not distinguish. He was dressed in black attire, as if he were attending someone's funeral. Perhaps he, too, was looking at the crowd and everything else that came with it. This deafening glory would be the old man's death, he swore. And just as the act of impure sin and butchery invaded Robi's mind, he could have sworn that the leader had looked at him directly, keeping his eyes on him.

I see you, he spoke. *I hear your thoughts. You're the reason Beriță died.*

Nicolae Ceaușescu raised a hand, and the crowd's screams turned into mere murmurs.

"Dear comrades and friends, I address you today to express my full appreciation for the work done by our people in the Socialist Republic of Romania!" the man whispered weakly.

Robi felt almost sorry for him.

Somewhere to the right, he saw the foreigners trying to jot down notes about the atmosphere around, as Timmy held out a small camcorder, nuzzling it behind his coat. He pointed it at Lizzie, as if he were holding a gun, targeting it at her core.

"Hey," Robi tried calling out, wondering if he could help them in any way.

If it meant causing a scene, God knew that he had waited for such an occasion for a long time! He placed his arms around his body, trying to warm up his palms. Then, as if he had instigated a chain reaction himself, he heard the people shouting as clear as daylight.

"*Libertate*!" a group of young men chanted.

Then, his ears heard the familiar sound of home.

"Timișoara! Timișoara! Timișoara!" called the young people all around. "*Libertate*!"

Freedom. His city.

They know.

He searched for his friends' gazes, and was relieved when Lizzie looked back at him. Her furrowed look was all the reassurance he needed — Tim looked back too, as the group of young people caused more havoc in the square.

In front of him, Robi saw a few girls holding up a Romanian flag with a large hole carved in its centre, and could distinguish their calls for freedom from the rest of the crowd. Robi stared at the man on the balcony, who looked frightened at the look of the people below.

"*Vă rog să păstrăm liniștea și ordinea*! I ask you to maintain your calm, and respect the order," Nicolae Ceaușescu coughed.

The crowd grew more violent — everyone was screaming, shouting, and some people were attempting to throw things at the balcony. Robi ducked, trying to shield Timmy's camcorder.

"Record everything," he shouted, holding Timmy's shoulder. "You want your clip?"

Robi stood back up, looking at Frankie and Lizzie. Without judging his own movements too much, he pushed Lizzie out of the way, shaking her body, as if he were violent and enraged.

When he got a glimpse of her expression, she looked more confused than startled — at least the camcorder had gotten a part of the footage that Lizzie could send to Berkshire and the newspaper in England. They would have their *outrageous* attack on the journalist, even if it wasn't real.

He looked around, measuring the panic in the place. In the far right corner, he spotted the *TVR* camera operators unplugging their devices and running for their lives from the students and young people.

Nicolae looked livid — he raised a fist in the air, as if protesting.

"This is a coup organised by foreign agents who want to destroy our country's independence and socialism!" he shouted.

Then, as if he had never been there in the first place, Nicolae Ceaușescu vanished back inside, for what Robi suspected was the last time in a long while.

Forty-Four

Nicolae

Bucharest, Romania — December, 1989

The sound of the women singing made his heart ache — the cavity of his chest felt wide all of a sudden, and although he stood still, he could've sworn that he was falling. Nicolae rubbed his temples with greasy fingers, patting them against his fur coat afterwards.

The women had made an exception for him, as they repeatedly told him; the gypsies were specific about who they were going to let on their grounds, and Nicolae's presence alone could be considered a disruption by many. He respected what they asked him to do, sitting with his legs crossed a few feet away from the giant bonfire that they had lit up.

Pagan nonsense.

But perhaps it was worth trying, his wife had told him. Put his prejudices about the gypsy women and the witches that had helped her over the years, despite how repulsive he found the Romani people. Maybe it was time to look beyond the opinions he had formed of these communities, the ones that he deemed below himself. A young girl who had been appointed as Nicolae's companion leaned in every once in a while, explaining the ritual and the procedures to him in low whispers. The woman in the distance chanted, her hands waving in the air.

"We release your pain to the birds, let the world cry through their song, so you may see what is to come," the young girl next to Nicolae translated, her voice melodic.

The rest of the women who had cornered Leana began chanting their own songs and prayers, sending a chill down his spine. A herd of crows flew up to the sky from the crown of the trees — Nicolae flinched at the sight of the dark birds that carried even darker sorrows upon their wings. Instantly, he was flooded with regret; perhaps he should have never come here. The journey back from Iran had been tiring, but nothing would send his mind to rest until he could be certain that this wasn't the beginning of the end.

The woman near the fire called out, sending Leana deeper into her seat than before. Nicolae could see his wife's body language: the agitated shakes in her hands, the way she trembled like a leaf under the bonfire's mighty light.

"What did she say?" Nicolae asked the young gypsy girl next to him.

She leaned closer, the clinking of her jewellery echoing through the open space.

"Can you not see? The spirits of the dead in Romania knock on your door, and blood comes down the road," the young girl spoke, her own voice crystal-clear.

Nicolae shuffled anxiously — *what was the witch doing?*

The woman's voice carried through the walls and the spaces between, while a sharp yodel escaped her throat. The rest of the women chanted, and after a couple of minutes, the young girl had left her seat next to Nicolae empty — her bare feet ran towards the bonfire, as she joined the others in song.

Nicolae felt protective all of a sudden, as he wrapped his fur coat closer to his torso; he sensed the chill of the December air howling through the barren homes, piercing his bones with each puff. The icy drops of water frozen above his head resembled the spikes of a great crown made out of the sharpest thorns, growing outward into his own skull — he was the king of the dead, and the leader of the damned.

Leana looked at him fiercely from over the rows of wooden seats, her gaze hot. Her face seemed unlike her own, to which Nicu blinked — she resembled a great orange-red demon from the gates of Hell, staring at him with hatred. Her lips parted, as if trying to make a sound, but he couldn't hear her. Nicolae stood up instinctively, looking around. He wondered whether the witches' spells and castings were affecting his dear wife, who was accustomed to visiting them so often.

Suddenly, Leana's eyes widened, pouring blood out of them instead of tears; Nicolae leaned down in fear, wishing that the gypsy women would stop their horrible singing. He covered his eyes, afraid of the demon that had possessed Leana — the light of the bonfire looked like the flames of Hell — burning hot, calling his name with each spit.

Nicolae hadn't realised that he was on the floor, screaming at the sight of the demon who had leaned in closer. Leana's deformed face dangled over him, his screams stuck in the centre of his throat.

"You will die," the demon whispered, making Nicolae shut his eyes tightly.

When he woke up again, Leana was standing by the fire around the singing women, looking into the void — there was no sign of the demon. The rest of the women hadn't even noticed that he had fallen to his knees as if in prayer, the demon's voice warning him of something that he wanted to consider impossible.

But as he looked at the trees, the demon's blood-filled eyes painted the crimson hue of the trees, the whistles of the wind carrying his own whisper. Three words, echoing clearly in his ears as if the Devil's voice was his own.

You will die.

Nicolae tapped his forehead with the damp cloth, the ice beginning to melt from the heat in his palms.

"You're making a mess," Leana took the ice from his hands and took it to the freezer in the suite again.

He used the end of his sleeves to wipe the water residue off the table in front of him, rubbing it thoroughly. His head didn't hurt as much, although he could still hear the gypsy women's song in his head.

Would he ever get away from their haunting sound?

"Leana?" he asked, making his wife snap out of the daydream that she seemed to have been lost in.

She gave him a hum of acknowledgement.

"Do you think we went too far this time?" he asked, his voice cracking a little.

He masked his recollection of the demon with bloody eyes with a cough, but Leana watched his body language as if he was exposed under a microscope.

"Is this about the demon?" she asked, looking at him with an amused smirk. "I told you, there was nothing there!"

He grabbed her wrist like a beggar beseeching her for her last penny, trying to make her listen.

"I know what I saw. It was a warning, Leana," he said, feeling like a madman. "Have we gone too far this time?" he repeated.

Leana took his chin in her hands, looking at him with a straight expression.

"For the Romanian people, nothing is too far, Nicu… all of this is for their own good — order, discipline, a world free of chaos. *We* are the victors in this game of cat and mouse, don't you see?" she tried consoling him, her face hardened.

Nicolae nodded; he had forgotten all his promises about not being a coward and about being the most outstanding leader that the Romanian people had ever seen. One crack in his confidence and it had all evaporated, like a snowflake melting on the windowsills of an old church.

"We'll get over this," Leana promised, urging him to stand up.

He felt relieved at the sight of people gathered underneath him for his speech; for reasons unknown, he couldn't fathom giving another speech after this one. He tried searching for the possibilities of the future, all the things that he had looked forward to in the years behind him. But no matter how much he looked, like a blind man in the darkness of a basement, all he could find was one thing — nothing.

There was *nothing* left.

He gathered the strength to walk to the door, where Florin waited to guide him to the balcony, where his usual speeches took place. The young man greeted him politely, and Nicolae watched him offer Leana an arm to lean on. She accepted quietly, without even giving him her usual devilish smirk.

"What do we do if they begin a riot?" Nicolae asked, imagining the angry mob beneath his palace, ready to come for him.

"The television people are all over the place... if they try anything, we will make sure it doesn't get shown all over the country. We'll shut it down instantly," Florin promised, laying out the rest of the plan for the speech.

"Good," Nicolae coughed, feeling like he was regaining the confidence of his former self.

Before Iran, before all this, before the rebels in Timişoara — he had been someone much more different. A man deemed untouchable, a strong figure for the nation. Now, despite the crumbling of the foundations of his regime, he still believed in the best. He was still a fighter and would continue being one until his last breath.

The balcony hall was full of military and police personnel, people who were there to control any situation — it made the weird feeling of a void growing in his stomach ease a little, as he unclenched his fists and looked at the open door of the balcony. In the crimson of the curtains around him, Nicolae could sense the demon staring at him. The murmur of the crowd beneath him sounded like a hive of bees buzzing in his ear over the whisper of the demon, who had been chasing him since his evening at the gypsy witches' home.

He shut his eyes before stepping into the balcony, the crowd beneath him shouting and cheering — whether they were cheering for or against him, Nicolae couldn't tell or differentiate.

The air around him seemed to grow heavy, his arms resting at his side. It took every vein in his body to raise his hand as a salutation to the crowd below, their cries growing louder with each step. He could spot a few Romanian flags underneath him — the clean, complete version of the flag, unlike the one with holes carved in its centre that the people from Timişoara were using in their movement. In the far right part of the square, some of the people were also holding portraits of him and Leana's faces, stuck on top of spikes and wooden sticks as if their heads had been impaled on them.

The Winter Sun made him nauseous — the weather was freezing, but the heat of the ground beneath him made the atmosphere warm and muggy. Nicolae touched the microphone, leaning in closer. He urged the crowd to calm down with his other hand, realising that the mountain of people was also gathered there for something else.

You will die, the demon laughed in front of Nicolae, its head dangling over the balcony like a corpse.

He blinked slowly, raising a hand again.

"Dear comrades and friends, I address you today to express my full appreciation for the work done by our people in the Socialist Republic of Romania!" he croaked over the cheers below.

He heard the crowd cheering, and someone in the distance whistled. The people accustomed to his speeches — he almost smiled. But to the left of the crowd, Nicolae spotted trouble even before his eyes were entirely focused on that side of the square. The entire space could have very well been a stadium or an arena, a place where people were ready to battle each other in his name.

Who would be the victor?

Nicolae's eyes widened at the boos and chants that had switched around as insults addressed towards him. People chanted "*FREEDOM!*" and "*TIMIȘOARA!*" above the few groups that had obviously been orchestrated to manage the situation in the face of a rebel escalating everything. And yet, there seemed to be more people shouting against him…

He tried to get feeling back into his numb jaw, swallowing dryly before he could speak his following words.

"Starting January 1st, we will increase wages by 100 lei for workers and pensioners!" Nicolae coughed, trying to mute every hum and buzz that screamed in his face.

The demon watched him, smirking.

Nicolae turned to see Leana — her face was livid, painted over with anguish. He looked down at the people who were whistling and singing the banned anthem, a few of them trying to interrupt the national TV broadcast. Instantly, someone — a *Securitate* agent, no doubt — pulled the plug of the broadcast cameras that were standing in front of Nicolae. He guessed that they were doing that with all the cameras; the nation didn't need to see this kind of undisciplined vagabonds.

Nicolae raised his fist in protest, knowing that people could still hear his voice on their televisions. He had blinded them from the torment of those fighting below his home, begging him to be crushed by the mob like an insect — but they still had his voice.

"This is a coup organised by foreign agents who want to destroy our country's independence and socialism!" he shouted, noticing how the mob beneath was attacking the military.

He could only hear whistling, insults, chants of freedom and other nonsense about Timişoara — even after Florin had dragged him back inside the hall. When the other man finally let go, Nicolae took off his hat and sat down, still feeling the waves that shook the very ground that they relied on.

Nicolae spat out in disgust.

"What happened out there, eh? Who gave those imbeciles permission t-to… People started to shout about the citizens of Timişoara?" Nicolae shouted, seeking an explanation.

Somewhere behind him, the demon chuckled like a madman.

"Sir, people are still outside. They have started to riot, even the television seems to be against us now," a young man across the hall told him, his glasses sliding off his big nose from nerves.

Nicolae palmed his face. He looked at Leana, who stood by the other man almost maternally, her arms to her side. She remained calm and calculated, unlike all the men in the room, who were split between those whose heads were hanging in shame and those who were waiting patiently for more instructions.

"Ask General Milea to continue using any kind of force. It's time to get to work," Nicolae said, standing up.

Florin leaned in closer to him then, and Nicolae paused.

"The mob won't let you remain safe in here for too long. The helicopter is ready for you," he said.

"I will be with you in a moment… take Leana."

Florin shook his head.

"I was told I can't go. For your safety — they're giving you someone else… someone from Milea's group, I think," Florin nodded.

"Very well," Nicolae nodded, leaving.

Less than a step behind, the demon followed him down the halls of Cotroceni Palace, dancing in the candlelight's shadows — for what Nicolae knew as his last time there.

Forty-Five

Dragoș

Timișoara, Romania — December 1989

When Nicolae Ceaușescu's broadcast got interrupted, Dragoș had jolted up from the couch, almost throwing little Ioana over the edge. He had held on to his cigarette box tightly, as if he was holding someone's hand in his from the rising anxiety.

"He left," he extended his arms, as if demanding an explanation.

Elena, who had just entered the living room with her sheepskin coat on, took a seat next to her daughter. She held Ioana's head on her shoulders, as if forcing her to fall asleep.

"I need to go," he said, taking out a cigarette from his box, pacing around the room like a madman.

Elena flinched at the words — she looked up at him.

"Please don't," she begged. "I can't do it anymore. Please," she broke down in tears again. "Losing another one."

"You haven't lost Robi, Elena. He will return soon, I am certain," Dragoș said, raising his hands. "I know what you will say. That he didn't call. How could he? He is busy, Elena, don't mourn him just yet," he added.

He had comforted the woman countless times in the last couple of days, and he would have done it all over again if he had to. But he couldn't hide behind closed doors forever. Things were changing quickly, and he had started to wonder about the other people in his line of work again.

For all your hard work.

"I'm sorry," he mumbled awkwardly.

Elena tutted.

"Be careful," she sniffed.

"When will you return?" Ioana asked Dragoș, forcing a smile.

"Tonight," he promised. "Don't think I forgot about your promise to me. Eminescu and his *Scrisoarea a III-a*... I remember these things."

Dragoș picked up his coat from the armchair, handling his cigarette box with care.

"Let me know if there's anything from Robi," he said, then made his way out into the frozen streets.

The day had gone more smoothly than he had expected. There were talks of the military joining the people's side soon, instead of the dictator's, from the whispers that Dragoș had caught in the square. People had nothing but speculations, but even these were worth a lot, fuelling the hopes of the ordinary.

When he returned home — or instead, what he now called 'home', for a short while, Dragoș wanted to do nothing more than crash down on the Professor's armchair. He had a few leftover bites of *mămăligă* in the fridge, along with a side of heavily salted *telemea* cheese waiting for him.

He arranged it all nicely on a plate, then cut the last tomato that he could find on the kitchen counter. Its top was crowned with mould, and he had chopped it with a scowl on his face. He took a few strands of green onions and put them on the plate, as if it was garnish.

There. This could be a Parisian meal now, he smiled to himself. Although he would've much rather had his mother's Christmas *sarmale*, and the *ciorbă de burtă* that Geta used to make at *Revelion*.

Then, he opened the Professor's cabinet above the stove, reaching his arm all the way to the top. He could feel the old jar's lid as he pulled it towards him. He nearly dropped it on the stove, but caught it just before it could touch the counter's edge — it had been a close call.

Dragoş undid the lid of the jar, bringing it to his nose.

Chamomile. With a hint of something else.

He poured some hot water over the tea leaves, letting them rest on the bottom of the porcelain teacup. It was almost perfect, he grinned — now, he just needed to sit down on the Professor's old armchair, and eventually fall asleep on it.

With a steady hum, Dragoş put the TV on and turned all the lights in the apartment off, waiting for it to switch from stand-by to the regular channel. He cut off a slice of his salted cheese, blended it with a spoonful of *mămăligă*, and took a bite of the sweet tomato and the bittersweet garnish.

It tasted like heaven.

After finishing the meal, he grabbed his tea from the counter, letting it rest between his arm and hand. He would've almost drifted off too, if it wasn't for the sound of the door unlocking that awoke him in a frightening stance. He turned the TV off with a quick flick and got out of the armchair. For reasons unknown, he wondered whether what he was doing was considered trespassing or not.

Robi?

He didn't dare say it out loud, though — he crept into the kitchen with silent footsteps, putting his plate on the counter. He hid his cup of tea somewhere in the sink, letting it blend in with the other dirty dishes.

Let it remain forgotten, he agreed.

He almost opened his mouth to call out Robi's name in anticipation — with a trembling upper lip, he coughed silently.

Then came the laugh.

A woman's.

Dragoş ducked under the kitchen table, trying to watch from underneath. He bent his knees, praying to hush his silent sighs and breathing. He could hear the woman's laugh growing louder with each step, bringing her closer to the kitchen door. Then, a man's voice interjected, their conversation indecipherable.

The woman turned the light on in the living room, coming close enough to the kitchen door for Dragoș to see her frame from behind. He let a short sigh escape his throat, a breath.

No, it couldn't be, he swore. But of course it was. He wished that it was anyone in the world but her — her loud tone of voice was only a reassurance for what his heart already knew.

"My God, Professor… you are amazing, truly," Florica Lupu laughed, throwing her head back.

Dragoș's ears went warm, his head fuzzy from the adrenaline. He wanted to jump and crawl, and strangle Florica for what she was doing to the poor old bastard. The Professor and Robi, by extension, were both in dangerous territory now. Only Dragoș could do something from the inside of the apartment, without causing too much of a scene.

"*Doamnă Lupu…* my dear Miss Lupu, you are just as amazing." The Professor's arm went to Florica's shoulders, then he ran it all the way down to her back.

False pretences, perhaps, he told his bewildered heart — Dragoș tried calming down, but it was no use.

Then, he looked back up from under the table and watched the Professor's hands go all the way down to Florica's bottom as he tightened his grip around one of her cheeks. She laughed back at him in excitement, then grabbed his chin in her hands.

"You are a mystery, my dear Professor. Who would've known that you were such a thrill to be around? *Un mister…* that is what you are," Florica giggled under her breath, in a way that Dragoș had known to be genuine.

He crawled from under the table all the way to the back window — the apartment was high enough for him not to perish from a fall. And besides, the giant oak tree was close. One leap to a branch, and he could be out and gone…

Who are you fooling, Dragoș?

No. He wouldn't lose hope just now. There was always more left of that.

Dragoș twisted the handle with his left hand — the squeak it produced felt like a thunderous roar that could be heard hundreds of miles away. Every breath he took felt like the echo of a whale's snoring.

But it was probably all in his mind.

All he needed was a couple more minutes to gather the courage that he needed to leap out and…

"Robert?" the Professor called from the kitchen door, reaching for the light switch.

Dragoș's body stiffened — he needed to jump right then and there. His hands grew sweatier by the second, and his back arched forward. Suddenly, the height of the apartment felt nauseatingly tall, and Dragoș's heartbeat began suffocating him. The bright, white light devoured him every inch, eating him alive.

He was exposed. And there was no more jumping now.

Fool.

"*Tu*? What are you doing here…" the Professor mumbled, as if talking to himself.

Dragoș heard the gun clocking first — he had avoided looking at *her*. But he did it anyway. Florica's soulless eyes watched him from head to toe in a shooting position, as if he were a stranger. He raised his hands in the air.

"I am Robi's friend… I am with him — he's coming back soon," he lied.

Florica laughed loudly.

"*Acuma sunteți prieteni, eh*? Now you are friends? First, you were the idiot who had to follow him and keep tabs on his activity. *Prostule*," Florica shook her head, slightly loosening her grip around the gun.

Dragoș's pleading gaze pierced through the Professor's face. He couldn't let Florica win him over with more lies and nonsensical flirting.

"Sir, I promise you… I never informed anyone about Robi's activity," Dragoș said, looking at Florica. "We wanted a different life, both he and I. And the riots and protests… they have already started," he put his hands down. "Florica, you can't frighten me anymore. You'll see. *În curând, nici nu veți mai exista*. You will cease to become relevant."

Florica scoffed in a bored manner. She almost rolled her eyes in frustration.

"Professor? *Cum doriți să procedăm*? How would you like me to proceed, sir?" she asked, straightening her back.

Dragoş's face grew pale. The Professor was in no position to be tricked. *He* was.

"Y-you're with *them*..." Dragoş whispered.

Florica grinned at him.

"Believe it or not, even I get my orders from someone," she smiled sweetly. "When they assigned you to watch Robi... who do you think gave the orders? Their father knew they would be a magnet for trouble, one way or another. *Nu am crezut...* I didn't think you were a cretin, too, Dragoș. Siding with them in this little game of cat and mouse... I was very hurt, you know?" Florica put on a mocking pout. "It started with the radio. Then the Professor had the honour of finding out about the foreigners when they came to Romania. Because I was the one who interviewed them, fool. Remember?" Florica explained.

Then he started laughing — it all made sense. Why Dragoş was watching Robi closely, as per Florica's request. Naturally, someone else was also doing his job. He never thought that it would be Robi's father that he would worry about, though.

"*Pizda mă-tii*," Dragoş swore in between his laughter, his knees nearly giving away. "Oh, you're something else, Professor... like our lovely Miss Lupu here said."

Dragoş's face grew hot, his vision becoming blurry. The Professor stepped closer to him, pulling out his own gun from his back.

"*Hai băiete*. Come on, boy, let's take this to the living room. Talk it out like civilised people," the Professor urged.

Dragoş did as he was instructed, bursting out in laughter. He felt the cold tip of Florica's gun touching his head.

"Come on now," Florica said as they all entered the living room.

"You know he died? Your grandson," Dragoș blurted out. "The body was taken away from Timișoara..."

The warm light in the living room was a welcome change from the harsh kitchen light. At least he was going to die with a nice view in front of him.

"What are you saying?" the Professor asked, facing him.

The older man looked at him, puzzled, studying his face for a hint of falsehood. The man had been around the terrorists of the *Securitate* long enough to recognise all the signs. Dragoş could only cry between the forced laughter, looking at his face in defeat — the truth seemed always to be harder than the made-up illusion.

Even Florica had lowered her gun, looking at the Professor's panicked expression.

"Beriţă. The imbeciles took him to *Cenuşa* Crematorium in Bucharest. Did the boy not even deserve a funeral?" he asked, breathing heavily. "How many young boys did you kill, Professor?" Dragoş added mockingly.

The Professor looked around the room as if he were lost, not taking Dragoş's words into account at all. The old man was experiencing a form of shock, which made him vulnerable.

Any moment now, Dragoş thought, sniffing in and wiping the salty tears from his hot cheeks.

"*Ferească-mă sfântul.* May the Lord have mercy," the Professor murmured, hesitation clouding his movements.

Dragoş watched him, then took a step forward. The Professor's instincts may have been slow, but he had noticed the man before it could have been too late for him.

"Coward! Liar!" the Professor shouted, pointing his gun once again, forcing both Dragoş and Florica to duck.

The sound of the gunshot was loud enough to make Dragoş's ears ring — the window breaking behind him seemed like a whisper in comparison. Dragoş leapt over the Professor, while the old man dropped the gun on the floor, frozen.

Dragoş's arm was wrapped around the old man's neck, and he held the Professor's own gun to his head. He gave Florica a grin, who was back in position. For once, Dragoş saw a mixture of fear and surprise on her face.

Not so sarcastic now, he smiled.

"Put the gun down," Dragoş instructed. "*Altfel trag în el.* I will shoot him," he added.

The Professor stood perfectly still, almost like a mannequin.

"Dragoş, Dragoş..." Florica tutted. "I thought you were a clever boy."

Dragoş walked backwards, aiming to get to the bathroom. He turned around the room, his gun glued to the Professor's forehead, while Florica followed him around like a lost puppy.

"*Nu înțeleg*... I don't understand. What was your purpose? Putting me in the middle of Robi's problems?" he asked no one in particular.

"*Ca să îl îndrum*," the Professor choked under Dragoş's weight. "I wanted to guide him. To learn how not to make the same mistakes that I had once made."

Dragoş kicked the bathroom door open and jumped in. He shut it before Florica could rush in, and shot her in the shoulder from the ajar space between the open door.

His heavy breath grew heavier by the second as he knelt. He watched Florica from the keyhole — seeing her scream in agonising pain made his stomach twist in knots. The Professor tried to loosen Dragoş's grip around his neck, and he finally gave up. The old man had little to no strength left; the shock had made him shift enough, and after all, Dragoş was the only one in there with a gun.

"*Dobitocule*," she whispered. "You fucking idiot!" Florica screamed louder.

He watched her pick up her own gun, aiming it at the door. Dragoş ran into the bathtub, which stood on the other side of the bathroom, parallel with the door. Even the biggest bullet couldn't hit him sideways.

The Professor ducked on the bathroom floor, hiding from the woman. He crawled towards Dragoş, who kept pointing the gun at his head, his hands shaking. Then, everything started becoming fuzzy.

It all happened much quicker than Dragoş had anticipated. Florica's heel had pushed the door open with a swing, making Dragoş's aim switch from the Professor to the woman. He had looked her in the eye, watching her bloody shoulder stain her yellow coat a bright red colour. He pulled the trigger, closing his eyes tightly.

But it was her bullet that hit him first.

Forty-Six

The Professor

Timișoara, Romania — December 1989

The gunshots had deafened him for a while, as he held the edge of the bathtub tightly. He dared look up from the sage marble floor and saw Florica lying in front of him, her head bent at an unorthodox angle. Blood poured down from her back, a perfect hole carved right through her skull.

Dead.

He didn't need to search for her pulse to be sure of that. It seemed strange to think of her lifeless body as something that, in its own way, looked beautiful. She was still herself — this was the only thought that offered him some shelter, when the sight of so much blood made him feel sick.

He was ready to vomit right there and then, the memories of a different floor and a different pile of blood and dirt clouding his brain like an early Winter morning's fog.

He looked at Dragoș, whose chest was growing red by the second.

"Did she hit your heart? Did she get it?" the Professor asked, shaking madly.

Still, he felt hopeful. Dragoș's gasps for air made him think bizarrely relieved. This was all going to be over soon enough — Revolution or not. The young man shook his head, panting heavily.

"N-no," Dragoş choked. "I don't think so," he added, pointing his gun at his head.

The Professor heard the satisfactory click of the gun, resting against the bathtub. He was on his knees, as if in prayer — but there was almost nothing that he could think of to say to God in that moment, despite being so close to smelling the sweet perfume of death.

It was lingering around that room right there, but also in the entire apartment. The whole building, the city — Romania itself reeked of death and decay, and the Professor could smell it under his nose as if the stench was nothing but his own shit and piss.

"Oh, come on, Dragoş. *Nu mai are rost.* There is no point. You will never survive this," the Professor spat, his legs giving way.

He sat down on the tiles, looking at Florica's still body. Dragoş whimpered, pulling his weight upwards. The tub had been slippery enough, and the pain was making him weaker by the second. The wound was never going to heal if the bullet was still inside.

He will die before he can make it out of here.

"I am terribly sorry," the Professor tried putting on a honey-like tone. "But under no circumstance can I let you leave this place alive. Neither one of us can, really."

"One of us can," Dragoş said, breathing heavily.

Dragoş looked him in the eyes, without a trace of fear on the young boy's face. He was only a little bit younger than his own Elena. A little older than his Robi.

"Tell me, is it going to be the wounded man who doesn't know how to apply pressure to the wound, or the man who doesn't even have a scratch on him?" the Professor asked, taking off his glasses.

Dragoş pushed the opening of his bullet wound, applying pressure on it. Still, the blood was flowing quickly. The Professor tutted.

He couldn't bear the sight of Florica's dead body — but the cruelty of his condition didn't let him look away from her face either. The perfect shape that the bullet had left behind, the blood on the marble floor, and the way that she looked like she was almost in a deep sleep, more peaceful than ever.

"Remember what I told you when you first came to my apartment? I asked you whether you were certain that this was the life you wanted. The kind of risk you were inviting into your life," the Professor coughed.

He eyed the gun that had fallen to the side in the motion of her fall, and he crawled to get it. Now, with Florica's gun in his hand, he was in a better position than the other two, by far.

"You would've pulled the trigger by now, Dragoş. But you're a smart boy. Even you know that I am the only one who can leave," the Professor said. "I am not an evil man, Dragoş. No matter what you think of me."

The gun going off again, and in such proximity, made the Professor scream. Then came the pain of the injury inflicted by the bullet, its metallic structure passing through his chest cavity.

"Try leaving now," Dragoş said, trying to get up from the bathtub. "I am not finished with you yet, Professor. You should know that it is your fault that Beriță died in the way that he did. *Your* people did that."

The young boy sniffed, his face growing teary again. The Professor's vision kept growing blurry, but he managed to distinguish the shapes on the boy's face.

He is struggling, he told himself. *Struggling to get out of here. Or we're both in Hell, and I am the Devil.*

Then it hit him.

No. I have already been to Hell. And back. And I made a deal with the Devil.

This was the last thought that the Professor remembered forming coherently, before the sharp pain of his leg bleeding out put him in a deep state of unconsciousness.

The year was perhaps 1954. Or was it 1953?

He had been so young back then! Perhaps even younger than nineteen. And the memory had played inside his mind like an old film reel so many times that time had imprinted its alterations on it. The only thing that he remained sure about to this day was that everything was hot, and the cart of corn had been way too heavy for him and his brother.

They had been leaving the field, or perhaps going to it? No — why would he be taking a full cart of corn *to* the field? Of course, they were going home.

And oh, Bernard was such a sweet boy! This much he could also recall with clarity. His kid brother, the only boy in the village who would have followed him to the end of the world. The other kids called him *'retardat'* — a retard. They chased him around with wooden spoons, throwing rocks at him from behind bushes.

But kids have a habit of being cruel, and Bernard had to accept it. If only he could've kept that stupid stutter out of his mouth, perhaps they would have been kinder to him.

Bernard, Barni, Beri, and finally *Beriță* — all the nicknames he had for the young boy, who at seventeen looked more like a skinny thirteen-year-old kid. Since the crops had been transported out of the country in increasing quantities, most farmers, like their own parents, kept very little food for themselves. The result had not only been malnourished children like Bernard, but also an increase in infant mortality rates.

So really, he was carrying the corn cart on his own, while his brother lingered around him like a shadow.

"C-c-c..." the boy stuttered, looking at the red sky. *"Cât mai durează, N-nico?* How much longer?" Bernard asked impatiently.

He had become so tired from the heat and the whole walk — he swallowed dryly.

"I don't know," he answered honestly. "I think we still have three kilometres to go, Beriță," he told his brother.

The younger boy sighed.

He couldn't tell whether they had walked for another five minutes or fifty, but by the time they were at the well that led to the village, they were both sweaty and dusty, craving a mouthful of cold water. Beri had been the first one to lift the rusty bucket of water, fishing it out with weak, bony hands. He made a cross — a habit of their beloved grandmother, despite how it was greatly frowned upon in some parts, and sat down to drink.

Nico — later nicknamed 'The Professor'- remembered the metallic taste of the water, wondering even then if they were *supposed* to drink water that looked and tasted like *that*. He had seen the mountainside of Herculane three Summers ago, where the clear water that came directly from the springs tasted clean and fresh, without any odour. Not like the well in front of them. Little did he know that he wouldn't see it well or its wretched water for another six months after that. And he would beg God to bless him with a glass of anything except what he was going to drink and eat, and shit and sleep for the remainder of that time.

"C-c-c-can I d-d-drink m-more?" Beri asked Nico, trying to snatch the bucket out of his hands.

"*Nu*," Nico warned. "You'll grow drowsy, and you will make me carry everything on my own. Like you always do," he grunted, throwing the bucket back into the well.

He heard it clink against the rocky walls, then splash into the dirty water.

"P-p-please, can we at least get some rest? *Am nevoie de odihnă*," Beri complained, kneeling on the hot soil, his palms against the concrete.

Nico sighed.

"Fine. But not for too long," he said with an alarmed look on his face.

Any day now, he told himself. Any day now, the police would come looking — that is, if their cousin Dani had snitched on them. Which he was more than confident about. Dani didn't keep things to himself very long, and the discovery of the yellowed excerpts from his personal diary would be no different.

The art of making it — a forgotten cup of tea, he had written. *The art of making a forgotten cup of meaningless, cold tea. That is pretty much what the ambition of our great leader Nicolae Ceaușescu amounts to. And soon, it shall all dry out completely.*

A couple of lines which he deemed harmless, among other confessions that he couldn't tell his priest about. And by all logic, they were completely innocent; no one was getting hurt. No one was to see them except him, and perhaps Beri — it wasn't like he was going to write a book on it, put up posters about and call Nicolae Ceaușescu '*ceașcă*' in public. The metaphors of forgotten cups and remembered cups were things he liked dwelling upon in his own solitude. Until cousin Dani had walked into his room, flicked through his books and pages with greasy fingers still stinking of *untură*, everything had been fine.

"What the fuck is this?" his cousin had asked, fitting the crumpled papers in his apron. "You are trouble. Big trouble," cousin Dani had said, holding his neck with his meaty fists.

"Give them back. Please," Nico had begged, remembering uncle Doru and aunt Marica's loyal commitments to the communist party.

His limbs had grown cold, while his face had lost its colour almost entirely — and not just because of Dani's tightened grip around him.

Every day since had been pain and struggle, leading up to the anticipation of the day that someone would finally knock on his door and make him go to prison for a while. The local one was just a nuisance like the others, usually imprisoning people who did not deserve to be there. He imagined himself behind those bars often, wondering how bruised and beaten he would return home, having to explain to his mother that all of it happened because of his own stupid ambition.

He had been looking over his shoulder for a long time, but it was never enough. The anxiety was continually rising to his throat, making his mouth as dry as the soil that had hardened under the red rays of sunshine.

He shut his eyes, resting against the well.

"N-n-n-n..." Beri stuttered again like a simpleton, and he opened his eyes. "N-n-nico?" he repeated, getting up.

Nico did the same. He could see it from a distance where they were standing — the car. He kept wishing that the well behind him was deep enough to shelter him from the incoming danger, but not *too* deep. There was a fine line between drowning and swimming. Seeing a car in these parts was as unusual as seeing an elephant in their cornfield.

He couldn't recall whether he had even seen one until then.

"You have to run," he told Beri, holding his head to bring his focus on him. "Listen to me. Run. Go home."

"O-o-o-okay," Beri said, shaking.

"Run," Nico repeated, waiting for the worst.

He watched his brother run away, holding his heart in his throat — something was buzzing in his ear, and he tossed it off his skin with a slap.

When he looked up again, the car had accelerated all the way to the path that led to the side alley, a way paved to the well leading to the main village.

The car's engine stopped suddenly, and in its absence, Nico noticed its sound for the first time. The roar it produced was loud enough to drown away the sound of his own blood rising all the way to his temples, while Beri ran behind him with the speed of a hound. His brother had thin, long legs. Perfect for getting away when needed.

His knees gave way when the stranger got out of the car, accompanied by cousin Dani.

"*Stai pe loc, băiete*," Dani warned. "Don't you move, boy. This won't take long."

"What won't?" Nico asked, kneeling protectively behind the corn cart.

Cousin Dani ignored him.

"Get the younger one," the stranger ordered cousin Dani, and he followed the instructions.

Nico saw Beri running into the *pădurice* behind them, hopeful that they had lost him. The young boy was innocent in all of this. The last thing he needed was to lose both of his mother's sons in one day.

The stranger got closer to him, and he flinched — the corn cart was not nearly big enough to protect him.

"Come on, boy. Don't make this tougher than it needs to be, eh? Your cousin Dani means well… we are taking you somewhere you'll learn about the world. A beautiful place," the man insisted, his voice almost calm.

"N-no," Nico stuttered, remembering Beri again.

"No?" the man asked, amused. "You don't get a choice, Nico. Get in the car."

How does he know my name?

"No," Nico shouted, pushing the cart of corn in front of him, and bolting in the opposite direction.

The other man was stronger, taller, and had all the crucial senses far more developed than Nico. He grabbed the boy with steady hands, holding him tightly in place.

"Now, Nico," the stranger said, revealing a small pocket gun from inside his trousers. "Get in the car, or your brother eats the next bullet that comes out of this."

Nico whimpered, kicking his legs — the heat, the corn, and his brother seemed to be the least of his worries, as he fought to be out of the man's grasp. He remembered the way the little bugs that he and Beri used to play with as young children would agitate their arms and legs whenever they were rolled up, their stomachs facing the sky.

That's what I look like right now, he tried biting the man's hand. *How much longer till he crushes me with his rock?*

"I found him!" cousin Dani called from the other side of the path, holding Beri with one hand.

The skinny boy seemed to lose all of his power, as he didn't even try to break out of cousin Dani's grip. He watched his older brother, the stranger's gun suddenly pointing to his forehead.

"Now, Nico…" the man began again. "Will you behave now?" he asked.

Nico nodded. Tears stained his face, and he tried to breathe through his mouth. The man let go of him, as if feeling his struggle.

"Get in the car," the man said, calmer than before. "Both of you."

The boys did as they were told, wiping off dust and tears from each other's clothes and palms before getting in the car. The stranger got in the driver's seat, while cousin Dani sat right next to him. After about forty minutes of continuous driving through the rural Romanian roads, Nico dared speak — for both of their sakes.

"Where are we going?" he asked, his throat dry.

The well seemed like a distant memory then, something he couldn't even draw out on paper properly if someone asked him to.

"A young boy like you deserves the best education, Nico. The words you wrote on those papers…" the man tutted. "Some of it is shameful, some is pretty bold. And some is what we call treason. Do you understand what treason means?"

Nico nodded, as did Beri.

"It means I am in trouble," Nico wiped his face with the back of his hand.

"That's where you are wrong," the stranger claimed. "You need to be re-educated, taught about the ways of our country. And our leader. Do you know that he is feeding poor orphan boys, children the same age as you? And you believe that such an honourable man's legacy amounts to nothing, Nico?"

Nico shook his head hesitantly.

"You must be taught," the man repeated. "Taught about what kind of great things this country has to offer — in exchange for loyalty. You will learn what that is, too, Nico. Very soon," the man smiled.

Next to Nico, Beri coughed.

"W-w-w-when… w-w-when are we going to go home? To see o-o-o-our m-m-mother?" he asked.

"Oh, very soon, dear boy," cousin Dani said for a change. "You have to stay with your brother for a while. I have taken it upon myself to make sure that both of you get the best education in the world."

The stranger slammed the brakes suddenly.

"How do we say when someone does something nice for us, boys?" he asked.

"Thank you," the boys answered in unison, and Nico turned to look outside the window.

"Where are we going?" he repeated his question.

The man could have turned his story around a few hundred times to avoid giving a straight answer, but Nico couldn't be fooled so easily. The stranger sighed, and cousin Dani pushed a smile.

"Pitești," the other man said, trying to contain his own enthusiasm about the place.

When Nico woke up again, it was dark, and he was sitting in the back of a damp cell, his face against the cold tiles. The bars in front of him were rusted and old, and there was nothing but a small bucket in sight — for pissing and shitting, he assumed. Apart from the tiny window above him, small enough to fit a house cat and nothing bigger, there was no sign of other sources of light.

Some school.

"Beri?" he called out in the darkness, wondering whether anyone could hear him.

"Nico?" Beri's voice spoke back to him, and he turned to face in the opposite direction.

It took his eyes a few minutes to adjust to the newfound darkness, but he could make out the shape of his brother's body after a while. For reasons unknown, he looked even frailer than usual.

"Are you okay?" he asked.

"Y-y-y-yes," Beri answered, kneeling. "I w-w-w-was awake… through it a-a-all."

Nico didn't understand – then Beri proceeded to explain. It turns out they *were* in prison. However, this is a unique type of prison. They were running new ways of educating inmates here — things that would one day be deemed *revolutionary*. That is what the other guards said upon their arrival, while Nico had passed out from heat exhaustion.

"You're telling me that they try new methods here?" he asked. "Like locking us up in the dark with nothing more than a bucket," he sighed.

"I-I-I… I think they a-a-are d-d-doing experi… experiments on i-i-i-nmates," Beri confessed. "I-i-it's what t-t-t-they s-s-said."

"Who?" Nico asked, but the bang of another cell's door made him jump.

Instinctively, he ducked, pretending to be asleep.

"Get up, boys!" a loud man called out. "*Haideți, puturoșilor*! Lazy bums," he shook his head.

He approached the cell doors one by one — when he got close to Nico, he could see that the guard had a long moustache, not shaved for a good couple of months.

Both he and Beri moved without hesitation — no matter what cousin Dani and the stranger believed, they were both good, disciplined boys. They were going to be well-treated in this new prison in Pitești, where experimental methods were being used to educate the inmates again. They would be out in less than a week for their amazing behaviour. Nico promised it in his head.

The guard paced up and down the hallway, all the way back to Nico's cell.

"Strip," he said with a smirk.

"*Ce*? What?" Nico asked instinctively.

The guard's eyes widened. He unlocked the cell door with the tiny twist of a golden key, which had been hiding inside his pocket until then.

"You don't say '*ce*' to your elders, boy..." the guard spat. "Did your whore of a mother not teach you that?"

The guard gave him a punch — hard and on his face.

"*P-p-poftim*? Pardon?" he corrected himself, taking a step back.

"Look at you... stuttering like your retard of a brother," the man said, running two fingers over his moustache. "Now strip."

Nico did so without any hesitation, trembling from head to toe. It was only when he took off his underpants that he discovered the stain of warm liquid that had escaped from within him in the guard's presence.

In the first few weeks at Pitești Prison, later remembered as *Experimentul Pitești*, Nico and Beri had faced various forms of beatings and bruisings from each of the guards. Beri was more vulnerable than Nico on most occasions, mainly since the guards had grown accustomed to making fun of his speech issues and his underdevelopment compared to other boys his age. There were belts and whips, ropes and chains, and various other instruments that Nico had never even seen in his life. They all kept shouting at them, trying to make them confess everything that they had ever done in their lives that could be linked to values that went against the system.

"Confess!" they barked, hitting them harder each time.

The most bizarre part was that Nico could see the pleasure on the guards' faces each time a boy would cry out in pain, or would start bleeding out from all the beatings. It was as if they were *enjoying* the types of torture they were exposing the boys to.

On his sixteenth day (or seventeenth, Nico couldn't tell exactly), he could feel his strength evaporating into thin air, despite not doing anything apart from being forced into beatings. He had heard many tales from other inmates, things whispered from wall to wall and from cell to cell in the unholy hours of the night, when the guards would finally leave them be for a couple of hours.

There were men whose soles were burnt after being forced to walk on coal, others who said that they witnessed fingers and toes being chopped off with chainsaws, although he was yet to experience such an occurrence. There was a middle-aged gentleman who resembled cousin Dani almost perfectly, save for the fact that the poor sod had no tongue. One of the guards (who was retired now, to Nico's pleasure) had cut it out one night after hearing the man singing an old church song. Nico knew the words to it, too, as did most Romanians; how could one be so offended over someone's *singing*?

All this for reasons like 'fascism' — Nico had heard that word once before, but it was said in the company of a friend of his who didn't quite know what it meant either. None of them did. And somehow, he was being accused of it, along with the rest of the men, some of whom were old enough to be his parents or grandparents.

"Confess, stupid boy," the guard had hit him one last time, and Nico remembered praying that he would die then and there.

One of the worst parts was that they never let them *die* — it was always enough to make you feel like you were about to go, but not enough actually to send you over the edge. This was worse than Hell.

"Fine," he raised a trembling hand in the air. "I'll tell you."

The guard put a thick leather boot on his face; his ugly, blond hair shone in the pale light.

"What did you say?" he asked, pressing his boot to his lips.

"I will confess," Nico shouted with all his might.

Then, he was taken to a medical assistant (the irony of it!), where all his blood was cleaned off, and he was even stitched up and given a few pills to soothe the pain. He hadn't seen his brother since the morning, which was alarming him slightly — the boy was so fragile that he could break any day now.

After a couple of minutes of waiting outside the room where he was given medical care, a man approached him. A younger, newer guard. He had never seen him on a shift before. He rose to his feet before the man could utter a word.

"Follow me," the guard said, looking a little surprised.

Nico obeyed, eyes glued to the ground. When the guard stopped, Nico almost bumped into him.

That's what I need. More reasons to get a beating.

"Sir?" the guard asked, letting Nico into a room that resembled an office. "*Domnule?*"

To Nico's great surprise, the man sitting at the desk was none other than the stranger who had driven him to this 'school' all those days ago. He stood in his chair, just as calm as he had been on the day that he had kidnapped Nico and Beri and brought them to this horrid institution.

"Leave us," he told the young guard, pointing at Nico to sit down on a chair in front of him.

Nico sat down in front of the man, feeling humiliated and small all of a sudden. After all the things he had endured, he still felt like it was his own fault — for not hiding his papers better, for writing them in the first place, for being with Beri when he knew what was going to happen, for not telling anyone…

The list only kept growing.

"I heard you are ready to be a good boy," the man spoke to him as if he were a four-year-old child, and not an almost-grown adult.

"I am ready to confess," Nico said, trembling.

"That's a *good boy*," the stranger said, leaning in.

He touched Nico's cheek with the gentle touch of a guardian or an older sibling, patting his skin with his fingers. He made mock kissing noises as if he were cradling a toddler.

"Now," he stepped back, eyeing Nico from head to toe. "What did you do?"

Nico paused, shame rising to his cheeks and painting them red.

"I said horrible things about our great leader. The honourable man Nicolae Ceaușescu, who is responsible for making us the great nation that we are today," Nico wiped his tears with his dirty sleeve, not for the first time that day.

"And?" the stranger persuaded.

"And…" Nico repeated dumbly. "And I was a traitor. I didn't know about loyalty," he said, repeating the man's favourite words.

"And what else?" the man insisted, putting a palm under his own chin.

He smirked.

"I was a good inmate, I promise. I haven't done anything else. My b-brother and I… we were both good here. This entire time," Nico rambled like a madman.

I lost the one shot I had, he thought, wishing he could punch himself in the face.

"You wrote something," the other man began, pulling out a stash of papers and old journals from underneath his desk. "You wrote a lot of shameful confessions in your notebook, boy. Things you should *never* do," the man insisted, looking embarrassed for him.

"W-w-what…" Nico wondered, trying to remember every small swing of his pen across his old notebook.

"You wrote this," the stranger said, pulling out Nico's journal from the desk, as if by magic.

Fucking Dani.

"You said you like touching yourself, Nico," the man laughed cheekily. "When you think of 'the beautiful face that was carved, as if, by the moonlight', you wrote it right here," the man pointed at the notebook, revealing its contents to Nico.

His black, neat handwriting was accompanied by a red, blood-like colour staining the line underneath his words. They had annotated his journal like it was a precious novel, forbidden to the regular individual to read, instead of the useless piece of garbage that he considered it.

The stranger laughed.

"Why are you so shocked? Is this not yours?" he asked.

"I-i-i-it is…" he admitted.

No point in lying to someone who already knew everything about your past.

"And here…" the stranger pointed. "You start talking about God and his mercy on someone as bad as you!" he laughed. "You didn't confess to me about these misguided actions, Nico! About the young boy who wants to escape into his stupid little books because God is too harsh on him and this country, and who cannot contain his sexual needs? What do you think you are? Some sort of Sadoveanu?"

"I'm sorry," Nico apologised between tears, not sure *what* he was apologising for. "I have done a lot of bad things in my life… I will do anything, please…" Nico begged, getting on his knees.

"Get up, boy," the stranger warned. "Come on, Nico."

He did as he was told, nearly losing his balance on the chair.

"Let me show you what we do to believers in this facility, Nico. What every 'man of God' will eventually have coming," he said mockingly, getting up.

Nico did the same, not daring to make eye contact with the older man. The stranger who knew him inside and out, perhaps better than his own mother. The stranger led him out of the room and down the corridor, making turns here and there — Nico couldn't find the courage to make sense of the directions around him. The institution was far too large, the time was far too little, and the eyes poking out and looking at him were too many.

The stranger walked up a set of stairs and into a long hallway full of cells like his own — the stench reminded him of his old home's pig sty, and he hated to admit that he was growing more and more used to it day by day. Unwashed inmates like himself stood behind the bars, looking at them from a safe distance.

When he approached the third cell, Nico saw a man in his thirties crouching down on the ground, peeling off his skin from his back. He was disturbed by the new person, and he couldn't help but continue looking at him. Holding up a shiny new piece of skin covered in pink blood and hair, the man put it inside his mouth, swallowing it in one go. He smiled at Nico — revealing an ugly, toothless grin.

He felt his stomach twist and turn, despite not having a single piece of real, solid food from the moment he had come there. Apart from the guard's scraps, very little was on offer — and it seemed that people on this side of the prison didn't even have access to that much.

The stranger stopped in front of a cell, perhaps number twenty-four or twenty-five, and he took out a key. He unlocked the cell doors, letting out two men who were wearing nothing more than a pair of old shorts.

"Time for our special dinner, boys," the stranger said, leading them back the way that he and Nico had just come from.

On his way out, the inmate from cell three waved at Nico.

"*Poftă bună*," the inmate laughed, and Nico was sure that the man was entirely out of it.

They walked from one side of the prison to the other for about ten minutes, even venturing out into the yard to shorten the distance to the other half. Nico hadn't seen the sunshine since the day they had been brought there — feeling it sting his skin was pleasant and unfamiliar, all the same.

They reached a massive open hall that resembled an event room, and Nico got a proper look at the men's faces. One of them was short and a little rounder at the middle — although he looked fragile, even by his standards. He was trembling like a leaf, partially from the fact that he was almost naked. The other one was skinnier and leaner, with a pair of grey eyes that watched all movement with intensity.

"Strip," he ordered, the same way that the guard with the moustache had done to Nico on his first day there.

The men followed instantly, standing barefoot and naked in front of them.

"Now, Nico," the stranger looked at him from a couple of metres away. "Here you go," he said.

He pushed an empty, rusted bucket at him with his left foot. Nico caught it, looking inside.

"Take a piss, Nico," he ordered. "Or a shit. Whichever one suits. I promise we won't watch," he laughed under his breath.

Nico had questions — starting with *what* was wrong with everyone here? He distanced himself a safe length away from the rest of the group, trying to shelter himself as much as he could.

"Don't touch yourself, Nico. We will know," the stranger said, bursting into laughter, as if he had just made an intimate joke that only he and Nico would understand.

Nico sighed under his breath. He stood in the corner of the room, leaning over his bucket with weak legs. After a couple of seconds, he managed to squeeze out a few drops of dark yellow piss, and he put his trousers back up.

He returned to the others with a shameful look on his face and a stench that would mark the room for a few days.

"What a boy," the stranger laughed, patting Nico on the back, and turning to the other two men. "Now, boys, Nico here is new, and we have to teach him about what happens to people who reject the fundamental truths of the world. Lost people. Like you," he smiled. "There is still hope for him, isn't there, hm?" he asked no one in particular.

The stranger took out a couple of objects from a cupboard that Nico hadn't even taken into account until then. He handed Nico a glass and held a thick, silver chain in his hands. On it, a pendant in the shape of a star dangled left and right, the stranger's fingers twisting slowly in the air.

David's star.

Nico had only seen a picture of it in one of his old history books. He recognised it as the symbol of the followers of Judaism, recalling what was happening to people of that faith less than a decade ago. In most parts of their country, such discrimination was still in practice.

The stranger coughed.

"Eli, *tu primul*. You first," the stranger said, pointing at the taller one.

The man stepped in front, looking pale and sickly.

"When we found you, you were wearing this as a symbol of your love for your faith and people, weren't you?" the stranger asked.

The man — Eli, shook his head and began shaking violently.

"No?" the stranger asked.

"Yes," Eli said. "Yes, I was."

The stranger applauded, and the echoes of his claps travelled through the open hall.

"You can have your necklace back. But you have to swallow it," he laughed.

Nico turned to face him.

"You have to swallow the *pendant*. The star and all," he repeated. "When you shit it out tomorrow morning, you can wear it around your Jew neck again."

The stranger sounded calm — and yet, he stepped in front and kicked Eli in the stomach. Eli fell to the ground, trying to regain his balance.

"Nico will make sure you swallow it," the stranger said, handing Nico the necklace.

Its weight felt burdensome in his hands, holding much more than met the eye. Nico's hands began shaking as he approached Eli.

"Please," he began, kneeling in front of Nico. "Please, don't…" he cried.

Nico looked at the stranger for some guidance — but the man had already moved on to other things, pouring Nico's piss into the glass that he had taken out.

"It won't kill you…" Nico tried reassuring Eli, taking the pendant out.

The star was big enough to feel like a lump in his throat, but nothing that a little force could bring down. Nico was trying to calm him. The fear and pressure would only exacerbate the situation.

"It *won't* kill you," he repeated.

"No talking to the inmates," the stranger warned Nico, his voice steady and calm.

Eli looked at Nico with the pleadings of a slaughtered lamb, begging him not to put him through the pain of swallowing metal. Nico insisted, handing him the star.

"Please," he mouthed.

Eli hesitated long enough, whispering prayers under his breath. He grabbed the necklace, and with one sudden move, he put the pendant in his mouth, ready to swallow it. As expected, the size of the star, which was half the size of Nico's thumb, made it hard for him to breathe. Eli held his throat tightly, gasping for air, and trying to undo the necklace.

There was a moment of relief in Eli's eyes after a few seconds, as he finally managed to swallow. He was ready to take his first gasp of fresh air — that's when the bullet hit him. Nico's bloodstained face looked at the stranger, who was pointing a gun at Eli's dead body — he had been watching him struggle long enough.

"Jew scum," he spat on Eli's bleeding head. "Now..." he wiped his gun.

The other man in the room was on his knees, his bare body facing the ground.

"P-p-please..." he begged the stranger, while Nico tried collecting himself off the ground.

"This is Andrei," he said, pointing the gun at the other man and looking at Nico. "Patron saint of Romania. Or some bullshit like that, they tried telling us in church long ago."

The stranger waved his gun around the room.

"Andrei liked telling people during Communion that praying to God for the lost cause of the country and leader would solve all their problems. Can you believe that, Nico? I think we deserve our own Communion here, don't we?" he picked up the glass of piss.

He waved at Nico, who could barely rely on his knees to aid him in taking a few steps towards the man.

"*În numele Tatălui, și al Fiului...*" the stranger began, beginning his session of mock Communion. "Come on Nico."

He insisted that they all prayed in unison to make the Communion valid. Nico and Andrei followed his lead, despite the mistakes he made in the prayer.

"I give you the blood of Christ," the stranger said, handing him the glass of piss and clocking his gun. "If you drink it all, I'll spare you from the fate of the Jew."

Andrei looked around, the same look in his eyes as Eli — they begged Nico for more, but he was just as helpless as any of them.

"N-no," Andrei said, trying to look directly at the stranger.

"Come on, Andrei, we don't have all day," the stranger insisted.

The man shook his head, and the stranger was growing impatient.

"Nico. Make him take the blood of Christ. Be a good Christian brother to your fellow inmate," he said calmly.

Nico held the glass with trembling hands, resenting the smell of its contents just as much as the other man.

"Make him drink it, Nico," the other man insisted.

Nico shut his eyes tightly, pushing the glass onto the other man. Andrei tried fighting back, but the stranger jumped in Nico's defence this time, holding his hands behind his back.

Nico pushed the entire glass down the other man's throat, feeling his own body begging him to throw up what wasn't even inside of him.

"God boy," the stranger praised him.

The bullet hit Andrei from the back, staining Nico with the blood of others once again.

Later on, Nico was returned to the cell, accompanied by a different guard, and a new present awaited him inside. Wrapped in a newspaper, Nico found an old book by an American author. In neat, red writing, an inscription was made on the front page, staining the following pages in the same devilish crimson.

"In the face of wolves, you can run — or you can join the pack."

Everything from that day on resembled a fever dream that Nico could recall bits and pieces of, not sure how much of it was real. He knew that the stranger would often visit his cell, sometimes when he was asleep. He would frequently wake up with a new book waiting for him by the door.

There were things he wished he could forget — the countless times that another Eli or another Andrei would be introduced to him, and the stranger, or some other guard, would make him do things with the purpose of 're-education'. Whether they meant their re-education or his own, he never asked. It's not like they were handing out grades and certificates with the promise of a good life.

He resented the times when another inmate had to make him do something against both their wills, but they always failed. In many ways, he was always the winner in every test or challenge that the Pitești Phenomenon had in mind for him.

They made him do it to Beri, too — with purpose, of course. He liked justifying it to himself; perhaps this was all right, and everything that they were doing would pay off one day. His stuttering fool of a brother would often find his head in buckets full of excrement, sometimes forced to consume them as if they were his meals for the day. They had made him walk on burning coal a couple of times, too, but luckily, Nico wasn't there to witness it. The worst he had seen was the night that Beri had not even told him anything about his day, the opposite side of his cell, sitting as quiet as a graveyard.

"Beri?" Nico had insisted, hiding his face guiltily.

The silence made his ears hurt. After a few moments of it, Nico bent down.

"*Mama* told me we will get out of here soon," Beri said.

The mention of their mother made him jump to his feet.

"When did you see her, Beri?" he asked.

"Today. And yesterday. *Mama* is always waiting for me after the guards make me do things, you know?" Beri claimed, clapping his hands. "She is the one who helped me stop stuttering. You didn't notice?"

Nico watched him in the darkness.

"What are you saying? Are you out of your mind?" he said, but Beri was already asleep.

That was the last time that Nico ever had a proper conversation with his brother.

After their release and the rounds of bargaining that Nico had made with the stranger and all the other guards at Pitești, the rules were going to be obeyed. The *Securitate* had agreed to let him pursue his interest in foreign books and philosophies under *their* control. He would go on to the University and become a professor, get paid good money, and never know hunger or fear again.

His re-education was successful, which is what cousin Dani bragged about six months after the hot day when he had kidnapped his family members and taken them to Pitești. The boys' mother was just pleased with the fact that her boys were home (especially when cousin Dani had handed her forged certificates from a 'school' in Pitești).

Beri never exceptionally returned home — sure, he was physically back home with their mother and everyone else. But the signs of his newfound madness were as evident as the prison that they were all living in. Perhaps Beri was one of the few people who knew that the extent of torment went beyond the walls of the Pitești Prison.

"At least his stuttering is gone," their mother had claimed happily, watching Beri refuse to get into the bathroom without Nico's supervision.

On the first day of the corn harvest month, Nico had gone into his brother's room to get him ready for the big event ahead of them. His mother was *already* there, as if she had sensed that her baby boy was no longer with her.

Beri's lifeless body was hanging from the ceiling, a chair pushed away from where he was tied up. His face was blue and swollen, his eyes bloodshot.

When the Professor woke up, he looked around the bathroom for signs of Dragoș, who had been bleeding out moments ago.

How long did I pass out for?

He looked in the bathtub, but the boy was not there. A trail of blood led all the way out of the bathroom and towards the kitchen door. The Professor leaned forward, trying to find him — the exhaustion, pain, and tiredness were making him sleepy.

His eyes shut again, passing out as before.

He never woke up again.

Forty-Seven

Robert

Timișoara, Romania — December 1989

There had been something tremendous about leaving Bucharest and returning home on the night train, as Robi sat down alone in the darkness. There was a silence inside him which haunted him more than the loud voices outside — at least one of them had an end, while the other was growing inside him like a parasite.

Saying goodbye to the foreigners had been simple enough. He hadn't lingered around for too long after the dictator's speech — apart from the jar of ashes sitting in his bag on the train, Bucharest had nothing else left to offer him. The weather was growing chillier by the day, his entire body feeling numb. Christmas was around the corner, he realised, which meant that all the good kids (who coincidentally happened to be the ones with wealthy parents) were finally going to get rewarded.

None of that for Beriță. Not that he ever had a lot to open on Christmas Day, though.

The thought made him open his eyes in terror, and he stared around the train, which had come to an abrupt stop. A man in front of him got up from his seat, looking around the compartment.

"What's going on?" he asked him.

"We are outside of Timișoara. A village called Remetea Mare. We need to walk from here, they are saying. No more trains going into the city," the man explained.

Robi sighed, getting his luggage from the seat next to him. It was almost dawn, and the fog outside was growing thick and heavy. He straightened his back and decided to walk out, directly on the tracks, where a few other people had done the same.

With his head hanging in the posture of an archer, Robi walked through the fields leading from the villages of Ianova and Remetea Mare into the city, praying that a Christmas gift would be around the corner.

The smell made him want to puke at the door — at least the people inside hadn't been in there for more than forty-eight hours, otherwise the entire apartment building would have been unbearable.

When Robi found his father's dead body, the place was entirely untouched. Apart from the dead woman who was in the same room as the Professor (the bathroom, which made Robi wonder why she was there in the first place), the apartment was as neat as ever. He didn't cry or scream, nor did he feel afraid. This wasn't a forced entry or the job of the *Securitate*. Unless...

Where is Dragoș?

Robi had found a few dirty plates and cups in the kitchen, the food in them starting to rot, just like the corpses down the hall. From the bathroom to the kitchen, a thin trail of blood led him all the way to the kitchen window, which had been left open. The front door showed no signs of blood or any other disturbance.

"Dragoș?" he whispered, looking at the oak tree in front of him.

Unless his friend had jumped out of the window, hanging off the thickest branch of the tree and down its trunk, Dragoș had no other way to exit the apartment. Of course, he knew that the place would be surrounded from all sides if the woman inside was a danger. More often than not, the *Securitate* had more than one person on the case. But why the Professor? Why now, after years of his father remaining clean?

Had Dragoș murdered his father and the woman?

No.

Dragoş was many things, as was the Professor. And perhaps the strange woman as well. But *none* of them seemed like killers. Not in the light that he had found them in anyway.

Later, he told the police (or the man who had shown up in civilian clothing, claiming to be police) that he was returning home from visiting a relative outside of Timişoara, and that he found his father's dead body in the bathroom. He hadn't even spoken to his sister yet, thinking of how this turn of events would play out on her. The officer responsible for the case shook his head and looked at the bloody tiles.

"Too many cases like this. Disappearances, random murders. I am so sorry for your loss," he said. "The army is on our side now, you know? They turned on them... we are finally going to get peace."

Robi looked at him.

"You're not joking?" he asked.

"No, no... I wouldn't dare..." the man put his hands up.

Robi visited Elena not long after. She only wept quietly, then retired to her room. She didn't utter a single word.

"Dragoş?" Ioana asked him, her eyes searching for clues and answers.

Robi only shook his head. His friend was nowhere to be found. Not in the neighbourhood, not at his old home, and not at the usual places he would go to. For a few days after the death of the Professor, Robi would often see Dragoş's face around the city — the trees, the wind, and the river all called his name.

But Robi could never catch *him*.

On the second day, the police officer revealed more to Robi about the mysterious circumstances of his father's passing.

"The woman... she was *Securitate*," he lowered his head. "There are other things... your father, he was involved with them."

Robi put a hand up, asking him to stop.

"Leave all the papers here. You've done enough," he offered, letting the man go.

It all made sense.

In the corner of the living room, he watched Ioana listen to every phrase that the police officer had uttered.

So much for sparing her innocence.

Christmas Day came sooner than Robi had expected, and there was still no sign of Dragoş. At two o'clock in the afternoon, just as Elena was setting up the table for everyone, the long-awaited gift was delivered to the family. It was broadcast on television, shown across the entire country for everyone to watch.

On the 25th December 1989, at precisely 14:50, Robi, Ioana, and Elena watched Nicolae and Leana Ceauşescu get executed on the national news.

Forty-Eight

Nicolae

Romania — December 1989

The helicopter had been in the air for about an hour before the pilot finally stopped turning back at them again and again, and actually uttered something of importance.

"We're almost out of fuel," he screamed, his voice sprinkled with panic.

Nicolae looked at the place below them, and his stomach twisted again. He was never fond of heights, despite being up there in the air so often. He turned to Leana, who was murmuring something under her breath.

"We should've stood at Snagov. Hold our ground there," Nicolae rubbed his palms together, avoiding the sight of the ground.

Leana shook her head. Their brief landing on the ground, about a mile away from their lakeside home, was not enough to help them plan.

"We were going to be arrested by the lunatics, Nicu. You are aware of that, right?" Leana said. "We should land where we can, and get the aid that is made available by the military. We can get shot down in the air if someone else sees us here," she suggested, pretending not to care about what came next.

The truth was, they were both frightened. Their children had gone into hiding, as well as their sworn allies.

Cowards. We cannot be seen doing the same.

Nicolae nodded at the pilot.

"Just land here. Where are we?" he asked.

"Titu, in Dâmbovița," the pilot shouted over the sound of the helicopter's blades chopping through the air.

Nicolae nodded again. He had been in those parts before. There was a military base a few miles away, where someone could have granted them protection. Instead of hiding, they would be saved and respected by people whom they could trust. In the back of his mind, Nicolae wondered whether Florin should have come with them instead of this pilot and the other people who were there to help them escape the Revolution situation.

In less than ten minutes, the helicopter landed next to a few patches of land and grass, cornering the field that guarded the small town of Titu. The surroundings had a few trees and bushes scattered here and there, enough to hide the helicopter that had just landed in one of Romania's quietest areas.

Leana waltzed out of the helicopter, holding the arm of the pilot. The young boy exchanged a few words with her, while Nicolae traced the ground with his eyes. They needed to reach Târgoviște, which was swarming with troops and personnel who had always been loyal to their regime and country. It was better than lurking around the untouched sides of the country, where the people were probably much more united against a common cause.

"We should get going," Nicolae said, trying to find the most stable path which would lead to a main road.

The pilot hummed.

"I will help you, Sir," he agreed, taking a lead towards the motorway that could take them to Târgoviște.

Nicolae exhaled heavily, waiting for Leana to join him by his side. He offered her an arm, which she accepted, and helped her onto the muddy path. Villagers often used these grassless paths to get from one village to another, avoiding the busy roads. For once, this seemed to benefit Nicolae as well. He hadn't walked through a rural site like that, with almost no guards and no dogs, since he had been a boy.

"Sir!" the pilot called after them from a few metres south, passing towards a road where cars could drive and also accommodate those on foot.

Nicolae and Leana fastened their pace, feeling a light breeze coming in from beyond the trees.

"Sir," the pilot repeated when they were closer. "I think we need to ask for a ride on the side of the road. There are no buses or trams in these parts, especially after the turmoil in the larger cities. And besides, Sir. It is almost Christmas. We might find a good soul willing to help you," the man said, tucking his hands into his pockets.

Nicolae scoffed.

"Captain, I admire your creativity! Maybe you should have been a poet," Nicolae laughed.

He looked around, waiting for Leana to be just as amused — she only looked at him with furrowed eyebrows, then turned towards the road ahead.

"You cannot expect the man you have been the leader of a country for twenty-four years to suddenly hitch a ride, General," Nicolae added in a little more serious tone.

The pilot shook his head.

"There are many people across the country who are very dangerous right now, Sir. If you keep your cover and have your story laid out clearly, they will never suspect that you are Nicolae and Elena Ceaușescu. People probably expect you to be driving in a limousine or riding in a helicopter. Excuse me for being so forward, but this is the best shot you have at your safety," the pilot said, taking a step back.

Leana nodded.

"We can tell them we are government officials. Mere workers who need urgent transport to Târgoviște for something that is top secret," she added.

The pilot pointed a finger at her agreeingly.

Nicolae didn't like the casualness of it all — this new pilot being their 'buddy' didn't sit right with him, nor did the following act that they had to put on to get to Târgoviște. But if it meant not perishing in the middle of nowhere, he was able to make a compromise.

"We can try," he said calmly. "But I doubt we'll find anyone today. It's almost Christmas, Captain. What kind of people are in these parts right now?"

It took them exactly thirteen minutes to spot a car that had been driving from the opposite direction and heading towards Târgoviște — a beautiful *Dacia* 1100 that paused right in front of them. The driver was a man of about forty-five or forty-six, dressed in a heavy Winter coat and a sheepskin hat. He smiled at the couple and the pilot through his twisted moustache and rolled down his window.

"Where to, *oameni buni?*" he asked.

The pilot stepped in front.

"Târgoviște. The gentleman and his lady are on their way to an important business meeting," the pilot handed him a note with an address on it. "Government thing."

The man nodded.

I cannot wait for all this to be over, Nicolae thought to himself, missing his home. He wanted to feel the silk of his sheets caressing his face, and the touch of his dogs' clean coats each time that he fed them. He missed being in the quarters of his own palace, where he could finally sit down and sip a cup of warm tea in front of the *sobă*.

"Get in," the man repeated, smirking.

"This is where I leave you," the pilot said, turning his head in the opposite direction, where the helicopter he had landed was waiting for fuel.

Nicolae nodded, then shook the man's hand.

"Thank you, Captain," he said, as did Leana.

The couple entered the car and looked around the empty seats. Apart from a few boxes of what they presumed were presents, which were on the front seats, the back seats were deserted. Leana stepped in first, confident and proud.

"Thank you," she said to the driver, then asked for his name.

"Marius," he responded, then proceeded to tell them that he was an engineer from the local town, working around the area and the surroundings near it.

"Very well," Nicolae said, impressed. "You are an honest man."

Marius eyed him from the rearview mirror.

"As are you, I am sure," he smiled. "So, government things, huh?" then the engineer asked. "Pretty rough place to be in right now."

"Oh, it will all be over soon," Leana smiled. "Everything is under control."

Marius glared at them carefully, blinking between his focused sight on the road and their faces.

"Is that so?" he asked. "Well, I'll be glad when everything goes back to normal," the man coughed.

They rode in silence for about fifteen more minutes, until the engineer took a right turn off the main road.

"W-where are we going?" Leana asked.

"I need to get something from the pharmacy here for my mother-in-law. You know how older people are... You need to get all their things sorted as if they are toddlers," the engineer laughed, and they joined him.

Nicolae cringed, looking outside the window.

They had entered the centre of town, where most of the shops were sealed off from the inside. In small towns like that, the vast majority of people would often leave their homes and businesses to be with their families — in both good times and bad. Nicolae wondered whether the Revolution or Christmas had a greater power to 'unite' people here.

The engineer parked in front of the pharmacy, and most of the spaces around were empty. There was very little activity in this part of town, although it was meant to be the centre. It fuelled Nicolae with uneasiness as much as it did with safety.

"I will be right back," Marius said, and left them to their own in the car.

Nicolae turned to Leana.

"What are we doing?" he asked, looking around.

"Relax. Târgoviște will help. Trust me," she reassured him.

"That man, the engineer — trustworthy?" Nicolae asked.

Leana laughed.

"There are people in this country who want to see your head impaled on a spike, Nicu," Leana said. "Of course, I do not trust him."

Nicolae shook his head, tutting.

"I think we should reward him somehow when we are home. For his services, loyalty. Hard work," he said.

"Oh, come on! Nicu," Leana tutted.

Nicolae's face straightened.

"I just think it's a good idea to really remember those who are with us now. In times of hardship," he explained.

Leana put a hand over his and looked at his face.

"I am here," she said.

Nicolae nodded — a moment later, the driver's door flung open, and the engineer stood back in his seat.

"Done," he said, adjusting his mirror.

He turned the engine on, then pulled out onto the Boulevard again. As they drove past the many stores and places around them, Nicolae realised a crucial detail about the engineer's errand.

There were no pharmacies on the road.

Right around the corner where he had walked to, though, there was something else that Nicolae had not seen before. As clear as daylight — a telephone booth.

When the engineer arrived in Târgoviște with the Ceaușescu couple in his backseat, Nicolae was already convinced that some havoc was awaiting him in the city.

Fucking Florin.

"You don't mind if I turn the radio on, do you?" the engineer asked, smiling through his front two teeth.

"No, no... go ahead," Nicolae urged him, looking out the window.

They rode through the city for a couple of minutes before they could reach the address the pilot had written down for them. As Nicolae watched the dense rows of buildings become increasingly sparse and blend into the surrounding trees and rural scenery, the radio caught his attention.

A special announcement was being made — the engineer turned it up.

"General Vasile Milea was found deceased in his apartment this morning. His

death has been ruled out as suicide. Officials found—" the announcement declared, and the engineer turned it back down again.

Vasile Milea was dead. The General who had helped keep the people in their place — he had *perished*? This couldn't be. And what a nonsensical excuse. Suicide. No one in their right mind would have believed that. Nicolae tried to contain his shock, while Leana watched the floor knowingly. Someone on the inside had gotten to Milea.

I'll avenge him. When all this is over, the traitors will pay for their lives.

The car came to an abrupt stop as the other man pointed at a warehouse in the distance. He opened the car doors for them, helping them out.

"*Până aici ați plătit*," he joked. "It was nice meeting you, Sir. And Madam."

They nodded, then shook hands with him respectively. The man didn't hang around very long, and soon enough, they realised why.

It didn't take more than a few minutes for police and military personnel to get word of their presence in Târgoviște. From inside the warehouse labelled '*Unitate Militară* 01417, two pairs of guards walked down the road, accompanied by them, their hands tightening their grips around their guns. Nicolae watched their mannerisms, wondering what their paranoia was all about.

This was *him*. They believed *him*, right? They had to!

"Nicolae and Elena Ceaușescu," one of them declared.

A statement. Not a question. The couple nodded, and Leana almost sighed in relief. Perhaps not everyone in the army had turned against them just yet.

"Arrest them," the man said, and turned his back to Nicolae.

To call it outrageous would have been an understatement.

On Christmas Day, Elena and Nicolae were to be taken in front of a 'judge' who would make a decision based on everything that they had been accused of doing to the country. They called their actions war crimes, genocide, and a few other terms that Nicolae had forgotten from the weight of different stresses.

With hands tied, as if they were truly some criminal imbeciles, the

Ceaușescu couple stood in front of a building in the outskirts of Târgoviște. Next to the old military unit was a train station. Nicolae watched the clock on the wall, wondering how much longer all this nonsense would take place.

When they were finally let into this mock 'courtroom', the judge inside was waiting for them with a glass of water by his side and a few papers on the desk. From all corners, the Romanian television surrounding the area waited with anticipation to hear what the court would decide. It made Nicolae nervous. But it was Leana who had it much worse.

Most of the boys who had grown up in orphanages around the country were sent to the army when they reached the age of enlistment. Boys who had lived from the Ceaușescu couple's money — Leana often called them 'her children'. So *much* of their funding had gone to them. They frequently reminded others of it, too — they had made these boys who they were today.

"*Copiii mei,*" she had cried for hours after reaching Târgoviște.

And Nicolae knew that she wasn't only thinking of their own three children — Zoia, Nicu, and Vali. Now those same men were plotting against them, the mother and father of the nation?

Nicolae watched the man in front of him. He had never met this judge before — or had he? This man was not on his payroll; this much was true. There were people. Some people operated in the Communist Party, some closer to it than others.

"In the name of the Romanian people, you are being tried for genocide, destruction of the national economy, and undermining the state," the judge spoke in a steady voice.

Leana began shouting at the guards around them, then, turning almost hysterical. Nicolae could not bear it.

"I do not recognise this court! I am the legitimate President of Romania!" Nicolae shouted furiously.

The judge did not look impressed. Leana's hair had lost its composure, and she looked around, frightened.

No one was listening to them.

"Romania does not recognise you. The people have rejected you!" the judge shouted.

Nicolae looked at the soldier in front of him and reached out his arms to them with great force.

"Traitors! Traitors, all of you! History will avenge us," he sniffed, his eyes begging for mercy.

The judge handed one of the soldiers in front a few papers, while a few other young men tried to contain the Ceaușescu couple in their place. The papers slammed against the table in front of them.

"I am not signing anything!" Leana shouted, fighting off a soldier with tears in her eyes. "I am your mother. I am the mother of the Romanian nation!" she screamed.

The judge coughed, holding their verdict between their hands.

"*Pedeapsa*. Your punishment is death by firing squad, with immediate execution," he ordered.

Leana began screaming. Nicolae looked around, pleading with them for some humanity. What kind of trial was *this*? Such serious offences, only to reach a verdict in the matter of a few hours?

A few more soldiers approached them, tying their hands even tighter and leading them to the other side of the building.

The execution site was chilly — almost freezing. This was not how Nicolae had imagined he would go. This wasn't the way *anyone* deserved to go. The television crew were filming everything that was happening now, as if Nicolae and Leana were animals at a petting zoo.

Had he not earned the right to die with his children and grandchildren by his side? After leading such a fruitful life, was he not also one of the people who should have seen death the way that it had been intended for him to see it? He wished he could explain all this, perhaps get someone to be a little merciful.

Defeat was close. Closer than ever.

"*Hai la lupta cea mare! Rob cu rob să ne unim! Internaţionala! Prin noi s-o făurim!*" Nicolae began shouting the Communist song that he had been fond of in protest.

Leana was trembling near him, trying to hum along to its melody.

"Shoot me first!" she spat on the ground, her teary face looking at the soldiers. "I have raised children like you!" she shouted, watching them get into position.

They raised their rifles, ready to fire at a moment's notice.

"History will judge us!" Nicolae shouted.

Then, bullets rained on him and his wife for the entire nation to cheer for.

Epilogue

Present day

A tall woman in red-bottomed heels walks around an office, pacing back and forth with anxiety. She clutches her coffee tightly, watching the city in front of her. Her suit, tailored especially for her, feels comfortable — good thing she had gotten it pressed in time for today.

"Come in," she commands when her assistant (presumably) knocks on her door a second later, making her turn around.

"The letter is here for you," the young assistant tells Miss Tina Berkshire.

"Thank you," she smiles, grabbing the envelope from her hand.

This piece of paper has caused her so much worry. Enough for her to reach out to her sister, Lizzie — they usually speak on Christmases and birthdays, since the age gap between them has been large enough for them to become even estranged at times. Tina unfolds the letter, sealing back the envelope and placing it on the table.

Dear Miss Ross,

I want to start by thanking you for your previous letter and for reaching out to me — it has indeed been a long time. It truly meant a lot to me to hear back from you. I apologise for the delay in my response — our local Poșta Română *is notoriously slow with timing.*

I am sorry to hear about the death of your beloved father. I am sure that he was a great man — I should mention that Ross Berkshire never published the stories that the journalists had brought back to him, if I recall correctly. We were told that he never approved it. I had written him countless letters on behalf of our family. Still, he was your father before he was a professional, so I am genuinely very sorry to hear about his passing. Cancer doesn't discriminate between rich or poor, man or woman, young or old.

Thank you also for the questions that you asked about our Revolution, your interest in this story, and your desire to publish it now. You don't need to be sorry for wanting to do this now. It's better late than never, as I always say. Your commitment to this is all that matters.

I'll start answering your questions.

Yes — I did meet Elizabeth when she came to Romania in 1989 with Frankie, the American. I remember both of them, although I had been relatively young back then. Lizzie had been very kind to my baby brother and me, although we couldn't speak to her much.

I am so happy to hear that she is doing well and working at the magazine in London now, focusing on the things she likes doing. The photos you sent are beautiful to see. Lizzie has aged so gracefully, and so has Frankie. Who would have thought that they would tie the knot? Their son Bernard looks like Lizzie's spitting image.

I will have to ask my daughter to send photos of my own family to you via e-mail. I don't like using technology much nowadays. It only reminds me more of how much I have aged.

Allow me to begin at the start.

After my brother was murdered and cremated without our knowledge or consent, things escalated very quickly here. You have to understand that it wasn't like this just for us, but for everyone in the country. And after Ceaușescu's execution, the political shift was rapid and not done with the care that it should have received.

Unfortunately, a lot of people who — believe it or not — were Nicolae Ceaușescu's right-hand advisors returned to Parliament not long after he was shot. After claiming that they had always been against the regime, their previous wrongdoings seemed to all be forgiven in an instant. As if everything was forgotten in a heartbeat. They benefited from a system that was corrupted and flawed, and this aspect hasn't changed even today. I will get back to it in a second — my train of thought is getting way ahead of me.

My brother, as you can imagine, never got the justice that he truly deserved. Nor did my family, or the families of all the other people, have been cremated and taken away during 'Operațiunea Trandafirul', *a military operation approved by Elena Ceaușescu. Hell, we don't even get a page in our History textbooks here dedicated to them, can you believe?*

I was looking through my daughter's books the other day, and the chapter about the Revolution doesn't even mention the martyrs who were sacrificed with enough detail for younger generations to be filled with horror about the subject. Our youth are not being taught about recent events. So to be honest, no. There isn't much that you can do to contribute to the non-existent memorials made for these people.

Our town square no longer bears a single mark of the Revolution, not even a plaque or a museum dedicated to the events that unfolded in this very city. They even want to hide away and renovate the bullet marks on the buildings there, as if none of it ever happened.

People speak of the times behind us, but not often in the right contexts, I fear. The other day, I was talking to my neighbour about the current political situation — not just in our country, but around the world. This sudden and bizarre urge and obsession that people have for various forms of extremism. An intoxicating kind of love for being oppressed. Romania is more divided than it was during the Communist Party's rule. We have been divided by hate, led to believe that everyone who is against our ideal way of thinking is our direct enemy, not our fellow Romanian brother or sister. In reality, the unity should be against one common enemy, as it had been during the time of the Revolution. I am not saying that the same brutality needs to occur, because violence doesn't solve as many problems as it causes — but there needs to be unity.

My neighbour had he audacity to tell me that she missed the way that things were before the Revolution. Mind you, she was only five when the dictatorship ended, not much younger than my brother Beriță. To think that she had an overly romanticised version of what occurred under Ceaușescu's regime (thanks to the nostalgic lens that some people view the period through) is, to me, utterly pathetic. The lack of human empathy is incredible.

She told me that she would have gladly picked a dictatorship over our current democracy, thanks to how people described Romania back then to her. The lie of 'equality' is pretty much that — a lie. Communist Romania had social classes, just like most places. The people who had it well back then remember it as the utopia that was fed to the gullible people, while the rest of us watched our loved ones burn.

I had excused myself to this, left her home without causing an argument. Fighting would have been nonsensical, and I am too exhausted to continue.

People here like to taunt everyone. And their frustration is justified. Despite the fall of the dictator, we have remained unchanged. The rulers, like I said, are the same. Corrupt, full of bland words that they call promises. I don't know what to tell you, Miss Berkshire, because the flaws of the system are too many to count in one letter. Half of us want to seek nothing but the future, while the rest are stuck in a loop of the past. Racism, xenophobia, and even discriminating against our own... these have become much common than before.

Our leaders wield the name of God like a weapon — they tell us that they are the faithful Messiahs, the 'chosen' ones that will bring our country back to its 'Christian roots'. Yet their actions don't spark an ounce of Christianity that my mother taught us about as kids, and the qualities that religion tells us to strive for. They lie and cheat, but the people believe their faces when they draw a cross on their own chests in front of thousands of flashing cameras, mocking everything that we believe in. You know what they say. Propaganda works best on a society that is easy to manipulate, one that is moulded by a spine lacking education.

Anyway, I will tell you more about my mother now. You asked a lot about her, but I'm not sure how much of this will satisfy you. The outcome of her future is, as you can expect, not great — for a woman her age, she looks at least ten years older. The worries have printed themselves on her face through scars and wrinkles. Time's spell did wonders for her, but I don't think that she ever healed from what happened to my brother in '89. Elena never married again, and my father never returned from the mills where he used to work — I never saw him again, but I heard from a mutual friend who knew him at the mills that he went away to Oradea, had children there... But it didn't last long.

My mother, on the other hand, looks like she is still fighting a Revolution inside her. Perhaps on the day that Beriță died, both of them died — but only one got cremated. My mother kept on breathing against her will, and she kept insisting that this had been a punishment for a grave sin that she had committed a long time ago. I never asked too much about it — she's suffered enough.

Nowadays, Elena spends her time reading and writing reports for children at school, as she will retire next year. In her free time, she sits around knitting things, usually with a cigarette hanging from her lips. Her outings typically consist of grocery shopping or taking plastic bottles to recycling centres in town. Her eyes have lost their spark long ago, and she is thinning more and more each year. My daughter says so, too. They have a much better relationship than my granddad and I did.

When the Professor's betrayal was discovered by one of our own, a row of shootings had taken place in his apartment, and he was presumably killed by Dragoș or the woman they had found in his bathroom, Florica. Even my uncle Robi deduced this much. Some of the hidden things we later found in his apartment only confirmed his involvement with the Intelligence, which explains why they never bothered my mum and uncle for so long.

Forgive me for being so blunt. I never doubted Dragoș's loyalties. The question of him being a traitor is not even something worth considering. As you asked, where did his body go? I'll tell you a little secret.

I had seen a man in the crowd at Beriță's funeral, among the many funerals happening around that time. He had looked at me while I laid flowers on his gravestone after the memorial service. With a short wink, the man had put a finger on his lips in a shushing manner, making me get up from my knees in an instant. I had run after him like I had never run in my entire life, praying and screaming Dragoș's name. The man had been quicker — lost in the woods behind the graveyard, becoming one with the trees. I can swear to you on my life that the man I had seen that day was Dragoș. I tried telling the others, but they had only half-believed me before, and then they never talked of it again.

I still see signs of his presence, believe it or not. Every time I go to his gravestone, where the empty grave with his name on it sits restlessly, I always find flowers on Beriță's grave. Apart from my mother and me, who visit together, who else would give a shit about our dead boy and the ashes that we buried? I have also found books — significant books, left in the most random parts of my everyday routine.

Even on the bench in the graveyard, or my doorstep. Things that shouldn't be are almost always solved, like a guardian angel is watching over me. I know that one day I will be reunited with Dragoș and ask him about the truth. About how he left, where he went, and what happened that night in the Professor's apartment.

My uncle Robi moved to Belgium, would you believe? He now has three sons and a daughter, and is married to a local woman in Brussels. I visit him from time to time, but even he hasn't stayed the same as before. For starters, his own kids do not speak Romanian at all, as if disconnecting them from their roots will erase what happened. He never speaks of Dragoș either, although he named his oldest boy after him. When I had made the observation, he had scoffed, pretending like the mere mention of our Dragoș was so unusual. He then tossed the whole conversation aside by saying that his wife had chosen the name anyway.

As if I were a fool.

Dragoș was the last friend that Robi ever had.

I miss our Robi. The one that you saw in those photographs from Bucharest — the boy who had his hair down like a rockstar, and dreamed of fighting for Romania. Now, he doesn't look too much different to my grandfather. The same round glasses and sweaters. Minus the betrayal, of course. But he is no longer the young revolutionary I had once admired.

He teaches geography and writes books about plants and rocks. He hasn't stepped in Romania for about five years, nd when he had, it was because my mother had insisted on it. I am sorry if this is all sad and disappointing to you., I know you were very eager to learn about Robi. I am not sure if he will give an interview on this now, as more than thirty years have passed.

As for Nicolae Ceaușescu, his oldest son is his only survivor. Even his dogs had refused to eat after his death, because only he had ever fed them. They died of starvation after his execution. I think there's something almost poetic about the brutality of an innocent animal dying like that — there wasn't much bliss after the fall of the dictatorship, was there? Elena Ceaușescu had much more control than history gives her credit for — there is a lot I can tell you about her when we meet in person.

When are you planning to come to Romania? Do let me know. I look forward to continuing this conversation over the phone.

All the best,
Ioana S.

Tina lets a sigh escape her. She turns on her laptop, looking up direct flights to Romania in the next few seconds. Then, she stops abruptly, a new thought rushing to Tina's bewildered mind.

She picks up her phone and dials her older sister Elizabeth.

Acknowledgements

Thank you, God, for making this book possible — and for showing me the dream in which I essentially saw this entire story unfold inside my head before I had a chance to write it down. Dreams have been my guide through life for as long as I can remember, and the privilege of witnessing something so personal and spiritual is unmatched.

My *biggest* thanks go to my mum, Anam, for supporting me all the time, through my highs and lows. Thank you for being here for me as my best friend, and for the incredible strength you have as a mother and single parent. And a special thank you for creating the lovely artwork featured on the cups on the cover of this book. You pour your heart into every painting that you do, and it means so much to me that you took the time to make that artwork especially for me. I love you so much.

Thank you, Laiba, my little sister, who is also sitting right next to me while I am typing up these acknowledgements, while we're watching Season 2 of '*Outer Banks*' together. Thank you for always coming to my defence when I need it, for being by my side, and for being my biggest supporter. You are literally my best friend in the whole world, and I love you the most, Bebe. Although my eyes are hurting like hell, I know I'll probably spend the next hour watching edits with you.

Thank you, Tony, for watching enough TV shows and films with me to inspire me to pursue the job I am doing today, and for listening to me talk about the things I love doing. I think you'll find parts of yourself in this book, mainly because of your love and curiosity for Romania. You're one of my biggest cheerleaders, and I cannot thank you enough for it.

Thank you to my childhood best friend, Amira Kalasli, for designing these book covers. Thank you for taking the time to make them, for blending all three of my mum's paintings into teacups, and for all the other amazingly creative ideas you have had for this. I wouldn't want anyone else to create this artwork, especially since I have known you for so long. You are one of my best friends, and I am truly grateful for you.

I want to thank all the current cast and crew at *Faizah Studios Ltd,* who are working so hard on developing our first feature film, '*The Long and Winding Road*'. My long-term goal has always been a career in cinema, and being able to do it with such a talented group of indie artists is the most significant opportunity of my life. I am also looking forward to developing this book into a film next year, especially after all the interest people have shown in it. Words cannot describe my gratitude.

Thank you to all the readers for choosing this book and for everything that they have done for me. I wouldn't be an author without you. I am overwhelmed by the number of people who are so supportive and loving — this book wouldn't be *anything* without you. Thank you for being a part of this journey.

I would also like to thank the amazing bookstores around the world, especially independent stores, for buying and displaying my debut novel at a time when I thought that being an indie artist meant setting myself up for failure. Being grateful and thankful for such excellent opportunities, and for being treated like a '*real*' author at the age of twenty-one, doesn't quite cover it; it is a privilege that not many people have. The future is indie.

Thank you also to the *love of my life*, Loki, who, unfortunately, cannot read these acknowledgements and has no idea that he gets a mention here. You're the best ginger tabby in the world.

Having a platform like this comes with a great deal of responsibility, and I hope that artists worldwide can start using their voices to address issues that we need to discuss more. I am determined to use my platform further to discuss problems and injustices from different periods of the world's history, without exception, including current world events that shouldn't be ignored. I pray that all the suffering around the world, from the people of Palestine to other forgotten nations that don't get any coverage in history, can find closure and an opportunity to have their voices heard.

A significant portion of this story highlights the very real side of the media's exploitation and dissemination of misinformation, as well as its failure to cover specific issues that require more attention. With enough artists uniting against this type of everyday occurrence, we can combat many more problems together. That's the final thought I'd like to end this book with.

Faizah Muhammad. 2025.

About the Author

Faizah Muhammad is a novelist, filmmaker, and astrophysicist whose work explores memory, identity, and the quiet intensity of human connection. Born and raised in Timişoara, Romania, to South Asian heritage, she draws on her multicultural background and fascination with the cosmos to craft stories that are both intimate and expansive, blending emotional resonance with visual precision.

Her second novel, *The Art of Making a Forgotten Cup of Tea,* follows lives intertwined in the upheaval of 1989 Romania, exploring love, courage, and loss in the midst of extraordinary historical change. Alongside her debut, *The Long and Winding Road,* it is being adapted into a feature film by her UK-based production company, Faizah Studios Ltd, where she serves as writer, director, and producer. Her short film, *The Height of Ignorance,* premiered at Pinewood Studios as part of the Lift-Off Global Network, earning recognition for its sensitive storytelling and visual elegance.

When she isn't writing or directing, Faizah watches films like a madwoman, obsessively dissects video edits on TikTok of her favourite characters, and eats an alarming number of prawns. She also teaches English, rescues cats, studies the night sky, and curates the perfect soundtrack for every heartbreak she writes. Her work blends imagination, empathy, and a sometimes irrepressible sense of humour, creating worlds where both the cosmic and the personal collide.

Also by Faizah Muhammad

The Long and Winding Road

June Dawson has always been the one who holds her family together. When her beloved Aunt Diana dies, June is tasked with fulfilling her final moving from Suffolk to a quiet village on the edge of Lake Como.

But she isn't making the trip alone.

Unexpectedly joined by her estranged father, the man who walked out years ago, June sets off on a road trip across Europe, where grief, memory, and unresolved silence fill the space between them. From ferry ports to empty hotel rooms, gas stations to winding mountain roads, each mile forces her to confront the emotional weight she's carried for too long.

The Long and Winding Road is a tender and lyrical debut exploring inter-generational trauma, mental health, estranged family bonds, and the quiet, painful work of healing. With emotional depth and understated beauty, Faizah Muhammad writes about the way we inherit both pain and resilience — and what it means to love someone while learning how to let go.

The Height of Ignorance — Short Film

Written and directed by the author.

Sisters Mariana and Ioana Dumitru are struggling to get by during the Communist period in Romania, in a time where every basic necessity is a luxury.

www.ingramcontent.com/pod-product-compliance
Ingram Content Group UK Ltd.
Pitfield, Milton Keynes, MK11 3LW, UK
UKHW051151301225
9805UKWH00003BA/10

9 781919 339801